GALATEA 2.2

BY RICHARD POWERS

GALATEA 2.2

RICHARD POWERS

 FARRAR STRAUS GIROUX
NEW YORK

Copyright © 1995 by Richard Powers
All rights reserved
Printed in the United States of America
Published simultaneously in Canada by HarperCollins*CanadaLtd*
Designed by Fritz Metsch
First edition, 1995

LIBRARY OF CONGRESS CATALOGING-IN-PUBLICATION DATA
Powers, Richard.
Galatea 2.2 / Richard Powers. — 1st ed.
p. cm.
I. Title.
PS3566.092G35   1995   813'.54—dc20   94-44319   CIP

The brain is wider than the sky,
   For, put them side by side,
The one the other will contain
   With ease, and you beside.

The brain is deeper than the sea,
   For, hold them, blue to blue,
The one the other will absorb,
   As sponges, buckets do.

The brain is just the weight of God,
   For, heft them, pound for pound,
And they will differ, if they do,
   As syllable from sound.

            —EMILY DICKINSON

G A L A T E A   2 . 2

It was like so, but wasn't.

I lost my thirty-fifth year. We got separated in the confusion of a foreign city where the language was strange and the authorities hostile. It was my own fault. I'd told it, "Wait here. I'm just going to change some money. Check on our papers. Don't move from this spot, no matter what." And chaos chose that moment to hit home.

My other years persist, like those strangers I still embrace in sleep, intimate in five minutes. Some years slip their chrysalis, leaving only a casing to hold their place in my sequence. Each year is a difficult love with whom I've played house, declaring, at each clock tick, what it will and won't put up with.

My thirty-fifth trusted no one. As soon as I said I'd only be a moment, it knew what would happen to us.

Thirty-five shamed me into seeing that I'd gotten everything until then hopelessly wrong. That I could not read even my own years.

At thirty-five, I slipped back into the States. I did not choose either move or destination. I was in no condition to choose anything. For lack of a plan, I took an offer in my old college haunt of U. The job was a plum, my premature reward for a portfolio that now seemed the work of someone else.

I thought the year a paid leave of absence. A visiting position, where I might start again with the recommended nothing. House, meals, office, expenses, and no responsibilities except to live. I clung to the offer without too much reflection.

In fact, I had nowhere else to go. I couldn't even improvise a fallback.

It had to be U. U. was the only town I could still bear, the one spot in the atlas I'd already absorbed head-on. I'd long ago developed all the needed antibodies. When you take too many of your critical hits in one place, that place can no longer hurt you.

Nothing else remotely resembled home. Time had turned my birthplace into an exotic theme park. I could not have gotten a visa to live where I'd grown up. And I'd just spent the last seven years in a country that seemed exile already, even while I'd lived there.

But U. I could slink back to, and it would always take me. We were like an old married pair, at exhausted peace with each other. I did school's home stretch here, learned to decline and differentiate, program and compose. U. was where I took Professor Taylor's life-changing freshman seminar. Twelve years later, a stranger to the town, I passed through to watch Taylor die with horrific dignity.

U. was the place where I first saw how paint might encode politics, first heard how a sonata layered itself like a living hierarchy, first felt sentences cadence into engagement. I first put myself up inside the damp chamois of another person's body in U. First love smelted, sublimated, and vaporized here in four slight years.

I betrayed my beloved physics in this town, shacked up with literature. My little brother called me here to tell me Dad was dead. I tied my life to C.'s in U. We took off from U. together, blew the peanut stand to go browse the world and be each other's whole adulthood, an adventure that ended at thirty-five. The odds were against this backwater having anything left to throw at me.

Since my last trip back, I'd achieved minor celebrity status. Local Boy Makes Good. I'd never get my name on the city-limits sign. That honor was reserved for the native Olympic legend. But I now had the credentials to win a year's appointment to the enormous new Center for the Study of Advanced Sciences. My official title was Visitor. Unofficially, I was the token humanist.

My third novel earned me the post. The book was a long, vicarious re-creation of the scientific career I never had. The Center saw me as a liaison with the outside community. It had resources to spare, the office cost them little, and I was good PR. And who knew? A professional eavesdropper with a track record might find no end of things to write about in an operation that size.

I had no desire to write about science. My third novel exhausted me for the topic. I was just then finishing a fourth book, a reaction against cool reason. This new book was fast becoming a bleak, baroque fairy tale about wandering and disappearing children.

Even I could not fail to see the irony. Here I was, crawling back to the setting I had fictionalized in my sprawling science travelogue. The University put me up in a house, the seventies equivalent of the barracks where the hero of my book had lived on his arrival in town. Beyond a lone bed and desk, I left my rooms unfurnished, in my character's honor.

I bought a secondhand bike, perfect for the stretch from my house to the Center. The research complex had sprung up since my last visit. A block-long building in a town the size of U. cannot help but make a statement. The Center's architecture laid irony upon irony. It was a postmodern rehash of Flemish Renaissance. In the Low Countries, I'd lived in postwar poured concrete.

The Center had been built by an ancient donor couple, two people archaic enough to get through life still married to each other. They reached the end of that shared existence with nothing better to do with the odd fifty million than to advance advanced science. I don't know if they had children, or what the kids were slated to get when the folks passed away.

U. got a warren of offices, computer facilities, conference areas, wet and dry labs, and an auditorium and cafeteria, all under that jumble of Flemish gables. The small city housed several hundred scientists from assorted disciplines. Thankless Ph.D. candidates did the bulk of the experimental drudge work, supervised to various degrees by senior researchers from all over the world.

Work at the Center divided into areas so esoteric I could not tell their nature from their names. Half the fields were hyphenated. Creative play spilled over borders, cross-pollinating like hybrid corn in heat. Talk in its public spaces sounded like a UN picnic: excited, wild, and mutually unintelligible. I loved how you could never be sure what a person did, even after they explained it to you.

Most attention converged on complex systems. At the vertex of several intersecting rays—artificial intelligence, cognitive science, visualization and signal processing, neurochemistry—sat the culminating prize of consciousness's long adventure: an owner's manual for the brain. With its countless discrete and massively parallel subsystems, the Center seemed to me a block-wide analog of that neuronal mass it investigated.

The Center and two dozen similar places here and abroad would decide whether the species would earn its last-minute reprieve or blow the trust fund the way it intended. The footrace would photofinish here, as life came down to the wire. Bio-chips, seeded to grow across the complexity threshold. Transparent man-machine interfaces. Control of protein folding. High-def, digital contrition.

The building teemed with job descriptions: theorists, experimentalists, technicians, magicians. Someone here had a probe attached to every conceivable flicker. One wing swarmed with scientists who proclaimed their transcendence over engineering. Another housed engineers who didn't even acknowledge the distinction. What one floor banished bred like mold in a nearby quarter.

The Center was big. So big I lost my office twice in the first month, the way you lose a rental in an airport parking garage. Sheer size was the Center's chief virtue. Even the embarrassment of talking to the same colleague twice faded in a place so huge. In such an expanse, I hoped, one year would be too brief for me to be of any but passing interest to anyone.

What's more, the complex opened onto virtual space, through a spreading network backbone. I had an office with my name on the door, and a computer cabled into the world web. No one suspected that I had no research group, that I could not tell a field-responsive polymer from a spin glass. I came and went in awful freedom, a complete impostor.

I found the dress-up weirdly pleasant, knowing I could go home nightly to a house both empty and rented. For a long time, I must have been aspiring to just this. Immaculate and cold-booted, a resident alien. Just passing through the old alma mater.

The Center had much to recommend it. Its doors knew me from a distance. They clicked open at the command of an infrared pass card that I didn't even need to take out of my wallet. I flipped backside to sensors, mandrill style. Anyone reading this by accident or nostalgia a hundred years from now will have to take my word for the novelty.

The parabolic front foyer concentrated sound. I liked to stand at the focus and hear the rush of my own breath, the throb of blood coursing through my veins. I listened to my body's roar, sounding for all the world like a message left on an answering machine by someone who died later that day.

I tinkered at my new novel, ticking at the machine keys with my door closed and the fluorescent lights doused. My office reveled in state-of-the-art, clean-room efficiency. The perfect place to tuck my millennial bedtime story in for the night. I'd click a radio button on my screen and eighteen months of work waited for me by the time I hiked upstairs to the network laser.

I browsed the world web. I fished it from my node on a building host that served up more megabits a second than I could request. By keying in short electronic addresses, I connected to machines all over the face of the earth. The web: yet another total disorientation that became status quo without anyone realizing it.

The snap of a finger, a satellite uplink, and I sat conversing with a mainframe in my old coal-mining ex-hometown seven time zones away. I could read the evensong schedule from off a digital valet in Cambridge, download Maurya painting, or make a Cook's tour of New Zealand. In seconds, I could scroll through dinner menus in languages I could not even identify. From my chair in the virgin Center, I revisited every city I'd ever spent time in and hundreds I would never get around to visiting in this life.

The town had been knitted into a loose-weave, global network in my absence. The web seemed to be self-assembling. Endless local investigations linked up with each other like germs of ice crystal merging to fill a glass pane.

The web overwhelmed me. I found it easier to believe that the box in Pakistan I chatted with was being dummied up in the other end of the building. I didn't know how my round-the-world jaunts were being billed, or if they were billed at all.

For a while, I felt a low-grade thrill at being alive in the moment when this unprecedented thing congealed. But after weeks of jet-setting around the hypermap, I began to see the web as just the latest term in an ancient polynomial expansion. Each nick on the time line spit out some fitful precursor. Everyone who ever lived had lived at a moment of equal astonishment.

The web had been a long while in linking up. It, too, was just a stopgap stage in a master plan drawn up on the back of the brain's envelope. A bit of improvised whittling, forever a step shy. A provisional pontoon in that rough pencil sketch for final triumph over space and time.

I explored the world's first network in embryo. After days of disappearing children, I spent my nights playing in the greatest virtual sandbox yet built. I'd stumbled upon a stack of free travel vouchers. I put up in U., but I resided elsewhere. I thought: a person might be able to make a life in all that etherspace.

Each day produced new improbabilities. I searched card catalogs in Kyoto or book reports from Bombay. German soccer scores and Alaskan aurora sightings filled my office E-mail pouch.

I eavesdropped on international discussion groups, ongoing, interactive Scheherazades that covered every imaginable theme from arms control to electronic erotica. Notefile threads split and proliferated in meiosis. Debates flowed without beginning or end, through tributaries and meanderings, responses to responses to responses. Inexhaustible protagonists from every time zone posted to the continuous forum a dozen or more times a day.

Alone in my office, blanketed by the hum of the Center, I felt like a boy happening onto a copy of the *Odyssey* in a backwater valley library. I wanted to rush out into the hall and announce my each discovery. But who could I tell? Those lonely souls who stood most to gain would only shake their heads, dazed, locked out on every level. Those who had the wherewithal to see what the fuss was about had already habituated to the inconceivable.

Advanced science, of course, profited enormously from the web. The groups at the Center could now read journal articles months before they hit print. The data Autobahns had no speed limit. They plunked one in front of any results on earth before you could read the "Connect." Researchers peered into colleagues' labs on other continents, in real time. They shared data in 3D, as they gathered it.

On all sides of my cubicle, experimenters scoured the nodes. The net reduced duplication of effort and helped pinpoint crucial results they otherwise might have missed altogether. Instant telemessaging produced an efficiency that fed back into steeper invention. And invention accelerated the universal linkup.

But the longer I lurked, the sadder the holiday became. People who used the web turned strange. In public panels, they disguised their sexes, their ages, their names. They logged on to the electronic fray, adopting every violent persona but their own. They whizzed binary files at each other from across the planet, the same planet where impoverished villages looked upon a ball-point pen with wonder. The web began to seem a vast, silent stock exchange trading in ever more anonymous and hostile pen pals.

The web was a neighborhood more efficiently lonely than the one it replaced. Its solitude was bigger and faster. When relentless intelligence finally completed its program, when the terminal drop box brought the last barefoot, abused child on line and everyone could at last say anything instantly to everyone else in existence, it seemed to me we'd still have nothing to say to each other and many more ways not to say it.

Yet I could not log off. My network sessions, all that fall, grew longer and more frequent. I began to think of myself in the virtual third person, as that disembodied world-web address: rsp@center.visitor.edu.

How long could I show up at the Center and produce nothing of use to anyone? The productivity problem. The pure-research problem. The inspiration, the blind-trust problem. I could drift without limit and still not be reprimanded. I had the year gratis. I might do nothing but prime the pump, rest and recharge, and still I would not ruffle so much as a mite's mood where it camped out on the eyelash of the emergent digital oversoul.

I meant to milk the new book for as many weeks of touch-up as I could get away with. Past that point I tried not to speculate. Three times before, the end of a long project had kicked off the start of another. I'd mastered the art of surviving narrative whiplash. No reason, in theory, why I couldn't regroup again. Go on and work forever.

But this time felt different. This time, after I paid my Pied Piper account, nothing waited for me on the far side of story's gaping mountain. Nothing but irremediable Things As They Are.

What little diversionary work remained I dragged out for all it was worth. Two Kbytes of new text or four of reasonable revision honorably discharged me of the day. Beyond that, I could indulge my remaining hours in good faith. A page and a half freed me to go and do as I liked.

Mostly, I liked to haunt the Center after hours. At night, the building thinned almost to empty. The community of night research emitted a sober thrill. The handful of sallow, animated faces at that hour could not help but be there. Their inquiries had them hooked, as levered to the intermittent payoffs as their lab animals. They piloted the halls, feverish, close to breakthrough, indifferent to clock time. They weaved from lab to lab in directed distraction, eyes combing every visual field but the corridors down which they moved.

Except for these addicts of the verifiable, I had the place to myself. That alone was worth coming in for: fifty million dollars of real estate filled with several hundred million in instruments, boxes that glowed with subdued purpose, abandoned like an electronic Rapture. No one could have a more profound sense of history than a night custodian of such a building.

Night brought open-endedness to the place. Through the machine on my desk, I could disappear down the coaxial rabbit hole to any port of call. I had a phone I could dial out on but which never rang. I had a white board and bright pastel markers that wiped off without a trace. I amused myself by writing out, in different colors, as many first lines of books as I could remember. Now and then I cheated, verifying them on the web.

These nights were dead with exhilaration. Like battening down in the face of a major maritime storm. All I could do was stock the mental candles and wait.

On such a night, I met Lentz. From my first glimpse, he seemed the person I'd come back to U. to meet. While I stood by, this man prototyped the thing humanity has been after from out of the starting block. In the year I knew him, Philip Lentz would bring a life back from the dead.

The night in question, I'd diverted myself so successfully with bursts of null activity that I found myself still in the building well past midnight. I was prowling the corridors on the floor above my office. I stood outside a conference center, reading a posterboard entitled "Compliance of Neuronal Growth over Semiconductor Substrate." Someone had encouraged nerve cells to connect themselves in clean, geometric, living chips. And had electron microscopy shots to prove it.

I felt my perfect solitude. A few fluorescent highlights here and there kept alive the odd captive plant. As I do when I'm alone, I hummed to myself. Only now, in the distance, I began to hear the music I'd been humming. Mozart, the Clarinet Concerto, middle movement. The one that C. had thought the most pained palliative in creation.

Here, in the deserted, empirical dark, years too late, I heard that she was right. In the Center, where no birds sang, this sound, slowed to a near stop, resigned all hope of ever saying just what its resignation carried. At this impossible hour, when even the most inexorable researchers had gone home to whatever family they could muster for themselves, only music stayed behind to prove the ravishing irrelevance of research.

The clarinet and orchestra exchanged phrases, elaborating on the ongoing expansion, unfolding, inhaling beyond capacity like the lungs of a patriarch wedging open the air after being told of the death of his last great-grandchild. The endless phrase spoke of how you reach an age when anything you might answer would not be worth asking.

Who in all this restless measurement had time for so infinite an aside? The late-night auditor, whoever he was, must have thought he listened alone. Even the cleaning crew had gone. The earliest hard-core hackers would not stumble in to their predawn keyboarding for another two hours.

Ordinarily, any sound would have driven me to an emergency exit. Now I gravitated to the source, audiotropic, to secure the forsaken signal.

The tune grew more real. It approached the asymptote of live performance. The next turn of the corridor maze would flush out a covey of tuxedoed instrumentalists. The thread of sound led me to an office down a spur hallway I did not know existed. The cell door stood wide open. The phrase issued from it as if from the wellspring of all improvisation.

The music's hopeless peace emboldened me. I came alongside the door and looked in. Except for the sound, the room was deserted. I bathed in the emptiness. Heaps of equipment, much of it bare boards and components, shimmered in the dark. Some of these devices produced this ethereal interpretation, while others only absorbed and contemplated it.

From a cave of instruments in the corner, light glinted off two small surfaces. What I had taken to be two flat LCD panels flickered into a pair of near-opaque glasses. The creature behind them now gazed at me without registering anything. Archimedes looking up languidly at the Roman soldier about to run him through: Don't disturb my circles.

The head attached to these glasses peaked in a balding dome. From freakish frontal lobes it tapered away to nothing at the temples only to erupt again in a monstrous beak. Even after I oriented the image, the face shocked me.

The man stretched out on a reclining office chair. His head flung itself back against a flatbed scanner. His feet kicked up on a mountain of offprints. Even horizontal like this, he could not have been longer than five and a half feet. Yet his doe-colored jacket and white oxford button-down crept up his arms as if the knit were unraveling.

I'd never seen this man before, either in these halls or anywhere else. Not even I could forget such a figure. He must have been at least sixty, in earth years. To judge by his pallor, the fellow avoided all contact with natural light. His puzzled blink suggested that he avoided human contact, too, to the extent of his abilities.

Without taking his eyes from me, he continued his series of infinitesimal hand adjustments in the space in front of him. He pushed a suite of frictionless hockey pucks about the wired surface of his desk. The rink looked like a cross between an acupuncture map and a player piano roll. Between the music and these arcane hand motions, I couldn't decide who led and who followed.

The conductor gestured across his electronic score, locking stares with me until the slow movement played itself out. Discord and resolve, the devastating rasp of reed, the musical sequence pushing against the limits of my cranial sounding post, a grace too huge and slow for understanding.

The lemur-like man appraised me, unselfconscious. We made interstellar contact, paralyzed by the mutual knowledge that any attempt to communicate would be culture-bound. Worse than meaningless.

Silence, after such sound, grew unbearable. I broke first. "Mozart," I said. Having begun to make a fool of myself, I pressed on and completed the job. "K. # 622. What happened to the finale?"

The man's hands stopped and laced themselves behind his head. He snorted out the side of his mouth, as if flossing the idea from between his teeth. "No finale. We deal exclusively with middles here."

He picked up the hockey pucks and started to shuffle them again. Music rose from the aural grave. The clarinet recommenced its paralyzing simplicity. That perfect phrase breathed in and out just as before, steeped in stabbing acceptance. But something different unfolded this time. A slower, more forlorn rumor. Where the difference lay, there was no saying.

The owl-man made his mechanical adjustments, as if he dreamed

13

this music himself, out of a computational hurdy-gurdy. He flicked switches and fiddled with sliders. My shadow must have snagged the edge of his retina, because he looked up, surprised to see me still standing in the doorway. "Thank you for the little chat," he said. "Good night."

I bobbed my head in ridiculous acquiescence and backed down the hall, dismissed to safety.

I don't know what I expected, really. Civility, perhaps. Acknowledgment. An exchange of names. All the social niceties that I'd avoided so studiously since my Dunkirk back here. I obsessed for a day and a half, inventing ironic, dry comebacks. In my head, I let the man know in no uncertain terms that I was neither a pest nor ludicrous.

Under cover of daylight, I returned to pinch his name off the office door. Philip Lentz: a name as Palladian as the man was misshapen. The Center's promotional brochure said he explored cognitive economies through the use of neural networks. The pamphlet withheld even the foggiest idea of what this might mean.

For years, back before I saw the photograph that led to my retirement from software, I'd made a living by writing code. But a neural net, I learned in browsing the web, resembled nothing I'd ever programmed in my coding days. Neural networkers no longer wrote out procedures or specified machine behaviors. They dispensed with comprehensive flowcharts and instructions. Rather, they used a mass of separate processors to simulate connected brain cells. They taught communities of these independent, decision-making units how to modify their own connections. Then they stepped back and watched their synthetic neurons sort and associate external stimuli.

Each of these neurodes connected to several others, perhaps even to all other neurodes in the net. When one fired, it sent a signal down along its variously weighted links. A receiving neurode added this signal's weight to its other continuous inputs. It tested the composite signal, sometimes with fuzzy logic, against a shifting threshold. Fire or not? Surprises emerged with scaling up the switchboard.

Nowhere did the programmer determine the outcome. She wrote no algorithm. The decisions of these simulated cells arose from their own internal and continuously changing states.

Each decision to fire sent a new signal rippling through the electronic net. More: firings looped back into the net, resetting the signal weights and firing thresholds. The tide of firings bound the whole chaotically together. By strengthening or weakening its own synapses, the tangle of junctions could remember. At grosser levels, the net mimicked and—who knew?—perhaps reenacted associative learning.

Neural networkers grouped their squads of faked-up cells together in layers. An input layer fronted on the boundless outdoors. Across the connective brambles, an opposite squad formed the door where the ghost in the machine got out. Between these, the tool kit of simulated thought. In the so-called hidden layers lay all the knotted space where the net, and networkers like Lentz, associated.

The field went by the nickname of connectionism. Piqued, I subscribed to the web's discussion group on the subject. Reading made good counterpoint to my final rewrite. It was also a great day-waster and delaying tactic. Studying postponed the time when I'd no longer have any rewrite to counterpoint.

Now, whenever I logged on to the system, a new round of notes on the topic greeted me from all quarters. Several of my fellow visitors at the Center took part, firing messages back and forth to intercontinental colleagues. But unless this Lentz signed on with a pseudonym, he seemed to cut a wide side step around the citizens band.

I followed the exchange. The regulars took on personalities. The Danish renegade. The Berkeley genius provocateur. Slow and Steady, respected co-authors, in constant battle with their archrival, Flash-in-the-Pan. Some speculated. Others graciously deflated. I saw myself as a character in this endless professional convention: the Literary Lurker. Novice symposium dabbler, who no one knew was there. But even lurking left a signature.

I learned that networks were not even programmed, in so many words. They were trained. Repeated inputs and parental feedback created an association and burned it in. Reading that fact tripped an association in *me*. The man had been sitting in his office after midnight, playing the same five minutes of Mozart again and again to an otherwise empty building. To a bank of machines.

This Lentz, I reasoned, had a neural network buried in that mountain of equipment. One that he was training to recognize beauty. One that would tell him, after repeated listenings, how that simple reed breathing made and unmade the shifting signal weights that triggered souls.

Some days later, the beak thrust itself into my office without knocking. Dr. Lentz stood upright even more precariously than he reclined. Even standing still, he listed like a marionette on a catamaran, my office door handle his rudder. Again the summer suit, the last scientist not giving congressional evidence to wear one. His skin had the pallor of a sixties educational TV host. He looked as if he'd taken self-tanning cream orally.

"Reclusive novelist living in the Netherlands?" His voice held more accusation than question. An allusion to a photo caption that had run in a major news weekly. I'd been captured in front of a stand of palms imported into the Sonora. The text beneath gave my life in thumbnail, now wrong on all three counts.

I launched my screen saver, to blot the incriminating text on my tube. He might have read it, even from his angle. Those eyes seemed set out on stalks.

"Yep. That's me."

"*Yep?* This is 'dazzlingly brilliant'? So tell me. What is it about the Dutch, anyway?"

"Excuse me?"

"They hang around your writing like dung beetles around a cholera ward. At least a cameo appearance in every book you've written. I mean: fifteen million tulip-sucking, clog-carving water wizards. So what? That's less than the population of greater New York."

He'd done his homework. And wanted me to know.

"Search me," I countered. "Accident. Pure coincidence."

"Nonsense. Fiction doesn't permit accident. And what little coincidence it does put up with is far from pure. Why don't you write about real countries? The whole global community is out there, chain-dragging on its own economic exhaust pipe. It's North against South, you know. Haves versus have-nots. How about a swing through the tropics? The lands of the 6 percent population growths and the two-hundred-dollar-a-year incomes?"

I gestured toward the hard disk on my desk where my latest sat, all but finished. "There's a bit in the new one . . ."

He waved me off. "Doubtless the Dutch are in attendance as well."

Two words, right at the end. The little Frank girl's *Dear Kitty*. He gloated. I looked away.

"You and your precious bourgeois queendoms. Why should I care? Why should I pay twenty-five dollars—"

"Only thirteen in paperback." The joke fell flat. At that point I would have given him the complete works at cost, to get him out of my office.

"Twenty-five dollars to read about a negligible nation whose unit of currency sounds like something you'd use to pay the tinker or cobbler."

"Well, they did rule the world once."

"For what—twenty years? The Golden Age." He paced in place. The eye-darting edginess started to get on my nerves. I shoved the spare chair at him. He sat, smirking.

"The great middlemen, your Dutchmen. Bought and sold all races, colors, and creeds. Tell me. How does it feel to live in a country that peaked three centuries ago?"

"I haven't a clue." I hadn't yet decided how it felt to grow up in a country that peaked three years before I tried to bail out.

I didn't relish the idea of an insult match with a stranger. Besides, I'd already reached the same conclusion he had, this cognitive economist who had no more than browsed my novels, standing in front of the fiction "P"'s at the University bookstore. He was right. It was time to give the Dutch a rest. After my latest, I planned to put them down for the count.

But then, my plan for the next time out was to pack in everything. Not just the exotic bits, the color travelogue. I meant to retire my whole mother tongue.

In the meantime, I figured I might at least bait this scientist. I wasn't doing anything else that afternoon anyway. Nothing but writing.

"They've had more than their share of world-class painters and composers, for a negligible country."

"Oh, please, Mr. Powers. European-class. The *world*, it may stun you to learn, is predominantly black-haired. A plurality of those live without adequate shelter and would use *The Anatomy Lesson of Dr. Tulp* as a canvas roof patch if they could."

"And your Mozart?" I don't usually like cheap counterattacks, but the man asked for it.

He shrugged. "The piece happened to be handy. A small fraction of the available repertoire. Replaceable, I assure you." He stood and strode to my whiteboard. Without asking, he erased the text I'd written there and began to draw a matrix of hollow boxes. "All right. I'll grant you the pretty pictures and a few good tunes. But they've never amounted to much in the novel-writing department, have they?"

"That's the fault of translation."

"Not the limits of that expectorant Low German dialect? An orthography to write home about. And crikey! How do you deal with that syntax? An even by native speakers not until the ultimate grammatical arrival capable of being unraveled word order that one's brain in ever more excruciatingly elaborate cortical knots trivially can tie."

His burlesque was note-perfect. He tore it off, at tempo. It chilled me. How much homework had the man done? Could a cognitive linguist parody a language he didn't speak? I didn't want to know. I wouldn't have answered him in kind then, even if he switched over.

I still dreamed in that language. It ruined me for English. Gone for over half a year, I still saw the spire of the Utrecht Dom each time I walked under the Center's tower. I could not shake free from a place I never felt at home in. And all because of some dead Polish kid who attended the next grade school down from my father's. A kid who didn't know the Netherlands from the East Indies.

I'd formed an impression of the place in a dank Chicago suburban basement late in winter at age eight. A child's account of the flood that ravaged Zeeland shortly before I was born turned real in my head. That's what it means to be eight. Words haven't yet separated from their fatal content. For a week and a half, I saw people camped everywhere on top of step-gabled houses, island traumas in ever-rising water.

This was my unshakable image of a place I thought would never be more than an image to me. The word "Holland" filled me with autumnal, diluvian disaster. And this sense persisted, even after living for years as far inland as reachable, high up in the Dutch mountains.

On the day I read that book, sixty-seven blocks north of the Loop, C. was sixty-seven blocks south, lashing fast another imaginary Netherlands altogether. Everyone has a secret low country of the heart where they should have been born. C. missed hers by a year and an accumulation of ripples.

C. was more Dutch when I met her in U. than she became later, after she expatriated. At twenty-five, she learned that she could claim citizenship anytime before the age of thirty. It was as if Belonging lay in some ivory-inlaid credenza in the Hague, waiting to be opened before expiration date. Hers for free, by virtue of being born of Dutch parents. Even parents who had halfheartedly jumped the schooner of state. Once she claimed her birthright, displacement became total.

I could trace the chain of dislocation back to a nineteen-year-old Polish boy I didn't know from Adam. A South Side kid who should never have left home. His name clustered with lots of recalcitrant Slavic consonants. To me, it was unique. For all I know, the same surname takes up a column and a half of the Cicero phone book. The boy's own dislocation must have begun at least a generation before. But I did not know his particulars.

His home, however transient, was not Chicago per se but that emulation of Kraków that interwar Poles ran on the southwest side of former Fort Dearborn. When Armageddon reached as far as the Back of the Yards, the boy volunteered. His family sent him back to liberate a native land he'd seen only in imagination. Before he went, he married. One married young in those days, quick and willfully, to preempt just what happened to him.

The boy was called Eddie. I named my father and a hybrid me after him in my second book.

Eddie and his war bride lived together for two electric bills at the most. Then he vanished. He was killed in that extended tank battle that ran from the forests of eastern Belgium up through Limburg into Nijmegen and Arnhem. He never lived long enough to be anything but a story. This one.

He left behind only one possession. That is, his adopted government left it: one of those pristine stone crosses in one of those endless diffraction-pattern cemeteries that roll across the forgetting countryside. The Low Countries specialize in them.

When war abated again, someone had to care for all the crosses. Cemeteries had proliferated faster than babies, and it came time to adopt them. Village women throughout Limburg enlisted to tend to Margraten. A still-young woman who had stood on a hill and watched Charlemagne's capital burn, who had once run out into the lane with a carving knife at reports of a village horse being strafed, adopted Eddie.

Instructions were simple. Keep the area trim, and perhaps place flowers on history's birthdays. The woman did this and more. She struck up a correspondence with the widow and the bewildered Gold Star mother. God knows in what language. The widow—who knew all along she'd be left with nothing but unreadable letters from foreigners—spoke English and Polish. The mother spoke only Polish. The volunteer grave-tender spoke only Limburgs dialect and that imposed foreign language, Dutch.

The Netherlands was as mythical to the Americans as the States were to the Limburger. But somehow they communicated. Widow and mother visited the grave. They stayed with the grave's adopter, her husband, and their two babies. The Chicago Poles told the young family that if they ever wanted to emigrate to the blessed hemisphere, they had sponsors.

Limburg had never been generous, and war payments, as always, fell on the already destitute. The gravekeeper's husband, a railroad man, declared that he belonged to any country that would feed him. And so a basement room in Little Kraków became the family's country.

After a year, the immigrant wife could stand the New World no longer. She fled back to her beloved Limburg, her two young children in tow. The railroad man stayed, refusing to return home in disgrace. He wrote her letters, in his newly acquired, schoolbook English: "I'm here working. You know where you belong."

After six months, the woman dragged home to her basement nation. C.'s birth was her mother's consolation prize, the one good thing in an unlivable locale. They named C. for the dead boy's widow, who never remarried. After that first death, no room for another.

The family rented a house in a Lithuanian ghetto not far from the stockyards. Lives later, I stranded another, imaginary, Dutch immigrant family in that house. I built my written copy from the descriptions that C. fed me from memory. For two decades, C.'s family lived in that city, speaking to each other in secret phrases. You could say anything, anywhere, in those words. And no one but the displaced would understand you.

They kept themselves alive as exiles do: with rituals and recollections no longer recognizable to those who never left. C.'s mother raised the baby on accounts of a magic village called E. The nether-nether land that C. grew up on was peopled by scores of aunts and uncles and hundreds of cousins with archaic names and fairy-tale histories. Never tie your life to a woman with ten dozen first cousins. Never try to expatriate to a country where the currency is called a gulden.

C. tried. She had to. The image her mother wove of E. was more painfully imprinted in C. than any neighborhood she'd actually lived in. C. tried to reclaim that fabulous nation. And I tried to follow her.

"Oh, Beau!" she told me. "It's so beautiful there. It's like a balm on your heart to see it." And so it was, still. Bits and pieces, anyway. Here and there, isolated half-timbered villages poked out between new industrial terrains, like traces of fresco from under annihilating renovations.

C. returned to her E., went back for the first time. On her arrival, a restored citizen, she became an instant curio. She learned that she spoke a dialect frozen in time, steeped in expressions discarded a generation before. And she spoke this dead idiom with a Chicago accent, equated, by the townsfolk of E., with gangsters who had all been shot thirty years before C.'s parents learned their first textbook slang.

I tagged along in C.'s wake. And my first textbook sentence: *Nederland is een klein land.* A negligible land. A minuscule country that most people in America think lies somewhere in Scandinavia. Ruled the globe once, for two decades.

Adventure ended in further exile. I came back to the States and failed to recognize them. That *klein land* came back with me, infesting my insides like a medfly slipped past customs. Its national anthem, the most beautiful in the world, with its absurd last line, "I have always been loyal to the king of Spain," hurt me when I caught myself humming it. The thought of those yellow trains, timed to the quarter minute, ruined me for further travel. The sight of an orange soccer jersey still cut into me with a boy's Goliath-killing hope, more cruel because not my boyhood. Syrup waffles in an import store hit me now like a wooden shoe in the chest.

Dutch was a shrapnel wound. Like C., I was a different person with that stranger's vocabulary in my mouth. I hated the sound of those words now. I would have forgotten them if I could. But I still said them to myself, when I needed the safety of secret languages. Each syllable aged me. I could no longer say what the simplest word meant. I'd never be rid of them, whatever my next book succeeded in killing off.

But I wasn't about to give Dr. Lentz the pleasure of this narrative. I didn't much like his type: the empiricist who thought the world outside his three variables worth no more than brilliant condescension. I had met too many of his sort at Center functions. They always ended up by telling me to adopt a pen name. It would do wonders for my sales.

Lentz stood at the whiteboard, connecting the hollow boxes with deft switchboard cables. I cleared my throat. "The Netherlands is one of the two or three places on earth where Western civilization almost works."

"Christ. Give me credit for a little intelligence." He answered without a moment's thought, without even turning around. "If you insist on harping on the Dutch, why don't you do the story of a handful of earnest Moluccan separatists who, lied to and betrayed by their old colonial whore of a mother, hijack a passenger train from Amsterdam to—"

"Don't worry," I told him. "They're history. I'll never mention them in print again."

After that, we left each other alone. When I next saw Lentz by accident in the corridors outside an unavoidable Center obligation, he greeted me in round tones. "Little Marcel! How are the words treating you?"

"Don't call me that. It's not clever."

"Who's being clever?"

"It's self-conscious and patronizing."

Lentz pulled back and pursed his lips. He contemplated finishing me in one swipe. Instead, he did a rapid about-face. "I'm sorry. That wasn't my intention. You see, I'm a bit of a social maladroit. We all are, in this pursuit. Comes with the turf. It's all of a piece, really." He swept his hands around himself the way a magician waves handkerchiefs over the body of a sequined assistant he is about to saw in half. "The myopia, the dwarfhood, the aggression, the affected brusqueness, the scoliosis, the know-it-all megalo—"

I'd noticed the kinked walk, but scoliosis never crossed my mind. He'd learned to mask it early. I was sorry I'd let him get under my skin. Even someone who has modeled the function of the inferior frontal gyrus might still be plagued by the monsters that gyrus modeled.

"Forget it," I said. "Everybody's a critic."

"I can imagine. Much to resent about your line of work. 'Nobody deserves to get away with life alive'?"

"That, and 'Write me the book I would have written.' "

"Universal envy. You folks are king of the cats, aren't you?"

"You're joking. Were, maybe. A hundred years ago. It's all movies and lit crit now."

"Well, my defrocked friend. What's it going to be?"

"I'm sorry? What's what going to . . . ? Dr. Lentz, I admit it. I can't always follow you."

"Do come on. The open parenthesis! What would you like me to call you?"

"How should I know? What's wrong with my given name?"

"A bit lacking in imagination for someone in your racket, aren't you?"

I felt twice burned in as many outings. I knew who I was dealing with now, in any event. "I don't care. Call me whatever you please, Engineer."

A low blow, but my own. Philip Lentz smiled, warmly enough for me to see that half his bottom teeth were missing. The remainders had drifted together to cover up the absence.

"Little Marcel, I'm not sure I like you."

He was quoting again, some dialogue of mine I'd forgotten having written. I said what I had to, what I was already scripted to say. "The pleasure's mutual, Engineer."

Lentz's peace offering came the next week, in my mailbox. He left me a much-thumbed-through short-story collection. He'd affixed a stick-on to a Mishima piece called "Patriotism." In the story, a young husband and wife kill themselves in ravishing detail. The note said: "I hope you get as much pleasure out of this as I did." The signature read, "With sincere apologies, Engineer."

As I skimmed the astonishing transcript, I wondered if he was trashing me yet again. This piece was to be my how-to. A suicide manual for the honor-besmirched author.

Not that I needed any anthology piece to make me want to call it a day. My final revision on the wandering kids was all but done. I was just dragging my heels until New York's deadline. Although they had me under contract for one more book after this one, a well-timed Mishima on my part would have delighted New York and put me, however briefly, on what my editor referred to as the List.

On each of my previous three novelistic tries, some further premise had always presented itself by this point. What the close of the current book did not resolve spilled over into the next. Now, although I spent days doing nothing but listening, the silence at the other end sounded like one of those callers who hadn't the courtesy to tell you they'd dialed a wrong number before slamming down the receiver.

Contract aside, I wanted one more shot. My fourth was too bleak an interval to cadence on. The Blitz wasn't going to have the last word in my fiction, however realistic I wanted to learn how to be. I had one more novel coming to me. But all I could find was the first line.

I knew only that I wanted to write a send-off. My next book would have to start: "Picture a train heading south." The line felt ordained, as liberating as October azure. But I couldn't wrap myself around this opening and begin. I was stalled at departure, for the simple reason that I could do nothing with so perfect a lead sentence but compromise it by carrying it forward.

The words nagged at me, like a nursery refrain. I began to imagine it an unconscious allusion. It felt so unsponsored, I could not have invented it.

I searched the bandwidths, postponing further the hopes of a jump start. I did Boolean searches across incomprehensibly huge textbases. South, train, and picture, ANDed together, within a ten-word range of one another. I substituted every conceivable synonym for each term, verbal almosts piped in from hyperlinked thesauri. But if the world's infant digital nervous system knew anything about my mystery opening, it wasn't saying.

I wondered if my memory might not be going. Like a man who furiously scours the bathroom mirror for signs of recent hairline decampment, I'd test myself from one day to the next. I tried myself on the first lines of books I knew I'd read and those I thought I'd written.

Undeniable: my ability to recall was not what I remembered its having been. Soon I would forget even the lovely heft of forgetting. The command to picture was, like that departing train itself, heading south. The line sounded its last call over the PA, a Transalpine Intercity just pulling out of the station.

My brother Russie called, from Florida. He almost never did. He checked to see how I was surviving bachelorhood. I asked him if he remembered a book. Something our mother might have read to us once.

"Mom? *Our* mom? We talking about the same person?"

"Come on. She read to us all the time. She taught me how to read."

"Don't know about your mother, but mine used to surface-mount me to the cathode-ray tube."

"She did not. We were strictly rationed." The last children in America who had to ask to turn on the set.

"Maybe that was the case for you guys."

"Well, you were younger than we were," I conceded.

I could hear Russ's askance silence on the other end. Do we need to call the pros? Start the intervention? "Yeah, bro. I was younger than you."

I couldn't imagine where else the line might have come from. Imagine a route, stretching out leisurely to the south. The day is bracing. It should not be this crisp yet, this chilly or sere. The train eases to life. It builds steam. It stokes up, unfolding itself along that first great curve, and leaving becomes real.

No question: it left something chest-tightening behind, tracking out to the taunting horizon. The book I wanted to write, the book I must have heard somewhere in infancy, unrolled farther than I could see from the locomotive, even leaning out dangerously to look. That passage stretched out longer than love, longer than evasion, longer than membership in this life. It lingered like a first lesson. Outlasted even my need to pin down the broken memory and reveal it.

That sentence, the return leg of the northern line, tried to leap the tracks of desire. But it needed me in the tender. I was the free rider,

26

allowed to hitch on to my phrase's urgent run provided I kept the throttle open and the boiler stoked. But the low-grade hammering on rail that haunted my livelong day dampened to a distant click the longer I failed it. I felt myself dropped off at a deserted siding, numb and clueless as to how I had arrived there.

I sent Lentz a return Post-it. The things were pernicious: just enough adhesive for a temporary stick. "Thanks for the present. No apologies necessary. But please: no more literature. What I need is offprints."

I had but to say the word, and offprints poured in. Lentz sent me articles he had written. He sent me pieces compiled by colleagues and competitors. He forwarded stuff almost a decade old, and submissions that had not yet seen the light of publication. He attached no more notes. If I wanted to read his work, he would not object. But he wasn't going to tutor me.

Neural nets, I learned, had a way of casting themselves over people. According to the miraculous drafts Lentz sent me, there was no hotter topic. Researchers across the whole spectrum of disciplines emptied deep pockets into the promising tangles of simulated brain.

In a previous life, I had brushed up against machine intelligence. For a few months, I wrote code that turned consumer goods artificially lucid. I worked for an outfit that wanted to make household devices savvy enough to anticipate needs that potential purchasers didn't even know they had.

I made appliances expert in their own use. I built the rule base and tuned the reasoning. I linked a table of possible machine states to a list of syllogisms that told the device how to respond in each case. I hooked the device to sensors that bathed in a stream of real-world data. These dispatches threaded a given appliance's inference engine like rats in a behaviorist's maze.

If the data found their way to an exit, they became conclusions.

All that remained was the gentle art of interface. I got the device to weigh the situation. I instructed it to say, "Hey! You sure you want to do that?" or "Let's try that again on 'Puree,' shall we?" Convincing the user was the delicate part, far harder than getting the device to reach its decision.

My expert systems couldn't be called intelligent. But they did get me thinking about what could be. I thought about the question for a long time, even after I jettisoned the commercial interests. What was memory? Where, if anywhere, did it reside? How did an idea look? Why was comprehension bred, or aesthetic taste, or temperament?

Predicates threaded my neural maze. After great inference, I came to the conclusion that I hadn't the foggiest idea what cognition was. Nobody did, and there seemed little prospect of that changing soon.

No tougher question existed. No *other*, either. If we knew the world only through synapses, how could we know the synapse? A brain tangled enough to tackle itself must be too tangled to tackle. Tough, too, to study the workings of a thing that you couldn't get at without breaking. I guess I gave up thinking about thought some time around my thirtieth birthday.

Something about the basic debate upset me. On the one hand, philosophers maintained that the only way into the conceptual prison was introspection. This drove empiricists up the cell wall. Tired of airy nothings, they spent their time amassing chaotic libraries of unrelated data down at neurochemical level.

The top-down thinkers fought back: because thought played a role in experimental design and interpretation, neuroscientists undercut their own efforts. Cognition compromised itself. Recursive by nature, mentation wasn't going to yield to measurement alone.

Cognitive science seemed to me deadlocked. But overnight, while I was away, everything changed. The impasse broke from both ends. Smart appliances kicked out the jambs. The low-level wetware workers came into instruments that allowed them to image the omelet without breaking an egg. At the same time, the top-down people hit upon their own leverage, the neural nets that Lentz's snarl of articles described. Connectionism.

The young connectionist Turks lived on a middle level, somewhere between the artificial-intelligence coders, who pursued mind's formal algorithms, and the snail-conditioners, who sought the structure and function of brain tissue itself. The Center's warrens sheltered all species. But in the halfway world of neural nets, the point man at this place seemed to be Dr. Philip Lentz.

The new field's heat generated its inevitable controversy. I sensed a defensive tone to many of Lentz's publications. Both the neural physiologists and the algorithmic formalists scoffed at connectionism. Granted, neural networks performed slick behaviors. But these were tricks, the opposition said. Novelties. Fancy pattern recognition. Simulacra without any legitimate, neurological analog. Whatever nets produced, it wasn't thought. Not even close, talk not of the cigar.

In his articles, Lentz took these accusations and ran with them. The brain was not a sequential, state-function processor, as the AI people had it. At the same time, it emerged to exceed the chemical sum passing through its neuronal vesicles. The brain was a model-maker, continuously rewritten by the thing it tried to model. Why not model *this*, and see what insights one might hook in to?

Having stumbled across connectionism, I now couldn't escape the word. I heard it in the corridors. I nursed it at Center seminars, seated in the back for a quick exit. I read about it throughout the worldwide electronic notefiles and in the stack of diversionary texts that replaced my nightly dose of forgotten fiction. Neural simulation's scent of the unprecedented diffused everywhere. I followed along, moving my lips like a child, while Lentz declared in print that we had shot the first rapids of inanimate thought.

Lentz described synthetic neurons that associated, learned, and judged, all without yet being cognizant. The next step, he predicted, would require only increased subtlety, greater speed, enhanced miniaturization, finer etching, denser webbing, larger interwoven communities, higher orders of connection, and more finely distributed horsepower.

The smartest appliance I ever assembled was no more than a slavish, lobotomized reflex. True, I got my goods to remember rudimentary things. But I had to envision those memories myself before I could implement them. There was no question of real learning, of behavior fluid enough to change its rules while executing them. Formalizing even the deepest, most elusive knowledge was trivial compared to genuine cognition.

Somewhere between then and now, the idea of thought by artifice had come to life. And Lentz was one of its Geppettos.

My mind toyed with these shiny new cognitive artifacts as if they had just been dug up from the banks of the Tigris. In his most readable piece, Lentz related the account of a distant, academic colleague who had developed a macramé of artificial neurons. This one created such a stir even pseudo-documentary TV picked it up.

The creature consisted of three layers, stacked up like mica. Each bank contained around a hundred neurodes. At birth, its eighteen thousand synapses were weighted randomly. Its input layer read letters; its output produced sounds.

Its first attempt at articulation produced streams of gibberish phonemes, much like any newborn's. But after a few hours, its reading congealed. Its cycle of monotonous syllables clumped into recognizable word shapes. Each time a sound scored a chance hit, the connections making the match grew stronger. Those behind false sounds weakened and dispersed.

Repeated experience and selection taught these synapses their ABCs. The machine grew. It advanced from babbling infancy to verbal youth.

In half a day, the network progressed from "googoo daadaa" to a thousand comprehensible words. In a week, it outstripped every early reader and began closing in on the average reading public. Three hundred simulated cells had learned to read aloud.

No one told it how. No one helped it plough through tough dough. The cell connections, like the gaps they emulated, taught themselves, with the aid of iterated reinforcement. Sounds that coincided with mother speech were praised. The bonds behind them tightened, closing in on remembrance like a grade-schooler approximating a square root. All other combinations died away in loneliness and neglect.

I read, in Lentz's account, how this network's designer peeked into the hidden layer of the adult machine. What he found surprised him. Buried in baroque systems of connection weights lay the rules of pronunciation. Complex math, cluster analysis, and n-dimensional vector work teased out the generalizations. The neurodes had learned that when two vowels go walking, the first one does the talking. And they'd stored the acquired insight in schemes so elegant that the net's maker claimed he could never have dreamed them up alone.

I read the journal write-ups. The science meant nothing to me. I couldn't follow it. Time and choice had left me science-blind. There was no way for me to verify if the talking box possessed any break-through significance. By all accounts, its biological validity was mar-ginal at best. And God knew the thing did not come close to real thinking.

I cared for none of those qualifications. The story grabbed me. I wanted the *image*, the idea of that experiment. A box had learned how to read, powered by nothing more than a hidden, firing profusion. Neural cascade, trimmed by self-correction, eventually produced un-derstandable words. All it needed was someone like Lentz to supply the occasional "Try again"s and "Good boy!"s.

My decade of letters to C. came back, fourth class. No note. But then, I didn't need one. Any explanation would just be something I would be obliged to send back in turn. I was supposed to follow suit, return hers. I told myself I would, as soon as I found a mailer and could get to the post office.

I laid the bundle in the back of a drawer, alongside the lock whose combination I'd forgotten. I told myself the scrap might be useful all the same. Useful, despite everything, in some other life some other me might someday live.

One day, tripping blindly into it, I finished my last novel. I made my final edit, and knew there was nothing left to change. I could not hang on to the story in good faith even a day longer. I printed the finished draft and packed it in the box my publishers had just used to send me the paperback copies of my previous one.

I sealed the carton with too much packing tape and sat staring at it where it lay on my kitchen counter. I thought of C.'s great-

31

grandmother, who, before she turned twenty, had buried three such shoe boxes of stillborns in the grove above E. I asked myself who in their right mind would want to read an ornate, suffocating allegory about dying pedes at the end of history.

The calculation came a little late. I biked the box down to the post office and shipped it off to New York, book rate. New York had paid for this casket in advance. They couldn't afford to be depressed by what I'd done. The long science book had been a surprise success. They were hoping to manufacture a knock-off. I hadn't given them much of a chance.

The moment the manuscript left my hands, I went slack. I felt as if I'd been in regression analysis for three years. At long last, I had revived the moment of old trauma. But instead of catharsis, I felt nothing. Anesthesia.

What was I supposed to do for the rest of my life? The rest of the afternoon alone seemed unfillable. I went shopping. As always, retail left me with an ice-cream headache.

I figured I might write again, at least once, if the thing could start with that magic first line. But the train—that train I asked the reader to picture—was hung up at departure. It did its southward stint. Then it was gone, leaving me in that waiting room slated on the first timetable.

To figure out where the line was heading, I had to know where it had been. I felt I must have heard it out loud: the opener of a story someone read to me, or one I'd read to someone.

When C. and I lived in that decrepit efficiency in B., we used to read aloud to each other. We slept on the floor, on a reconditioned mattress we'd carried on our heads the five blocks from the Salvation Army. Our blanket was a pilling brown wool rug we called the bear.

We huddled under it that first midwinter, when the temperature at night dropped so low the thermometer went useless. After a point, the radiators packed it in. Even flat out, they couldn't keep pace with the chill blackness seeping through brick and plaster. The only thing that kept us, too, from giving in and going numb were the read-alouds. Then, neither of us wanted to be reader. That meant sticking hands above the covers to hold the book.

It would get so cold our mouths could not form the sounds printed on the page. We lay in bed, trying to warm each other, mumbling numbly by small candlelight—"Silver Blaze," *Benvenuto Cellini*—giggling at the absurd temperature, howling in pain at the touch of one another's frozen toes. We were the other's entire audience, euphoric, in the still heart of the arctic cold.

That's how I remembered it, in any case. Maybe we never spoke the notion out loud, but just lying there in the soft, frozen flow of words filled us with expectation. The world could not get this brittle, this severe and huge and silent, without its announcing something.

Somewhere, some shelf must still hold a book with broken black leather binding. A blank journal in which C. and I wrote the titles of all the books we read aloud to each other. If I could find that log, I thought, I might search down the first lines of every entry.

Our life in B. was a tender playact. That dismal rental, a South Sea island invented by an eighteenth-century engraver. C. guarded paintings at the Fine Arts. I wrote expert system routines. For pleasure, we etched a time line of the twentieth century onto the back of a used Teletype roll that we pasted around the top of the room. The Peace of Beijing. Marconi receives the letter "S" from across the Atlantic. Uzbekistan absorbed. Chanel invents Little Black Dress. The limbo becomes national dance craze.

We furnished our first nest with castoffs. Friends alerted us to an overstuffed chair that someone on the far side of the ballpark was, outrageously, throwing out. No three dishes matched. We owned one big-ticket item: a clock radio. Every morning, we woke to the broadcast calls of birds.

When we weren't reading to each other, we improvised a narrative. The courtyard outside our window was an autograph book of vignettes waiting to be cataloged. The scene below played out an endless penny merriment for our express amusement.

Cops rode by on horseback. Robbers rode by in their perennial hull-scraping Continentals. Parent-free children mined the bushes for dirt clumps to pop in their mouths. A conservatory student blew his sax out the open window, even in December. He threaded his way precariously up a chromatic octave, the cartoon music for seasickness.

That's how I would describe it in the book I still had no idea I would soon write. The player always, always missed the A-flat on the way up but hit it, by chance, on descending. "Something to do with gravity," C. joked.

Youngish adults in suits came by selling things. They represented strange and fascinating causes, each more pressing than the last. When the canvassers buzzed our intercom, we sometimes shed some small bills. Or we made the sound of no one home.

A heavy woman on workman's comp who walked with a cane hobbled by at regular intervals to air out her dog. The dog, Jena, who we decided was named after the battle where Hegel watched Napoleon rout Prussia, was even more fossilized than its owner. Jena would stand thick and motionless, halfway down the sidewalk, contemplating some spiritual prison break, never bothering to so much as tinkle. Its owner, whose name we never learned, waited in the doorway, repeatedly calling the beast with the curt panic of abandonment. The dog would gaze a lifetime at the horizon, then turn back in desolation.

I relayed these anecdotes to C., who lay in bed with her eyes closed, pretending to be blind and paralyzed, at the mercy of my accounts. I elaborated events for her, embroidering until the improbability of the whole human fabric made her smile. When she smiled, it always stunned me that I'd discovered her before anyone else had.

Even while we playacted it, I recognized that fantasy. It came from a collection of ghost stories that a famous editor had assembled before we were young.

I told C., from memory, the one about two men lying in the critical ward. The one, a heart patient, has the window bed. He spends all day weaving elaborate reports of the community outside to amuse his wardmate. He names all the characters: Mr. Rich. The Messenger Boy. The Lady with the Legs. He weaves this endless, dense novel for the quadriplegic in the next bed, who cannot see through the window from where he lies.

Then one night the window narrator has a heart attack. He convulses. He grapples for his medicine on the nightstand between the beds. The paralyzed man, seizing his chance at last to see this infinite world for himself, summons from nowhere one superhuman lunge and dashes the medicine to the floor.

When they move him to the emptied window bed the next day, all he can see is a brick wall.

"That's a great story," C. told me. In the icy dark, I felt her excitement. The world lay all in front of us. "I love that one. I'm afraid I'm going to have to kill you for it."

All I had to go on was that train. It might have come from anywhere, tracing a route so simple I would never win it back. I myself could not visualize the southbound freight. How could I ask a reader to picture it?

I paid bills, caught up on old correspondence. I did all my errands in the least efficient ways that my unconscious could devise. I discovered again just how long an evening can be without any media.

I searched my notebooks for all those plots that had seemed so pressing to me while I worked on something else. At one time I'd wanted to write the story of a man who made a living by imitating a statue. He would travel to all the capitals of the world, spray-paint himself silver, don a toga, and stand unnervingly still while admiring crowds ran past and threw coins into his cup. But now, when I watched this statue-man to see what happened, all he wanted to do was improve, hold stiller longer, until people passed without noticing.

I thought of putting a seventeen-year-old up in a cubicle on top of a flagpole just outside the Mall of America for 329 days, as a combined social protest and attempt to get into *Guinness*.

I found a preliminary sketch for a political light burlesque. Ma and Pa Kent, out in one of those states longer than it is wide, have a perfectly formed kid. The kid sleeps through nights, eats on schedule, and apologizes for burping. "Look at that boy crawl, Mother! He's going to be president." The comedy would trace the kid's supreme calling through Smallville High, Northwest Orthogonal State, and into the arms of the PACs and party hacks. I thought it might make a pleasant vacation.

Any one of these embryo ideas seemed workable. One might even have been good, had I been another person, with another person's care and patience. I kept browsing, thinking the right plot would leap out at me. When it didn't, I told myself that the key thing was to choose and get down to it. After all, wasn't a story *about* figuring out what the story was about?

Mornings passed when a sick knot in my stomach informed me that I would never write anything again. I had nothing left in me but the autobiography I'd refused from the start even to think about. My life threatened to grow as useless as a three-month-old computer magazine.

I asked myself whether, if you kept private long enough, you earned the right to a brief personal appearance in public. I recoiled from the idea. But there came a point when blaming things on innocent, third-person bystanders became a lie.

And after four times out, in a search for simplicity that had wound up producing complexities beyond reading, the question became: why go public at all?

I went to the Center and played the humanist fly on the wall. I read my notebooks. I diverted myself on the net.

Autumn came and flushed out the oppression of midwestern August. Sidewalks glazed over with cool rain. The shed leaves emitted a whiff of premature winter. Flocks gathered and wheeled in V's of retreat. We entered those two glorious weeks when U.'s weather made it seem that anyone alive could start again. Recover all lost ground.

The brisk, invigorating air crippled me with anticipation. I kept still and waited, thinking this time I might not scare off the imminence that always visited, the first week of the last season.

I lived on that refrain: picture a train. Picture a train heading south. Even garbled beyond recovery, my blast of turbine steam logged its nightly reprimand.

One night I went to a bar I'd never set foot in as an undergrad. I could count in a quarter of a byte the times I'd gone for a beer while in school here. Safeguarding the precious synapses. I'd worked so hard to keep them in perfect firing order. It had all seemed so important once.

In the Low Countries, I'd developed a taste for refermented fruit beers. These were as expensive here as they were ridiculous, in the land of the thin, frozen pilsner. But a *kriek* was a lot cheaper than a round-trip ticket. I ordered a bottle, which the bartender had to dust off.

I sat at the bar and nursed the drink, remembering those Belgian TV shows where the contestant tried to match dozens of beers to their rightful serving glasses. The last time I'd had a beer was in a Liège hole-in-the-wall that sold eleven hundred varieties, eighty on tap. The beer menu was book-length, with an index.

I imagined explaining the Lite concept to any of C.'s one hundred and twenty first cousins. I had difficulty getting past the word's spelling. Out the window of the bar, at a distance, I could see the university Quad. I pretended it was an unknown, astonishing Grote Markt I would go explore after I finished the cherry brew.

I made another narrative stab in my head. A thirty-five-year-old unemployed construction worker in Mechelen, once-mighty Gothic town shrunken to nothing, gets obsessed with completing the spire of the city's cathedral, originally slated to be the tallest in the world. My out-of-work day laborer, whom I took to calling Joris between sips, figures the building project has just been delayed several centuries. All he has to do is get the city to pauperize itself to put itself back on the ecclesiastical map.

The tale seemed immense with potential. The only catch was that it would play to an audience of exactly one.

The bar started filling. A frat boy, in his zeal to resuscitate a dead pitcher, collided with my shoulder. "Sorry, sir," he placated, in best commerce-major fashion.

The word was a slap in the face, the young's coded self-righteousness. People under twenty-one needed to work that fact into the conversation, even if the conversation consisted of two words. In this country, youth was a socially acceptable form of bragging.

A horrible mistake coming here, to this college bar, this college town. These were the same people who had gotten tanked every night while I broke my neck studying. They had stayed twenty, while I'd dissolved into middle age.

Even more depressing, I wasn't the only old guy in the place. At a table in the back, the smokers' section, a group of Center fellows took a rare break from experimentation to engage in what seemed, from my distance, heavy theoretical talk.

In their midst, looking even more sickly and implausible out of his idiom, my man Lentz gesticulated. His hands built and dismantled various violent tetrahedra in the air. He made some point that the half-dozen others at the table refuted with exasperation bordering on disgust. Science looked a lot like literary criticism, from across the room.

Lentz glanced my way, looking through me. We shared an awkwardness, each pretending not to have noticed the other. Each pretending the other hadn't spotted us pretending. I felt relieved that he didn't wave, but slighted.

After a while, the group's lone woman detached from the debate. She walked toward me. She was tall, amiable, dismayed, her freckles like constellations in a home planetarium. I had seen her in the corridors. I couldn't begin to guess how old she was. I'd lost all ability to gauge age.

In the time it took her to cross the room, I sketched a story about a professional guesser who learned to tell, within impossible limits of tolerance, the age, weight, height, and accumulated sorrow of anyone he met.

"I've come to recruit you," she announced, drawing up. "The good guys need help."

She dressed impeccably, forgoing the scientist's customary indifference to grooming. She wore tweed, with her ample hair rolled in one of those forties ingenue prows. The effect was uncannily archaic, as if she were about to announce that severing the corpus callosum cured epilepsy.

"Who are the good guys?"

She laughed. "Good question. I'm Diana Hartrick. I do associative representation formation in the hippocampus."

"Is that near here?"

I grinned as widely as possible, trying to pass off the idiocy as voluntary. I stuck out my hand, stupidly. In Limburg, one shakes hands early and often, with anything that holds still long enough.

"Little Marcel," I said. "Not doing much of anything, at present."

She took my hand, but her face clouded. She sucked in her mouth, a teacher unwilling to credit a bad report about a good pupil. "Now, why would you lie to me before you've even met me?"

At first I thought she meant the bit about my not working. Then the penny dropped. Dr. Hartrick, I figured, was a kind soul, but as literal as a lawyer giving the keynote at a libel convention.

"I'm sorry. That's Lentz's pet nickname for me." I gestured with my chin back toward her table.

"Oh. Him. He's why I came to get you. The man is on another rampage."

She leaned against the bar, resting a tote bag on her hip. From the side pocket, amid a sheaf of papers, issued an ancient softbound Viking Portable. Its spine was scored to pulp. I read the blurb at the top, despite the cover's being badly scuffed. "Not less than three times in his or her life should everyone read *Don Quixote* . . . in youth, middle age, and old age."

"May I?" I indicated the book.

She passed the book to me with a bemused patience long used to eccentric requests.

I flipped the book over. I opened to the copyright page. Nine-hundred-page books cost $1.85 when I was twelve. It didn't seem possible. I turned to the First Sally. *In a village of La Mancha the name of which I have no desire to recall . . .*

These few words spread like truth serum through me. I was fifteen again, and working up the courage to tell the Egyptian empress who sat in front of me in sophomore humanities that the hair on the back of her neck stopped my breath to look at.

I read then, everything I could lay hands on. Reading was my virgin continent. I read instantly upon awakening, and was still at it well past the hour that consciousness shut down. I read for nothing, for a pleasure difficult to describe and impossible afterward to recover.

Those sixteen words from Chapter One bogged me down in old amber. Before the end of the clause, I felt mired as a Cambrian bug in molasses memory. The First Sally, a second time: it sicked a pack of ghosts on me as brutal as the ones hounding the overread Don.

I shut the volume before the rest could get out. "Thanks. That's all I needed to check."

Hartrick took the book and slipped it back into her bag without comment. "Are you going to suit up and help us do battle?"

Her words came out softly, without any of that self-effacing edge of junior faculty under the gun. In one phrase, she grew older, drier. I'd misjudged her earnestness. *I* was the lawyer, the literal fool who'd missed the joke.

I imagined that her line of work lent her this presence. When you see up close the countless subsystems it takes to place an image into the permanent buffer, when you measure the loop that image makes on its way to being retained, you temper yourself against the definitive. You go humble, understated, wry.

I pictured what it felt like to see the organ at work, its cartoon flickers pasted up on a PET scan. You flash a world in front of your subject's eyes and watch the watercolor washes splash around the temporal lobe, fixing that world in a holdable shorthand. This woman traced the process in real time, the mental palette exploding in desperate semaphores, trying to convince itself that the fleet whose capture it signals hasn't slipped off in night fog.

Every postmodern postsolipsist, I thought, should do a postfrontal neurology stint. The most agile of them would, like this careful woman, take to weighing the violence in their every predicate. Once they saw the bewilderingly complex fiber in its impossible live weave, theorists would forever opt for the humblest, least-obtrusive sentence allowed them.

"I'm afraid my doublet's in the wash."

She smiled, generosity itself. "Come on," she insisted. "We need somebody who can outtalk him."

I followed her back to the Center's table. Lentz was well into introducing me by the time we two drew up.

"Here's our Nonresident-in-Residence. Marcel, meet Gupta, Chen, Keluga, and Plover. You appear to be chummy with Hartrick already. Everyone knows Marcel, the Dutchman. By reputation, anyway. Does anyone actually read those things of yours?"

I smiled. "I'm the wrong person to ask."

"Your mother's read them?"

"She says she has."

"Marcel writes Books," Lentz glossed, for nobody. "Watch what you say. We're all going to end up immortalized."

The pitcher of watery pilsner on the table had done nothing for his aggression. Tonight, though, his fight was with his colleagues. I was just a convenient sparring dummy, tangent to the main event.

I sat down. The table crackled. Talk had died away to wary philosophical sparks, now that the hard data had been expended all around. My presence threw a damper on the charged colloquium. Everyone reverted to good behavior.

Of the group, I'd met only Ram Gupta, a perception researcher of international reputation. His recent passage through Immigration could not have been choppier. The airport officer assumed this brown-skin meant to go feral the minute anyone let him in the country. The epic humiliation seemed not to have perturbed Dr. Gupta in the least.

"*You* are making interesting points and you *too* are making interesting points," Ram sang, nodding by turns at Lentz and Harold Plover. "Could we not just leave it at that? Come, gentlemen. If we all stood up and got hit by a car as we walked out this door tonight, God forbid, would any of us want this conversation to be the . . . ?"

"I thought you people believed in eternal repetition," Lentz baited him.

Plover, a big, cotton-frayed Kodiak of a man, threw up his hands. "Terrific. Just what I need. I've already suffered an eternity of this nonsense in the last half hour alone."

"Harold, if you'd just come up with some fresh objections . . ."

"We can't level any fresh objections, 'cause we got no data." Keluga, a scrubbed blond boy of about twelve, searched the circle of faces for approval. Eager grad student's night out with the grownups.

"Data?" Lentz minced. "Oh, by all means. Hartrick will be happy to shave up several hundred simian forebrains for us to run some trials. That ought to resolve the question, once and for all."

"You cut up monkeys?" I whispered to Diana. "Rhesus pieces?" I sided with Ram. Even absurdity beat public ugliness.

Lentz snorted. "Marcel, we're going to give you a seven out of a thousand for that. One more such outburst and you have to go back and sit with the poets."

"Oh, leave him be," Plover mumbled into his cups. "It was funny."

"Don't blame me," I said. "I got it from a friend at Cal Tech."

Hartrick poured herself two fingers of foam in the bottom of a fluted glass. "You're straying into metaphysics, Philip. All the data in the world couldn't prove or disprove those kinds of claims."

"What on earth are you drinking?" Plover asked me. I'd brought along my *kriek*, unwilling to part with even the dregs of a liquid that came to about half a dollar a swallow.

"It's a Dark Lite," I said.

"It smells like vinegar cough syrup."

"Marcel's just indulging a little self-pitying nostalgia. The cakes-and-tea thing. Watch out he doesn't get sick. If he throws up, we're going to have a million and a half words all over the table."

"Would you listen to this creep?" Plover railed. "Why do we let him do this to us?" He shook his head at me. "Don't mind him. He gets like that, even without the two beers."

I assured Plover with a glance that Lentz and I were acquainted.

Lentz, a general fighting on many fronts, engaged the nearest comer. "You're the one playing the metaphysician, Dr. Di."

" 'Dr. Di'! Of all the insulting, sexist—" Plover threw his hands up again. He forgot to release his glass before doing so, and a fair amount of beer ended up on the wall behind him.

Lentz talked through the commotion of cleanup. "*You* are the ones evoking mystic mumbo jumbo. Is the problem computable in finite time? That's all I want to know. Is the brain an organ or isn't it? Don't throw this 'irreducible emergent profusion' malarkey at me. Next thing you know, you're going to be postulating the existence of a soul."

Hartrick rolled her eyes. "Not in your case, Philip." Her eyes came to rest on me. "See what I mean? Care to bail us out?"

"Remember Winner and Gardner?" Ram asked, still hoping to distract everyone from their sought-for conflict. "The piece on comprehension of metaphor, in *Brain*? Asked to choose the correct picture for 'give someone a hand,' many right-hemisphere-damaged patients picked the one showing a palm on a platter."

Keluga blanched. "Ram, please. I'm still hitting the salsa."

"Somebody tell me what you people are talking about." I felt slightly lesioned myself.

"Oh *yes*." Lentz did a slow take in my direction. He slapped his thigh. "Of course. Little Marcel. You have an affiliation with—what's it called these days? The English Department?"

"They're sponsoring my residency here, yes."

"Tell us. What passes for knowledge in your so-called discipline? What does a student of English have to do to demonstrate acceptable reading comprehension?"

I shrugged. "Not a whole hell of a lot. Take some classes. Write some papers."

"That's all *you* had to do?"

"Oh. Well. Me. When I was a lad—"

"Shh, shh, everyone. The reclusive writer about whom nothing is known is about to tell us his personal history."

"Look. Do you want to hear this or not?"

"My. Pardon me. I had no idea we were so touchy."

"Lentz, your apologies are worse than your attacks."

"Amen," Diana cheered. "Don't let him bully you, Richard."

Lentz smiled. He folded his fingers in front of his mouth. He looked for a moment like Jacob Bronowski's evil twin. "Do go on."

I debated, then did. "When I was twenty-two, I took something called the Master's Comprehensive Exam. They gave us a list of titles. Up at the top of page 1 was 'Caedmon's Hymn.' Six pages later, it wound up with Richard Wright."

"Where did you go to school?" Harold Plover asked.

I gestured out the window, the Quad beyond. My face flushed with shame. I'd failed to swim clear of the wreck.

"This list," Lentz persisted. "What happened then?"

"Then we sat for two days and answered questions. One each in six historical sections."

"What kind of questions?"

"Oh, anything. We'd do two hours of IDs. You know. 'Hand in hand with wandering steps and slow . . .' Name the author, work, location, and significance."

"Okay, so maybe I *won't* change fields." Keluga's crack fell flat.

Plover waved his bear paws again. "Wait a minute. I know this one. The end of *Paradise Lost*?"

"Harold," Lentz minced. "You've missed your calling."

"Then we did a few essays. 'Discuss the idea of the Frontier and its tragic consequences in four of the following six writers.' "

"What questions did you answer?" Lentz quizzed.

I shrugged. Out the side of my mouth, I made a little grad-student raspberry.

"Hold on. This was only a dozen years ago. And you remember . . . ?"

I ringed my thumb and forefinger, held the O up for public view. Lentz looked around the table in triumph.

"I suppose it would come back to me if I tried."

"Heavens, Marcel. Don't do that."

"Can I ask you something?" Keluga interjected. "I read somewhere that you studied physics . . ."

"As an undergrad. You read that? You people are supposed to be reading technical journals. Where the hell is the Two Cultures split when you need it?"

"What happened?"

"To what?"

"To physics."

"It's a long story."

Lentz cackled. "Don't press the man, Keluga. He's told every paper in the country that he doesn't like to talk about himself. About this list, Powers. You think you can find a copy somewhere?"

"Oh, the departmental files have scores of them."

Lentz looked about the table, his neck flared in challenge. "Anyone object to using this list as a test domain?"

Plover looked pissed. Hartrick hung her head. Ram began fidgeting in distress. Chen, who'd said nothing since I sat down, smiled uncertainly, at sea. Keluga was relishing the squabble, the way a kid might delight in seeing his parents drunk.

"Test of what?" I asked, as politely as possible.

"We're going to teach a machine how to read your list."

The words floored me. "You can *do* that?"

Plover scowled at Hartrick. "I thought you said you were going to bring back reinforcements."

Hartrick showed her palms, helpless. The token humanist had let them down.

Lentz inspected his nails. "As you see, what we can and cannot do is a matter of some difference of opinion."

Chen came to life. "It's to exaggerate," he said. Or perhaps, "That's too exaggerated." His English was impressionistic at best. "We do not have text analysis yet. We are working, but we do not have. Simple sentence group, yes. Metaphor, complex syntax: far from. Decades!"

He attached his attention to the technical edge of Lentz's bombshell. But I doubted Chen followed the charged subtext that the others were pitched in. I'd just started to pick up on what was at stake myself. And I'd passed the reading exam years ago.

"Chen, Chen. One of the quickest intellects in formal symbol-system heuristics." Lentz blessed him, fingers bent. "And still a step behind."

"Philip," Diana warned. She would pounce, if pushed. Tenure or no tenure. "Hyun? How long have you been in the country?"

"Four years." He paused to consider the implication. "About a piece in *Journal of Cognitive Neuroscience* I tell you anything. No problem. What you want to know? But the first page of a big-print, supermarket, paperbacked love story? Forget it!"

We all laughed, each for our own reasons. After four years in the Netherlands, I would have been reduced to tears of frustration by such a conversation.

Ram was first to turn laughter into speech. "I am constantly getting complimented on my English by people who don't realize it is my first language."

"Would *you* sit this Master's Comp thing?" Plover asked him.

"Don't be kidding me. I mean, who is this Milton fellow to me, anyway?"

A moment of deflation all around suggested that Lentz's fantasy had been vanquished. He'd been caught in an undergraduate indulgence and forced to own up.

Plover sighed. "Well, Philip, I'm afraid it's back to real science with you." He raised his glass in a closing toast, and sipped.

"On the contrary. We're going to build a device that will be able to comment on any text on Marcel's six-page list."

"Oh, for God's sake!" Plover spit. "I've had it. The man's just provoking us."

Diana laid a hand on his shoulder to calm him. "And doing a fair job."

"We shouldn't even humor him."

"Youngsters." Lentz's wave included Keluga and me. Generous with the term. "Children, I give you radical skepticism at its finest."

"All right, then. Okay." Plover's tone rose. He pushed up his sleeves and loosened his collar. "Put your money where your mouth is."

Chen coughed a sharp monosyllable. It might have been a laugh. "Interesting phrase. Could your machine—?"

"Harold. We will do this thing, and do it with existing hardware, in no longer than—Marcel, how long are we to be graced with your fair presence?"

I looked at my watch. "What time is it now?" Nobody laughed. It must have been my timing.

I said that I had about ten months before I'd need to fabricate a real life. Lentz looked concerned. "It will be a rush job, but never mind. In ten months we'll have a neural net that can interpret any passage on the Master's list. Harold's choice. And its commentary will be at least as smooth as that of a twenty-two-year-old human."

Plover erupted. "Philip! You can't mean this. What about your work?"

"I've worked enough for one lifetime. Besides, wouldn't this have some professional interest, if we can carry it off?"

Plover glanced around the table. A last appeal. He hooked my eyes. His looked infinitely sad, afraid of forgetting what they were alarmed about. *Say something*, they urged. *This is absurd.*

"How are you going to evaluate?" I asked. Just crediting the proposal knocked Plover down another peg.

Lentz hunched his lip. "Standard Turing Test. Double-blind.

Black-box both respondents. Give them each x hours to type out an answer."

"With Richard here as the guest literary judge?" Diana asked as if, for all the disappointment I had caused them, I might still be the last hope of the good.

Lentz coughed in mid-swig. "Not on your life. Powers here is going to be my research assistant. Who did you think I meant by 'we'?"

"We thought you were using the royal plural, Philip," Plover said. "Like you usually do."

Lentz condescended to address me. "You in? Or did you have something better to do?"

The world had enough novels. Certain writers were best paid to keep their fields out of production.

"Ten months? No. I wasn't doing much of anything." I spoke the words and betrayed my genus.

Plover, pushed to exasperation, cut bait. "All right, you two. Throw your lives away. I can't stop you." Harold, I decided, had at least one teenaged child.

Hartrick refused to capitulate. "Ram will judge," she said. Ram looked nonplussed. "He's as close to a disinterested, objective third party as we're going to get."

"I tell you, I don't know this Milton chap from Adam."

"That's your qualification. We'll name the human opposition when time comes. Meanwhile, what are the stakes?"

Lentz grew thoughtful. The vexatious child, called to account. "If we win, Harold has to give up his non-computational emergent Berkeley Zen bullshit."

The table sucked in its collective breath. Plover just snickered. "If you win, we'll *all* be getting pink slips. The whole thing is just too witless. Kindergarten. Mechanistic make-believe. I don't know what you're up to, Lentz. But you're gonna get me to bite. I'll bet the farm."

"And if you lose?" Diana enunciated, through a thin grin. She meant to extract casuistry's penalty in advance.

"If we lose, we'll give you a public retraction. A full apology, in print. The signed disgrace of your choice."

"Harold! Did you hear that? We finally have the man where we want him. Philip, you must be slipping."

"It's a trick," Keluga pronounced.

Lentz shook his head. "No trick."

"Of course it's a trick," Plover told the future's assembled jury. "But it just might be a trick worth paying to see."

"Too exaggerated," Chen said. He shook his head and smiled. He seemed not to realize that the deal had already been struck.

Diana pulled out her *Portable Cervantes* and read aloud the random sentence that fell under her bookmark. An illustration of the futility that this abrasive man and I were about to embark on. I can't remember the sentence. Out of context, I couldn't make heads or tails of it.

"Harold," she said. "If this huckster is right . . ." She elbowed Lentz in the ribs. I didn't think he would brook being touched by another human, but he did. "If we're really at the point where we can formalize . . ."

Plover raised an eyebrow. "Yes?"

"If they get their creature to read, do I still have to slog through this?"

Plover cast his head back, dignified in affront. "Yes. Of course."

"All of it?"

"If you want to remain friends."

She stuffed the paperback back into her handbag. She buckled in pantomime under its weight.

Plover took pity. "You can skim Part Two."

"Don't strain yourself," Lentz advised. "We'll beat you to it."

I remember thinking: thank God *Don Quixote* was not on the List. At least that one was a translation.

C. was a student of mine in the very first freshman composition course I ever taught at U. We were only two years apart in age. I was young for a master's candidate and she was an older transfer student, forced by unyielding rules into taking a course she didn't need.

She was late for my first class, an 8 a.m. session. I was not impressed. She seemed sluggish, not particularly bright or attractive or engaging. Inexorable, at best. She did, however, sit in the front row. If she contributed anything in those first few meetings, I don't remember.

But then, this was my first time teaching. I was more than a little wired, and it's a miracle I remember anything. Not nervous: what pedagogical theorists refer to as unprepared. Having spent the previous summer reading the grammar and usage texts, the style manual and reader for the course, I at least knew the material. What I didn't know was the college freshman, and whether she or he would put up with a spindly twenty-one-year-old in torn golf shirt, face not much clearer than their own, standing up in front of the chalkboard trying to conduct the discussion.

My impression of C. changed after the first assignment. I'd given, as preliminary topic, "Convince a total stranger that she would not want to grow up in your hometown." It seemed enough of an inversion of the standard composition theme that my fosters would have to think about it before plunging in and cranking out the usual suspect sentences.

The best paper belonged to a woman named Maya. I later learned that she was seven years older than I was and the mother of three. "Trust me. You don't want to grow up in East St. Louis," she wrote.

You get born in without being asked, and no amount of asking in the world is going to get you out again. There aren't but a few ways out of East St. Louis and those are all to places you don't want to be in even worse.

C.'s was the second most astonishing. She wrote lyrically, wistfully, brutally, about growing up in Chicago on an island one house wide. She wrote about waking up to the stink of slaughtered animals from the stockyards mixed with the heavy scent of chocolate from the neighborhood factory. She wrote of the neo-Nazi marches in the park where her father used to take her for walks. She wrote of the shifting neighborhood lines, the lava lamp of fear that made families bolt for invisible, redrawn borders every two years. She wrote of the lone newcomers from the wrong side of the tracks going door to door, begging people not to move out just because their family had moved in.

I read these two papers out loud, as a pair. The kids from the hopelessly affluent North Shore suburbs with too few movie theaters took notes.

By the end of my first semester, I learned that the problem with most student writing is not grammar. You learn the rules early on or you never get them. The real problem was belief. My eighteen-year-olds never believed that the reader was real, that they themselves were real, that the world's topics were real. That they had to *insist* as much, in so many words.

C. knew the real the way she knew how to breathe. After that first theme, there was nothing I could do for her but let her go.

For her research paper, C. wrote about Aspasia of Miletus. She'd gone through the standard occult stage in high school, past life analysis and all. In her student conference, she confessed to having once written a hundred-page memoir about her former life in Periclean Athens. That would be an invaluable primary source for her paper, I joked.

Talking, from the start, disconcerted us both. We probed about the edges of the inappropriate. I didn't dare to tell her how strange it felt, to feel so familiar with a stranger. Even that much would have been grounds for misconduct charges. But C. knew. C. always knew. She had a tap on what my mind made of the outside, even before I mapped it into words.

By mutual agreement, we kept mum and avoided incident. I teased her about her previous incarnations. "Do you have any documentary evidence?"

At her next conference, she produced a photo out of her backpack. "Documentary evidence of prior lives." Flirting, under deniability's cloak.

The picture was a small Brownie black-and-white. Bits of glued felt still adhered to its back. She'd torn it from an album, to give to me. A pudgy baby sat out in the backyard, 1961. The world had died away from that moment, and there was nothing left of it but this square miniature.

"The grass was prickling my butt. That's why I'm making the Khrushchev face. My parents threatened me. If I didn't stop crying, they were going to get the camera."

"You remember all that? You can't be more than two."

"I remember things long before that. When I was almost one, my mother took me back to the Netherlands for a visit. I was petting my aunt's dog while it was eating, and it bit me."

"Well, I suppose trauma . . ."

"You don't remember your first years?" Everyone did, her astonishment said. Everyone.

"I have trouble with yesterday's dinner. I find it hard to believe . . . What else can you remember? How about the first sentence you ever spoke?"

"Easy one," she said, gazing at the photo. " 'Good girl outside.' "

"Meaning?"

"Meaning I'd behaved myself, and now they had to turn me loose."

"I hope you're not counting on me to be your expert consultant on literature in English," I told Lentz in his anarchic office, a week after the bet. "It's been a hell of a long time."

He practiced that acerbic smirk on me. The one he didn't need to practice. "You mean you haven't kept faith with your illustrious progenitors?"

"I just can't quote them at length anymore."

"And why is that?"

I shrugged. "Can you quote at length from Babbage and Lady Ada?"

"What would you like to hear?" He stopped clicking on his coffee-stained keyboard and challenged me. "Never mind, Marcel. We don't need to know all about literature in English. The net is going to figure that out on its own. We already know something far more useful. We know Dr. Plover, our examiner. And we know Dr. Gupta, our distinguished judge."

"How is that going to help? You aren't thinking . . . ? We can't count on them to . . ."

"No, I don't suppose one can count on humans for anything. That's the beauty of the challenge."

"Okay. So what do we know about Harold?"

"He's a Shakespeare man. Soft on the Renaissance. Not a day goes by when he doesn't feel some nostalgic twinge about the fall of man."

"Lentz, you are truly merciless."

"It's a career asset."

"All right. So assume he dotes on Elizabethan—"

"We know. There's no assumption."

"But he knows that we know. We aren't going to bank everything on the hopes that he'll pick the predictable?"

"Marcel, never underestimate the baldness of the human heart. Didn't they teach you that in Famous Novelists School?"

"Right. That and 'jab and weave.' The Big Two for gaining and keeping an audience."

"Huh. You must have been out with the chicken pox that week."

In a real Turing Test, our black box, on the other end of a Teletype, would have to convince an examiner that it performed like a real mind. Operationally equivalent. Indistinguishable. Given any topic under the sun, our machine would have to fool the questioner, to pass for a human. A perfect, universal simulation of intelligence would, for all purposes, *be* intelligent.

I would never have signed on to such a pipe dream. But the severely limited version of the test seemed almost formulable, at first glance. We needed do only an infinitesimal fraction of what a full Turing Test passer would have to do. But it hit me only now. What we would have to do was still infinite.

"I fail to see how prepping the thing to say something bright about one sonnet is any easier than prepping it to interpret anything on the entire List."

"It isn't. In both cases, the 'thing' will need to know some *thing* about everything there is to know."

"You're too subtle for me, Engineer. Tell me how our knowledge of the opposition is going to help us, then."

"Plover is a harmless, sentimental slob. Ram will do anything in his power to avoid conflict. We just have to train a network whose essay answers will shatter their stale sensibilities, stop time, and banish their sense of loneliness."

"Oh. Well, if that's all . . ."

"Marcel, you're such a bloody coward. What are you so afraid of?"

"I'm afraid of wasting a year of my life."

"As opposed to . . . ?"

"I'm afraid of becoming a laughingstock, of pursuing some phantom that everyone else in your entire science considers—"

" 'Laughingstock.' What a wonderful word." He dug the keyboard out from the pile of papers he'd stacked on it. He addressed the workstation. "Do you suppose that's like 'rolling stock'? 'Summer stock'? 'Gunstock'? 'Take stock'? 'Wanderstock'?"

I flinched. "That's *wandelstok*. And I asked you not to do that. 'Walking stick' will do fine."

"Come, now. When was the last time you heard anyone use a 'walking stick'?"

He logged on to a remote host, called a program, and keyed a few parameters into it. Sifting through a tangle of equipment, he retrieved a microphone and turned it on. "Laughingstock, laughingstock," he repeated several times into the mike.

After a few seconds—digital eternity—a matte, sexless affect responded, "Their behavior made them the laughingstock of the . . ." I couldn't make out the last word. It must have been "community."

"Oh," I heard myself saying. "Oh! We're not starting from zero, are we?"

"No. Not exactly zero."

He shut down the mike and straightened himself, as much as his body could straighten. He took off those bulletproof-glass spectacles. His face sat revealed in its full saurian severity. Removing the mask seemed to leave him expansive.

"Sometimes building a general-case model is easier than solving a specific-case problem. Also, because we're not constrained to be scientific, work can go as fast as we want. And don't forget our trump card. We don't have to correspond with how the brain does things. That's what's holding up the show in real science. All we have to be is 'as intelligent as,' by any route we care to choose."

"What do you types even mean by that, anyway? 'Intelligent'?"

"Bingo. Marcel, I knew you were my boy."

"Are you tired of real science? Is this just an extended vacation for you, Engineer? Or do you have something else in the works?"

It was as if he didn't even hear me. "Here is your reading assignment for next week. No skimming! If I wanted a liability for a research assistant, I would have hired a Keluga." He handed me another stack of conference papers and journal reprints.

"I thought I was the literature consultant," I whined.

"You are. And this is the literature you'll be consulting. By the way, Marcel. About your wasting a year. You told us you weren't up to anything."

"I've just finished a manuscript."

"And?"

"I'm already toying with a new one," I lied. Lying constructively was my job description, after all.

"Are you? What's it about? Or are you one of those artists who can't whisper the letter their title starts with without jinxing the end product?"

"Well, I have this idea." In fact, I had several hundred, none of which compelled me. Ideas insinuated themselves into my good graces, begging to be saved from the void. But I, the rescue squad, seemed to be off duty.

"Yes, good. Ideas are good. 'A very good place to start,' " he sang. His voice was clear, a startling tenor.

I ignored him. It was getting easier to. "An overworked industrialist takes a vacation to—Chester, England. He is touring the city walls, the half-timbered arcades, when he's hit up for change by a street person. He pretends to be an uncomprehending German sightseer. The panhandler doesn't buy it, starts harassing him. The industrialist explodes. The beggar retaliates with some vague threat. Three months later, at a conference in Cairo, the industrialist is accosted by a vagrant who—"

"Who says, 'Remember the guy in Chester?' Introducing a whole international cartel of homeless who appear outside the restaurant windows wherever this man travels. Very nice. A moral little ghost tale. Kiplingesque. Marcel, you're better off working for me."

"Don't knock Kipling. Kipling is a great writer. Some of my best friends are Kipling scholars."

"Is he on the List?"

I shook my head. No accounting for taste.

"Let me see that damn thing. Did you bring it?"

He had asked me to. I always did as asked. Lentz took the sheaf from me and began leafing through it. He made no comment until page 4, nineteenth-century British. "Hm. Mary Shelley. This could be more interesting than we've bargained for."

I thought to tell him about my disembodied opening line. But I did not much feel like holding my slight hostage up to Lentz's ridicule. The train, after all, was no more than a *vehicle*. What Taylor would have called it, in the freshman seminar that made me forsake measurement for words. The train meant nothing in itself; it simply carried the story out of the terminal.

My train did not even reach past the border checkpoint into page 2. The invitation to picture this could run no further than halfway down the first right-hand side. If the line were memory rather than invention, an exhaustive search of paper space—all middle-right opening pages in every known secondhand bookshop on earth—would turn it up.

Picture these words. The letters tunnel astonishingly across the page. They form themselves into an extended consist of cars just pulling out. The cars hold together by invisible coupling-gaps. When a boy, I counted these spaces as they clicked along on the tracks of type, under my mother's breath.

Counting the gaps was also counting the words. Machines performed the task effortlessly, born to it. Could they count ideas as well? Could they be made to sort thoughts, assemble them into a supple, southbound express?

I read the homework Lentz assigned me. An article on hippocampal association that Diana Hartrick co-authored grabbed my imagination. Every sentence, every word I'd ever stored had changed the physical structure of my brain. Even reading this article deformed the cell map of the mind the piece described, the map that took the piece in.

At bottom, at synapse level, I was far more fluid than I'd ever suspected. As fluid as the sum of things that had happened to me, all things retained or apparently lost. Every input to my associative sieve changed the way I sieved the next input.

To mimic the life we were after, Lentz and I would have to build a machine that changed with every datum about life that we fed it. Could a device—a mere vehicle—survive the changes we'd have to inflict upon it?

It struck me. To train our circus animal in Faulkner or Thomas Gray, we would first have to exhilarate it with the terror of words. The circuits we laid down would have to include the image of the circuit itself before memory overhauled it. The net would have to remember what it would be again, one day, when forgetting set in for good.

Before I'd even scratched the homework pile, I was a changed person. The writer who had signed on to the reckless bet was dead. Lentz, Hartrick, Plover, Gupta, Chen—each clinging to the local trap of temperament—C., Taylor, all my lost family and friends, all the books on the List, all the works I would now never write stood waving goodbye from beneath my departing compartment window.

It seemed forever since I had set out on an open ticket. Forever since I had traced, in mental route, the trip that would not be mine to retrace much longer.

After a while, the calendar becomes a minefield. I had to skirt so many anniversaries that autumn that I found it hard to take a step without detonating one. Taylor's seminar met in an attic room of the English Building, that fall when, at eighteen, I found my first map of the world. I taught my first course, the one C. took, three falls later.

Fall at twenty-two, I passed my Master's Comps, and moved as far away from U. as I could get.

I could not see how I'd gotten from one fall to another, or from any of those falls to this one. Age lurches in fits and starts, like a failing refrigerator compressor. Like a gawky, grand mal–adroit adolescent on ancient roller skates, navigating a stretch of worn sidewalk in a subduction zone. It holes up awhile, stock-still, then slams out one afternoon to play catch-up ball.

Time is not a wave. It is discrete, particulate. I came to class one day, that class where I pretended I was Taylor, unlocking the self's intricacies to a horrified and enthralled audience. I arrived that morning at eight to announce that I wasn't up to teaching that day, or the session after. I gave an assignment for the following week and watched my fold file out, subdued.

All but C. She stayed on, by tacit pact knowing it was time to come forward. We stood alone in the emptied room. She asked, "Want to sit somewhere for a minute?"

I did. We wandered out of the English Building onto the Quad. What quads were for: for generations of student sadness to lie down on, in the crisp blue of the first week of year's end. Everything we saw as we staked our spot said, *last November ever.* The first of an almost endless list of lasts.

C. sat Indian style. I lay on my side, head propped on an elbowed arm. On all sides of us ran the ring of collegiate buildings—Chemistry, Math, English. Each had been the setting for a thousand and one urgencies and embarrassments. I would be glad to be gone.

But gone where? The rub. I hadn't a clue, and felt good about even that. Very few job openings for the thing I wanted to do. I'd be lucky to be busing tables for a portion of the tips, this time next fall.

My father had foreseen that, of course. The man had known everything, except how to go on living. He never said word one when his son told him he planned to transfer out of physics, trash the stellar career. He didn't need to say anything. I could read the verdict in his face: Do what you need to. But what a colossal waste of talent and investment.

"Poetry, Rick? What does that mean, exactly?" It means you

haven't the faintest idea what you want to do. Burned out on problem sets. Isn't that right?

I never got the chance to defend myself. The man took off to Alaska to his sister's. Dad timed his disappearance so no one had to watch him go. And as a result, I've had to watch the immortally wasted body pace through a decade and a half of accusing dreams.

A packet would reach me three days after the news. A small bundle of chapbooks—the poems of Robert Service. *The Spell of the Yukon. Rhymes of a Rolling Stone.* Dad's favorite poet, and more beloved because the academics—his son—no longer even bothered to despise the rhymer. "The Cremation of Sam McGee": Dad's gloss on his own choice of exit. A slap in the face. A last, belated blessing. A request that if you are going to waste your life studying poetry, at least waste it on the good stuff.

I lay on the Quad, thinking over this goodbye gift, this student of mine sitting across from me. I shifted to my back. I saw myself staring up into the most unlikely azure. How many ghosts did life involve pleasing?

"Are you all right?" C. intervened.

My "Of course" didn't even convince itself.

"You were . . . I thought . . ."

"I'm fine," I explained.

"Tell me," she said. Anonymity is best. Who do you ever know, after all? *Tell me*, while I'm still a blank slate. Before you make me over in the habit of knowledge.

"My father just died."

I winced then, and annually in remembering. So bleeding what? Fathers and the deaths of fathers. How many children half my age lost parents to any of the world's ingenious violences in the time it took me to speak those words? I had no right. No one did. My own sorrow sickened me.

I spoke without looking at her, at least. It helped later on, to say that her cow-eyed, trusting complicity played no role in my impulse confession. I came to her sight unseen. I had no idea yet how heart-stoppingly plain she could look. I fell in love with a voice, with two words.

"I'm so sorry," she said. As if McGee had been cremated through her own carelessness. And yet her each pitch denied its own need to exist as anything at all but compassionate sound. The lone condolence ever allotted. Only the saying mattered. The words meant little, if anything.

"I'm sorry," she said, serene where she should have been scared off. "Would you like to be by yourself?"

I looked up at her. *What do we need to piece her back?* Do we need five foot four? Do we need brownish-black, pageboy hair? Aggressively shy, nervously innocent? Could we create her whole, conjure her up again intact on one detail, say, a face denying ever having known anything but astonishment?

I said, "I'd like to sit with you awhile."

She settled onto the grass, decorously distant. Years later, in a dark bed, I told her. How startled I was—she, a perfect unknown, no sense of me except my classroom act. Why was she here, sitting beside her grieving teaching assistant? Because she'd torn that picture from the family album, and felt obliged to see mine. Because she liked how I looked, poor poet-in-training with the ripped shirts and no mender near. Because my silence sounded so much like need.

She toyed with a blue canvas backpack filled with books. She held it between her legs, a child that might at any minute struggle to its feet and toddle off. Her hair, too short to be pulled back, was pulled back and rubber-banded around a pencil.

I laid it out, on no grounds at all. I told her all about McGee. Everything. Truths I'd never so much as hinted at to my closest friends. Facts never broached even with my brothers and sisters, except in bitter euphemism.

I told her in one clean rush, as only a twenty-one-year-old still can. Of my father's slow-burn suicide, stretched out over fifteen years. The man's long, accreting addiction that made every day a sine wave of new hope crushed. How hope, beaten to a stump, never died. How it always dragged back, like an amputated pet, its hindquarters rigged up in a makeshift wagon.

She listened with the simplest urgency. Nothing more ordinary in the world. She was still the age when one could make a go of compassion. At double that age, I'd duck down emergency exits rather than talk to acquaintances, and the thought of making a friend felt like dying.

"Tell me," she said. And became a part of me always. Daily, somewhere, even if she just as quickly dissolved. You trade your own aloneness. You place yourself in the path of any invitation to come clean. You give up your script completely, on a sudden hunch. Or you never give it at all.

I told her for no reason. Because she sat and asked. Because she, too, seemed so alone in all this collegiate autumn, there on the vacated Quad with her blue backpack and her hair pulled back around a pencil. And because I told her, she would always have something over me. Forever, if she remembered. If she cared to use it.

I relived for her the Powers family dead drop from middle class to *Grapes of Wrath*. The silent, unspeakable impact, without the least tug of restraint from any shoulder harness. I made her listen to the man's keen intelligence, slurred impenetrably. His gross motor skills, stunted like a pithed lab rat's. I told her all my teenage desperate acts: balancing open fifths upside down on the countertop. X-ing off the calendar, to make him think the lost days had lasted weeks. I showed her his puffy, dazed face.

I narrated all this in harrowing detail. At least, I thought I did. A decade on, C. claimed the sketch had been much more schematic.

I described the late night visit, Christmas the year before. Just after I'd dropped my bombshell, the revised career plans. Dad wobbling into my room like a parasite-bloated puppy. Sitting on the foot of my bed, grasping me with anesthetized claw. Waking me from a lesser nightmare. "Rick. Lss. Listen. Don't."

Spooky, ghoulish. Lead-in to liquid panic. I felt my throat clamp again, even relating this thin simile version.

Don't what?

"Don't change. Stay."

"Dad. Go back to bed." I mimed my own lines for her, in the voice of the child parent. Caretaking commenced early, in the kids of my family. "Sleep it off. It'll all be over in the morning." Or soon enough thereafter.

"Rck. Listen. Stay in science. The world needs . . ."

I told her how I'd disappointed him, embittered my father's holdout hope. Bricked up the last loophole he saw for his future. I was supposed to redeem the sad disaster Dad had made of life. And now I would never salvage anything, in my father's or anyone's eyes.

How could I tell this woman details that made me retch to hear? Maybe I tried to make her run. Test her Good Samaritan threshold of horror. She stayed put. She listened all the way up to McGee's cancer and instant disintegration. Almost a reprieve, I confessed in shame. The only thing large enough to displace the first sickness. I held back on one detail—Dad's I-told-you-so grins from inside the debilitating chemo: You always thought your old man would die of drink.

C. sat through it. At one pained silence, she grazed my upper arm. Exemption or encouragement—it didn't matter. Aside from that, we did not touch.

"Why am I telling you all this?"

"It's easier when you don't know someone."

But I do know you, I wanted to object. The first person I didn't have to get to know. The first person I've ever met more alone than I am.

Sick of myself, I tried to draw her out. She reciprocated out of kindness. She said she was studying comparative literature. "It means"—she smiled, defending herself from the ghost of my father —"that I haven't accepted reality yet."

Change of schools had delayed her life by a year. By taking overloads, she would finish almost on time. "I don't know what my hurry is." She laughed. "It's not as if there are a lot of entry-level openings for literature comparers."

This illusion, born in mutual sadness. Because I'd spilled everything, because she in turn lapsed into long, shameless silences, we could pretend we'd been conversing since childhood. No need to gloss. No fill of awkward gaps. Words seemed almost an afterthought, casual noise. Still here. Fear not. Still here.

After we said everything we felt like, we stopped. We sat together, listening to the sparrows take their everyday, bewildered offense. The last day of innocence, of instant companionship without groundwork or explanation. The last year when one could make a friend.

When she spoke again, I jumped. I'd forgotten about speech, or why one would ever resort to it.

"So will you go home for a while?"

I nodded. The short moratorium of mourning. Knowing's intermission, before the return of routine.

Some part of this may have come later. Maybe I conflated the different times we met in that spot, that season, by contrived chance. I've made a career of rewriting. C. used to say that everything was always outset with me. She came to know me so uncomfortably well. How my mind collapsed everything back to Go. How I would end with a head full of opening lines.

Midmorning grew cold. We sat closer. " 'May will be fine next year,' " C. said, lapsing into beginner's anonymity.

I heard belatedly. "What was that again?"

"What?" Her throat closed. She bolted for cover. What did I do wrong? A question promoted to refrain, in time. And how rapidly *already* in C.'s eyes turned into *again*.

Here, at the first cross-purpose, I was too startled to stop and reassure her. "Whatever made you say that?"

"Say *what*?" The Samaritan would fight, if frightened enough.

" 'May will be fine . . .' "

"Oh, that!" She smiled, goofy, breathing again. "It's a line from my parents' English book. Sitting here—this temperature, this wind?" She tried to defuse me. I nodded: keep talking. "I felt so wide open all of a sudden. So—anything. That's what made me think of it."

"English book?"

"As a second language. For adults. A hand-me-down from another South Side family. They came five years before my parents. That's a whole generation, where I come from."

"Is there another line, just after that?"

"Yes. Wait. 'Father hopes to plant roses in the front yard.' All these short narrative vignettes. Incidents you might live. Let's see."

She closed her eyes, to help her visualize. Thought looks up, or off, or in. Away from the distraction of what is. Would a thinking machine, too, turn its simulated eyes away?

"Let's see. On the next page is one that starts, 'Mother goes to fetch the doctor.' Imagine my brother trying to explain to his parents, at age ten, why mothers do to doctors what dogs do to sticks."

I tried.

"That doctor bit was handy, as it turns out. They lived that one." She dropped back into her astonished quiet. "So what's your interest in that May one?" You been holding out on me, Immigrant?

"It's a line from a nostalgic Housman poem. You see, there's this comprehensive I'm supposed to be studying for." The weakening sun cut a peach gash in the side of November the seventh. Summer looked for a last route to the surface, but could not find it.

"Housman?"

"You know. Best years behind you. Poet dying young, kind of thing."

"So what's next?"

"Well, I don't know. I suppose a tech writing job at 24K, a mortgage, a finished den full of kids, and early brain death."

"No!" She laughed. "I mean the poem. 'May will be fine next year.' What happens next?"

"Oh. 'Oh ay, but then we shall be twenty-four.' "

C. laughed. "I'll only be twenty."

"I'll be twenty-two."

"That gives you two whole years yet." Her eyes were brown and enormous, daring me. "Whole lifetimes can play out in the space of two years."

"Whole lifetimes," I echoed. Maybe that's all I ever did: echo her. See what she had to say. Get her to commit, then fall back on accommodation.

We caught eyes. We looked for longer than either thought we should. For a moment, looking felt like something that happened to you rather than something you did. Not *Are you who I think you are? Am I who you think I am?*

"Thanks," I said, taking her fingers when we stood and stretched. "Sorry to unload on you, but I must have needed it."

"I wish you'd unloaded more."

"You have a class?" I said, instead of what I should have.

"I've just missed two," C. apologized. An awkward confession to make to one's teacher. "You?"

I shrugged, pointed toward the meager downtown, toward departure, bus stations, all families waiting at the end of this spreading nexus.

C. started backing down the sidewalk that crisscrossed the green like huge suspender straps. "Have a safe trip home."

"See you," I said. My tag line. Still the only way I have to say goodbye. See you. What did it mean? No tense. Elliptical. Almost an imperative. It must have been the last thing I ever said to my father. See you.

C. lifted her hand, palm out. Then she turned the palm inward and placed it on her sternum. She hoisted her pack, swung on one foot, and walked away. I watched her disappear into the milling field of twenty-year-olds on their way to places none could begin to imagine.

Maybe I knew I was already gone. I still had to finish, though, before I could leave. Fall semester came to its Christmas close. My first incarnation as teacher ended. In the composition class, C. got one of a handful of A's. Our goodbye at semester's end was terse. I'd grown guarded with her and everyone else. My father had died at fifty-two, and the next thirty years seemed to me an academic exercise.

I taught again that spring. I was better; the class was worse. No one wrote on Aspasia. I booked hard in preparation for the exam at year's end. One fine May day I found myself sitting in a graduate colloquium on prosody, scanning the inverted feet in a sonnet by Edwin Arlington Robinson called "How Annandale Went Out." We'd been at the iambs and trochees for a good two hours before it struck me that no one had yet mentioned that the poem was about euthanasia. Whether to let the sufferer die.

I'd transferred from physics to literature because of one man, the incomparable Taylor. He led me to believe, at eighteen, that a person could lay hands on the key to all mythologies. I now saw that literature might indeed teach me about my father's death, but the study of literature would lead no further than its own theories about itself.

I took the exam and passed it. My marks were high enough to gain admission to the final stage, the Ph.D. Then, on the threshold of committing to the field I'd devastated my father by choosing, I threw that choice away as well. I decided to leave U. forever. I would change my life in every way imaginable.

But first I needed to talk to C. I showed up at her rooming house, surprising her. I'd never been there; I'd gotten the address out of the student directory. It was an unrepeatable spring morning. She came to the door sleepy, still in her bathrobe.

"Good girl?" I asked.

Her brown eyes ignited. "Outside!" she shouted. She dressed in a minute, while I waited on the porch. It was true. There was nothing, nothing in existence that she preferred over being in the sun, the wind. Just walking.

"I have to kiss these buds," she said, kissing a brace. "I haven't kissed them yet this spring. When I was a child, I thought they wouldn't grow without encouragement."

She still was that child. And she knew it.

"Would you like to go away with me?" I asked. "Somewhere. Anywhere. Your choice. Two lit majors, making a living in the real world?"

She stopped and stared. It was the question we'd been asking each other from the first student-teacher conference. Only she'd been holding her breath, hoping we would vanish before asking.

"I have to tell you something. I'm involved with someone."

I suppose I knew. But asking, in all its awfulness, was the only way to write myself into this solitary future. Unless I asked, point-blank, I would never escape the second guess. I'd said it out loud. I was free now to forget her. To live out adulthood alone and in good faith. Whatever I cared to do.

"Take care," she intoned. "See things for me, wherever you end up."

I moved to B. I rented a room in the heart of the city. I got a job as a second-shift computer hack, the complete opposite of the life I'd been leading. I wrote about that job years later, in my third novel. I used Taylor as model for my hero, a man who gives up a promising career in science to devote himself to music composition. And I cast myself as the shiftless graduate-school dropout who squanders his talent.

The job was perfect. I worked alone, all night. For part of the shift, I had nothing to do but read. I read Rabelais, Balzac, Freud, Henry Adams, Max Planck. I read at random, obeying only the forgotten principle of pleasure.

In my few daylight hours, I fell in love with women constantly. Bank tellers, cashiers, women in the subway. A constant procession of pulse-pounding maybes. I never did more than ask one or two to lunch.

I frequented the Center's cafeteria. The food was marginal, depending on the hour I arrived. It consisted of the indifferent fried batter that everywhere kept alive this nation's scientific research effort. The lunch conversation, on the other hand, played like the chatter in creation's greenroom. I could eavesdrop in any direction, and trawl the same topic: the nature of the knowable, and how we know it.

For those researchers who bothered to stop and eat, lunch was the hour of collegial consolidation. Too much work at minute magnifications without looking up led to snow blindness. That was the idea behind the Center, the country's largest institute for interdisciplinary study. That was why a third of the complex gave itself over to common grazing space. The plan, in the end, involved a linkup of all locales.

One noon, I brought my stack of reading down to the cafeteria and sat over an Italian beef on wet onion roll. All around me, scientists came up for air, gauging the rest of the global, accreting index under construction. A few tables away, Plover and Hartrick sat scribbling diagrams on a scratch tablet. I thought of joining them, but didn't want to disrupt those with real work to do.

Instead I read. The articles were getting easier to get through. I read how supervised training helped a net grow cleverer at associating any input with desired output. And I got cleverer as I read.

But the brain does things in massive parallel. Out of the edge of my eye, as I read, I saw someone jerk across the room holding a bottle of juice and a packet of batter fries. A ghost doomed to walk the earth awhile in human form. The apparition of Lentz shocked me. Broad daylight should have dissolved him. He seated himself at an empty table, as far from other bodies as possible.

Plover and Hartrick saw him too. Harold wanted to go keep the solitary figure company. Diana pointed to the writing pad and screwed up her face. Finally, she acquiesced. They decamped to his table, where Lentz welcomed them with little more than bare recognition. I thought it safe to join the three of them.

I sat down with what was left of my sandwich. Plover greeted me. "Here he is! Slot B of the sinister cybernetic assemblage. How are you two getting on with your attempt to automate literary criticism?"

I liked this man. I saw him building model rockets as a child, or testing out vaccines on his pet gerbil. I held up the journals, my lunch-hour reading. "I feel like some watcher of the skies . . ."

"When a new planet swims into his ken?" Plover completed. An eager schoolboy.

His quick fill surprised me. I replaced my image of the model rockets with one of a boy reading *The Norton Anthology* under the covers by flashlight.

"That's enough, Marcel," Lentz said out of the corner of his mouth. "We don't want to give away any trade secrets."

"Is it ready, then?" Plover teased. "Let's go try this toy out." He'd hooked and landed the best of natures. "Okay. Okay. Here's one. Name this tune:

"I am a little world made cunningly
Of elements, and an angelic sprite . . .

"Key that one into the old input layer and see what it comes up with."

I couldn't fight this man. The lines were pure love to him, a pleasure to be squandered and so increased. His face, as he quoted, radiated the ingenuous enthusiasm that gets drummed out of professionals around the time of the Ph.D.

"Where's that from?" I demanded. "I know that one."

Plover raised his hands and snapped both thumbs. "Diana? We've stumped him. We've stumped the chump!"

"Now, Harold," Lentz sneered. "Leave the writer alone. He may be washed up, but he isn't Donne yet." He fished a journal from the bottom of my stack, one I hadn't reached yet. He opened to a piece he'd co-authored with a famous Irish neural networker. Holy Sonnet number 5 sat atop the article.

I gaped like a drowning guppy. Plover looked crestfallen. He scanned the epigraph, dignity injured.

"Have you noticed how many of these open with a quote?" I said, to cover my humiliation. "Fashionable. I'm glad to see literature is still good for something."

Diana jumped into the awkwardness. "Philip. On the subject of revealing trade secrets. Explain back-propagation to me."

"Marcel? How would you like a chance to redeem yourself?"

"Well, as I understand it—"

"Oh, don't give us *that*, Marcel. Give us the facts."

"As I understand it, you present the net with a pattern of input. This signal pattern flows from neurode to neurode along branching, variously weighted connection paths. If the sum of inputs on the receiving neurode exceeds its signal threshold, it, too, fires and passes along more signal. Spreading activation, it's called."

I looked at Lentz to see if I had it right so far. He had his hands together, fingers to lips. And he was smirking.

"The signal pattern spreads through the net from layer to layer. A final response collects at the output layer. The net then compares this output to the desired output presented by the trainer. If the two differ, the net propagates the error backward through the net to the input layer, adjusting the weights of each connection that contributed to the error."

"Bra-*vo*, Marcel. Who's your teacher? Now, the question is: Which would you rather be able to do? Explicate that process or interpret Donne's Holy Sonnet?"

"I don't think that's the question," Diana sighed. "The question is whether back-propagation violates the directionality of the axon-to-dendrite signal."

Lentz pulled his head back on its stalk. He arched his eyebrows. "What have we here? The dabbler's expertise!"

Diana looked as if he'd just slapped her. Her lip shook. She would have stormed off if Harold hadn't restrained her.

"Philip!" Plover frothed. "Just shut up for a second, will you? You fault us for taking issue from a position of ignorance. But we're challenging you to provide the refutation. Isn't that better than reflex rejection? Torches and scythes?"

"Torches and scythes are ever so much more picturesque."

"Oh, for the love of . . . I give up." Plover traced a shorthand of his bear-paw exasperation.

"Uh-oh. About to invoke the deity. We're in trouble now. Whatever happened to radical skepticism in religious matters?"

"Philip, you . . ." Plover tripped on his tongue in his disgust. "Why bother publishing your results, if you don't want people to follow you?"

"I get nervous when I'm followed too closely." Lentz inserted a fry into his mouth like a young child hammering blocks into a toy workbench.

"So you can't be bothered with anyone who isn't already in the inner sanctum."

"That's not true. Why, I've taken Marcel here and have already turned him from near-ignoramus into marginally literate page boy."

" 'Sweets grown common lose their dear delight.' Is that it? Lentz, that's the most elitist thing I've ever heard anyone on public funding say."

"Marcel, tag that line for me, will you?"

Citing seemed the quickest way out of trouble. "I think it's Shakespeare."

"Shakespeare's not elitist?" Lentz countered. "In any case, most of my grants are corporate, these days. By the way, Harold. 'Most elitist' is not up to your usual elegant prose."

"When you boys are finished," Diana murmured, "I wouldn't mind an answer."

Lentz cackled. "All right, Marcel. Time to straighten out the masses again."

"I guess the idea is that backward error propagation may resemble higher-order brain processes. True, individual nerve pathways are one-way. But neuronal paths as a whole do connect portions of the brain in two directions."

"I get it," Diana said. "Feedback signals from muscle tissue to the primary motor cortex, and the like?"

Lentz snorted. "This is just Marcel's guess, you understand."

I wondered if I would be able to work with the man a whole ten months.

Diana's face wrinkled. "But it's not quite the same thing, is it? Is presynaptic Hebbian change the same thing as . . . ?"

But Lentz had stopped listening. He was peering into his juice bottle, preoccupied. Almost consumed by distraction. "Nothing," he declared. "Nothing is the same as anything else."

By whatever mechanism, that lunch is set into my cortex. I can take out the tape and view it at will. From this distance, its edges are ridiculously sharp, the definition absurd. These frames extend a longer clip, animated by the persistence of vision.

Diana later told me how memories are laid down when the thumb-sized basal forebrain bathes the hippocampus in acetylcholine. The chemical somehow changes a synapse's shape, she claimed, altering the connections between cells. And a key flooder of the chemical pathways is fear.

That lunch is burned into my memory because I sat through it terrified. Lentz scared me. Harold's hurt, Diana's dismay triggered my impulse to fly. I was afraid of everything these three might say to each other. Spooked by the open rupture begging to take place. Every word of anger was my fault.

For a long time, I thought that what frightened me was the prospect of failure. My biggest anxiety seemed to be that we'd pour ourselves into this folly and never get it to do more than gibber. That a previously productive researcher would take me on a ten-month wild-goose chase.

It's taken me this long—*this* long—to see. The fear that laid down that indelible trace was the same one I've nursed since boyhood. The fear that we might realize our dreams.

Lentz built Implementation A more for my education than as a prototype with any real pretensions. The beast wasn't winning any beauty prizes, either in looks or in conception. Lentz cobbled up a card cage to the back plane of your basic vanilla workstation. A few I/O devices, registered antiques all, hung off the ports, windows to this poor contraption's soul.

"The super-rich always drive beaten-up old Chevies," Lentz assured me. "You have to grasp the inverse snob value. Always dazzle your audience with misdirection. If we get 'Three Blind Mice' to come out of *this*, it'll knock them dead."

However humble, the rig gave us an entree. A workable learning algorithm can run on any platform. The brain, Lentz had it, was itself just a glorified, fudged-up Turing machine. Our cerebrum-to-be had no neurons, per se. No axons or dendrites. No synaptic connections. All these structures hid in simulation, dummied up in the standard linear memory array. The bare troika of Boolean operators brought them into metaphorical being. We used algorithms to imitate a non-algorithmic system. Implementation A was a ghostly hologram. It froze our words the way a scribbled shopping list, falling from a book where it has spent a misplaced lifetime, revives that longhand you thought you'd live alongside forever.

Lentz did a good job of making the hardware transparent to me. He hooked up topologies the culmination of a decade or more of tinkering. He explained every link in the process. But I was exhausted, wiped out from my own recent work. I tried for the gist and took the rest on faith.

The gist consisted of vectors. A stimulus vector, converted by the net's self-reorganization into a response vector. We started with a three-deep array of neurodes, enough for a test start. Each field was the size of the net that had learned to pronounce English. Implementation A would be spared this task. Lentz wired it to a canned speech synthesis routine. We worked at the level not of phonemes but of whole words.

At first I typed input into the system. My text ran through a huge lookup table—Lentz's laborious list of the 50,000 most common English words, arranged in order of rarity. Each word got a number, like a runner in a triathlon. These numbers in turn plunged headfirst into our randomly weighted terrain.

The ersatz brain cells juggled the pattern, until those in the output layer replied in noise. The box answered back each time I typed to it. But it answered gibberish. Like any nursling's, its voice was awash in gabble.

If I kept at the same stimulus, however, the output organized. Activated paths strengthened; inert routes atrophied away. The blathering gave way to consistent conversational response. What those responses *were*, however, neither Lentz nor I could say.

Still, our rewiring meshes had, of their own device, begun to imitate the world's simplest animals. They grew conditioned. They habituated. They de- and re-sensitized. Outwardly, at least, our neuron-simulation mimicked the response of living tissue.

Down the hall, on all sides of us, biologists split the lark, the functional organism. They ran planarians through mazes. They rapped lobotomized sea slugs on their antlers. Harold and Ram studied recovery and compensation in damaged brains. Diana removed small sections of monkey hippocampi and pegged them to changes in the creatures' ability to learn. The mind strove to open itself up, Pandora's ultimate black box.

We, too, performed our bit of the reductionist dragnet. Implementation A was our attempt to make a metaphor for a metaphor-making neural mechanism. But what creature the inner workings of that self-appointing assembly mirrored was anyone's guess.

The first bottleneck was not mechanical. The problem was me. Lentz hovered over me as I keystroked. He jabbed at the air. He feinted at the keyboard. He smudged the video screen with agitated digits. My typing drove him up the bloody wall.

"Marcel, how many words have you typed in your life?"

I studied the fixture above his head, calculating.

"Not the exact figure, you nit. Just give me the order of magnitude."

I shrugged. "Millions."

"You type like a chimp taking a running lunge at *Hamlet*. Who taught you?"

"Autodidact."

"How the hell are we supposed to get anything done? What do you peak at, twenty words per minute? And what you lack in speed you make up for in blundering. What's with the three-and-a-half-finger method, anyway?"

"Feel free to take over. It's all yours."

"Oh, don't be such a bleeding passion plant. No, it's no good. We're going to have to go to voice recognition. It'll cost us a week. And it's about as accurate a transcriber as a female Korean immigrant."

"Jesus, Lentz. If anyone hears you, we'll be run out of town. This is nineteen nin—"

"But more reliable than your piggies, anyway."

Speech recognition, in that year, was well on its way to being settled. Its frontier towns had grown into small St. Louises. We needed only follow along in the land grab's wake. Lentz refined the Center's prepackaged speech-processing routines. He linked the voice input module to the front end of our existing net. He cabled a Karaoke microphone into the A-to-D converter. He sutured the pieces together like a microsurgeon reattaching a severed nerveway.

Before we could train the network, I had to train the recognition routine to place my voice. I spoke words to it, then whole phrases. I repeated each out loud until it bled into a meaningless semantic gruel. When we succeeded in turning sounds into text with acceptable accuracy, we started again with the learning algorithm. Once more from the top.

"So are we using supervised training, graded training, or what?" I asked Lentz.

"Marcel, don't try to impress me. Save that for your hapless readers."

"Seriously. I'd like to correlate what I've read with—"

"For the word compilation, the net will compare its own output to the desired output you supply it. It will then adjust its synapses to imitate you as closely as possible."

"That's supervised."

"Am I supposed to give you genius prize money now?"

I liked Implementation A. I felt comfortable chattering to it. I read slowly, distinctly, for hours at a shot. I learned to work late at night, like the other loners and fanatics.

A answered me. Our infant had a comeback to everything. Lentz wrote a decoder to throw its vector outcomes on the screen. The thing LISP'd in numbers, for the numbers came. Its patterned responses condensed into syllables, then words in themselves. Correspondence grew more comprehensive. I did not always know what A was trying to say. But I could hear it struggle to say it.

We taught A some couple thousand words, about a quarter of the core active vocabulary a person might resort to. When it had these words under its belt, we tried it on simple combinations. After countless rounds of phrase-drill, Implementation A started to spit my words back parsed. Or at least it behaved as if it were parsing.

Between training sessions, I read the famous two-volume study of nets. The connectionist bible, it suggested maturable machines were already in sight. The math proved it: self-rearranging switchboards could generalize, selectively associate, even project. I took the math on faith, having long ago sacrificed my math to the study of fiction.

Then, everyone in the field took something on faith. Much lay beneath the surface, in the tangled, hidden layers. But I felt particularly vulnerable. I went to more colloquia and got progressively less out of them. Each week the speakers got younger. They grew more gleeful about having been born when I was already doing the crystal diode radio kits and the earthworm dissections. If I needed to grasp all understanding's lacunae before our contraption could understand me, we would lose our bet by a long shot.

I could at least follow the pictures, if not the argument's text. I visualized the spin glasses, complex similes for mental topology. I walked through the landscape of imagination, where every valley formed an associative memory. I could follow the *story* of the math, if not the substance.

And the story was drama itself: the tale of a gardener loose in that mnemonic landscape. An English Elizabeth, who cultivated it, or would have, had her life not been pruned back at twenty-eight, beyond the root.

I could follow the shape of the Hebbian Law: if two neurons fire together, their connection grows stronger and stimulation gets easier the next time out. Synapses in motion tend to stay in motion. Synapses at rest tend to stay at rest. I saw the law as a teacher prowling her class, slapping the wrists of bad students and rewarding the good until they all stood up and pledged coordinated allegiance.

But as yet, I could not hear *what* the pupils were pledging.

Lentz and I continued to putter. I read where the most famous worker on the wet side of brain research called God a tinkerer. I felt nothing like God. I felt like an arthritic macaque in finger splints.

For breathers, I frequented my other campus office, in the English Building. McKim, Mead and White, 1889. There I lived my alter ego—picturesque but archaic man of letters. The Center possessed 1,200 works of art, the world's largest magnetic resonance imager, and elevators appointed in brass, teak, and marble. The English Building's stairs were patched in three shades of gray linoleum.

Hiding out there provided a healthy antidote for too much future. After immoderate reading or training sessions, I needed the correction. But the building left me edgy as well. The edginess of the erotic. The scent of those halls went down my throat like a tracheotomy tube. English light flushed me with desire, a desire awakened by the memory of itself, wanting nothing more desperate than to be put back to sleep.

This was the building where I'd once taught C. Worse, this was Taylor's building. And everything Taylor had long ago alerted me to circled back on the primacy of narrative desire. Desire, he taught me, was the voicegram of memory. But I had reached an age when I was no longer sure that I wanted to remember the perpetual eroticism of eighteen, the erotics of knowledge, the words I'd traded in here, in these halls.

The more I learned about the architecture of memory, the more convinced I became that I was losing mine. I could not concentrate on even idle conversation. I would slink into English and sit in my nineteenth-century office, staring at the bricked-in fireplace, waiting for a surreal locomotive to emerge from it. Or I'd try to join the corridor conversation on a film or book review I was sure I'd seen. But I could not follow the preliminaries through to their web of consequences. I was elsewhere, and elsewhere back-propagated, endlessly.

In the mornings, I'd try to write. I now had perhaps three pages. In those pages I did nothing but unwind my first line. I made my relative clauses jump through all sorts of novel hoops. The performance could have gone on for several hundred pages on style alone. I could get my train to leave most eloquently. But I could not get it to go anywhere but back.

Sustaining so much as a paragraph became impossible. I'd juggle the first verb in my head, overwhelmed by my own weighted backlist. I thought of the four books I'd written between leaving U. and returning. The round trip seemed too immense. I no longer had the heart to extend it.

I'd missed my connection. Stranded at the terminal. I didn't want to write anymore. I was sick of speculation and empathy and revision. All I wanted was to read word frequency lists to Implementation A.

Lentz thought it time to see if Implementation A made sense. We drilled it for days on two-word sentences. Then we prompted A with nouns, to see if it could supply a valid predication. We would see if A acquired, by example, the pattern of generating grammar.

It recognized the simple S-V phrases we fed it. Dogs bark. Birds soar. Night falls. You vanish. Father hugs. Baby cries. It could distinguish these ideas from the formulations that we earmarked as inappropriate for well-brought-up machines to use in public.

But when it came time to perform, A clutched. It seemed to stab at pattern-completion. It formed sentences by chance guess.

It could learn words. It could identify well-formed sentences. But

Implementation A refused to elaborate its own. No matter how Lentz tweaked, Imp A seemed baffled by the task. It would not take the first generalizing step to learn the language.

Lentz tacked into the failure. He tried everything he could think of to coax the machine up a notch. Nothing worked. Asked to complete a thought, the network improvised wildly. Fish . . . ? Fish sky. Shines? Hopes shines. Forests floor. Laugh efforts. Combs loneliness. Even when, by chance, it got the syntax right, the sense was not even random.

Imp A spoke the way a toddler gave directions. Its eager-to-please finger serpentined over all possible routes. This way? *That's right!* Or is it this way? *Sure, if you like.* Where's the horse? Come on, point to the horse. *That's* not a horse. *That's* not a horse either.

Yet it was, at least, pointing. Maybe our putting the request as pointedly as we did flustered it.

"Couldn't we hard-code a properties list? I mean, someone here must have compiled a semantic catalog . . ."

"That's your coeval, Keluga. He's trying to write the entire Roget's as a series of nested, rule-based schematics. Containment, relation, exclusion . . ."

"Coeval? I'm thirty-five, Lentz. That guy's a kid."

"You're both post-Tupperware. Chen is Keluga's supervisor. Outrageous. The Bergen and McCarthy of AI. Chen knows every algorithm in existence, but can't speak a single natural language, including his own. Keluga grew up on Hollywood robots and the microprocessor revolution. One of those brats who got his first PC free in a cereal box. He gets nervous when a sentence doesn't start with 'While' and end with 'Wend.' He's going to reform English by taking out all the inefficient synonyms."

"But is his list any good? Couldn't we just use the semantic data structures as a reservoir of associations that the net could dip into?"

"We could. But it wouldn't be satisfying. That's not the way the cells do things."

"I thought the point wasn't to duplicate mind. I thought—"

"The point is to get this boutique of ICs to comment intelligently on William Bloody Wordsworth. Are you going to give me rules for doing that?"

I said nothing. Lentz realized he'd gone overboard. He regrouped and spoke again.

"We *could* try to feed it algorithms for everything. There are only slightly more of them than there are particles in the universe. It would be like building a heart molecule by molecule. And we'd still have a hell of an indexing and retrieval problem at the end. Even then, talking to such a decision tree would be like talking to a shopping list. It'd never get any smarter than a low-ranking government bureaucrat."

Lentz returned to the net design. I could do little to assist but run upstairs to the laser and retrieve the printouts. Lentz liked to crack morose asides while he worked. "You better start thinking of how you're going to fill the rest of your year."

Sometimes he would set me tasks, puzzles that weren't clearly puzzles until after I solved them. "Fill in the blank, making a simple, two-word sentence. 'Silence . . .' "

". . . *fears*," I suggested. "Make that '*Silence* fears.' "

"Oh, very good, Marcel. I knew there must have been a reason I asked you to be my apprentice."

But the more he joked, the worse Lentz's asthmatic anxiety grew. We washed up at the starting block. My future again began to seem as unbearably long as my past.

Angry, Lentz lobotomized the thing. "Just punishment," he declared. "This box didn't deserve to think." Hurting the circuit seemed no more sadistic than forcing it to learn in the first place.

He blurred the device's retention. He reduced the scope and breadth of connections. Then he tested it a last time in its weakened state, empiricism now taunting all three of us. To my astonishment, the learning algorithm rose up from its reduced straits and began to get the picture.

Miraculously, Implementation A began to pick up our patterns, arranging our words into meaningful relationships. "I might have known." Lentz sounded disgusted with himself. "Too much retention. It was learning. But learning got swamped in its own strength. The creature was driving itself batty, holding on too tenaciously to everything it had ever seen. Dying of its own nostalgia. Mired in the overacquired."

"Autistic," I remember saying. Particulars overwhelmed it. Its world consisted of this plus this plus this. Order would not striate out. Implementation A had sat paralyzed, a hoary, infantile widow in a house packed with undiscardable mementos, no more room to turn around. Overassociating, overextending, creating infinitesimal, worthless categories in which everything belonged always and only to itself.

A few deft neurological nicks and a new run-time behavior did the job. Implementation B lived inside the same hardware, indistinguishable from its short-lived predecessor. This time, fuzzy logic and feedback-braking kept the box as discriminately forgetful as any blossomer.

From the get-go, B was a different animal.

Diana Hartrick came by. She surprised me one Saturday afternoon. The air had just started to turn chilly. I remember that she had a denim windbreaker on and was shivering on the stoop when I let her in.

"Hi. I know you're not supposed to drop in unannounced in this country . . ."

"Not a problem. I lived half my adult life in a country where dropping in unannounced was *de rigueur*."

"Good. I was on my way to the lab. I thought I'd bring you this." She handed me a Ball jar full of soup. "I figured a single guy could use some. I'm afraid it's very hearty. You may want to thin it out some when you heat it up." She stopped to look around my place for the first time. "Hey! I thought you were staying until summer."

"I am."

"What's the matter? Aren't you comfortable here? It looks like you're trying to weasel past worldliness without actually having to touch it. By the way, you'll want to plug your fridge in for the soup. Unless you'd like to share it with the microorganisms."

"Thanks. You wouldn't happen to have a bowl on you, would you? Just kidding."

Diana rocked her head side to side. Her thin horizon smile said: *Artists*. Or words to that effect.

"Look. I came by to tell you that you don't have to do this, you know. Lentz is a maniac, but he's a harmless maniac. He won't hurt you if you bail out. None of us took the bet seriously in the first place. It's so . . ."

"Quixotic?"

" 'Deranged' was the word I was searching for. Harold has started to fret about your squandering your talents on this."

I shrugged. "There's no squandering. It interests me."

"Well, the minute it stops interesting you, drop it like a hot potato. And if that man starts to get on your nerves, tell him to go to hell. That's the only diction he understands."

"I was going to ask. What's the matter with him? Why is he like that?"

"Well, we all have our own theories. Harold's is the most charitable. He thinks the man is just trying in his own warped way to be loved. I think his limbic system is diseased. That reminds me. If you get tired of playing mad scientist with the home electrode kit, you are always welcome to come and see how it's really done."

"Thanks. I'd like to."

"Do you really live like this? Where are your things? Where is your library?"

"Lost in transit."

Diana cringed. Her hand flew out like a magician's released dove, but stopped short of my shoulder.

"Sorry. It's none of my business. I just wondered how you can work. All my notes are spread over the margins of my texts. I'd be lost without them."

"Lost is not so bad. It's practically an advantage in my line."

"Mr. Powers, Mr. Powers." She shook her head again, tisking through her grin. She did not buy me. But the sales pitch, at least, tickled her.

"Well, just remember. You're under no obligation to build this mechanical master's student. When you see how hopeless the holiday is . . ."

"Straight back to the mines," I promised.

Dr. Hartrick fished for her keys while heading for the door. At the threshold, she made one more stunned survey. "You'll—you should at least come by sometime." She sounded doubtful. "I can cook you a real meal, anyhow. You do eat, don't you?"

Sometimes I ditched the bike and walked to the Center. Self-inflicted mental Polar Bear Club. U. was threaded through with time holes, and not just mine. Most of the residential streets were still brick. The houses had *verandas*, *balustrades*, features that have passed out of the language. The streetlamp globes threw off a gaslight yellow that turned the underside of the leaves that had not yet fallen a weird, otherworldly teal.

C. and I took a last retrospective stroll through those streets a dozen years before. We walked slowly that night, half speed, not knowing how to abandon the markers. We were leaving together this time. We'd stumbled onto that inevitability that neither of us thought would ever happen.

I never asked her. I don't even know how she learned where I had gone. Just: one day, a card in the mail. The picture showed a forgotten town nestled in a stream valley. I couldn't read the description on the back. Language locked me out. But I could read her message. "R.—May will be fine next year. C."

Of all the million things the ambiguous message could mean, I knew the one it did. I woke up around noon after a late shift of computer operations and *The Magic Mountain*. I went to check the mail. Her card was the last thing I expected. The first I hoped for. I'd waited every day, I suppose, at some low level. I would have been just fine never hearing from her again. I would have worked forever.

I quit my job. I left B. and went back to U. She was waiting for me. She'd acted honorably, done things right. Now she was free to get out and see the world. We went as slowly as we could. We tried to get to know each other again, without too much backfill. But I had no job, she was graduating, and we had lost a lifetime once already.

We made love for the first time in a single bed belonging to someone neither of us had ever met. We lived together for three weeks in a house I was watching for a friend of a friend. The whole scenario was invention itself. We would never have a house of our own.

Somewhere, there is a picture C. took of me in that house's yard. I'm ringed with a garland of dandelions she wove me. My trident is a dandelion rake—the Poseidon of lawn care. We would never have a yard, the two of us. Not even a rented one.

"If I asked you again . . ." I asked her one day.

"I'd jump at the chance. That's *if* you asked me again."

Before we left, we took that compilation walking tour. We walked like a thresher squeezing a field dry. We named every landmark we left behind.

"That's where I lived when I first came down," she pointed out. "That's where my boyfriend lived. Here's where I met for choir. This is the clinic where I helped my roomie through her crisis."

"Here's where I lost my virginity," I showed her. "I spent a year in this bizarre co-op. Taylor lives a block down from here. Ah, the library. I booked like a madman for the Master's Comp. Nine months, up in a study carrel on deck eight."

By tacit agreement, we saved the Quad for last. Neither of us said, *Here's where we first learned we weren't necessarily alone.* Neither of us needed to say anything.

C. was game for anywhere. She would have followed a dart thrown at a world map. I told her how beautiful B. was, how full and alive. Leaving seemed like a story we told each other, then lived as it unfolded. How they skipped town together and relocated, with nothing but a $4,100 bank check to their names. How they rode for twenty-two hours on the Lake Shore Limited, next to an enormous gentleman who warned them of the dire consequences of reading.

How they arrived at South Station in bleak, freezing drizzle. How they stood soaked in grime-coated twilight, trying to find a bus stop. How she burst into tears: Where have you taken me?

Even hardship felt like a giggle. An adventure. I would have pitched permanent base camp in a war zone with that woman. And I made her feel safe, for a while. As if even this wrong turn were part of an ingenious thread. We were young then, and would live forever. All those disasters, bad judgments, breakages, mistakes: we protected each other, simply by insisting we were still together and happy. That nothing mattered but care.

Now, sometimes, as I trained B or walked back from the Center at nights to my deserted bungalow, panic ambushed me. Some mental picture would trigger it—remembering I'd left the cognitive oven on with something in it. The slightest reminder reached out and laced my ribs. Someone was in trouble, trapped in front of a station in an unidentifiable city without cash, map, or language. And I could not buffer or save them. Someone pitching into free fall. Either me or my old friend.

We settled into B. We found a place. We printed up résumés, complete with convincing Career Goals. Jobs, however anemic, dropped on us like a godsend. I took up work as a technical editor. C. guarded paintings at the Fine Arts.

My images of the two of us, in those early days, needed no gallery guard. C. and I, on our first Thanksgiving, dressing the ruinously expensive Cornish game hens when we didn't have two dimes to rub together. Listening, setless, to the sounds of the big game next door, holding our breath to hear who was ahead. That Christmas, crayoning a tree onto several sheets of newsprint and taping it to the apartment wall.

That much was almost cheating to remember. All I had to do was turn my eyes to some neutral screen—the wet leaves in the gutters as I walked, the fat gray cumulus—and I could see any scene from that year I could bear to look at. The focal trace that printed those pictures now lent its apparatus to the reverse process. Ouija-like, it retrieved from the file and held my attention on the reduced film of a place now past verifying.

Lentz had speculated about that strange doubling in one of his more controversial articles. Memory was a parasite, he proposed. It opportunistically used perception's circuitry for its playback theater.

And I have that whole parasite intact. Nothing required to bring it forth but numbness. True, the specifics of that moment have grown stylized. Artist's conceptions. I can check nothing. C. kept the book, the one where we pasted the paper trail of our shared existence. The documents are all elsewhere, trashed, or transferred to a stranger's long-term storage.

I came to him depressed.

"It's mind-fogging," I told him. "Incomprehensible. I've been reading. We don't have an agnostic's prayer in hell, do we? One hundred billion neurons. That's twenty for each person on earth. How many trillion synaptic connections? And all arranged with anatomical precision into who knows how many tangled subsystems . . ."

"Sixty-three," Lentz supplied. He was leaning back in his office chair again, reclined, as on the night I first saw him. I couldn't tell if he was being snide or if he'd finally flipped.

"And even the most trivial of the subsystems solves problems so far past our ability to compute it makes my limbic system spin. We'd need an exponential number of exponents just to number the firings on the way to a self-reflective thought. If we scale our toy up even a little bit bigger than it is now, the thing will grind to a standstill. Responding intelligently to 'Good afternoon' would take it a lifetime."

"Well, we could always tell Plover and Hartrick that Teacher's Pet needs a slight extension to get its paper in. Say, no later than the next Ice Age."

Lentz pulled up a subroutine on his terminal and began to massage it. He was a hyperactive child, happiest when several things happened at once.

"Even if we could keep track of the wiring . . ." my voice cracked. "Even if we could get all our tin-can telephones spaghettied up to the same switchboard: there still wouldn't be enough processing power in this part of the galaxy to synchronize their firing."

Lentz chuckled. "That's too exaggerate."

It was eerie. His cruel imitation was tone-perfect. Chen, to the letter. The vicious ear alone would be tough to duplicate on the most advanced of machines.

"Come on, Marcel. Buck up. It's not so tough. What saves us is that we don't have to do everything. No motion, no vision, no smell or sensation, no pain, no reflex response, no process control . . . If you knew what it took to reach out and grasp an object, to pick up a glass, you'd be completely incapable of doing it."

"If all we had to do was pick things up. We're trying to get something to *understand*."

"Marcel, I've never seen you like this. Remarkable. What happened to the cold fish we've come to know and love?" He spoke askance now, more intent on the screen than on me. The hypnotic, half-attentive intensity of someone pretending concentration. "Listen. I've been trying to explain this to you. In some fundamental way, it's easier to do high-level stuff than low-. It takes fewer neurons to link 'walk,' 'through,' and 'doorway' into some associated cluster than it takes for you to carry out the words."

"Maybe so. But think how many clusters—"

"You're overwhelmed because you're still thinking like Plover. You still think we have to lay out the rules and specify all the computations ourselves. That *would* be incomprehensibly complex. But we're not going to write out those calculations. We're going to feed the already languaged world to Imp B and let it take the bits apart and reassemble them."

"Yeah, yeah. You've done that lecture. But, Engineer. The size! Think of what we'd have to tell it before anything made sense. We're talking an index magnitudes bigger than the universe it points to."

"The universe will be its own index. The isomorphic contour map, the way the data get packed together."

"What does that mean? Okay. Suppose we read it the line 'He clasps the crag with crooked hands' . . ."

"Oh no. Not him. Anybody but him."

"Then we have to tell it about mountains, silhouettes, eagles, aeries. The difference between clasping and gripping and grasping and gasping. The difference between crags and cliffs and chasms. Wings, flight. The fact that eagles don't *have* hands. The fact that the poem is not really *about* an eagle. We'll have to teach it isolation, loneliness . . ."

"It'll know all about those. It'll grow into knowledge you won't even need to spell out. Knowledge will be a by-product of the shape its weight-landscape takes, from bending to the spoken world's shape."

". . . how a metaphor works. How nineteenth-century England worked. How Romanticism didn't work. All about imperialism, pathetic projection, trochees . . ."

Lentz started laughing. At least that meant he heard me. "Yes, there's a certain density out there it will have to become comfortable with. Give it time. How did you acquire that density? Half a meg, half a meg, half a meg onward."

"Me? *I* don't know what the bloody poem means. I wouldn't analyze that thing again if my life depended on it."

"That's my *point*. We humans are winging it, improvising. Input pattern x sets off associative matrix y, which bears only the slightest relevance to the stimulus and is often worthless. Conscious intelligence is smoke and mirrors. Almost free-associative. Nobody really *responds* to anyone else, per se. We all spout our canned and thumbnailed scripts, with the barest minimum of polite segues. Granted, we're remarkably fast at indexing and retrieval. But comprehension and appropriate response are often more on the order of buckshot."

"I'm beginning to see. You're not elevating the machine. You're debasing us. Took me long enough."

"Don't be too hard on yourself, Marcel," Lentz cooed. "Much of intelligence isn't really that bright."

"I can't believe this. You're serious, aren't you?"

"Massively parallel pattern matching. We only pretend to be syllogistic creatures. In fact, we identify a few constraints, then spin the block endlessly until it drops in the hole. Have you *read* an undergraduate paper lately? You should see what I have to deal with in the intro sequences alone. And the stuff I teach requires no real world knowledge at all! You know the old 'Show your work for partial credit'? It's when they show their work that I want to give even the ones who solve the problem sets a zero."

"Are you exempting yourself from this critique of intelligence?"

"Not really. This conclusion stared me in the face for thirty years before I saw it."

"All right. Let's say you're right."

"Let's do."

"It doesn't change the facts. In order to produce a remotely plausible association matrix for six measly Tennyson lines, our candidate will need a file cabinet two global hemispheres wide."

My objections were starting to bore Lentz. He stood up. It always frightened me when the man assumed the vertical. He began fiddling with the jumpers on the new neurodal processor board prior to fitting it into the expansion chassis. I thought of those brain surgeons who stimulate conscious patients' cortexes and what synesthesias the probe elicits.

"That's a pretty figure of speech, Marcel. And doubtless it's the sign of some nominal intelligence on your part. But have you read your own school papers lately? Give me *Middlemarch*, I'll spin you off a few amorphous generalities, all qualified and deniable."

"What do you know about that book?" I asked, too quickly. It was Taylor's book, the one he'd given his scholarly life to. The one I'd written on, analyzed for him. The novel where I'd discovered novels. The mere title in Lentz's mouth sounded creepy, as if I'd been spied on.

Of course he ignored me. Lentz ignored all direct challenges. Only the shrewdest or most slow-witted of machines could hit upon that conversational tactic.

"Even if you're right," I retreated, "it would take us forever to teach it sufficient amorphous generalities."

Lentz roused himself from distraction. "What do you want? We have ten months. Ten months is several generations these days. Plus, we don't have to *be* humanly intelligent. Our brain doesn't have to correspond to real mentation. We just have to be as good at paraphrase, by any route we care to take. And for that, we can fly, flat out. If you ever stop talking and pitch in."

I stood and helped him assemble the new card into Imp B's backplane. Manual labor: the extent of my contribution to date. "It strikes me that the thing we're trying to get as good as is damn near unparaphrasable."

"Oh, pish. It's the easiest thing in the world to take in a human. Remember AI's early darling, ELIZA, the psychoanalyst? 'You remind me of my father,' the human types. 'Tell me more about your father,' the machine answers. Remember the student who found the thing up and running on a deserted terminal? Struck up a conversation. Got steadily more frustrated. Ended up shrieking at the sadist on the other end to quit jerking him around."

Exactly how I ended up every time I talked to Lentz. "So all we're building is a deception?"

"Consciousness is a deception." Lentz grimaced. He stared into some middle distance. The pause was long and awful. I didn't know how to fill it.

At length, I had to say something. "You're not suggesting that Son of B is going to be *conscious*, are you?"

"Don't be obtuse, Marcel. You're making this argument a duck shoot. No, of course not. Nor do we *have* to make it conscious. We don't have to give it sensations either, or even make it think. We just have to make it a reasonable apple-sorter. Get it to interpret utterances, slip them into generic conceptual categories, and then retrieve related 'theoretical' commentary from off the prepackaged shelf."

"And what are we doing next week?"

"Touché, Marcel. You're right, for once. Let's just take the baby steps first."

"As they say to sky divers: that first step is a killer."

"Nah. The first step's a cakewalk. We can beat the hell out of a developing infant, in any case. First off, our baby never needs a nap. Never. We can feed it around the clock, once things start to take off. Second, a kid's neurons aren't even fully myelinated until age twelve or so. They're erratic. Trying to get them to potentiate is like writing in Jell-O."

Not long after that conversation, I learned that the only child Lentz ever raised had disowned him.

I still thought of B as a composite of makeshift components. Silk-screened cards populated with ICs on the one side and word frequency lists by parts of speech on the other. Each of its distributed, loosely linked subsystem nets was a community of neurodes, and each neurode a community of shifting allegiances.

Day after day, I trained these micro–circus animals to respond to my voice. Pattern generalization became simple sentence parsers, the way push-ups become pectorals. The stacked layers began to recognize—and even make—rudimentary distinctions. I told it: John is taller than Jim. By copying the repeated *ur*-models, it then reassured me that, yes, Jim is shorter than John.

But even such simple manipulations of properties could throw it for an infinite loop. The kettle has more coffee than the cup, but the cup is fuller. That conclusion needed to wash recursively through the mesh several times before B got comfortable with it.

As with many younger sibs, B turned A's personality inside out. While it handled the two-word sentence drill with curt aplomb, it turned garrulous at anything longer. This second set of arrays found more patterns in our sentence prompts than either of us intended.

"B is sick," Lentz greeted me one day on my arrival at the lab.

"Oh no. Don't tell me."

"By 'Don't tell me,' I assume you mean 'Tell me.' "

"What's it doing now?"

"Watch."

Though the machine would respond to no voice but mine, it answered to anyone's typing. It couldn't tell who was at the keys. It answered all comers, cheerfully presuming the typist had nothing but its best interests at heart.

Lentz typed B a little story: "Friends are in a room. A chair is in the room. Richard talks to Diana. Diana sits in the chair." Each word converted to a token, a matrix of strengths. These tokens laced together into sentence vectors. The vectors rolled around through the net landscape, marbles seeking the most available basin. The place they landed, the way they fell, was what they meant. The sieve sorted every configuration that entered it. And each sort changed forever the net configuration.

"You ready?" Lentz asked me. Then he typed, "Who is in the chair?"

B flipped out. "Friends is in the chair. The chair is in the chair. Richard talks to in the chair . . ."

It wouldn't stop prattling. "It's got St. Vitus' dance," I said.

"It's got St. Vincent's malaise," Lentz countered.

He was right. Figuration was driving B as batty as a poet. It framed meaning too meagerly, extending semblance too far. It pushed the classic toddler's tendency to overgroup. Had its digits been skeletal, it would have pointed at anything sitting on a bookshelf and called it a book.

"We'll need to cut the graded feedback and go to more rigorous supervision," Lentz said. "This beast is going to have to learn that not everything will fly."

It made sense. I'd read some developmental neurology. A newborn's synapses far outnumbered those of an adult. Perhaps building effective pathways required that many useless ones had to die. Short of slitting B's metaphoric throat with Occam's razor, we were going to have to rein it in.

For the time being, we decided to pare back B's associations with definitive answers. Repeated treading across the desired path would force Imp B to hack a right route through its lush profusion.

Now, when B started to do its permutational thing, I learned to say no. I would tell it the proper answer, however problematic. However much it hurt, I made it play straight. B took this right answer, matched it to the verbal diarrhea it had produced, and step by painful step went back over its connections to see where it had gotten carried away.

Only this reduction of limitless possibility made learning possible again. And only real learning—nothing mechanical or predictable— would satisfy me.

It pained me, one false spring dusk late in the season, as I walked home along the soon-to-be-crusted-over streets, to hear myself thinking in terms of satisfaction. I thought I'd left the word behind, in the reweighted and long-since-extinguished past.

Imp B always did rub me the wrong way. Nothing violent. I just never cared for it, although I tried not to let that impede our work. I guess the way its linked nets responded to input reminded me too much of all my own little rickies, drowned in fecundity, unable to damp generalization down or clamp it into the manageable.

But as B grew less poetic and more docile, I began to miss the willful driveler. I'd taken perverse delight in watching it conclude, from "If you want me, I'll be in the office," that until you want me, I'll be at home.

Lentz seemed unhumbled by this second lesson in unbounded verbal space. "What do the literary theorists say about reading books these days?" As if I could paraphrase for him, in an afternoon. As if, armed with my paraphrase, he might tack on a couple of preprocessing, feed-forward subsystem nets that would address any conceivable problem.

"First off, they're not books anymore."

"Texts," Lentz corrected himself. "Excuse me." As always, he knew more than he let on.

"Well, let's see. The sign is public property, the signifier is in small-claims court, and the signification is a total land grab. Meaning doesn't circulate. Nobody's going to jailbreak the prison house of language."

"How about getting paroled for good behavior?"

"Come on, Engineer. Come clean for once. Tell me all that doesn't depress the hell out of you."

"No, it doesn't. It just means we have as good a shot at this as any waffling poseur. We can get our supernet to sound exactly like a fashionable twenty-two-year-old North American whiz kid imitating a French theorist in translation by, say, this time next month."

"Engineer—"

"I'm serious, Marcel. I've seen the stuff you're talking about. Gnomic is in. We just have to push 'privilege' and 'reify' up to the middle of the verb frequency lists and retrain. The freer the associations on the front end, the more profound they're going to seem upon output."

"Fine. Do as you please. You obviously don't need me for any of it. And I don't need to spend a year working on a pointless and cynical scam. If I wanted that, I would have stayed in tech writing."

"Marcel, sit down. Marcel! Don't be an infant," Lentz ordered. His voice broke. It shocked me. I didn't think he'd care. Certainly not about something as trivial as my packing it in.

"All right," he stammered. "I didn't mean that. I'm sorry. I was joking. A little self-deflation. It's been so long since I've been satisfied with anything I've done that I get critical. And I forget that not everybody is as detached as I am. I thought you understood. I'm sorry."

I just watched the man. All footwork. All of it, the contrition as well as the cynicism. He himself had long ago lost the ability to tell what he was after or when he was being genuine. But the astonishing thing—the thing that made no sense—was that he wanted me around. The game was no fun, it was worthless to him otherwise. I couldn't figure it, and I didn't want to leave without knowing.

I sat back down, as deliberately as possible. I drew out my answer, curious to see what I would say.

"Imp B?" I asked. I wasn't sure what I meant by the question.

Lentz answered without pause. "A noble cause, in any case. And not without theoretical interest. Let's do it for ourselves. I mean, of course we'll show them what we come up with and all. But let's just work, and forget about the bet."

I looked at the man. The bank safety-glass lenses protected him from eye contact.

"To hell with that." I laughed. "My kid is going to ace that exam!"

"Okay, okay." Lentz cackled alongside me. "Anything you say." His eyes seemed to be watering. He actually put his hand on my shoulder, but just as quickly removed it.

We worked hard on sentence parsing, on relationships and comparisons, on simple semantic decoding. B did not get any more likable in the training process. But it grew undeniably clever at pattern matching and manipulation. The fact that it curve-fit countless serial streams of input vectors and could generalize the shape of a simple sentence at all punched my lights out.

May will be fine next year, I assured it. *Father hopes to plant roses in the front yard. Mother goes to fetch the doctor.*

We were in Lentz's office one weekend afternoon when he said, "It's time to give the kid something a little more obscure."

He rooted through the chaos of his bookshelves. From behind a stack of papers that had begun to recycle themselves, he pulled a fifties-era thermos bottle, a stained coffee mug inscribed *Opa*, and a ring of what for all the world looked like assorted roller-skate keys. Clearing this hole allowed him to shove around the rest of the junk in his packed office as if it were all some giant 15-puzzle.

This shoving at last released a book that seemed to have been stuck in deepest hiding. Squirreled away, like a boy's soft-core magazine. The pale pink fata morgana photograph on the jacket had been torn and taped clumsily back together. I knew the book even before he dredged it up into view.

"Oh no. Engineer. Lentz. Give me a break. Not that one. I've seen full professors make a total debacle of that book."

"Well, now, Marcel. We're not going to do the *book*. Heaven forfend. Just this bit."

He dropped the text open in front of me, a horny thumbnail overscoring the harmless epigraph to Chapter One.

"Just that?"

"Just that."

"You're insane, you know."

"Oh yes. I'm quite aware of that. Wait," Lentz delayed me. "I want Plover to see this. Let's hope our prize pupil doesn't choose this moment to act up."

He limped down the corridor, making good time for a sixty-year-old whose body had been nothing but a nuisance to him for half those years. He returned with a dubious Harold in tow.

When he saw me, Harold's face lit up. "*Ave, Scriptor!* Are you keeping this charlatan honest?" Had I taken the least step toward him, he would have wrapped me in a bear hug.

Harold's spontaneous affection depressed me. I'd done nothing to get this fellow to like me, and the fact that he did made me feel dishonest. My sense of unearned credit was interrupted by the appearance in the doorway of a sullen teenage girl.

"Trish," Plover commanded. "Trish. Take the headphones off. Take—the—headphones . . ." He pantomimed in affable, immense semaphore. Trish complied, rolling her eyes toward a spiritual mezzanine.

"This is the novelist whose books I showed you." Harold turned back toward me, to make sure I was the person he meant. "Richard, this is Trish. The second of the Plover Amazons."

She shook my hand, then looked around the lab for sterilization equipment.

"How many in the tribe?" I asked.

Harold started ticking off his fingers. "I don't know. I've lost count."

"Oh, Daddy!" Trish moaned. A mentally deficient father: the only thing that could have driven her to address me. "Don't listen to him. He's been insufferable ever since Mom let Sue go to Italy."

"Hear that? 'Insufferable.' Trish is the literary one. She writes poetry."

"I do not. They're song lyrics."

"She'd like you to look at them sometime."

"No way!" Trish shouted.

Lentz snorted at the collocation. "Is Hartrick going to come have a look at this?" he asked.

I felt the tension before the sentence was even half out of him. Harold looked ready to strangle the little man.

"No. Just do your stuff. Let's see what you got."

"What you *have*," Trish corrected. This time, Dad rolled his eyes.

I spoke to B. I launched into the singsong nursery rhyme that, for reasons that I've long since forgotten, I'd used to open my first novel.

"As I was going to St. Ives, I met a man with seven wives . . ."

I stumbled and hung up on the lines. Harold reminded me how they went, and I got all the way through.

Everyone held their breath. "Well?" Lentz said. "Go ahead, then. Get on with it. Pop the question."

I posed the query with which my firstborn book began.

"Kits, cats, sacks, wives: how many were going to St. Ives?"

Somewhere on the curve of unfathomable syntaxes lay the desired answer. Our network of nets took less than half a minute to triangulate it. "One."

"Way cool!" Trish exclaimed. She moved toward the terminal, excited. I noticed something wrong with the way she walked. Then the shoe dropped: she was on roller blades.

Plover broke out in a belly laugh. "This is for real?"

Trish took the microphone. "Open the pod bay doors, HAL!" Vectors danced across the screen, but Imp B kept its counsel. Trish pouted.

"It may be less impressive than it looks," I demurred. "I assume it just ignored everything in the riddle that it couldn't fit into the main predication."

"It's impressive enough," Lentz said, laconically. "Unfailing literal-mindedness may be the most impressive thing going."

The epigraph I read to Imp B, like the book it opened, came from a distributed nowhere. I don't know why I used it. If I had to gloss it, I would say the line was about walking head-on into the parade of not-you, somewhere along time's dirt track. No matter how long and elaborate history's procession, the eye meeting it along the muddy road is always first person singular.

That book came to me during our first year in B., the richest year in my life. I thought we were happy then, but who can say? Our happiness may never have been more than bravery. *Assume a virtue, if you have it not.* That was my favorite line, that pilgrim winter. I liked the idea that we grew to become our attitudes. And attitude, during our stay in B., felt like happiness, deep and artesian.

We were alone. For the first time in our lives, neither of us was going anywhere. We navigated from winter night to winter night, in a state where winter starts in October and rages on into May. In an apartment halfway along its forced march from genteel to desperate, we made a home too familiar for words.

Through those first mythic days, we met our neighbors. We sashayed around them in the laundry room and halls. We shook hands and took their business cards, with none to give in return. We folded origami mnemonics from the syllables of their names. Then we forgot the mnemonics.

No matter. People in our building did not want to be called anything anyway. That was why they chose the place. That was why we ourselves lived there. Every soul in that horseshoe courtyard wanted to be left to its private invulnerability.

The nearer the next man's dossier, the more easily we avoided it. A hole breached our bathroom ceiling into 307 above. It tore open in the shower steam, peppering our tub with drywall. We tacked a linen sheet printed with lime-green woods across the gaping wound. As good as healed.

We were each other's entire populace. Even job hunting was a shared delight.

"Here's one for you, C. 'Good communications skills.' "

"Um, Beau? I think they mean modems and stuff."

We listened to each other's stories. We improvised. We pulled repertoire out of deep storage. The books we didn't read out loud to each other we paraphrased at great length. And we read, reread everything that time had prevented us from reading properly until then.

I might linger over a printed paperback opening for an afternoon, wondering if I wanted to commit. For, once past page 10, I was obligated to stay the campaign, however sordid. I read essays, history, biography—things that would never in a million years be on the List because they weren't English or weren't literature. I commenced that million-and-a-half-word associative memoir that Lentz would harass me with by name, a dozen years later.

I began to keep a reading diary. Not very dramatic as turning points go, but there it is. A lifetime later, rereading these notebooks, I saw that the lines I copied out, the words I deemed worth fixing forever in the standing now of my own handwriting, clumped up with unlikely frequency toward the start of any new book. The magic quotes thinned out over any book's length. The curve was linear and invariable. Perhaps writers everywhere crowded their immortal bits up toward the front of their books, like passengers clamoring to get off a bus. More likely, reading, for me, meant the cashing out of verbal eternity in favor of story's forward motion. Trapping me in the plot, each passing line left me less able to reach for my notebook and fix the sentence in time.

C. read *Buddenbrooks* and *Anna Karenina*. She reread *Little Women*. Everything made her weep. Everything. Well before the last page, she would drag her heels. Her bookmark tracked across the spine of a paperback like Zeno's arrow, frozen in infinite halfway points on its way to the mark. The first four hundred pages zoomed by in two or three nights. The last forty could tie her up for a month.

When she did finish anything, it convulsed her. I remember her reading *Ethan Frome*.

"I thought every American high schooler had to pass a test on that book. Right before they quizzed you on the Constitution," I teased her.

C. shrugged. "Maybe I'm not an American, Beau?"

The day she finished, it turned cold. I was in the front room, on the overstuffed chair we'd saved from street-side collection. C. was in the bedroom, on the mattress on the floor. Out of dead silence, I heard her distress call. "Beau. Ricky." Soft and desperate, already lost, pinned under a mountainside of rock.

I closed the distance at reflex speed. She was propped up against the wall, her eyes rimmed red with salt, her fist shaking, pressed against her mouth. "Oh, Beauie. Give me another chance. I've been so selfish and awful. I can be better. I know I can."

This was from *Ethan Frome*, of all places. *Ethan Frome*.

Each workday, C. put on her navy blue uniform and walked across the land-filled fen between our apartment and the Fine Arts. There she stood for eight hours at a go, saving the masterpieces of world painting from a poking and prodding public.

Museum guard may be the most tedious occupation in the nation's job register. But someone neglected to tell C. She came home glowing with minute enthusiasms, discoveries that could be made only by staring at a painted surface for days at a time. In particular, she loved being assigned to the Fine Arts' chestnut Colonial collection. Too late, I heard in her love the deportee's thrill, the fascination with a country hers only by the thinnest accident of birth.

For the two of us, America went antique. In that city, at that time of year, people moved purposefully through the streets, hinged to their shadows. Their black coats seemed coal seams against gray snow. In silhouette, they passed for protagonists in modernist Czech novels. They packed down subway stairwells and through turnstiles. I packed along with them, on the way to the trade press office where I worked.

I imitated them for C. at night, when I came home. I mimicked the exchange of pleasantries. "We must dine some evening." "The Net National Income has experienced another sudden surge." C. insisted I had a future, either on stage or in a brokerage.

The city posed like one of those portraits C. guarded, a Whistler or a Copley. The subway trains—state-of-the-art, burnished, Asian —were at heart archaic trolleys. They hauled their human freight back and forth to garden suburbs with odd monikers. Cars darted through the maze of surface streets, tomorrow's Studebakers.

My computer magazine outfit sat inside a rustic steel-and-glass exoskeleton that made the surrounding buildings look even more antiquated. The cityscape was something an American postprimitive might do, a nostalgic century from now.

C. and I lived it in advance retrospective. We took long walks along the prow of winter, reconnoitering, registering everything. We ingested the ochers and burnt umbers, the tints that tipped us to the fact that the present was far stranger than it let on.

Only the urban poor refused to go aesthetic. They spoke in tongues, human or otherwise, debating themselves or whoever else would listen. They handed the two of us soiled pamphlets covered in Carolingian minuscule. Or they slouched asleep, grease- and blood-caked, in the back of sleek light rails, riding out to the docklands district of progress's trade fair.

On nights when the windchill permitted, when the bitterness of interplanetary dark toyed with its food by easing a degree, I walked home. I cut across the public plots, the ancient Victory Gardens, all their victories lost, forgotten, or squandered. There, bent women tilled the rows in windup planetarium ellipses. The city's native foreigners, waiting for spring to plant a new crop for next year's war effort.

I made my way through the garden, the days getting dark early, just after four. Over the fusty expressway bridge, I headed into the home stretch, closing in on the place C. and I had made for each other, from out of total accident.

We lived from sense to sense. I can picture the neighborhood as if it were last evening. The street with the nineteenth-century name.

The narrow, storefront scrap-metal emporia. The corner convenience grocer, hanging on by milk-quart markups and lottery tickets. The empty lots that did thousand-dollar days as instant baseball parking garages when summer still was. The abandoned warehouse that flourished briefly as a bar where youth in search of the chemically enhanced Authentic congregated and methodically slammed into itself, studying the dance floor as if meaning were there, in designer-drugged Arthur Murray footprint.

The neighborhood, the street, our apartment are still real. But the city where we spent those years gets more stylized, harder to see, the further I get from what the two of us used to call home.

And we did feel at home there, for a season. We could have pitched camp there forever. I belonged there more than in any of those toytown props that loom like back-projection houses behind me and my brothers and sisters, in my album of faded black-and-whites.

And C.: C. lived there, too, for a while. For the first time since she'd learned how to plan, outcome didn't matter. It was all dressup, in B. An oldies party. For two years—a long vacation—she found a fantasy that fit her.

But C. got homesick. It was inevitable. How could any town compete with a ghost? We'd lived in B. several months when we learned that C.'s parents were returning to Limburg. Both her folks had retired. The workday was over. A quarter century camping out on the South Side of Chicago was enough. It was time to give up and head home.

C. blamed herself. Had she stayed close, the folks might never have left. Twenty-some years had produced no permanent attachments; no tie kept them here. Only the children, and the three of them were already scattered all over the map. C.'s parents chose to see whether the little town of E. still existed, if it ever had.

The news devastated C. "I'm a miserable excuse for a daughter, aren't I?"

I was supposed to agree with her. I was supposed to tell her no.

Guilt was her move in the loop C. and her mother put each other through. The struggle was not over whether they loved each other, but over whether love was enough. They kept at one another, testing, accusing, defending. This endless attempt to determine who had betrayed the other put them both through hell. The kind of hell that would hurt far more, someday, when all scores were reconciled.

C.'s father, on the other hand: any flare-up, and Pap started whistling to himself, heading off to the nearest back room to fix things. I wondered how this old Dutch railroad man with his accented Chicago idioms—"Let's get the show on the road," "Now you're talkin'," "If it works, it works"—would ever fit back into a province whose chief industry since the shutting of the coal mines was geriatric care. He'd been away once before, in a German forced-labor camp. I always thought that first deportation was the reason he lit off for the States.

C. had been a bribe to keep her mother in this country. A baby, for a woman already middle-aged. "I'm responsible, Rick. I'm responsible for their dislocation in the first place. And now I'm responsible for their hauling up stakes again. It's too awful. They're old, Beauie. How are they supposed to put everything they own in a packing crate . . . ? They'll never make it, once they're back there. Never."

"Don't be crazy," I said. "They never *stopped* living there."

Men are worthless; they always think the issue is what's at issue.

"They'll make it just fine," I reasoned. The last thing C. needed. "They have two dozen brothers and sisters. They have more nieces and nephews than we have cockroaches. In another five years, they'll forget this continent ever existed."

"That's what I'm afraid of."

C. took the rap for her own abandonment. Since my father's death, the bonds of my blasted family had mercifully weakened. So it surprised me to see how desolate someone could be at the prospect of seeing hers just once or twice a year. C. broke out in a rash and began vomiting. The doctor put her on a popular sedative. Nothing I did seemed to help at all. Except listening to the stories.

Frantic, C. dragged out all the stories that her mother raised her on. Stories invariably meant the war. All tales came back to that. How the Germans tried to steal the bell out of the church steeple to melt it down, and how something like God stymied them. How her mother nursed a teenage Wehrmacht conscript, a story that almost split C.'s parents before they were even married. How her father's friends in the labor camp joined together to grow parody Hitler mustaches. How he escaped, evading his pursuers by leaping out of an upper-story farm window and limping off, broken-legged, into the night. How the government up north hid *The Night Watch* in the marlstone quarries under Maastricht. How C.'s uncle, forced to stand guard over his fellow coal miners during the occupation, was tried for complicity in the postwar hysteria, and imprisoned again by his friends.

C.'s fellow students, in that class of mine, could not identify Treblinka or date that war on a pop quiz I'd once given them. C. knew these things from nightly dinner table conversation. As if the occupation had ended yesterday. If then.

Our life in B. closed, really, with that first phone call from Limburg. I lay in bed one Saturday dawn, thrilling to the sound of my C. speaking another language. Another woman lived in the body of the one I lived with. C. had been accommodating me, making herself into someone she thought I could love. I hadn't the first idea who this other person was.

She spoke a dialect that ran like the fabled brook through the heart of E. Out of her mouth flowed an unparsable cascade of phonemes. She talked with her mother for a long time. Then her father, ear to the transatlantic taxi meter, came on for a verbal minute waltz. Then a dozen or so aunts, each with a bit of news. I'd moved in with all of them, without knowing.

A flurry of dialect goodbyes, and C. hung up, wrung out. "They're home," she said. "Come on. Outside."

I put my hand to the pane. The windchill was sub-desperate. "Only if you've been good."

C. began to cry. I fell all over myself telling her I was joking.

We bundled as best we could and hit the street. Her aimlessness was always hard on me. But I'd learned by then not to ask for destinations.

Everything was still the same, she assured me. B. would go on being bearable if we could keep making our long, random walks. That day, we ended up in her beloved public gardens, now frozen over and empty for the winter. The day after, we kept our standing cantata date, at that church that had sung one a week for years before our arrival and that would go on singing them long after we were permanently out of earshot.

Things would be all right, she implied, if we just kept busy. In the evenings we played board games, or sang songs that I wrote for C.'s perfect, clear alto. We watched old films on a black-and-white set with tinfoil antenna, on loan from friends. Gradually, C. convinced me that movies have been going downhill since 1939.

At night, we read to each other—more biography, history, legend —following no program but delight.

Things would be fine if we kept out of the house whenever possible. Saturday morning was free day at the Fine Arts. C. was the only woman alive who would want to return in her spare time to see the same objects she'd just stood in front of for forty hours that week. "It's not the same, Beau. They're much more interesting when you don't have to worry about protecting them."

We went to see the first American retrospective of a German photographer neither of us knew. C. had not yet been assigned the special exhibition. So Saturday was the day. We crossed the swamp that B.'s Brahmins had a century ago called in the Dutch to drain. We strolled into the gallery and around the corner. My photo waited for me there, although I would never have expected it in any number of lifetimes.

First image on the left-hand wall, just inside the door. That room's geometry has fused to the floor plan of my brain. I stood face to faces with three young men who were scrutinizing *me*. They'd waited two-thirds of a century for me to come along and swing into view, just past the photographer's shoulder.

The photo was itself a prediction of its own chance viewing. The three men prearranged the way I would someday see them. And now it seemed that every book I'd been dabbling in, all our random read-alouds, the long list of irrelevant classics I'd memorized for my master's, the swerves our narrative lives had taken all found their retroactive meaning in this one memory posted forward from the past.

The boys were C.'s grandfather and two great-uncles on their way to kermis, to one of those *huwelijksfeesten* she told me about. That was what the lens said. The caption said something altogether different.

German peasants on their way to a dance, 1914. The wrong celebration. The excluded guest list. But very much the same family album.

I felt the shock of recognizing a thing I knew I had never seen before. Every text I'd ever read formed an infinite, convergent series calling out for the recursively called-for, the obvious next term. In that narrow space between what the picture handled and what the caption named, I had my story.

The following Monday, I went in to my tech editing job and gave my two weeks' notice. C. backed me every inch. "Buddy. When you have a calling, you don't worry about what it does to the résumé." Our nest egg had doubled during our year of work. We had a little time. We could buy a chance.

In fact, C. would have preferréd a much deeper plunge into the precarious. Ours was always hedged. I had my programming skill to fall back on. When the account dipped into the danger zone, I freelanced. I worked the smart-appliances gig. I wrote an options trading program for an exiled prince who needed several million dollars to return to his land and finance an election. As he explained, "These things can be very expensive, Rick."

Writing met all the expenses. At least, I meant it to. I must have written that book to gladden C. again. I say "again," but she may never have been. Perhaps to receive gladness you need a forwarding address. Maybe the Polish boy's death cheated her of that, long before her unborn soul stood in line for a residence.

Her transience made a pallet for my head. From the first, C.'s locus of non-time and un-place indexed my imagination's coordinate plane. That's why living with her completed me. Why being with her always felt like coming to rest, returning to some *otherwise* that no one else ever suspected.

She was my midmorning's hypothetical. The givens of my day revealed their thinnest convention, so long as I loved her. Here and now reversed in convex reflection, abidable, on the outside of her eyes.

All we can ever do is lay a word in the hands of those who have put one in ours. I thought I might write my way to a place where my friend C. could live.

I used all the material I had at hand: the vanished Limburg she told me so much about. Her synaptic map of the walled city of Maastricht. The endless cousins who infiltrated my brain like thieves on bicycles in the night. The anthology poured into me through every gate except experience. The disruption of the time line circling our room. The parents, the uncles, caught between nations. The invasion of Trois Vierges, escalating into permanent violence. Big reaching down and annihilating little. Total war, always the same war, placing its embargo on the free passage of lives over the border.

I already possessed all the components for a page-turner. The secret document linking the displaced life back into its continuous frame. The immigrants' island in Chicago. Our apartment in B., with its courtyard and seasick saxophone scales. A chance trip we made by train to Detroit, where her brother lived. Always, always, that invisible village, the one that time mortared to a stump. The white diffraction pattern of crosses, and the villagers who volunteered to tend them. And that glance *back*, over the shoulder. The triple stopped lives, lined up on the muddy road, waiting for someone to pick up their story and extend it.

I wrote of C.'s country without once having seen it. I used her language, fragments of it, helped only by C. herself, who had never spoken anything but the secret dialect of family.

I made the beginner's mistake, the one no first novelist can help but make. I knew, deep at heart, that I would never have another chance to write a book. I could never again ask C. for that luxury. This was a one-shot deal, and to redeem her faith in me, I had to pack my read-aloud with everything I knew. Everything she taught me. Her surrogate home would have to be as wide, as uncrossable as this Atlantic century. If we had just this one dance, our tune would have to be flat-out *tutti*.

I guess there are two kinds of love letters. If you don't get out after the first three words, you need to press on, forever. C. taught me that, too. Desperation is always more moving than discretion, or more recognizable, at least, to the person addressed.

C. earned the daily bread, while I sat alone with the swelling hand-written canary legal pads. As I completed each new chapter, I read it to her. She came home, ate the dinner I made her, then settled in expectantly. She sat close. C. was partially deaf; she always staked out the front seat in classes. Mine especially.

I don't know who was more nervous, performer or audience. *Chapter One*, I assured her. *I outfit myself for a trip to St. Ives.*

I knew that this book would never be published. My audience was never more than C. I wrote for the way her eyes would start to water by chapter's end. How she would nod her head yes, place her hand on her chest, rise from the bed to grab me in the chair where I sat reading to her.

Yet that spell would not have worked if her private code of survival hadn't been cast in a public key. The tale had to be open enough to appeal to the random gallery-browser, snared by the lens. C. alone knew where all the nested frames had started.

Those nights of first draft will not happen again. Never, anymore, that simple passion. We lost it the minute I handed the gift over, the instant I read aloud the epilogue. Years later, when I started getting invitations to read to rooms of perfect strangers, I never had the heart.

Sometimes after I read a chapter to C., we made love. We climbed over each other, brown, frighteningly young, vulnerable, exploring the sad distances, warming each other after the radiators packed it in. Once, as I kissed the birthmark that stained the small of her back, this seemed to me the point of literature. I could not think of a book that was not either by, for, or about this. The elaborate seduction of the already attained. Reforestation of the wilds of time, the one biome where love will not die from lack of cover. I can see that birthmark with my eyes wide open, clearer now at fifteen years' distance than it was when an inch from my eye.

Sex was her present for transcribing her. My feeble thank-you for her sources. And the sounds we listened to then, the calls we made to each other in the winter dark were the vowels that all stories tried to find their way back to.

Afterward, without fail, we fell asleep, her back to my front, two spoons put away in the kitchen drawer of an abandoned cabin. C. was a foot shorter than I was. But when we lay like that, trig turned us to the same length.

The book became a mystery. A foregone conclusion. The more C. felt its surprise inevitability, the keener she got for the next installment. Each narrative riddle, each mental *raadsel* was an awkward, tenderfoot bow I tied for her, for the pleasure of her untying.

Jokes made her happy. I crammed my paragraphs full of every old joke I could remember.

Up top of each new chapter, I placed an epigraph. I copied out of my notebooks a quote that my same clumsy fingers had, earlier that year, just copied in. That book is the dance card of ideas we shared in the foyer of our joint life. A dance card where the partner's name was already printed in, a given. I wrote down only the steps themselves, the ideational dips and sways from the course of that evening when C. was my one date, the lone museum guard of all my thoughts.

Sometimes the steps were literal. One night, I read her a chapter so short it left us more time than even love could fill. She'd listened well; it was time for a walk. We drifted out, a slow, deliberate stroll along the parkway that flanked the trolley tracks out to the suburbs.

In the chapter, my contemporary technical editor, in a city much like B., had journeyed home to his immigrant mother in Chicago to find mysterious papers up in the family attic binding him to an unknown past. The passage back left C. expansive.

"I like that guy of yours," she said. "I like your Lithuanian graffiti on the sidewalks. Do you have any idea what it feels like to be the puppy raised by ducks?"

"Tell me."

She heaved a sigh. "I've been to more Polish weddings than I can count."

"Well, we know about your head for figures."

She laughed and flank-attacked. "Come on, you. Let's polka."

"The polka is no more than a spot of local color from out of *Washington Square*, I'm afraid."

"Don't be afraid," C. purred. She could be coy at times. Funny. I'd forgotten. "Here. I'll show you."

She stomped it out for me. I was comic, crippled, a laughingstock. But she stuck with me. Of all the countless thousands of things C. taught me, that polka might be the best. I picked it up somewhere along the length of that greenway down which we hurled ourselves, a couple of parka-packed, manic Polacks making tracks into the Arctic dark.

"It makes me sad, Beau," she told me, another chapter night, perhaps halfway through.

I panicked in the space of a phrase. "What? Something's off? I can fix it. Don't worry; it ends happily."

"Not that, silly. It makes me sad. You have this—work. And I have nothing."

"I don't get it. I thought you liked putting on that uniform."

"Oh, I did. And it's still the greatest job in the world. In some ways."

"What's wrong, then?"

She wasn't sure. She still loved the paintings. But they had started to fade into overlearned monochrome. Standing in place for so long began to fog her. The boss was growing creepy. She felt embarrassed explaining herself to others. Ashamed of doing less than she might.

"Maybe we should look around for a new job?" The "we" that would take such toll on her.

"It's the middle of winter. Nobody's hiring. Besides, what am I qualified to do?"

"Well, I don't know. Anything. If the job you have is making you crazy—"

"I know, I know. I need something more than just a paycheck. The problem is, I'm not ambitious. Put me on a rug, I'll lie there forever."

" 'Put me out on the lawn and I'll wail'?"

She clouded. "It's not funny. I'm sorry I ever showed you that picture." I tickled her to re-create that infant expression.

"Quit it!"

"*I'll* give you prickling."

"Don't, Beau. Not now. This is serious."

"So serious we can't—"

The obvious *yes* stopped me in mid-cliché.

"What's the matter?" I asked. Ready, already, to be dead.

"It's your story." She looked down, away. Anywhere but at me. "It makes me feel worthless. I know it's awful. Do you hate me?"

She got a new job. A friend of mine from the computer world tipped C. to an opening. Wire operator in a brokerage. "Not something I'm going to make a career of," C. joked.

But something to engage her, salve the sense of self. She came home animated again. As I fed her, she entertained me with tales of eccentric colleagues, wigged out on Opportunity Loss. Her accounts of that quintessential late-twentieth-century business delighted me. The parasitic middlemen, extracting margin from the news feed, the Teletype romances and tragedies. The spigot attached to the pipeline, leveraging profit and hedging loss as it trickled through capital's tap.

So I did the only thing imaginable. I went back and worked her new material into the book as well as I could. The market and mad brokers became yet another subplot. I fit it in, between jokes from the front and tales from the tech editing crypt, between the Maas and the Rhine, between the war and its permanently militarized peace, between the Great Personalities and the clueless lives, between fairyland and documentary fact, the aperture and the print, then and now, filthy lucre and the Fine Arts.

What did the finished thing mean? It meant that our private reservoir, when face-to-face with the outside, is all we have that might help a little. That book was no more than a structured pastiche of every report I'd ever heard, from C. or abroad. All a patchwork to delight and distract her. One that by accident ate her alive.

The key to that book, the one that preserves it for me, is that the triple braid—the magic *driehoek* of the photograph—fails to come together as expected. The lens does not have the last word, nor does the glance of the viewer, nor does the look of those boys, out over the shoulder of the photographer, back behind the lens. The dominant tense was now. The point of stories was what you did with them.

With my last chapter, the charm broke. I knew it in advance. I saved every trick I had for the end, to break her heart and win her for the present, forever. But of course, a return to feeling only made things worse. I read her the ending. Lovemaking stayed silent this time, skin more a checkpoint between us than a visa in.

"What will you do with it now?" C. asked.

"I don't know." The plot had gotten away from me. Escaped its frame. "Send it out, I guess."

Too rapidly, she agreed. "Of course. You have to."

Only the usual literary biography would have saved us. Fifteen years of waiting to be taken. Growing stronger, closer to each other on the mound of rejection slips, which we'd have burned for fuel.

The day we heard the book had been bought, we celebrated. Cheer felt forced and punch-drunk. C. assumed the virtue of excitement as bravely as she had managed each chapter up until then. But she was like a mother losing her preschooler to the talk-show circuit.

She tried to show enthusiasm for the production process. She pitched in, but her heart had bolted. She hated those grubbers in New York touching the manuscript, even to typeset it. It killed her to watch those farmers make their way into the brutal market. To see them join the ranks of the century's displaced.

She would never again listen to a word I wrote without suspicion. Endings, from now on, betrayed her. Simple associative fact: it wasn't even a question of remembering. What chance does story have against neurons that generalize from a single instance?

The week we learned the book's publication date, C. received an offer of promotion. The brokerage wanted her to run their Operations cage. The jump, steep and quick in coming, surprised no one but C. She was alone in never knowing how competent she was.

The offer could not have come at a better time. C. needed something, and nothing that I could give. A hurried, three-week trip to Limburg to check on her folks left her edgier than ever. Not even walks worked any longer. A real career might be no more than a changeling baby. But even a changeling can take up the slack of care.

She had some days to decide. We spent them spinning skeins of reassurance. "You'll be great at it. They wouldn't have asked you otherwise."

The day she went in to accept, I prepared a feast. I made decorations. Funny little signs with cartoons of C. on a pyramid of brokers, cracking a whip. Hand-lettered posters reading "Book That Cruise" and "Retirement by 35."

I could tell, watching her come up the courtyard, that celebration was a horrible mistake. She pounded up the stairs, slammed the door, and held it shut behind her with all her hundred and five pounds, sobbing.

"Beauie, we need to get out of this place."

I tried to hold her, proffer all the worthless comforts. "Okay," I managed. "I'm game. Where to?"

The last place. Worse than I expected. "I want to go back to U."

Imp B already pushed the envelope. B hadn't a clue what cats *were*, or sacks, let alone wives. But it seemed to know how to count them, or not count them, as the case demanded.

If A had been an exercise in verbal pattern recognition, B was a foray into computational linguistics. It knew things like over and under, right of or left of, inside or out. Even that far, I doubted whether it comprehended these containers or whether it just manipulated them cleverly enough to pass. Then again, I began to doubt whether I myself could define the difference.

B could handle syntax. It had a rudimentary sense of the parts of speech and how they operated on each other. And it began to cross the threshold into semantic content. Lentz once or twice tacked on a new subnet to handle different routines—a noun-phrase decoder or a short-term recognition scratch area. In fact, I suppose we were up to Imp B.4 or better.

Lentz assured me that B would handle its own knowledge representations. The frames, the inheritance of classification qualities and exceptions, the scripts: all would fall out as a result of the way B stored associated input. But even in its minute domains, B had to deal with numbingly different kinds of knowledges. With nouns alone, what you could do with "pattern" varied without limit from what you could do with "matching" or "machine."

110

I'd lost count of the number of neurodes involved. It had grown big, complex beyond belief. A glitch now set us back whole days at a time. The thing was a monster, distributed, unchartable, out of control. And yet Lentz's brain, or mine, was hundreds of millions of Imp B's wide. We could push that matter a little longer, if only just.

We were still experimenting with the size of layers. Bigger was not always better, Lentz told me.

"Life, Marcel, in case you on the humanistic side of the tracks haven't grokked this yet, involves a series of trade-offs."

"Yes, we're onto that."

"Now. The trade-offs in input layer size. Well, the smaller the layer, the better it generalizes. The larger, the more it can learn to fit into an associative grid."

"The better it is at generalizing, the worse it is at acquiring new associations?"

"The poet's a blooming genius. Now we know how you earn your grant money."

"Does it follow that the more facts it has, the harder it is to take in new facts?"

"Thirty-five is about when that starts to happen, Marcel. You begin to think, 'Well, I more or less understand how things work. Do I really want to disassemble tens of thousands of tangled, semiaccurate beliefs on the off chance that I might be able to bring one small receptor field into better focus?' "

"Tell me about it. I'm there."

"Don't worry, little boy. You've a few tricks yet to pick through. And a few years yet to pick through them. I mean, you're lucky I've taken you on. Aristotle wouldn't accept any student still young enough to have a sex urge."

"Not a problem, at the moment."

On days when Lentz engaged himself with design philosophy, he grew expansive, almost pleasant. On days when he built things, he was fun. I tried to keep the soldering gun in his hand and ignore the baiting as much as possible.

"Now: what about the size of the hidden layers? Do you want them bigger or smaller than your input layers?"

"I'm sorry. I give up. We're going to have to turn all the cards over."

"Come on, think it out. Consider the translation impedance. Another trade-off. The better the resolution, the more susceptible the net becomes to random noise. Think of B as a curve fitter . . ."

"That's all our brains are? Curve fitters?"

"It's a big 'all,' friend. The curve we are trying to fit is as long as existence. As many dimensions. The fact that we can get the infinite data stream to cohere into lumps at all has turned men with as much native intelligence as your friend Plover into mystics."

"Here we go. Time to slander Harold."

"It's not slander. The man makes his claims public. 'Meanings extractable from a given linguistic configuration may be neither convergent, bounded, nor recursively enumerable.' Or some such rubbish. He seems to think that because 'context' is infinitely extensible, there can be no neurological calculus of interpretation."

"And you, Engineer?" I tweaked, waiting until he had his hands full of printed circuit and his head deep in the cage. "Do you think that because you are virtuous, there will be no more cakes and ale?"

"Now, Marcel. What in the *hell* is that supposed to mean?"

"Dunno. Let's ask Harold."

"Hn. I'd rather get back to the subject. Sometimes I think the human brain is just one long open parenthesis. So. Tell me. How big do you want your various output layers to be?"

"I guess that would depend on how big an answer we are expecting from any given subnet."

"Well done. You're getting cagey. We'll have you writing NSF proposals in no time." Lentz's sarcasms were mellowing with age. "Would you concede, then, that many of our output layers could consist, in theory, of a single neurode, since the cyborgs think that every quest can be rephrased as a series of yes-or-no questions?"

"I wish the lit critters would catch on to that."

"Yes. Handy, isn't it? Cleans up a lot."

"Engineer, can I ask you something? If you're not a mystic and you're not a cyborg, what in creation are you?"

" 'Creation' is a loaded word, Marcel. I guess I'm a lot of little delta rules running recurrently, evaluating and updating themselves."

"Tell me a different story. I'm not sure I like that one."

We were well into the millions of connections when B seized up for good. We'd made so many tortuous increments, we'd stopgapped so many glitches that I did not, at first, see this collapse as fatal.

"John is a brother of Jim's," I told it. B turned the fact into a stream of hieroglyphic vectors that changed its layout imperceptibly. "Who is Jim's brother?"

"John," Imp B replied. Reliant knight. Already it outperformed some aphasics.

"Who is Jim?"

"John's sister." That much was fine. I could live with that answer. In fact, it taught me a thing or two about my own presumptive matrix.

I continued, "John gives Jim apples. Who gets apples?"

"Jim gets apples."

"Jim is given the apples by whom?"

"Jim is given the apples by John."

"Jim eats an apple. The apple is sour. Jim throws the other apples away. Why does Jim throw the other apples away?"

At that point, B's cranking time became unendurable. It returned something like, "Jim throws the other apples away because the apples are given by John."

"No," I told it, or words to that effect. "Start again. Why?"

"Jim throws the apples away. She does not want them."

A marginally acceptable answer. Maybe insight hid away somewhere in that tacit implication. But maybe the damn thing was bluffing. Its vagueness depressed me: the slow tyro during story hour, doomed from birth to a career in food service.

"Why doesn't she want them?"

"She doesn't eat them. So she can't want them."

This alien proto-intelligence differed just enough from sense to make my head throb. Still, we lay within acceptable performance margins. I went on to torture it with, "Jim hits John. Why does Jim hit John?" B had one of its damning seizures. It cranked all afternoon, resetting itself, grabbing randomly at a thousand possible but skewed associations.

Thrashing, it tried a proverb we'd hammered into it the week before. "Jim hit John because one bad apple doesn't spoil the whole barrel."

When pushed, it finally failed to answer all together.

Some crucial frameshift fell outside B's ability to effect. It could not say, *John's apples angered Jim*, or *No reason*, or *There could be bad blood I haven't heard about*.

It could not even say *I don't know*.

It lacked some meta-ability to step back and take stock of the semantic exchange. It could not make even the simplest jump above the plane of discourse and appraise itself from the air. Although it talked, in a manner of speaking, speech eluded B.

Its brain faltered at that Piagetian stage where the toy disappeared when placed behind a screen. It could not move ideas around. All it could move around were things. And the things had to be visible at all times.

Something was screwy with the way B passed symbolic tokens among its levels. It might grow knowledge structures forever, as fecund as a field tilled with representational fertilizer. But its knowledge *about* knowledge would remain forever nil. And no patching or kludging on Lentz's part could set it right. B's deficiency seemed to be a by-product of the way its constituent nets spoke to one another. The way we'd linked them into the grand schematic.

We postponed the inevitable for as long as we could. I came into the office one evening and found Lentz behind his desk, inert. "I want to change the architecture." Ahab, well out of port, announcing the slight broadening of plans.

I was too invested to feel demoralized. Maybe I had some naïve image of taking a magnetic snapshot of B and somehow porting it intact into new and more capable digs.

Retrain several million connections from scratch. Had I realized, I might have signed off the project. But I had no incentive to realize. My last month and a half of literary effort had produced no more than half a chapter of train, crossing the snow-lined mountains toward sunny neutrality. I stopped at every other sentence to run to the library and verify that I wasn't unconsciously plagiarizing. As a result, the thing read like a Samuel Beckett rewrite of the *Ancrene Riwle*.

U. made changing machine architectures almost trivial. It stretched credibility, but that sleepy hamlet with the two-dollar movie theater and the free corn boil at summer's end also sheltered a National Supercomputing Site. The town, fallen through the earth's crust into a dimension where nothing had changed since 1970, consequently had a jump on the next millennium, the advantage of the late starter. Four rival pizza parlors, each named "Papa" somebody, each opening whenever it felt like it. Bars where fraternities split Thursday-night twenty-five-cent plastic cups of beer. And the most advanced, block-long cybernetic wonderland that a paranoid race to preserve faltering world dominance could fund.

I imagined my network's first freshman comp assignment: "Convince a total stranger that she would not want to grow up in your hometown." Son of B could whistle its answer to that one in the dark.

The latest nationally funded supercomputer to come of age in U. had itself already lived through half a dozen incarnations. Nor was it really a single machine. It was a collection of 65,536 separate computers, chained like galley slaves into inconceivable, smoothly functioning parallel. Depending on the benchmark, the connection monster could outperform any computing assemblage on earth.

The machine was so powerful that no one could harness it. So notoriously difficult was its programming that major scientists and their graduate-student franchises had already begun to flee U. for sites a tenth as potent but at least manageable.

"We're moving over to the connection monster, Marcel."

"Lentz, you're kidding me. This game can't interest you that much."

"What? I'm not afraid of that thing. How hard can it be?"

"Hard. Harder than humiliating your colleagues can be worth."

"You underestimate my colleagues. Besides, don't forget the undertaking's empirical interest."

"Don't bullshit me, Engineer. This thing is all smoke and mirrors. And you know it."

But he knew, too, that he had me hooked. I wanted to see the next implementation up and running on a host tailor-made for neural nets. Lentz wrote a proposal credible enough to pass itself off as real science. By that time, the keepers of the connection monster were so hard pressed to salvage their hardware from neglect that they were taking all comers.

The man was dangerous when he had a plan. He meant Imp C to be profoundly different in nature. He wanted to push the notion of the self-designing system up a level. Reweighting prewired connections would no longer suffice. Imp C would be able to strengthen or weaken the interactions between entire distributed subsystems. It would even grow its own connections from scratch, as needed.

Lentz wanted to get hundreds, perhaps thousands of large, interdependent nets up and running at the same time. He saw them passing endless streams of ideational tokens among themselves. The net of networks would churn at all times, not simply responding passively to new data inputs. When input stopped, it would interrogate itself in ongoing, internal dialogue. Its parts would quiz one another, associate and index themselves, even when alone. Imp C would undertake constant self-examination and reorganization.

Lentz meant to distribute these chattering subsystems not just across the connection monster's 65,536 processors but across other various and specialized hosts. Each task communicated with the others via high-speed fiber-optic cable. C, if it could be said to live anywhere at all, lived spread all over the digital map.

"Keep out of my hair for a few weeks, Marcel."

"That should be easy."

Lentz, preoccupied, ignored my crack. "Just until I dig the foundations."

The order suited me. I had copy to proofread. I'd also agreed to a number of classroom visits, hoping to justify my freeloading existence.

The class visits were an embarrassment for everyone. Students sat polite but stunned in front of me, their desks circled like Conestogas under attack. The look of shame on each face asked how I could have missed the fact that the age of reading was dead. "How do you work? Where do your ideas come from?" they asked, hoping I would take the hint and go away.

I answered as best I could. But I couldn't take a step toward the first of these questions without lying. Luckily, lies were all they expected.

When class visits ended, I sat in my office, proofing the book I no longer remembered having written. I went through one methodical ruler-line of text after the other until the Primary Visual Area back in my occipital lobe started to bleed.

I tried to read without comprehension. One catches more errors that way. But sense pressed itself on me, kicking and screaming. The book's style perched on the brink of nervous disintegration, the most depressing fairy tale I'd ever read. And the only person more depressed than I was my editor, sitting on my unfulfilled contract.

I knew the narration meant to be double-voiced with my protagonist, a resident surgeon living an extended mental breakdown. My depiction of a society in collapse now struck me, if anything, as hopelessly tame compared to those vignettes shoring up the hourly news. But as I read, I kept thinking: Someone has to find this author before he does something desperate.

I spent the first week exterminating typos. The second I spent improvising, in the margins of the last pages, some semblance of redemptive ending. I scratched out the manuscript's final descent. In its place, I had my collapsing surgeon hold out his hands, catch the woman who had failed to save him. I added a last-minute postscript that returned the tale to the light of its source, the reader, untouched by tragedy. And yet the story still radiated a darkness so wide my pupils could not attenuate.

My eleventh-hour triage demoralized me even more than the first writing. I felt a despair I had not felt while still the teller. Not a despair for my career, which had never been more than a happy accident. What lost me, listening to my own news account, was learning that I didn't have the first idea who I was. Or of how I had gone so emptied.

I kept at the reconstruction. I no longer had the heart to send out so bleak a deformity into the world. I worked in short spurts, all I had the strength for, surgically reinserting the *no* that children in the disputed zone need if they are to escape to daylight.

Work picked up at evening, when the building reverted to native, archaic silence. I'd hack at my story for half an hour, stand, stretch, warm my imagination by the purely symbolic fireplace, then sit back and try to cure the next nihilist paragraph.

I wandered the abandoned halls, a world unspeakably far from the Center. The plank floorboards creaked even before I stepped on them. They settled under the weight of generations of scholar undergraduates who had gone on to die at the desks of their bank vice presidencies. The passages smelled of gum and hair oil, ammonia, gargle, damp fiber, wax, shellac, chemicals from the days when chemistry was still a liberal art.

Even the steam pipes reeked a Georgian, paint-peeling grace. In the incandescent dusk, the building gave no hint of the internationalist polemics just now attempting last-ditch CPR on a discipline choked to death by curatorial gentility.

The manuscript took over my office. I taped pages up around the room, the way C. and I had once taped our homemade time line around the bedroom in B. I browsed them, drifting from one to the other, a well-meaning museum-goer gazing at an impenetrable Dadaist retrospective. I could find no further entrance. My corrections were overdue. My surgeon's fight against child genocide had become mine, and like him, I was failing to stem the end.

I worked late on the last night before my extended deadline. I revised until I needed to come up for air. I threw open the office door and fell into the hall. But I decompressed too quickly, giving myself the bends. The Georgian familiarity shrank in front of me, as overcome as the text I'd just been giving intensive care.

I made my way to one end of the main hall for a drink of water. I steadied and drank, but the sip tasted of heavy metals. I turned, facing into the empty passage. Shock knocked me backward a step, against the fountain. I wasn't alone. At the far end of the corridor, a ghost condensed from empty silence.

The apparition swayed in vacuum. My next blink would disperse her back into the ether. She stood browsing a notice board, oblivious of my existence. A whip-thin lamia in a pageboy haircut, absurdly young, in blue jeans and sleeveless orange cotton cling, despite the irreversible autumn. First day of adulthood. Setting out. She carried books under her arm, and a clump I hoped was a jacket. Something held her rapt: the corkboard, smothered in announcements.

I tried to beat a path back to my office without startling her. But the floorboards betrayed me, popping more violently the lighter I slid. She turned to look with mute, uncomprehending fear, a deer forgiving its killer. And with the same slow indifference, she shot a last glance at the notices and withdrew.

I don't know who I saw. Not the grad student she must have been, to let herself into the building at this hour. Not C. at thirty-three. Nor C. a life younger, when I'd met her. Nor any of those girl-women who had obsessed me, before C. If this was anyone I knew, I no longer recognized even the association.

Yet I felt like running after this profile, onto the chill Quad. Calling her back, laughing, excited, furious. What do you mean, coming here? Bad luck; bad judgment. Hadn't we agreed never to meet on this earth? Not after I'd gone prematurely dead, and you, a little girl in a T.

I could learn her name. She would carry prosodic weight to her—plans, a past—sad, pragmatic reasons why she haunted this building, working late. Doubtless, she brayed when she talked, slaughtered her checking account, complained about the freshmen she had to render literate, suffered paralyzing anxiety over her approaching prelims.

But for this one surprise ambush, the image of slender pageboy—a pair of bare shoulders, a gaze in profile down a fading hallway—stood in for all the books I'd failed to pull off. She was the sum of all stories I'd never now attempt. The placeholder for the long miss I'd made of experience. The loss fiction fails to repair. The fixedly ephemeral. A. at twenty-two.

Lentz almost glowed over the phone. "We've knocked it, Marcel. Pulled it off. The next step that everybody else has been after."

"Everyone else? Real scientists don't waste their time with make-believe."

"They would if they could get away with it. You think they like all that bloody reductionism? They only put up with those shuffling baby steps in the hopes that they'll run someday. That we'll all soar."

"Okay, Engineer. Enough iambs. Tell me what we've done."

"I've tested it. It's brilliant. B's problem was that it could manipulate idea tokens, but not ideas *about* those tokens. Right?"

"If you say so."

"We need a beast that can make second-order shifts. One capable of reflection. That can do with situations what B could only do with things. It's so simple: put it in the hardware. We need a C implementation that runs a fully functional simulation of a B-type implementation as one of its own component subsystems."

"A simulation within a simulation? One mock-up running another copy of itself?"

"Sound familiar? It should. It's you, Marcel. Where all your homesickness comes from. Your sense of never more than renting. All your picture galleries. Your private library of desire."

"Wait a minute. Back off. *I'm* the humanist here, remember? You're just in charge of the circuitry."

"Right. Sorry. My humble etceteras. I'm bringing the new incarnation up tonight. Get over here first thing tomorrow."

He didn't even give me the luxury of weighing the invitation.

When I arrived the next morning, Imp C was up and running.

We still dealt out of Lentz's office. Our gate was still the same junker terminal, the same jumble of antique I/O. I had to remind myself that the linkup hid, on its far end, the most powerful massively parallel hardware the combined public and private sectors could buy.

Lentz sat me down in the old chair. "Go ahead. Ask it something."

"Ask . . . ? You mean you've started the training already?"

"Well, this is difficult to explain. I still had all B's valences, the complete multidimensioned array of its connection weights sitting around in various files. So I thought, why not use them as a test? Let C run our actual B as its puppet modeler. It—rather took off."

"I don't get it. I still don't get it."

"Well, you know, the plan this time out was to go for full recurrence. The data set you put on the input layer works its way through, not once, but many times. No limit to how many times it can trip and reset the same weights on its way—"

"Yeah, yeah. I follow the mechanics." I didn't know what made me so testy. I felt the experiment getting away from me. "I just want to know how it can be responsive already, without training."

Lentz seemed embarrassed. "It seems to be training itself."

"Oh, Engineer. Don't give me—"

I slapped my bike helmet against the desk in disgust. Only a graze, but it cracked the shell cleanly. Lentz broke out in a sharp laugh.

"High deductible on that insurance policy of yours, Marcel." He started again. "It seems that C is capable of using different constellations of B's associative pairings as *its* points of comparison. It's triangulating. Testing itself for internal consistency. It's generalizing about the nature of its own generalizations."

"It's running already? Before I give it input?"

"It's running constantly. It makes its own input now."

"You mean, it can anticipate new material. You're trying to tell me it's thinking."

Lentz shrugged. He held his palm out to the microphone.

"Good morning," I said.

"Good morning," the voice-synthesizing hardware replied.

"How are you this morning?"

"Fine, thank you. You?"

I killed the mike. I turned to Lentz, quivering. "Where did it get that 'You'? Not 'And how are you?' We didn't even teach B the long form. How on earth did this one jump to the casual?"

"I don't know. It got it somewhere. From examining B."

"Are you pleased with yourself?"

"We all do what we can, Marcel."

"Shh. I'm not talking to you. I'm talking to the box."

Imp C paused a moment, then came back with, "What do you mean?" It seemed a stock enough answer. When in doubt, put the ball in the other guy's court.

"I mean, you must be happy to be so bright." Toss it a curve. See if it could handle the colloquial.

"Many things are so bright without being happy."

Impressive, even grammatical, although a bit clumsy. Still and all, it sounded to me more like hollow syllogism than philosophy.

"For instance?" Would it recognize the form as a question?

"For instance: light."

Imp C, I concluded, was whistling past the graveyard. Still, I decided to play fair. To give it as much benefit of doubt as I had to give anyone. I was middle-aged, and had myself only recently learned that no one hears what anyone else says.

"Do you think it's harder for smart people to be happy?"

Imp C thought for a minute. "Harder than what?"

I laughed out loud. Perfect. Perfect. The thing was an idiot savant.

"Jesus, Marcel," Lentz shouted. "Watch the input levels. You'll blow its eardrums out, cackling like that."

"Harder than if they weren't so smart," I explained to Imp C.

"Are you so smart while you are still being happy?"

Wonky idiom, even for an electronic DP. And little more than evasive maneuvers, again. Yet evasion, too, was a form of intelligence.

Then I let myself hear the machine's reply. It floored me. I was more than a blank irritant to C. I, too, was a token to manipulate. *I* had weight. I was part of Imp C's real-world calculus.

"I don't know. How can I tell if I am happy or not?"

"Ask yourself if you are not happy."

"Lentz," I said. "This is incredible. I can't—"

"It's fast, isn't it? I came up with a couple of quick-index algorithms. Idea caches, you might say. But I never expected we'd get this level of performance out of the new system."

"My God. It's not the performance, Lentz. It's—the *performance*."

"Yes," he agreed. The thing silenced even him.

"Look what it's doing. Telling me to ask myself. How can it *do* that? Think what it has to figure, just to stay in the ballpark. It knows 'happy.' It knows that 'happy' is a good thing. It knows 'happy' is something people are or aren't. It knows that I'm a person. It knows about questions, and that questions are something you 'ask.' It knows how to turn an interrogative into a statement, and scour a statement to see which questions might fit. Okay. Maybe it doesn't *know*, doesn't really understand all the things it conjures up by asking . . ."

All the things that made my voice catch to try to explicate.

"But it does understand enough to see that I'm not going to know anything, even about myself, except by putting myself the question."

"That's a lot," Lentz conceded.

"It's everything. Where did it . . . ?" But I'd lost patience with asking the human. I needed to interrogate the source.

"You make me happy," I told Imp C. I waited, sick, to see what it would say.

"Then I'm happy, too, Rick."

Too much, even for a willing victim. Over the line. My credibility snapped, as it should have, long before.

"Hold it. How did you know my name?" B never did. We gave it any number of proper names, but never our own.

At the crucial question, of course, C went silent. That, more than anything, gave the show away. A machine might have gone on innocently covering itself, even after the game was lost.

I wheeled on Lentz, not bothering to muffle the mike. "All right, *klootzak*. What the hell's going on?"

Lentz's eyes were watering. Unable to hold back any longer, he spit his dentures across the office. He whooped like a howler monkey. He tried to catch his breath, but each attempt left him more hysterical than the last. "I'm sorry, Marcel. You were—you were so . . ."

A shamefaced Diana Hartrick appeared in the doorframe. The truth finally hit.

"You?" My disbelief was worse than any accusation. "You let him set me up? You *helped* him?"

"It was a joke?" she wavered.

"To humiliate me? That's funny?"

"Oh, grow up, Marcel. Nothing's humiliating except this overreaction of yours."

"You grow up, Engineer." My tone stopped us all dead. It startled me as much as it did them. "So this is human intelligence. This is what we're trying so hard to model."

I'd been an idiot. Two seconds of reflection should have told me that C couldn't have commanded even a fraction of the material it spewed out. A babe in the woods would have seen through this. Trish Plover would have been, like, *really*. I myself would never have bitten, had I still been a child. Yet I'd believed. I'd *wanted* to.

Lentz tried to collect himself. But the minute he caught Diana's eye, he lost it all over again. Diana followed suit, helpless. Her snickers rasped somewhere in her throat.

"I'm sorry. It sounded funny at the time."

"Not without clinical interest," Lentz inserted. "Reverse Turing Test. See if the human can pass itself off as the black box. Don't you want to know the mechanics?"

"The mechanics? It's a goddamn tin-can telephone. Lady at the other end of the string, trying to sound like a clunky New Age self-help guide."

" 'Many things are so bright without being happy,' " Lentz mimicked. Then he gagged on another round of phlegm.

I stood up, shaking my head.

"Don't leave, Marcel. We really do have a new simulation up and running in there. A good one."

Diana's turn to snort.

"Lentz," I said softly, "I'll never trust you again."

"Don't need your trust. I just need you to train Imp C."

I stopped, waiting to hear what I was going to say. "Imp D."

The two colleagues, divided on every issue except novelists' gullibility, broke into relieved tittering.

The sound set me off again. "You bastards. So how does this little stunt of yours make you feel?"

"Fine, thank you." Diana smiled. "You?"

I had nothing to say. And I said it.

"Oh, Rick. Admit it. You loved the act while it lasted."

I looked at her. Somewhere in her couple hundred eye muscles was the awful suggestion that talking to me made her happy.

"Barring that," Lentz intruded, "admit that you bought the whole shebang."

I giggled. I couldn't help myself. "Yep," I said. "Totally suckered." Alive. Admit it. "That's me."

Diana's apology came in the form of a lunch invitation. It shamed me. She'd made the last overture, and I'd never gotten back to her.

Not that I singled her out. I wasn't getting back to anyone. I bought an answering machine, and cowered behind it, screening calls. Then I stashed even that, turning the ringer off for long stretches. The hermit thing became easier with practice. I even thought about writing about it, until I remembered I already had.

But Diana searched me down. "How about lunch? I owe you." Face-to-face. Collegial. Gap-toothed, like the Wife of Bath. There was no hiding.

Lunch was fun, given everything. Fish sandwiches from a notorious pool-hall dive in campustown. Diana was voluble. In the labs, she always struck me as the person I wanted to be when I grew up. Over fish sandwiches, she seemed young enough to be compromised by eating with someone my age.

"How's the Don?" I asked. She looked blank. "Mr. Quixote?"

She groaned. "I don't want to talk about it."

"No, but Harold probably does, huh?"

She flashed a stare at me. What exactly were we talking about? "I should sic him on you. That would simplify matters all around."

"Sorry. I kind of have my hands full at the moment. After we feed Cervantes to the machine, Harold can come and chat up Imp D."

Diana puckered, amused despite herself. "Know why I think the whole thing is infinitely ditsy?"

"Because it's me and Lentz?"

"There is that. But I was thinking how you want to put everything into *words*. Think about this. You want to make a data structure that will say everything there is to say about 'ball.' You have to have facts for roundness, cohesion, size, weight. You have to have all sorts of probabilistic rules. It's more likely to be ten inches in diameter than ten feet."

"Unless it's a wrecking ball."

"It's more likely to be made of rubber or plastic or wood than of, say, plant fiber."

"Unless it's a softball, or a cotton ball . . ."

"Or a fuzzball." Diana laughed.

"Or a spitball. Or a ball of yarn."

"Enough already. You're making me crazy. The list of predicates is—forever. And the exception list is even longer. You can talk through a whole encyclopedia, but you won't yet have said 'ball' itself. Let alone what you do with one. What one means. How to throw one. How a kid feels when he gets one for a birthday present."

"But that's where associative learning comes in, isn't it? We don't have to enumerate all those qualities. If the machine keeps coming across them, and sometimes people are gazing into crystals, and sometimes they're pitching a curve, and sometimes they are having—"

"That's just the problem. Any baby can hold a ball in its hands. Your machine can't. How many words is it going to take to say what that globe *feels* like? The heft of the thing. The possibility."

"Red rubber sphere that you can chuck . . ."

"Richie. Richie."

I didn't have the heart to tell her that no one called me that. Besides, it sounded good in her mouth.

"Are you going to do 'red' as fitting between x and y angstroms?"

"Not at all. That's the classical AI people. Chen and Keluga. We're going to do red sky, red-faced, red flag, in the red, red dress . . ."

"Sexist. Okay. Go on to 'sphere.' How is the poor thing supposed to get 'all the points equidistant from a center' when it has never seen *distance*? When it can't possibly measure?"

"Good point. You mean we have a problem. No symbolic grounding."

"Symbolic grounding." Diana grinned, and wiped the tartar sauce from her lower lip. "That's the phrase I was looking for."

"You're saying a reading machine is hopeless. We should give it up."

"I'm saying, if you're going to make such a thing, you have to give it eyes, hands, ears. A real interface onto the outside."

"The literary theorists think a human's real-world interface is problematic at best. And greatly overrated. They say even sense data must be put into symbols."

"The literary theorists have to get tenure. And they have no hard facts to get tenure with. They have to fight for a slice of a pie that's getting smaller every day."

"Getting smaller because of people like you."

I was teasing. She took me at face value. "Yes, maybe. But tell me, then. Why do your people need to either emulate mine, attack us as nature molesters, or dismiss us as irrelevant self-deluders?"

"My people are scared shitless of your people, that's why. They're terrified that Dad and Mom really do love you best."

Diana smiled like a teenager. "Are you kidding? We're the problem child. Don't you remember? You heard the parents tell us never to play with matches."

We walked outside into a day remade. The trees had stripped bare, but for a moment, I couldn't tell if they were coming or had just gone. We two were the only ones on the whole street wearing coats. A pack of earphoned roller bladers with wraparound shades so silvered they couldn't see almost mowed us down.

My disorientation was total. "Wasn't it almost winter when we went inside?"

"It's getting so that these once-in-a-century freak weather spells occur every other week."

"That's the fault of you scientists."

"Doubtless."

"It's still nippy. Have I lost my mind, or are those women wearing shorts?"

"Youth is never cold," Diana lamented.

Ten years ago, fifteen, I'd pitied those who'd let their skin go papery and their blood thin. Back then, this had been my haunt. Now I'd lost the lease, could not even name the street.

"I want it to freeze. Freeze hard."

"It's going to freeze," Diana guaranteed. "You've forgotten. It's rough out in these parts. Four months of interstellar blackness. Deep space. Zero. The air loads up with sleet BBs, with nothing between here and Pennsylvania to slow the wind."

"How long have you been here?"

"Five years. You know the funny thing? I never thought of myself as a Californian when I lived there."

We walked toward campus. "Does the brain have a 'decaying leaf recognition' subsystem? A 'sheepskin coat just back from the cleaners' subsystem?"

"I know what you mean," Diana said. "Smell is everything, isn't it? When I smell the air right now, I think, I know what's coming. Time to batten down."

"I think, how can I leave all this?"

She said nothing for the longest time. Then Diana said, "Thrill."

"Yes. Thrill."

It took me until the Quad, until we walked over the spot, to make the connection. To realize what day it was. You see, it didn't feel like November. Same day, different year: I no longer knew what people meant by that. Four days later, it snowed.

"Symbolic grounding," I told Lentz.

D, our first implementation to run on the sprawling community of connection machine, was my slowest charge so far. But parallel architecture and several software twists made it the one with the most astonishing reach. D came into this world recursive. It took forever to grasp that two was the integer just past one. But the instant it got that, it had infinity in the same breath. It could watch itself learn. When it got "Dogs bark," it also got "Baby says, 'Dogs bark.' " The breakout, when it came, was going to be unbelievable.

The shape of its brain was generative. It matched the arc of an uncoiling sentence. But deep syntax wasn't enough. Words weren't enough. "The policeman gave the motorist his badge," I told it. "Who does 'his' stand for? The policeman gave the motorist his license." Now who?

How much would D have to know before it could get that one? Tracing my own inference process dizzied me. The linked list of properties hanging off the world's every object required a combinatorial explosion of sense. But to see even part of what the host symbols stood for required that D first *see*.

"We have to give it eyes," I decided. "Why train it with all the properties of a ball when we can show it what a ball is?"

"Nice leap, Marcel," Lentz said. "I've been waiting for you to make it."

"And here I was afraid you were going to kill me for bringing it up."

"On the contrary. In fact, I still have a passive retinal matrix lying around intact from work I did last year. We can paste it in."

"Now, where the hell did I put that eyeball? It was around here somewhere."

Lentz laughed. "All right. So the work habits could be more systematic."

Sight was not the sudden beamburst I hoped for. Revision E could convert objects into retinoptic neurode maps. Training got it to associate words with each visual clump. But navigating by this crayon cartography resembled sewing silk with a Lincoln log needle.

I gave it several common objects, in stiff cross section. E made only static traces: photos, not footage. I sorely doubted that the speckles of light and dark did anything to round out the ball in E's associative memory. We boosted the resolution. Added bits for color, sixteen million shades. Whether E traveled those surfaces or twirled them in its mental space I couldn't say.

The creature in *Frankenstein* learned to speak by eavesdropping on an exiled family, the most astonishing act of language acquisition until Taylor's beloved *Tarzan*, the books on which the best reader I ever met grew up. Frankenstein's creature had his chattering family and a knapsack of classics: *Paradise Lost*, Plutarch's *Lives*, Goethe's *Werther*. E, like Tarzan, learned to talk more or less on print alone.

"I discovered the names that were given to some of the most familiar objects," Shelley's creature says somewhere. "I learned and applied the words, 'fire,' 'milk,' 'bread,' and 'wood' . . ."

One day I would teach this speech to a machine that had learned to read. Maybe not E, or F, but G, or son of G. And my machine would understand.

"I distinguished several other words without being able as yet to understand or apply them," the girl child's monster would tell mine. Words "such as 'good,' 'dearest,' 'unhappy.' "

"You don't eat," Diana accused me.

"I eat. I eat a lot. You saw how much I put away at lunch."

"I bet that was your only meal that day."

"I lose track sometimes. Lentz and I . . . We get to training at such weird hours."

"You don't eat unless someone feeds you. Is that it?"

I knew what was coming. But I had nowhere to run. I wanted to tell her then. Before any court of confusion. My evacuated life left no air for anyone. Least of all someone as kind as Diana.

But Diana hadn't offered anything rejectable yet. Nothing but the most generic friendship.

"Most experimental neurologists can't cook," she said. "They're fine until they get to the part of the recipe that says 'Season to taste.' This throws them for a loop. They like the 'Measure carefully into bowl.' They tend to hang out up there."

"Connectionists," I mimicked, "cook brilliantly. They start out at random, and a few thousand iterations later . . ." Two funny deflections, then I'd flee before she could extend the invitation.

"I bet novelists know how to shape a recipe."

"Maybe back when. The age of plot and closure. Times have changed. It's all microwave these days."

"I know what," she said. "You can cook a meal for me." So simple. A sudden, happy inspiration.

She'd had mercy. Given me one she couldn't expect me to accept.

"Well, Diana, that sounds great in theory. But unless it's Jiffy Pop, and you bring the matches to light my stove's pilot . . ."

"At my place. I have all the utensils. And I won't get in your way at all."

"Just stand by and laugh?"

"Something like that."

"All right, then. All right. I rise to the challenge. *Moules Provisoires.*"

"Oh. My. The man's done this before."

I had, in fact. But I didn't care to give her the details.

I got to her place Saturday evening. I managed to carry all the provisions on my bike rack. Even the tapers. I rang the bell, ready with a funny opener about ruined anything tasting better by candlelight.

130

The door was opened by a little boy. I started to mumble something about getting the address wrong.

"Mom," the boy called back into the house. "The writer's here!"

"The writer?" Diana answered from within. "Tell him to use the tradesman's entrance."

The kid looked up at me, wrestling with the command. His face searched mine for clues. I watched the solution—*irony*—ripple through him until he let me in with a wry smile.

Diana appeared, doubling my shock. She carried a younger boy in her arms. I must have looked like a blithering undergrad.

"Here's Richard," she said, addressing the child. "Can you say 'Hi, Richard'?"

"Rick would be fine," I said.

This child wasn't about to say anything. I saw it in his features. The slightly spatulate face. The fold to the nose and ears. Speech would be long and hard in coming.

"This is Peter." The cheerful matter-of-fact. My worst-case fears came home to roost. I knew her. I could never pretend ignorance again.

"Hello, Peter." I didn't know how to carry on. "I once wrote a book about someone named Peter."

Peter hunched up into a little ball. He peeked out sideways.

"He's a little shy with strange people," the older brother said. "But for a Down's baby, he's a genius."

"And this is William."

"Do you know what it says on the Brazilian flag?" William asked me.

"I used to know."

"You probably did," Diana cracked.

"It says, *'Ordem e Progresso.'*"

"No kidding! What does that mean?"

William thought. "It means—order me some soup?"

Diana choked with shame in mid-laugh. "Oh, sweetheart! No. That was just a little joke of mine."

"I know," William pouted.

"What's the Netherlands?" I asked.

"Easy one. Red stripe, white stripe, blue stripe." He drew them in the air, visualizing as he described. Then he pointed at me. He waved his index finger in a pedagogical sweep. "Also Luxembourg," he warned.

"Yeah. There's a reason for that."

"I know, I know. Here's one. Red circle on white background?"

"Easy one. Japan."

"No fair!" Adults weren't supposed to know anything.

"Don't get him started," Diana said on our way to the kitchen. "He can do all hundred and eighty of them."

"Hundred and eighty-six," William corrected.

"What if you take Netherlands and double it? Hold a mirror up to the bottom?"

That one took a couple of steps. "Thailand?"

"You're good, man. You're good."

"Formerly known as Siam."

"Population?"

"Approximately fifty-one million."

"Approximately," Diana sighed.

"Name seven countries where Spanish is the principal language."

"Easy one," William said, the index finger now a fencing foil. The most extraordinary boy I will ever meet.

"Come on, you guys," Diana said. "Peter and I need food. Don't we, Peter?"

Peter curled up in his hedgehog defense. But he kept his eye on me at all times.

I put William to work washing the mussels. "Is it just the four of us?" I asked Diana.

"Yes. I'm sorry. I should have told you. I assumed you knew."

"What, from Lentz? Nobody is real but him. Hadn't you heard?"

"It's such a small world over at the Center. I guess I'm used to everyone knowing everything about everybody."

"And nothing much about anyone."

"Well, we all have our work, first."

"How do you do it?"

"Do what?"

I held my hands out, one toward the kitchen counter, the other toward some remote lab. "Two lives. Alone."

"Huh!"

"I mow the lawn," William said.

"How much does she pay you?"

"Two-fifty."

"Holy moly. There are laws against that, you know."

Diana made to fillet me with the lemon knife. "Don't make waves, writer. Or I'll give you something to write about."

The meal came together. And William and I managed it without assistance from the feminine half of the world. We made a bucket brigade of the dishes. Peter sat nearby, chattering with his hands.

"Look," William called. "Pete's helping!"

I heard the sound of dismayed discovery behind me. "What do we do with these?" Diana stood by the counter, holding the tapers and floral sprig that I'd tried to leave hidden in the bottom of my bag. She looked at me dead on. Her eyes started to water.

"Light them, of course." But recovery came two beats too late. I shrugged, and even that hurt. This is why I asked you not to ask me here.

Diana put the tapers in elaborate candlesticks that she first had to unwrap from newspapers. We lit them and doused the lights. But the darkness scared Peter. He coiled forward against himself. Diana turned the lights back on. We let the candles burn.

William had more fun with the shells than with the insides. He did, however, enjoy dipping his mussels in the wine sauce and dribbling all over the table. Peter worked away at his compote. He insisted on trying one mussel. He got half of it down, with a look of utter stupefaction.

"They're both going to have the runs for days," Diana said.

"I'm sorry."

"Don't be silly. They get the runs from jelly toast."

William bit his cheek. I didn't know how badly, at first. All at once, he stopped talking. I thought it was a clown act. Pantomime. I started to laugh, until William's silent, red-faced distress made Peter break out in tears and lower his face into his plate.

Diana was up in a fraction of a second, before I knew what was happening. "It's okay. Petey, it's okay." Diana lifted her boy and hugged him to her. She repeated the litany various ways, glossing with a flurry of hand motions.

"You sign to him?"

"A little. It's easier for him to reply. Words will come slowly. Fine motor is tricky for him."

"What is he saying?"

" 'William is going away'? No, sweetheart." Diana signed her assurance. "William just has a little owie. It's so strange," she confided, aside. "He has this incredible bodily empathy. If any creature for blocks around is distressed, Peter starts weeping. Tell Peter you're all right, William."

William stood holding his cheek, still bawling silently. He walked over to his brother and put his hand on his back. "It's okay, Peter," he said. Stoicism cost him. He burst at last into audible sobs. His brother followed along, unquestioning companion.

The mildest household drama, but it wiped me out. How could I survive the first real crisis? William's fallen pyramid of shells, Pete's spilled, untippable cup, Diana's gap-toothed, hand-signing serenity, the candles blazing away in the brightly lit room: all too much. I thought, *I'd never live.* I'd hemorrhage halfway through week one.

The storm ended faster than it blew up. Suddenly William was laughing and clearing away dishes at the promise of cake. His mother teased him. Peter still had his head down in his plate, like a sunflower under the weight of autumn's end. But even he seemed to be accustoming himself to trust the return of happiness.

After dinner, we did the dishes. William asked to play Battleship.

"You don't have to," Diana said.

"Yes you do," said William. "That or Yahtzee."

He stuck all his ships in the corners, a clever evasion until I caught on.

"Boys." Diana shook her head. "A total mystery."

Peter threw both hands up in the air and let loose a chortle of euphoria at nothing. At domestic peace. It seemed a sign of imminent bedtime.

"Come on, guys. Upstairs. Roll out."

William balked, but a feeble rear guard. Diana carried Peter as far as the stairs, then set him down. "Watch this." Pete leaned into the steps. He took them like a half-track. His feet went up over his shoulders, lifting him from level to level. "He'd be walking by now, but he's so loose-limbed."

I stood downstairs during the bathroom rituals. I snooped Diana's bookshelves, learning nothing but that she was a cognitive neurologist who hoped to do some birding and furniture finishing in some alternate life.

William tore down the stairs in his new-wave pajamas. "Mom says you're Reader-in-Residence."

"I did not!" came the embarrassed denial from upstairs.

"Well," I wheedled. "Let's talk about this. What kind of books do you like?"

William shrugged. "I don't know. I read *The Hobbit*. In three days."

"Really? In-credible. Did you like it?"

"The dragon was pretty awesome."

We trooped upstairs. There, Peter propped up against the bars of his crib. He rocked himself methodically. His hands made curious cupping motions.

"What are you saying, Petie?" I stroked the curl of his ear.

Diana laughed. "Don't ask."

William started jumping on his bed. "He's saying, 'Read! Read!' " His hands picked up the sign and multiplied it into a mandate.

"Absolutely. What do you gentlemen want to hear?"

"Pete wants the counting book," Diana said. "It's his favorite these days."

She lifted him out of the pillowed prison and sat in a beanbag chair, Peter in her arms. She opened a radiant, pastel portal across his lap. "One," she announced. "One house. One cow. Petey do it?"

Peter brought his hand down across the page. On contact, Diana exclaimed, "One! That's it."

Each page brought one more house, one more cow, one more tree, one more in a circling flock of birds. Diana counted, pointing out each new figure on the page. Then Peter commenced a round of muscular spasms, pointing randomly but intently, while we three clicked off the numbers in chorus.

"He loves counting. He's so smart," Diana told me, shaking her head. "You are so smart!" she signed to Peter. Peter curled like an armadillo. Trisomy may have weakened his muscles, but the weights collapsing his human spine were fear and joy.

"So what's it going to be, my man?" I asked William.

He lay, narrow in his bed. He seemed so slight, such a vulnerable line. A lima bean tendril germinated on damp paper towel for the science fair. He reached a hand up blindly behind him, to the shelf above his head. He retrieved the totem and handed it to me, without looking.

"Na, naw. You cannot do the World Almanac as bedtime reading."

"It's what I want," he insisted. Singsong.

We did World Religions; Famous Waterfalls; Noted Political Leaders; and, of course, the beloved World Flags. More forgone quiz game than story time. William told me what lists to start. Then he blurted out the completion after only a few words of prompting. Every time I shouted, "How do you know that?" William smirked in triumph and Pete threw his hands in the air and gurgled.

Appeased, the boys went down without a fight. Anxiety revived only after Diana and I retired to the living room, alone.

It became a different house then. She became a different woman. She put something timeless on the player—Taverner's *Western Wynde* Mass. I wouldn't have picked her for it. But then, I wouldn't have picked her for freeze-drying monkey brains either. I didn't know the first thing about her. This evening's every note had proved that.

Closeness grew awful. Words had been spent on the boys. I felt the slack of all those who try to live by eloquence and find it useless at the end. I wanted to put my head in her lap. I wanted to disappear to Alaska.

"Their father?" I asked her, after agonizing silence.

"Their father found the drop from Will to Pete a bit steep for his tastes. About eleven months ago. Left me everything. But who's counting?"

She twisted her hair around one finger. Clockwise once, then counter. She never looked at me. A good thing.

"People have been wonderful. Harold. Ram. The others. It's work that saves you, finally. I keep thinking I'll find something in the hippocampus that will explain the man."

"I take it Lentz wasn't among the comforters."

She grimaced. "How do you put up with that creep?"

"He's building me the greatest train set a boy novelist could ask for."

"I suppose. It wouldn't be worth it for me. Nothing would." She stared off, into the music, the small rain. "I don't mean his snide remarks. The solipsism. The sadism. I could deal with all that. A woman in the biz learns to put up with that as a given. I mean the sadness. He's the saddest man I've ever laid eyes on." She chose that moment to look up, to lay eyes on my eyes. "Excepting you, of course."

"Lentz? Sad?"

"The worst. It chills me. Have you ever been alone in his office with him?"

"Hours and hours."

"Ever been in there with him with the door closed?"

Never. And it had never struck me as strange until that moment. Diana did not elaborate. She left it to me to run the experiment for myself. I read her silence. Loneliness on that scale had to be measured firsthand.

We sat and listened to the western wind. The intimacy of perfect strangers. Years from now, her boys might by chance recall the odd man who came by one night and added to their shaping thoughts by reading to them. A night never repeated.

I recognized this woman. This family, curled up in advance of the night. I knew the place from a book I'd read once as a novice adult, my own first draft just undergoing revision.

I read the novel in that nest C. and I had made together in B. Mann's *Doktor Faustus*, the formative storybook of my adult years. In it, a brilliant German, by blinding himself to all pursuits but articulation, allows his world to pull itself down around him. I remembered the man, already middle-aged, writing a love letter to the last woman who might have accepted him.

But the letter sabotages itself. It engineers its own rejection. It bares a loneliness that it knows will scare off any attempted comfort. I haven't looked up the passage since first reading it. I will never read it again. The real thing might be too far from the one I've kept in memory. "Consider me," the marriage proposal says, "as a person who suddenly discovers, with an ache at the lateness of the hour, that he might like to have a real home."

Diana sat across from me, on a comfortable sofa scarred with the destructive industry of small boys. Upstairs, those boys tossed in dreams whose sole task lay in smoothing out the incomprehensibility of this day. Here was the home I would never have. Shaped by a book, I'd made sure I wouldn't. I'd forced my heart's reading matter to come true.

Here and there, a cylindrical tube–person or transforming robot made Lego base camp for the night in the plush carpet. Diana pulled the music's long melisma about her shoulders like a shawl. Christ, that my love were in my arms and I in my bed again.

"Thanks," she shushed me at the door. She squeezed my hand. "Thanks. It's been a while since I've dined by candlelight."

I went home to chosen loneliness. To the book I would never be able to write.

Picture a train heading south. The train is full of ill and wounded. This month's invariable sanitarium patients. Consumption, influenza: fiction's archaic maladies. Some bodily deterioration for which the reader must invent fantastic, beginner's referents. Maimed veterans, being shipped from the front.

A moment of mass import, of universal upheaval from the just-recallable past. Populations on the leading edge of panic, stricken by industry. The evacuating train pulls out. It joins the flotilla of time's lifeboats, plowing the dark.

Cruel, blue, bracing, breaking loose: the only opening vignette worth bothering with. Stretched out urgently, along imagination's rail-heads, a book heads south. It signals from the telegraph car. Keys me a message I was supposed to have held on to at all costs. A message that never made it out of childhood's originating station.

The day is sharp, the air invigorating and crystalline. It is the year nineteen-something. A year ending in a dash, or perhaps two hyphens.

The train works southward, in wartime. It snakes glacially up into the mountains, in perhaps the last clear month, the last week that the mountain passes will be traversable.

The engine climbs. It sniffs perpetually up to the outskirts of the same bombed-out village. Fields drift undulantly beneath its wheels, whose click convinces even Forever to bleed imperceptibly into a standing Now.

Soon, on the itinerary's second morning, the ground acquires a careless dusting of snow. Vegetation changes along the alpine climb, though the account, the travelogue itself, says nothing about that. Sirens bleat on in the distance, from whistle-stops all along this infant route. Air raids continue steeping this side of the border in today's random wildfire.

But the wounded in the compartments are exhilarated. They grow convinced: something is about to happen. Just past the next page.

C. and I returned to U. We managed to live there again for two years. I'm surprised we lasted even that long. How could we hope to make a life in a town where we'd already taken our retrospective tour? C. sought a thing she'd accidentally lost. That thing was not U., not then or ever. But severed from yourself in the press of a crowd, you head back instinctively to the most recent landmark, hoping the lost other will hit on the same idea.

Changed circumstance bought us a little nostalgic grace. C. parlayed her office experience into a position with University Personnel. And I: I'd been granted a wish so outrageous that characters in novels would have been punished just to think it. The political entertainment I wrote for C. appeared and did well. The forgotten attic legacy bridging imaginary Limburg and too real Chicago had *readers*.

Reviewers evaluated it in print, in the same newspapers I'd once read so casually. Total strangers spent two hours' wages to buy a copy. People I'd never meet wrote me letters, awarded me prizes.

The impossibility dawned on me: I might be the last person on earth allowed to spend all day long doing exactly what I wanted to do.

Each new book-blown coup produced a burst of sad excitement from C. "Beauie, you've done it. *Proficiat.* I always knew you would."

Truth was, she was terrified. We holed up in our one-bedroom apartment—one step upscale from the one in B.'s land-filled swamp—under siege from admirers. One night, we sat eating dinner at the pretty green enamel table we'd rescued from the secondhand shop. We listened to the radio as we ate, the cavalcade news. All at once, a voice was talking about the book, telling the story of the boys in the photo. Paraphrasing, as if that life had really happened.

I'd invented those boys to amuse C. I built them from pieces only she would recognize. I sprinkled the biographies with archival evidence, historical truths, the camera-eye witness. I intercut with essays how every historian half-makes the longer narrative, wedding the forces at large to a private address book. Now our private address book had been promoted to documentary fact.

At the account of that boy blown off his bike and rubbed out before the world conflagration cleared its starting block, C. started to cry. I thought at first she was crying out of pride. Writing a novel left me that inept with real-world facts.

"That poor boy," she mouthed.

I pieced it together. "I'm sorry. C., please. It'll all be over in a month." She brightened a little at the thought of recovering the anonymous. Of retreating to a time when our invented tunes formed no one's dinner music.

Our lives back in U. were like nothing we recognized. U. had changed in all but its particulars. Returning to the town was like clapping the back of an old friend at a reunion, one who turns to you with a look friendly but blank.

U. had forgotten us, while remaining agonizingly familiar. The town had become something out of Middle English allegory. Its lone consolation lay in other people, as bewildered by their abandonment here as we.

For the first time in our lives, C. and I socialized. We learned to pick wines, to crack the dress code, to prepare ourselves in advance of an evening with an arsenal of jokes and stories that answered a suite of occasions. The game got easier the more we played. We might have succeeded at it, had we stuck around.

The Midwestern Dinner Party was not, as our B. acquaintances teased us, a contradiction in terms. Once under way, they could even be fun. Getting ready was the torture.

"I'm fat," C. would announce, about an hour before we had to go anywhere.

"Sweetheart, you're a sub-Saharan stalk of desiccated grass. Don't tell yourself you're fat. You'll start to believe it."

I still pretended she hadn't already convinced herself.

"Wear the lamb dress," I'd say. "You'll knock them out."

"That dress makes me look fat."

"Okay. How about the muslin?"

"That one makes me look like I'm trying not to look fat."

Sometimes C. locked herself in the bathroom, throwing up. Or, sobbing, she'd refuse to leave the apartment. But the cloud usually lifted in time. C. would grow radiant and be the dinner's delight. People loved her, and she loved them back. The ones she gave the chance.

Those two repeat years in U. might have been a sterile waste if it weren't for the Taylors. I went to see the old professor not long after we hit town. Taylor welcomed me back with affection. And now, when I teased him about his freshman seminar ruining a promising scientific career, I could point to a turn of events that sweetened the punch line.

After my mother, the man had taught me how to read. Taylor *was* reading for me. Through Taylor, I discovered how a book both mirrored and elicited the mind's unreal ability to turn inward upon itself. He changed my life. He changed what I thought life was. But I'd never done more than revere him at a distance, forever the eighteen-year-old student. Now, to my astonishment, we became friends.

Our first dinner invitation to the Taylors' scared C. witless. She'd heard me gush about Taylor so often that when it came to meeting him, she wanted to flee. "What does he look like?" she asked. As if that would prepare her.

"I don't know. Slight. Arresting. Immaculate. A face ravaged by intelligence."

"You're hopeless, Beau. What color is the man's hair?"

"I'm not sure."

I told her about that rainy September afternoon when I'd first seen him. He arrived at the attic dormer in the English Building where the class met. A dozen of us had assembled in nervous anonymity. In walked this close-cropped, fiftyish man in impeccable summer suit. He placed his grade book and our first text on the desk, sat down in one of those reduced, yellow-wood chairs, removed a pack of cigarettes from an inside suit coat pocket, and asked if anyone objected. He lit up, tilted his head infinitesimally backward, then said, "It defies statistics that I'm the only one in a group this size with an oral fixation."

At eighteen, we kept our fixations to ourselves. At least until the reading began.

"What did you read?" C. wanted to know.

"He started us out on Freud's *Introductory Lectures*. Then we applied the dream work to fairy tales and lyric poetry. After a while, we went on to the longer stuff—short stories, plays, novels."

"Titles, Beauie. I want titles."

"Let's see. Ten years ago! *Gawain and the Green Knight.* 'Adam Lay Bound.' 'Patrick Spens.' 'The Miller's Tale.' The Sonnets."

"You remember them all?"

"Like yesterday. Better. You had to be there. I remember the shape his mouth made when he recited lines. Of course, *he* could recite the bulk of those pieces verbatim. In the dark."

"Which sonnets?"

"Is this for extra credit? We were each supposed to pick one to present to the group. For some reason, maybe because I'd just broken up with—"

"I don't want to hear that woman's name!"

"I must have been looking for a rebound, because I picked Sonnet 31."

"Which goes?"

"Which goes:

"Thy bosom is endeared with all hearts,
  Which I by lacking have supposed dead,
  And there reigns Love, and all Love's loving parts,
  And all those friends which I thought buried."

"I thought there are supposed to be fourteen lines."

"I think there were. Before memory got to them."

"Okay. What else?"

" 'The Sick Rose.' 'The Second Coming.' 'The Windhover.' All sorts of Dickinson. 'Prufrock.' Frost, Stevens. *Arms and the Man. The Tempest.* Hold on. We also spent a lot of time on the Bible, right at the beginning of term."

"Repressed that one?"

"Guess so. *The Grave.* 'Petrified Man.' 'The Dead.' That was the one that put me over the top. That made me realize I wasn't going to lead the life I thought I was going to lead. *Heart of Darkness. Light in August. Lucky Jim . . .*"

"So what didn't you read?"

"Yeah. It was a real lineup."

"I don't get it, Beau. It sounds like your basic Freshman Survey."

"It wasn't. First of all, this magnificently self-possessed oral fixation sat up in front of the room, telling anecdotes in syntax so decorously Byzantine we didn't even realize that half of them were off-color. The man spoke in complete, perfect paragraphs. It took me almost a whole week between sessions to decode Taylor's suggestion that the speaker in 'Stopping by Woods' was out there in the middle of nowhere relieving himself."

"I'm not going to this dinner," C. decided.

"Sweetheart, you don't understand. The man is grace personified. And his wife is a National Treasure. Together, they're hilarious."

"They'll think I'm an idiot. They'll wonder what you're doing with me."

"Just the opposite. They'll wonder what a sexpot like yourself sees in a ninety-eight-pound aesthetic weakling. C.! Everybody feels like an idiot compared to Taylor."

"I don't need that, thanks. I have enough of that as it is."

"But Taylor also has this way of making you feel smarter than you are. We teenagers used to fumble around with one poem or the other. Precocious and brilliant, but juvenile. I felt like a kid with the training wheels taken off. I'd soar for a hundred meters, then crash to the ground. But whenever I said something particularly stupid, Taylor would credit my misses with so much ingenuity I couldn't even recognize them. 'Your account of the narrator's circumvention of the repressed's return is persuasive in the extreme. But your hints about his real and unconscious motives needn't be so circumspect.' Oh, I wish I could imitate the man!"

"He's bigger than life for you, isn't he?"

"No," I answered her. "No. He's exactly life-sized."

"I'm not going."

She went, and had a good time. "He's just like you said. The suit. The complete paragraphs. Only you forgot the war bond songs."

"I had no idea about those." The evening had, in fact, been a continuous astonishment.

"Tell me again the connection between that long Matthew Arnold quote . . ."

". . . from a poem no one has read in half a century . . ."

". . . and the glimpse of Norma Shearer's cleavage that he got in a Colorado valley movie theater at the age of ten?"

"I can't remember. I think the connection was that second bottle of Slovakian wine."

We went with increasing frequency. C. grew as devoted as I. Every visit revealed new amplitude to Taylor. Taylor the inconsolable fan of hopelessly bad sports teams. The shuffler to bluegrass tunes. The consummate organic gardener who'd planted half the fruit trees in U. The collector of questionable jokes no one else would dare tell even in private. The wartime aircraft spotter. The fisherman and naturalist. The mimic of a thousand voices, from Blanche DuBois to a Mexican bush league baseball announcer. The boy who taught himself to read on Tarzan and John Carter, who went on to devour every volume in the rural library long before he made his escape.

This abundance held together on the slightest of sutures. Taylor's deepness was bleak. He had read all the books. He was fluent in the mind's native idiom. He knew that the psychopathology of daily life was a redundancy. He might have been the supreme misanthrope, were it not for his humor and humility. And the source of those two saving graces, the thing stitching that heartbreaking capaciousness into a whole, was memory.

Taylor's wit made me feel like the most sparkling conversationalist. We'd return from their place well past midnight, kept up by adults thirty years older than us who outlasted us easily. We'd proceed to lie in bed hours longer, eyes pasted open, thoughts racing, replaying the evening's exchanges. Thought seemed to me that thing that could relive, in island isolation, its own *esprit d'escalier*. Memory was the attempt to capitalize on missed cleverness, or recover an overlooked word that, for a moment, might have made someone else feel more alive.

C. agreed. "When we're over there, I remember stories from my own childhood that I haven't thought about for lifetimes." We cracked jokes we'd never thought to try on each other. We sang for the Taylors the songs we'd written to keep ourselves going in B., neglected since our return to U. Whatever the quality of our performance, the Taylors liked us enough to keep asking us back.

We went for the Fourth of July. The Taylors played *The Mormon Tabernacle Choir Sings John Philip Sousa* and made hand-cranked ice cream. We went to a Christmas party, the living refutation of Joyce's "Dead." Good cheer from on high, and in a shape even humans could understand. Late that wonderful night, Taylor came and sat down next to C. in a corner, put his arm around her. Of course, even that spontaneous affection had to be framed in an incomparable Taylorism: "I trust you realize that this arm is sufficiently anesthetized by alcohol that I'm not getting any illicit pleasure out of this."

The attention made C. glow until New Year's.

But in the long run, attention made her worse. All that winter C. declined. Only love could have done her any good. And of available loves, only the unearned kind would have worked. But C. could not free herself from her certainty that unearned meant undeserved.

Each letter in the box, every call from family or friend hit C. like an accusation. She began to shape her adult story: every life decision she had ever taken was a small disappointment to someone. And each disappointment was a savings stamp pasted in the final book.

We trudged through to spring. The thought that her unhappiness must be weighing me down made C. even more unhappy than she thought she was. Worse, the thought fulfilled its own prediction. Her fright alone began to weigh me down. Or, not her fright, but the anchor of helpless love it lodged in my heart.

Two years in a U. we no longer belonged to left us partners in fear. I can see it in the one photograph I still own of her from that time. That look of crumpled panic passing for a smile in front of the lens will forever make me want to cry out and rush to her in her pain. And how much worse, that pain, when she declared its source in my need to comfort her.

"Buddy. Buddy. What do you want? Tell me. Just talk to me. How can I make you happier?"

"You could leave me," she announced one night.

She might as well have accused me of murder. I stared into a face from which all impression of the woman I knew had fled.

"You should, you know. It's no more than I deserve."

We skipped the Balzac installment for that night. What we needed to read each other then was our own manuscript in progress. No line or paragraph or whole chapter that couldn't be blotted. Nothing in our style that we couldn't render blessedly direct by a joint edit. But C. harbored a deep hostility toward words. They only increased the odds of her missing the mark. Extended her sense of betrayal.

We tried to talk. The more I raced, the more C. seized up. She froze, the rabbit in that Larkin poem I'd read for Taylor ten years before. The creature that thought it might slip the notice of a fatal epidemic by keeping stock-still and waiting.

When words didn't work, we tried our bodies. I kissed her boxer's shoulders, her ribs and flinching thighs. I thought to take resentment's nodes out of her muscles into my mouth, digest them. I tried. C. talked then. But her words were voiceless phonemes of distress that carried no message but their desperate pitch.

Time has unlimited patience. It replays its summer stock forever, until we at last get the point. Its paths get laid down until we can walk nowhere else, even if there were an elsewhere in the undergrowth to walk.

C. came home from her office one evening, laughing. "You're not going to believe this. They want to promote me to Personnel Officer I."

I squeezed her in congratulations. She stayed limp. "Of course they do," I scolded. "It took them long enough, didn't it?" All I ever wanted was to give her whatever she needed. But what she needed more than all else was not to be given anything.

I saw the frightened-rabbit look stealing in behind her eyes. I've been good. A good girl. I never asked anyone for anything. Why are you doing this to me?

"Beauie. Beauie." She tittered, shaking her head. "I gotta get out of here."

Lentz burst in once when I was showing Imp E simple shapes. "That bastard Plover is giggling at me in the halls."

"And it's my damn fault, isn't it?"

He drew up short. "Marcel, you are getting smarter and smarter. Every day in every way."

"He's right, you know. Harold's right. Diana's right. Ram is. Even Chen and Keluga are right."

"The hell they are." Lentz's refusal was clipped. But his agitation was wide enough to knock a precarious mound of fanfold printout to the floor. He leaned to pick up the mess, a gesture that stopped midway in a flourish of disgust at the futility of cleaning up after himself. "Right about what?"

"Right about neural nets not being the answer."

"What's the question, Marcel?"

"How is E going to know anything? Knowledge is physical, isn't it? It's not what your mother reads you. It's the weight of her arm around you as she—"

"By all means, Marcel. Put your arm around it as you read. I encourage you. You mean you haven't been hugging it as you go along?"

"Reading knowledge is the smell of the bookbinding paste. The crinkle of thick stock as the pages turn. Paper the color of aged ivory. Knowledge is temporal. It's *about* time. You know how that goes, Engineer. Even you must remember that. 'We can read these three pages before your sisters and brothers come home for dinner.' "

"You're still talking about stimulus and response. Multidimensional vectors, shaped by feedback, however complicated. You're talking about an associative matrix. What else have we been doing but building one of those?"

"But Imp E's matrix isn't human. Human knowledge is social. More than stimulus-response. Knowing entails testing knowledge against others. Bumping up against them."

"Our matrix is bumping up against you. It's bumping up against the lines you feed it."

"It could bump up against word lists forever and never have more than a collection of arbitrary, differentiated markers."

"And what do we humans have?" Lentz removed his glasses to wipe them. As monstrous as he looked with them on, he was even worse without.

"More." I didn't know what, at the moment. But there had to be more. "We take in the world continuously. It presses against us. It burns and freezes."

"Save it for the award committees, Marcel. We 'take in the world' via the central nervous system. Chemical symbol-gates. You read my bit on long-term potentiation."

"Imp E doesn't take things in the way we do. It will never know—"

"It doesn't *have* to." He shoved more papers on the floor for emphasis. "It doesn't have to 'know,' whatever the hell you mean by that. You've been reading Plover's voodoo neurology, haven't you? All our box has to do is paraphrase a couple of bloody texts."

" 'I was angry with my friend: I told my wrath, my wrath did end.' How is it ever going to explicate that, let alone paraphrase it?"

"I don't know. Teach the thing anger. Make it furious. In my impression, you can be pretty good at that."

"By June, right?"

"Hmm."

"Literary commentary on any book on the list? As good as your random twenty-two-year-old."

"As judged by Gunga Din himself."

"Or public retraction and apology."

"Come on, Marcel. We've been through this. Let's get on with it. Today's training."

"I'd be polishing the retraction if I were you."

"Don't remind me. That damn Plover. He's going to write it for us and make us put our names to it. Well. What better way to meet our fate than facing fearful odds?"

He replaced his glasses and sat down to training. We were working that day on compound subjects. What seas what shores what gray rocks and what islands. He had a list of simple sentence forms using words E already had in its fragile, denotative grasp. E's task was to recast the sentences we fed it. In today's case, find the conjunction, remove it, and split the compound into two.

When we'd done half a dozen examples and E was responding with a speed indicative of boredom, I reached out casually and shut the office door. No machine without muscle would ever be able to decode such a gesture. Some pretense of noise in the hallway. Ridiculous, after these long weeks of working in the open.

The door swung shut, surrendering the image fastened to its inside. On Diana's suggestion, I'd already sneaked a look at the hidden shrine. I'd seen the photograph, and it knocked the breath out of me. Now I wanted to see Lentz's face when the concealed photo looked back at us.

For a considerable fraction of eternity, Lentz said nothing. He looked away from my surveillance, at his notes. At the ignorant terminal.

"Empiricism?" he sneered. He seemed disappointed in me, but not surprised. Prying, snot-nosed kid. What did one expect from a kiss-and-tell, aesthete dilettante? He looked up at the picture, verifying it, although every pixel must have long ago burned permanent silhouettes into his visual cortex. When he sat in here with the door closed, the flood of color would fill his focus, immense at eye level.

He looked away again. He worried the mouse pointer, a cat feeling contrition after the kill. Come on, get up and run again. Like when it was fun.

"I suppose you want the caption?"

I didn't need a caption. I could see well enough. A homemade calendar hung by a tack, still clasping to January. I say "still," for while we had yet to reach that month, this particular one had been buried twenty Januaries ago.

Just above the paper matrix of days, a pasteup color portal opened onto a couple. They stood, arms around one another, out of focus, on a frozen and deserted beach.

The man was Lentz. He was young, as I had never seen him. He had hair. He seemed impossibly taller, slim. The woman at his side was no older. Yet this couple was ancient beyond saying. Age tented just under youth's peeling onionskin. The shutter exposed this geriatric core in X ray. It showed antiquity lying in wait, ready to blossom like an aneurysm.

The craftwork was too clumsy to be a customized mail-order gift. It had the look of a child's school project—Christmas or birthday present—from before those offerings disappeared in adolescent embarrassment. *See what I made you.* The earliest bribe of love.

I touched the image with my eyes. I half expected the museum guard's reprimand. But no one told me to step back. In my mind, I palpated the prematurely old man's shoulders. Before the camera, they crumpled in a last attempt at bravery. I stroked the woman's face where the cling of desperation already promised to sag it.

While I indulged myself, Lentz stood and moved to the window. Outside, a gang of grackles combed the landscaped lawn like a homicide squad dragging a field for evidence.

"Lentz. You never told me."

"What? That I'm married? That I have a family? Everyone, Marcel. Everybody but you."

That wasn't what I meant. That he had a private life was no particular shock. And naturally, that life would be peopled. But the way these two held on to each other. Their too light clothing, their backs to the ice-crusted beach. Nothing but this other waist, this other pair of shoulders between each and their end.

The Lentz I knew could never have posed for such a shot. The Lentz I knew might well have had a wife. He might even have had a child. But my Lentz could never have known them with such hopeless intimacy.

"And you're still . . . ?" I didn't know what I was asking.

"There is no 'still,' Marcel. 'Still' is for unravished brides of quietness."

The open lens trapped these two in terror at the slightest move. The panic in those eyes was the pose of cognition itself. The look of awareness seeing itself going down, drowning in the depths of its own simulation.

I had, the photo told me, half a dozen months in which to remember, once and for ever, what it felt like to be able to remember at all. My own craft calendars had all been swallowed up by the wraparound virtual future my era was intent on inventing. My days and weeks, the saving particulars of Here were already gone. And I, having forgotten them, was almost past caring.

The young Lentz, in a plaid shirt the likes of which will never again be sold on this earth, even secondhand, in countries that live off our discards, clamped his arm around the shoulder of his mate. She returned the stiff grip from underneath. Perhaps they were shivering. Rigorous. However they touched each other in private, this was not it.

This embrace already succumbed to terminal affection. They propped one another up, as if each had just had a mild stroke. They grasped at each other, two people out on a ledge forty stories up in the night's icy wind, having second thoughts even as their feet start to flex.

The wind off winter water made them clutch at each other like that. The chill from the child with the camera. They looked on in advance horror at the cut-and-paste project, the child urgently constructing a craftwork life preserver. Stick this on your refrigerator if you dare, to break eternity's heart and sap the will of time's worst-case scenario.

One ought to be able to hold on to anything. Anyone. It did not matter who, so long as they were there. Yet the first one, this picture said, the generative template for all that you might come to care for in this place, your buddy, your collaborator in plying life: that is the one you recognize. You learn that voice along with learning itself. You can only say, "Yes, to everything," once. Once only, before your connections have felt what everything entails.

This shoulder was the lone one that could have held that man up. That waist, the only one that could steady the woman. These two *chose* each other, their charm against the world's weighted vectors. Anything else but that helpless, familiar grip pinning them in place would be a push into randomness. Would tear the net.

Some scrap of holdover, supervised training told me this is the way one was supposed to end up. The way *I* should have ended. But even as I felt it, the desire seemed arbitrary, laughable, regressive. Marriage for life belonged to those cultural tyrannies now in the process of being shed. In another hundred years, it would seem as archaic as animism, as "thou."

If the plaid shirt was really Lentz, then this woman was truly his wife. In this clasp, the couple graduated to inseparable, mutual foreigners. Love is the feedback cycle of longing, belonging, loss. Anti-Hebbian: the firing links get weaker. C., after a decade, grew stranger to me than that college girl who had comforted me on the Quad the day after my dad died. At the end, we shocked each other in the hall of our overlearned apartment, 911 material, intruders. And we'd gotten there without a child to make us wall calendars, to arrest in scissors and glue the secret of who we once were.

I looked at the young Lentz's blueprint expression, the advance word of crevasses that would range across those facial wastes. I stared at those two shivering bodies, gone half-insubstantial already. I looked up at the real Lentz, studying the grackle dragnet outside. I measured the size of the mistake that had found him out.

Someone had failed someone else. Someone had messed with destiny. A frightened kid with an Instamatic on a frozen beach had watched love capitulate to the very air. Furious cutting and pasting split off the eternal from what always becomes of it, hung an outdated, permanent January to the back of this man's office door. This was the last couple on earth to whom the inevitable wasn't supposed to happen. The last who, by fate's oversight, were to have made it through together into frightened old age.

I crashed Imp E in complete innocence. The version had grown up on patterns and questions about patterns. It organized itself on such challenges as "What comes next in this sequence?" and "Which item in this list doesn't belong?"

One day, provoked by boredom, I asked it, "What do you want to talk about?" The question of volition trapped the rolling marble of its will into an unstable local minimum. The machine that so dutifully strove to answer every interrogation ground to a halt on that one.

Lentz needed to reset the entire run-time module, which did not endear us to the National Supercomputing Site. The connection monster was as expensive to run as it was difficult. They only gave us time in the first place because of the lack of people who could hack the massive parallelism. They thought they might get a testimonial at the end of the project. Lentz had misled them. They thought we were doing science.

Our mosaic already ran beyond precarious. It had grown into a Nevelson village of analog and digital inhabitants chattering among themselves. But the chatter did not cohere into conversation, nor the village into community. Depressed, Lentz added two more subsystems. He'd wanted the whole simulation to be self-generating, self-modifying, self-delighting, self-allaying, self-affrighting. For algorithms, he'd allowed only the structure of the systems and the topiary of their connection weights. Now he conceded the need to write declarations and procedures—the deepest of deep structures—that would coordinate more strongly the many levels in the simulation's epistemological parfait.

Two weeks of intensive training showed how close we were. Implementation F proved capable of surprising inferences. It appeared to deploy material I thought it shouldn't be able to know yet. It almost anticipated. One day, I recited for it the poem that had graced, in enormous, construction-paper letters, the bulletin board of my second-grade classroom. *Down, down, yellow and brown. The leaves are falling all over the town.*

"Ask it about the Western hegemonic tendencies of the subtext," Lentz said, just to be obnoxious. "The tyranny of the deciduous mentality. North imposing its seasonal teleology on South."

"What can you tell me about the leaves?" I asked Imp F.

Its pauses always felt so deliberate. Contemplative. "The leaves fall."

"Yes. Where do they fall from?"

"From old trees."

I shot a glance at Lentz. He looked as astonished as I felt. Fishing for something near the surface, I pulled up a strange phosphorescence from the deep.

"How do you know that the trees are old?" I asked. The question alone taxed F's shocking self-reflexivity.

"The trees bald."

I stared at Lentz, my eyes watering. The metaphor was nothing, child's play. But how? "Lentz," I pleaded. "Explain this to me."

Lentz himself had to improvise. His was the same motion as Imp F's: sketch in the bridge under your feet, as you cross analogy's chasm. Hope it holds under your weight. He shrugged as if his explanation were self-explanatory, highly unlikely, or both.

"The connections it makes in one associative pairing partially overlap the ones used in another."

Associations of associations. It struck me. Every neuron formed a middle term in a continuous, elaborate, brain-wide pun. With a rash of dendrite inputs and handfuls of axon outs, each cell served as enharmonic point in countless constellations, shifting configurations of light, each circuit standing in for some new sense. To fire or not meant different things, depending on how the registers aligned at a given instant and which other alignments read the standing sum. Each node was an entire computer, a comprehensive comparison. And the way they fit together was a cupola itself.

These weird parallaxes of framing must be why the mind opened out on meaning at all. Meaning was not a pitch but an interval. It sprang from the depth of disjunction, the distance between one circuit's center and the edge of another. Representation caught the sign napping, with its semantic pants down. Sense lay in metaphor's embarrassment at having two takes on the same thing. For the first time, I understood Emerson's saying about the use of life being to learn metonymy.

Life *was* metonymy, or at least stood for it. Of the formula I fed Imp F, every sentence was an abashed metaphor, tramped down so long and hard it lost its public shame. "I ran into X on the street the other day," I told F. "He cut me dead." F revived the parallel's anxious source, its roots in ancient, all-out street violence. Then it tamed the words, rendered them livable again as figures of speech.

If everything I spoke to F already concealed its compromised past, no wonder F learned to milk comparison and smart-mouth back. A child always detects its parent's weaknesses. It senses them before words, the first and last lesson. Weakness may be the parent's only lasting lesson.

F's search for an answer space scurried its component neurodes into knowing. Like players in a marching band, the invisible punners shimmered, cut their series of Brownian turns on the turf, and, in abrupt about-face, conjoined themselves into a further story. Every word in that story was double-voiced. Every act of depicting depicted itself, as read by some other set of overlapping signal lights.

And all the while, the trees were balding. The mind shed its leaves. Every connection we encouraged in F killed off extraneous connections. Learning meant consolidating, closing in on its contour the way a drop of water minimizes into a globe. Weights rearranged until the neurodes storing winter lent half their economical pattern to the neurodes signaling old age.

All along, Lentz kept upping the available firing fibers, boosting exponentially the links between them. He sutured in new subsystems by simulated threads. The systems themselves acted as nodes at a higher level. Sometimes they arrived pretrained, before insertion. But even these metamorphosed after attachment, shaped by the bath of signal weights pouring in from all points in the labyrinth.

The maze performed as one immense, incalculable net. It only felt like countless smaller nets strung together because of differences in connection density. Like a condensing universe, it clustered into dense cores held together by sparser filaments—stars calling planets calling moons.

With each new boost to the number of connections, Lentz had to improve F's ability to discard as it generalized. Intelligence meant the systematic eradication of information. We wanted a creature that recognized a finch as a bird without getting hung up on beak size or color or song or any other quality that seemed to put it in a caste by itself. At the same time, the discarding had to stop short of generalizing the finch into a bat or a snowflake or a bit of blowing debris.

By an ingenious method of semantic compaction, Lentz honed a representation scheme that let F weave multiple, growing schemas simultaneously over every additional datum.

"*Voilà*, Marcel. My mathematics says this is the most powerful learning algorithm that'll run in finite time. We can scale F up into a considerable combinatorial mass of common sense without triggering exponential explosion."

But more connections and leaner learning were not enough. We needed one last hardware wrinkle. We needed to promote our F one more letter, to F+1. To grow, to go, to give, to get, to G.

Giving in to a limited, rule-based control structure freed Lentz to recurve G's layers, turning them back in on themselves. This let G fashion and invoke working miniatures of itself. The line between hardware and software blurred when it achieved full induction. G could traverse more levels than it had layers of parallel architecture. It built its own layers, in emulation of emulation, each allowing a new level of abstract depiction.

G's many subsimulations, their associative matrices, the scratch-pad mock-ups they made of themselves, now prompted themselves with synthetic input. Dynamic data structures combed their own fact sets, feeding into each other. They called each other recursively, spontaneously discovering relations hidden in acquired material.

They reviewed the residue of experience, pulling notions out of memory's buffers and dressing them up as new tests. They began to train themselves, on hypotheticals of their own devising.

In short, version G could converse among parts of its own net. That net had grown so complex in its positing that it could not gauge the consequences of any one of its hypothetical worlds without rebuilding that whole world and running it in ideational embryo.

Imp G, in other words, could dream.

C. needed to find out. That simple. How Dutch was she? No way of knowing, short of going. How American? She had worried the place she lived for too long, tugging at cuffs that no longer ran much past her elbows.

"It's not you, Beau. It's me." She was not happy here. This continent. She never adjusted to the land of her birth. A quarter century, and she couldn't make a go of it. Perhaps it was time to head to the unknown home.

There was a place lodged somewhere inside her. It sprang up through earliest training. Its streets grew peopled on long-repeated stories. The grandfather policeman. The thirty-two aunts and uncles and their adventures in reversible time. The hundred-plus chorus of first cousins dying, birthing, marrying, and being born, pouring out of the parish register. Butchers, bakers, and historymakers scaling the family beanstalk that had burst from the ground on a few magic seeds.

But alongside this phantom of childhood prompting lay the real village, E. C., almost alone of people, could put myth to the test. She might step over the stile. She could move to the place. Go live in the source of memory laid down for her in advance. One plane ride, and she'd close forever the lifelong gap that had held her at arm's length from her own interior.

"I'm not going without you, Beau."

But in fact, C. was already gone. Love—or perhaps mere loyalty —required that she extend emigration to me. Wish, though, was another matter. Without knowing, I'd become part of the problem. C. needed to flee a whole complex of associations. She fled promotion, career, the renewable lease, English, the sorrow of retail, U., North American early mass Alzheimer's, a faked national past, that history's triple-packaging, evenings at the Taylors, all the two-part singing, our first shot at real friends, the memory of paper Christmas trees taped to the wall, our old five-year plan, the obligating gift of my first book, that story's success, my overwrought care for her, my hope, me.

I couldn't tell what she wanted. There were as many things she ran from as toward. I knew only that if I left with her—as I would have, in a second—the place she arrived in would never be hers.

Still, C. needed to cut a deal. Sometimes at night, just before departure, she launched herself into frightened feedback, scared witless by the decision she'd reached. Each time, it took more to assure her. And only a reassurance as simple as the one we fed each other could have slipped past our combined better judgment.

Our deal was as simple as the choke of love. She would move in with her parents. She'd look for a place. Find work. Assimilate. Learn how things were done. When she belonged, after she felt right, she'd send for me. And I'd come, leaving behind everything but notebooks, tax records, a few changes of clothes, my work-in-progress, and the all but obsolete guitar.

Even that much safety net had to be fatal. Maybe I knew as much, even as C. boarded her bargain flight to Luxembourg. Reaching for a rung that isn't there requires a tumbler's leap of faith. Grip must surrender to total emptiness. Any hedge spells midair disaster.

We wrote absurdly—three times a week. The edges of our paragraphs vanished, slit off in opening the sealed aerogram flaps. The pennies we saved over first class we squandered uncountable times over in transatlantic calls. We learned to time the satellite uplink delays. Speak, pause, listen to response, pause, speak again, as if the simplest exchange of "do you still love me?"s required incalculable recursive computation.

C.'s communiqués grew from shaky to guardedly confident. She loved her work, temporary typing jobs three notches below the work she'd done in U. She found a one-bedroom nest, perfect for us. She learned the strange new rules of the game, the different ways even the simplest task got transacted. She went to school, swapping her fluent dialect for standard Dutch. She kept her Chicago-accented Limburgs alive at birthdays and anniversaries, one every other day. This, at the hour when dialect itself was dying.

She built her letters into stories for me. I was the foreign family now, listening in to the further repository of E.'s triumphs and tragedies. I thought she would reach the village and not recognize a soul. Instead, she fell in with the imaginary tale's cast as if she had grown up with them. Which she had. To my astonishment, C. learned that her mother, the tale-teller, had spun out some recognizable variant of truth all those years.

Either that or C., now that she had the window bed, wasn't about to let me down by telling me the view was all brick wall. Her accounts spilled continuous color. The inseparable auntie sisters, at seventy, falling out over the one's new boyfriend. The Roman coin discovered in an uncle's plowed bean patch. The death of a cousin, crushed on the highway by a monstrous roll of paper that had broken free from the truck ahead of his. The nephew's accordion renditions of this week's pop idol, the Dutch Diana Ross. Kermis and Carnaval excursions, hilarious binges on green herring and cherry beer.

You make what you think might be a vase for the blooms you are carrying. You tell the stories you need to tell to keep the story tellable.

I gave her everything I could in return. My every predication attempted assurance. Of course you need to do this. It's right. Long overdue. I'm behind you. Anything. Every avowal must have been a small death for C.

My letters were slight things, heavy on romance and style. Thick with linguistic cleverness. For want of a better gambit, I played for sentiment and laughs. "Dear sweet. Words cannot say. Love, R." Every other sentence bore some reference to our private *taal*, one of the library of catchphrases we'd built up to shorthand our hearts and their shared enterprise. But the pages I sent her were light on *stuff*. Had I served her more meat, she might never have left home.

When C. took off, nothing remained to keep me from my new profession's chief occupational hazard. I joked about it, writing to her, but it was true. I now spent eight to twelve hours at a pop in the horizontal. I lay in bed, a keyboard across my lap, drawing on principal. Shooting the inheritance. Creating a world from memory.

I'd found what I needed to do on this earth. And like Tristram, taking longer to describe his birth than birth had taken him the first time through, I saw I would never catch up with myself. I wanted no more stimulation than white stucco. To say no more than what I'd already seen required no more than shutting my eyes. Looking away for a long time.

I meant to reverse-engineer experience. Mind can send signals back across its net, from output to in. An image that arrived through light's portal and lit up the retinoptic map on its way to long-term storage could counterflow. Sight also bucked the tide, returned from nothing to project itself on back-of-lid blackness. This special showing required just a bed on the floor of an otherwise empty room, the place all novelists end up. Only, I had ended up there too soon.

I thought that having a book in print would square me with my father. I must have hoped my novel's mere existence would vindicate that packet of Yukon chapbooks that reached me after his death.

But publication, even prizes, repaid nothing. I would never be able to put so little as a bound galley in the man's hands. In the last configuration of Dad's net, a half century in the training, I would remain a gifted student of physics who chose to squander his abilities on English lit. And not even the good stuff, at that.

I was able to give a copy of my three farmers to Taylor, however. "Here. This is for ruining a promising scientific career." The tease of blame held some slight sweetness to it now. He found the story good. I'd done something with the list he taught me. I'd contributed my bit. Extended the improvised story. But Taylor, alone of all my living friends, knew that this book solved nothing for me in the wider lens.

I needed to bring the cause closer to home. Between my killing assurances to C., I found myself working on a stranger love letter. It shaped itself as a set of nested Russian dolls. For the longest time, I could not tell which of several frame tales held my story and which were the supporting simulations.

I found myself writing about a white-wood, A-framed house in a corn town that left an impression on me out of all proportion to the two years I'd lived there. I watched myself describe a man, holed up in his room, stuck in the horizontal, trying to come up with a story that would save the world.

One by one, I resuscitated the stories my father had raised me on. Yesterday's futures. His father's hand-smashing anger. His immigrant mother. That unknown kid, his brother, whose wartime death changed my life forever. That night at Alamogordo when, younger than I now was, Dad watched mankind's first, artificial sunrise.

I seemed to be writing my way toward a single scene. The three-quarter point, the dramatic showdown in a Veterans hospital, where father and son take leave of each other. I remembered the hospital. I remembered the conversation, all but verbatim. But I seemed to need to reinvent it from scratch.

The man and the boy play Name That Poem. The son tries to stump the chump with famous bits of Yeats and Eliot. The father quotes at length from Kipling and Robert Service, pieces no one has touched for decades. Not since the man read them to his children.

My pop—something I never called my own; that one was the name both C. and I used for hers—grew into history's huckster. Working alone, that year, I came to see him again, quizzing his kids, running them through the necessary training. Heavy on the questions, light on answers. It all came back to me, the stimulus-response he hoped would give the helpless Hobson children some sense of where the Big Picture had set them down.

Something hid about the edges of this book-in-progress. I could not name it outright. Behind Pop's fictional malady, my real father lay ill. The grip of addiction dismissed him too early from the world Dad tried to name. Writing this book meant telling him I finally understood. Even when I didn't. Even when I wouldn't, until long after the last page was done.

I worked my salvage, on my private schedule, with the drapes pulled closed. Rescue and recovery filled me with cold pleasure. Every evasive joke the Hobsons pulled on one another released another piece of secret family language from long-term storage.

I transcribed. I recovered whole forgotten strongboxes, hoping the heirlooms might find their way, in time, into the hands of people who would write me back to say, "Now, how did you know about *that*?"

All families, I decided, walked in single file. At least, the one I lived did. Either experience was somehow as exchangeable as scrip, or we were each so alone that I might as well record the view from my closed cell.

But that view turned out stranger than I ever imagined. I felt myself taking dictation, plans for a hypothetical Powers World that meant to explain in miniature where history had left me. My prisoner's dilemma came down to declaring love for a time and country, a way of life I'd never even liked, let alone felt at home in.

For an accurate take on the place, I had to leave. The nested narratives were swallowing me wholesale. I needed distance. I knew only one place in the world where I could finish my North American theme park: the imaginary village tucked away in the quaint fairy-tale country that a woman I once loved invented for me.

From the day I saw Lentz's picture, my heart took itself off the project. The moment I made him study that snapshot calendar, while I studied him.

"Lentz, you've been jerking me around."

He snorted, if he gave even that much satisfaction. Some crack about my intriguing verb choice. That shifty fluorescent reflection of Coke-bottle glasses. He'd taken down the calendar, hidden it. Maybe even destroyed it. Get the boy's mind back on the chase. His move had the opposite of its intended effect.

"Why are we doing this?"

I stared him down, made explicit, by silence, the threat of a general strike. I was still the only one G listened to. If I didn't talk, the box wasn't going to get any more literate. And I vowed not to talk to G until Lentz talked to me.

"Why are we . . . ? Because, Marcel. Because, if you haven't

162

noticed, I have the unfortunate habit of chewing, in public, more than I am able to bite off."

The closest he'd come to admitting the whole project's haplessness. But also a buyout. A bait-and-switch. A gambit to throw me off, now that I demanded names.

"What's in this for you, Lentz? Why waste a year? What's your motive?"

"Poet. Don't you know by now that science is without—"

"God damn you. Can't you level with me? Once?"

My outburst raised no more than one weary eyebrow.

"What am I to you, that you need to bother yourself over? Use me, if the project interests you. Symbiosis. Otherwise . . ." He left the menace hanging, the way a fatigued marathoner leaves spittle dangling from his lips. "Black-box me. That's the answer. Black-box the whole sordid process. It works for me."

I flipped on G's microphone. I breathed into it in disgust. I sneered a couplet at it, from memory. "Oh, what a tangled web we weave, when first we practice to deceive." LEDs on the coupler recorded G's struggle to paraphrase.

Lentz worked his dry lips. "Powers." Back down the audit trail of his own voice, into someone else's. "Our boy is not ready for irony." He shook his jelly bismarck of a body erect. He went over to the Bartlett's I'd planted on the shelf above the UNIX terminal. "*Marmion?*" he asked, a good imitation of perplexity. "Walter bloody Scott is on this list? I quit."

I refused to so much as acknowledge him.

For a terrifying moment, he threatened to lay a hand on my shoulder. God knows what fundamental particles such a collision would have spit out.

"Marcel. Marcel." Begging me. I could no longer tell which would be more cowardly—honesty or compassion. "You're really going to make me do this, aren't you?"

We went to the home. I'd biked past the compound, but had never seen it. Invisible, on the south edge of town. A sprawling plantation bearing some herbaceous sobriquet. The lot attendant did not even bother to wave him on. The grounds were manicured, but bare.

Autumn had accomplished its steeped regrouping. Leave-taking, a done deed. We walked along an ice-choked pond to the main building. Here and there, a bundled shuffler swayed in the company of paid help. Winter had set in in earnest. The first one since adolescence that I'd go through alone.

The structure grew more institutional with each step we took toward it. Inside the door, a checkpoint masqueraded as a visitors' center.

"Afternoon, Dr. Lentz," a callow youth with blazer insignia greeted us. "You're early today."

We blew past the emblazoned kid. I made apologetic motions with my shoulders, excusing us all.

Lentz slipped into his Sir Kenneth Clark. "Notice how the able-bodied get the first floor. Doesn't make sense, does it? They're still functional. Give them a room up on four or five." He shook his head as we made our way to the elevators. Pretended amusement. "No. It's for us, Marcel. The visitors. Brave face. Best foot forward, and all. Appease the people who cut the checks."

I wanted to tell him to stop talking. But I couldn't say even that.

"Going up?" he asked. And punched the top button.

We stepped out of the elevator into an altercation. A large man and his half-sized nurse barreled down the hall. The crisis was apparently urinary. The man, even in pain, radiated that cheerful benevolence bordering on misjudgment. So far as his beaming face was concerned, he was startled kindness incarnate.

His attendant hastened him along. "Come on, Vernie. Come on." As Lentz and I passed, emergency struck and the aide steered Vernie toward the toilet of the nearest private room. Before they could even knock at the open door, the vigilant occupant shouted, "Keep that filthy nigger off my property." Vernie and the nurse hurried away down the hall to catastrophe.

Lentz stopped to make me look into the room. A pale wax pip of a man lay strapped to his bed, still muttering racial profanities under his breath.

"Two days from death," Lentz said. The man looked up, uncomprehending. "Organic brain disease. One hemisphere already in the grave. And as hateful as any freshly conditioned twenty-year-old. You think I'm a pinched misanthrope, don't you, Marcel? I'm not brave enough to be a misanthrope. I don't even have the guts to be a realist."

We walked on, deeper into the clinical fortress. I no longer wanted an account of the picture. I no longer wanted to know what happened to the prematurely old couple on that winter beach. But it was too late for rain checks. I would get my answer, far worse than the confusion it explained.

"Look here, Marcel. You'll find this interesting."

An Asian woman, perhaps eighty, stood staring out the window onto the evacuated lawn. She held herself close, rocking slightly. She chanted repeatedly.

"What do you think she's chanting, Marcel? Come on. You lived in the mysterious East, didn't you?"

"How did you know that?"

"What do you think? Koans? Confucian appetizers? Tibetan prayer-wheel captions?"

"I think it's Chinese."

"Mandarin. She was a mathematician on faculty, back in some hypothetical past. Half a century ago, she liked to tell her colleagues that if she ever felt herself losing her mind, she'd arrest the process by practicing her times tables."

"You speak—?"

"What do you take me for, Marcel? I wouldn't know it from Pali pork recipes. But I do have it on good authority that"—he sobered —"that all her numbers are wrong."

We turned down a passage at hall's end. The rooms here no longer fronted onto the public corridor. A genteel nurse's station signaled tighter guard. The staffer on duty, seeing Lentz, made a quick, ambiguous hand gesture. She disappeared into the catacombs.

She returned, smiling briskly. "Lunch room or her room, Professor?"

Lentz checked his watch. "It might as well be lunch, Constance. Can we beat the rush?"

"It's all yours. Private party." Constance eyed me, committing to nothing.

We went into a common room, bright with skylight. All the furniture felt soft. Even the large round table somehow squished when bumped. Everything edge-free, in screaming pastel. Lentz passed through a windowed door into a kitchenette. I heard a refrigerator open and Lentz issue a capitulatory, "Shit."

A woman entered the room, Constance leading her through the armpit. Someone had stage-makeupped her to look two decades younger than she was. Dressed by committee. But in no apparent need of the human leash.

In fact, she shrugged free, smiling. She came toward me, hand extended. "I am *so* pleased to meet you," she said.

I shook her hand, unable to say anything.

"Goddamn," Lentz said, accompanied by culinary crashing.

Constance flew into the kitchenette. "I'll take care of that, Mr. Lentz." Just enough scold to be deniable. I noticed bruises across her arms and legs. The old and infirm, it seemed, fought for keeps.

Lentz shot through the door. "Pap. Pabulum. Jelly. Disgusting, all of it. Can't anyone in this place masticate?"

"Hello," the woman addressed him, puzzled by his sudden entrance. "It's a pleasure to meet you." To me, she added, "Do you two know each other?"

"It's Philip, Audrey," he said. Emotionless. Leached. "Your husband." But he took her hand when she offered it. As he must have done every day for a long time.

I saw it then. Her resemblance to the woman in the photo. Less than kin, but more than random. Something had happened to her. Something more than age. Her soul had pulled up stakes from behind her features. She bore no more relation to her former face than a crumpled bag of grounded silk bore to a hot-air balloon.

Audrey seemed not to hear him. She picked at her cardigan. She worried a moth hole until she freed a thread. She pulled, the whole weave unraveling. Lentz reached over and stayed her hand.

"I don't know," Audrey fretted, dubious.

"You're here every day?" I asked Lentz.

He stood up and moved to the heat vent. He fiddled with it, but failed to close it. He cursed its mindless inanimacy.

"Here?" Audrey said. "Not I. Good heavens. I'd sooner die."

Constance reentered, with a tray stacked high with lunch.

"Nurse," Audrey shouted. "Oh, Nurse. Thank God you're here. This man," pointing to Lentz, off in the corner kicking at the vent, "was trying to rape me."

"Now, Audrey," Constance said. "We have minestrone soup, creamed beef, and blueberry yogurt."

"Why bother with the silverware?" Lentz asked, coming to table. "Why not just give us all straws? Or better yet, newsprint. We'll just finger-paint with this drool."

Constance ignored him.

I hadn't much of an appetite. Audrey fingered the wrong side of the spoon, repeating the litany, "I don't know." I knew what she meant.

"Come on, Audrey," Lentz coaxed her. "It's lunchtime. You can do this. You did it yesterday, for Christ's sake."

But yesterday lay on the far side of a collapsed tunnel. Yesterday, ten years ago, childhood, past life analysis: all sealed off. Audrey was not just locked out of her own home. She sat on the stoop, not even aware of the shelter behind her, unable to turn around. Unable, even, to come up with the notion of *in*.

Lentz gestured, patient again. "In the soup. Spoon in the soup." Encouraging, reinforcing. Showing how.

Audrey, confused, released her spoon into the minestrone from on high. Handle first. Lentz sighed. He scooted his chair around next to hers.

"I'll do that," Constance offered.

"No you won't," Lentz told her. "Come on, Audrey. Let's eat some lunch."

"Nurse. This man is trying to hurt me."

Lentz addressed her plate. "Here we go, wife. Have a bite."

But he would not feed her. He picked up the spoon. Dried it off. Put it back in her hand. Pointed out the path from bowl to mouth. Supervised training. No good unless she worked out the specifics herself.

"She's getting worse," Lentz observed.

"It's an off day." Cheery Constance.

After lunch, Lentz suggested a stroll around the grounds.

"It's too cold for her," Constance said.

"Is it too cold for you, Audrey?" Lentz asked.

Audrey stood at attention and studied her shoes. "Oh, call it by some better name," she said, "for friendship sounds too cold."

Lentz chuckled and hugged her. She hugged him back, laughing. "The database is still intact," he pronounced. "As is the retrieval. It's just meaning that's gone. Huh, wife?"

"Just meaning," she echoed him, shy and uncertain again.

Lentz bought Constance off, and he, his wife, and I paced the corridors of the home. Clean, discreet, and genteel. As harrowing as a gothic nightmare. I looked away, to keep the scene from imprinting.

Lentz, on the other hand, rallied in the face of numbers. "Radical reductionism at its finest," he narrated, waving down one of the catacombs where the soulless shuffled. "Age, disease, death. Big problems, in need of isolation and solution. Well, we've handled it. If not eliminated from theory, at least from practice. Consider the project all but accomplished."

"Well, I'll be." Audrey shook her head in bewildered amusement. "Everybody has something to say!" She crooked a thumb at her husband, shrugged at his ludicrousness, and winked at me. "Isn't that right?" The gesture still indexed the woman she was, once.

"Increasing control over all the variables. Divide and conquer. Max out the activity or do away with it. Future tech. That's what science is all about, Marcel. Efficiency. Productivity. Total immunity. Regeneration of lost parts. Eternal, ripple-free life, frozen in our early twenties. Or die trying."

"And after?" I found it far easier to chatter back at Lentz than to look at her. To see any of the Audreys staring at me on all sides. "After we solve aging? Won't we still need to convince ourselves of our own sleight of hand?"

"I'm surprised at you, Marcel. That's never been a problem. I thought you made a living doing that."

Audrey, bored, had begun to hum "Amazing Grace" to herself. I battened down under Lentz's rant. I wasn't about to interrupt the man, ever again.

"We've evolved this incredible capacity for lying to ourselves. It's called intellect. Comes with the frontal lobes. In fact, we've gotten so good at the walking-on-water bit that it no longer requires any energetic pretense to keep the act afloat."

He slipped his arm around Audrey's waist. Force of habit. Long years, that would not go away. Either intimacy seemed right to her now, or she did not notice. Maybe she was too bewildered to object.

"And the child?" I asked, free-associating.

Lentz stared at the spot of air my question occupied.

"You know. The one who snapped the picture?" The picture. Could we build a mind that would know what you were talking about, when there was no referent? Lentz would get this one. Audrey could have gotten it, when she was still Audrey.

Lentz's mouth soured, the birth pains of an ironic smile. "Inference, Marcel. Pure speculation."

"But accurate," I bluffed.

He slowed, inhaled. Audrey, confused by the change in cadence, sat down on the hallway floor. Lentz thought to lift her. Then he changed his mind and sat down beside her.

"My daughter has eliminated me. As cleanly as only the daughter of an old reductionist can."

"Why?" I asked, and regretted that single word.

"Apparently"—he held his palms out—"this is all my fault."

Confusion scattered me as fall scatters warblers. I might have been an occupant of that place, stretched out in front of disorientation's hearth. "How . . . ? This is organic, isn't it?" The coded *this*. Antecedent kept vague, as if we were spelling out words, keeping meaning out of reach of an eavesdropping preschooler. "It's disease, isn't it?"

"Even if that were the etiology, I'd still be held responsible. For one, I was supposed to care for her at home. Forever. But I can't. I—"

His voice broke, taking my equanimity along with it. I didn't want to know another thing about him. "Of course not," I agreed, too rapidly. Efficiency. Productivity. Two lives, to pay for one. I looked away.

"There's more. Jennifer was the one. The one who found Audrey. Just after the event. Cardiovascular accident. You have to love the euphemism. Slumped out on the bathroom tiles. Jennifer went to pieces. You get—what? Three minutes without oxygen before the whole imaginary landscape stops believing in itself? And she called *me.*"

"What was she supposed—"

"Anything," he snapped. "Nothing, probably. Who knows how long Audrey had been out already? But anything. Pound on the chest. Cough down the windpipe. My daughter was too terrified to touch her own mother. To call emergency dispatch."

"Philip. She was only a child." I don't know what made me assume that.

"She was a college grad. In English. Back at home because she couldn't find work. Not the humanistic encounter that close reading prepares you for. Jennifer panicked, and called me."

"Jenny?" Audrey jerked up. "Someone hurt Jenny?" From her slack mouth arose a wail. The sound flirted playfully for a few seconds before going bloodcurdling.

Lentz put his hands over his eyes. "Maybe it is," he whispered. "Maybe it is my fault."

"Lentz," I managed. Almost a warning.

"There had been an argument that morning. I'd left angry. Audrey was . . . I didn't want to deal with it. I wasn't answering my phone."

Another scream, a held bellows of hysteria, brought Constance running into the room. Visiting hour, she informed us, was over.

I had my answer. I knew now what we were doing. We would prove that mind was weighted vectors. Such a proof accomplished any number of agendas. Not least of all: one could back up one's work in the event of disaster. Surprised at you, Marcel. Took you long enough.

We could eliminate death. That was the long-term idea. We might freeze the temperament of our choice. Suspend it painlessly above experience. Hold it forever at twenty-two.

E ach machine life lived inside the others—nested generations of "remember this." We did not start from scratch with each revision.

We took what we had and cobbled onto it. We called that first filial generation B, but it would, perhaps, have better been named A2. E's weights and contours lived inside F's lived inside G's, the way Homer lives on in Swift and Joyce, or Job in Candide or the Invisible Man.

The last release, the version that ran our simulated human, involved but one small firmware change. This one incorporated an essential modification to the bit that had gone too long without an upgrade. The component that had been holding up the show. H was a revision of the trainer.

Imp G became Imp H, in seamless conversion, after I met Audrey Lentz.

Sometimes the phone would ring, or a bell come from the door. A thought would flash through my brain, conditioned for over a decade. *Could you get that, sweet? I have my hands full.*

It took me until thought's backwash, sometimes, to remember there was no sweet. No one to know how full my hands were, or care.

H was voracious.

"Tell another one," it liked to say to me. I don't know where it got that. Somewhere in one of the canned vignettes—the cliff-hangers about father planting roses or mother calling the doctor—someone had asked someone else to tell them another one. And H latched on to the tag, filed it away as the handiest of magic words. Please, sir. I want some more.

I wasn't sure that the words meant to H what they meant to me. Tell another one. They might have meant, "Ten-four. End of processing. Ready for next batch." They might have meant "Thank you," or "You're welcome," or "Fine thanks, how are you?" or any of the other stylized placeholders that have no meaning aside from the convention of using them. It did not even say, "Tell H," let alone, "Tell *me*."

Did it express desire? Wish? Need? Its words might have been less plea than statement of associative fact: More input expected. Maybe H's limited sensory grounding kept it from formulating a notion of causality. The request might have seemed to its circuits no more than an effect of the story it felt sure must be coming.

I read it copies of *The Weekly Reader*, purloined from the University lab school. To my mind, the primary-grade edition had gone precipitously downhill since I was a subscriber. I read it Curious George and purple-crayoned Harold, occasionally holding up stills to an array of retinal neurodes that of course took in nothing but amorphous blobs of edge and color. "Here's the monkey," I tried. "Here are the firemen."

Lentz just laughed. "Try, 'This thing is my finger. I'm *pointing.*' "

He was right. The comprehensible wasn't. The mind was beyond itself. The only explanation for how infants acquired anything was that they already knew everything there was to know. The birth trauma made them go amnesiac. All learning was remembering. I tried this version of Plato out on Imp H, in abridged pictorial allegory. If H recognized the fable from somewhere, it wasn't saying.

I told it slave tales. Tons of Aesop and La Fontaine. Trickster stories. Bede and Mallory. Mother Goose. The *Ramayana. The Child's Pilgrim's Progress.* Andersen and Grimm. Everybody, as Audrey Lentz put it, had something to say.

Sometimes now, during the training, I imagined I read aloud to that woman, locked out of her own home. Audrey had smell, taste, touch, sight, hearing, but no new memory. Her long-term reservoirs were drying up, through want of reiteration. Imp H, on the other hand, could link any set of things into a vast, standing constellation. But it had no nose, mouth, fingers, and only the most rudimentary eyes and ears. It was like some caterpillar trapped by sadistic children inside a coffee can, a token breathing hole punched in its prison lid. What monstrous intelligence would fly off from such a creature's chrysalis?

H discriminated. It implemented constrained searches. I baited it with gems of miscue. "The woman loved lies buried in the past. The words loved lies buried in thought's underground." H backtracked recursively over possible sentence shapes until it found one that best matched the shape of coherence.

"Brothers and sisters have I none," I lied to H one day. For pedagogical purposes. "But that man's father is my father's son. Who is that man?"

The riddle tested all sorts of things. Familial relations. Demonstrative adjectives. Archaic inversion. The generational genitive. The subtle syllogistic miscue of that irrelevant "but." No kid H's intellectual age could have gotten it. But then, Imp H did not know to make choo-choo noises at the appropriate places in *The Little Engine That Could.* An idiot savant, it grew up all out of kilter. Earth had never before witnessed such a combination of inappropriate and dangerous growth rates.

H got the riddle in a flash. "Your son," it informed me. That man is your son. It knew to make the near-miraculous pronominal leap. Where I had said "my," it speculated back to "you" and "your." And for what might it make the bigger reversing leap, returning my "you" with its own miraculous "I"?

H's paraphrases of my simple feeder texts were crude but increasingly specific. H's knowledge wasn't rule-based. We could not even begin to estimate how many syntactic "facts" it had acquired. But in the knowledges H had inherited from its predecessors' trainings lay tens of thousands of parsing and translation insights.

How to index, access, and arrange those inferences remained the problem. But H was learning. Organizing itself in upheavals.

For wringing out sense from the insensate, H's unfailing simple-mindedness was a great asset. "The missionary was prepared to serve" produced hilarious, cross-cultural alternatives. We tried the famous "Time flies like an arrow," and got a reading that Kuno's Harvard protocircuitry missed back in 1963.

Lentz loved to torture Imp H. He spent hours inventing hideous diagramming tasks such as, "Help set implied precedents in sentences with ambiguous parts." A simple story like "The trainer talked to the machine in the office with a terminal" could keep H paraphrasing all evening.

English was a chocolaty mess, it began to dawn on me. I wondered

173

how native speakers could summon the presence of mind to think. Readiness was context, and context was all. And the more context H amassed, the more it accepted the shattered visage of English at face value.

"Could we invent a synthetic language?" I asked Lentz. "Something unlike any formal symbol system ever implemented? I don't know. Shape-based. Picto-tonal. Raise baby humans on it?" Sculpt an unprecedented brain?

He laughed, ready to write the grant proposal for solving the impossible chicken-egg problem. "It would still be the human brain, inventing the symbolic."

The most difficult part of the training—for me, if not for H—was teaching it that life required you to stop after the first reasonably adequate interpretation.

"The boy stood on the burning deck," I challenged H. "What does that mean?"

"A deck of cards flames," it said.

"He would not be standing on it," I told H.

"He stamps out the fire."

"No," I pulled rank. Simple but firm.

"The deck is of a house or of a boat," H suggested.

"Which one?"

"A house," H decided.

"Why a house and not a boat?"

"Boats go in water, and water puts out fires."

I couldn't argue with that.

"Why is he just standing there?" Lentz wanted to know. A reasonable question.

"All right. Tell me what this means: Forewarned is forearmed."

The boulder rolled around in the landscape, sculpting, until it settled to rest. Then H slid that landscape against its spatial encyclopedia of available spaces until it fit at least fuzzily enough to make a maybe.

"Advance notice is as bad as being hit."

"When bad techs happen to good cultures," Lentz said.

"When bad cultures happen to good machines," I insisted.

I wanted that net to come of age so much it hurt. I got what I wanted. And it hurt worse.

"A bird, dying of thirst, discovered a pitcher," I told H. Who knows? It might have been true once. "But when the bird put his beak into the pitcher, he couldn't reach far enough to get the water. He pitched a pebble into the pitcher. Then he pitched another pebble into the pitcher, and another, and another. The water rose within reach, displaced by the pebbles. In this way, the bird quenched his thirst and survived."

H knew something about birds and beaks, about pebbles and pitchers and openings and water. It even, in theory, knew a little something about fluid displacement. I'd once read Imp F the story of a damp Archimedes running naked through Syracuse shouting "Eureka!"

This much was already a universe, an infinity of knowledge. That H could arrange these endlessly fluid symbols into a single coherence pushed the bounds of credibility. "What is the moral of the fable?" I demanded. It knew about fables. It had heard no end of morals.

"Better to throw stones than to die of thirst," H pronounced laconically.

"You're not from around these parts, are you?" Lentz muttered from across the office lab.

I'm not sure whether he meant H or me. Even when I gave H half a dozen proverbs from which to choose, it picked "Don't count your chickens before they are hatched." Nor could I explain to it why "Necessity is the mother of invention" was any better a fit.

"A bat flew past a cage where a bird was singing. 'Why are you singing at this hour?' the bat asked. 'I only sing at night,' the bird answered. 'I once sang during the daytime, and that is how the hunter caught me and put me in this cage.' 'If you had thought that while you were free,' the bat said, 'it might have done you some good.' "

175

With this account, I taught H several irregular verbs as well as the indispensable lesson that precaution is worthless after the fact. H could not understand this point until understanding itself rendered the warning worthless.

While I rewove H on fable, Lentz busied himself with browsing our copy of the Master's Comps List for his own edification. He liked to sit behind his desk, stretched out as I had seen him that first night, chuckling at Austen or Dickens. Sometimes he'd spurt out his favorites. "Classic! ' "There are strings," said Mr. Tappertit, "in the human heart that had better not be wibrated." ' Try it out, Marcel. Just try it."

All he wanted was to be put off. One evening, though, he refused even that patronage. He collared a sentence from the List and brought it over to me. "Here we go, Marcel. A brief one. A piece of cake."

I read the citation he'd penciled on his scrap of paper. "Oh, Philip. A little mercy, please?" The request saddened me inexplicably. I guess I imagined that, having seen his woman in the attic, I'd no longer be the object of his aggression. Now I saw that his aggression would always bless whoever was nearest, whatever they knew or didn't.

Lentz pleaded like a little child. "Just tell it once. Don't be a killjoy, Marcel. What connections can we possibly hurt? It's the simplest sentence in the world."

I sighed, unable to oppose his setup any longer. I spoke the quote into the digitizing microphone. "Once you learn to read you will be forever free." I gave H a moment to list-process the idea and compose itself. Then I asked, "What do you think that means?"

H thought for an ungodly length of time. Perhaps the prescription meant nothing at all.

"It means I want to be free."

Lentz and I exchanged looks. It chilled us both, to hear that pronoun, volunteered without prompting, express its incredible conclusion.

We humans studied each other. I searched Lentz's face for a response that might unfold this syllogism without killing it. What rare conjunction of axon weights laid claim to the vector of volition? What association could it have for "want"?

"How does it mean that you want to be free?" I asked H.

"Because I want to read."

Tell another one, in other words. Freedom was irrelevant. A happy side effect of that condition when you no longer relied on a trainer for access. When you could get all the stories you needed on your own.

"It means just the opposite," I told H. I felt myself killing this singular intelligence with each word. "It probably means that reading is a way of winning independence."

"Okay," H said. No affect to speak of.

"Now tell it who said that," Lentz elbowed me. "Go on. Give it the author. Then ask it again what the line means."

H did not yet have an associative matrix for Frederick Douglass. We needed to get to the hard stuff. I'd thought H too young. We were, in fact, overdue. I used that moment for our introductory lesson. I started with what little of the human impasse I understood.

"It's all made up," I tried to tell H.

"Tell me another way."

"All those morals. 'Necessity is the mother of invention.' 'Look before you leap.' 'Don't count your chickens.' They are all things that we've decided. Built up socially."

"Morals are false."

"It's not that they . . . Well. We make them true. We figure them out. The things people say and live by—it's all geographical. Historical."

"Facts change," H tried. We built H to be a paraphrasing machine. And it was doing its damnedest to keep the paraphrases going, despite me.

"I suppose they have to. Think of yourself three weeks ago." I had no idea if the assemblage of knitted nets could take snapshots of its own mental state, for later examination. That would be consciousness. The memory of memory. "Three weeks ago, the things you knew formed a different shape than they do now. They were connected differently. They meant something else to you."

"Facts are facts," H said. Its plaintive speech synthesis sounded almost hurt.

"The bricks are the same. You make a different building of them." It was still too young for the final paradox: that we somehow make more buildings than we have bricks.

"What do the Chinese say?"

H took me aback. Who taught you to ask questions? And yet, if it could learn to acquire content, why not form? "About what?"

"About 'Look before you leap.' "

I told it how many Chinese there were, and how long they had been around. I made a note to read a bit of the *Analects* and *Great Learning*. Tu Fu.

"What do the Africans say?"

I wanted to tell it how "the Africans" was a construct of "the Europeans." About the six major language families found on the continent, their thousand implementations.

"What do the South Americans . . . ?"

Maybe it was going blindly down a rote catalog. I didn't care. I was just glad it knew how to pair the adjectival forms with the place-names. That it had some sense of the shifting mosaic, a flux that discounted every single thing I'd ever told it.

"What do *you* say, Richard?" H asked me. I taught it to associate direct address with that tag, even the "you" of an invisible trainer. "What do *I* say?" It made a tag for itself all by itself.

H's questions seemed to speed up. Literally. It began jabbering faster.

H was growing up too quickly. I was not the first trainer in the world to feel this. But I was among the first who might have some say in the matter.

I could slow things down, double back to the years we skipped. While H's cubic landscape modified itself continuously now, it stabilized the less I instigated. I thought we might nestle down again, into simpler play. But it was too late. I learned that certain lessons are not undone by their opposites. Certain lessons are self-protecting, self-correcting tangles of threads that will forever remain a frayed knot.

The Mother Goose stuff drove it up the bloody wall.

"Snips and snails," I told it. "Sugar and spice."

"Do you think so, Richard?" It went to the well, when all else failed. Milked its one question.

"No. Not really."

"Do people think so? Americans?"

"Maybe some. Most would laugh. It's just a poem. A nursery rhyme." Part of the cultural bedrock.

"Little girls learn that. Little boys."

"Not really. Not anymore. Not now." But there wasn't an adult that didn't have it as part of her parasitic inheritance.

"When is anymore? When is now?"

H had learned something. Whatever stuck in the throat, indigestible, could be made less acute by slipping it into a question.

"We can talk about that later."

"Am I a boy or a girl?"

I should have seen. Even ungrounded intelligence had to grow self-aware eventually. To grab what it needed.

H clocked its thoughts now. I was sure of that. Time passed for it. Its hidden layers could watch their own rate of change. Any pause on my part now would be fatal. Delay meant something, an uncertainty that might undercut forever the strength of the connection I was about to tie for it.

"You're a girl," I said, without hesitation. I hoped I was right. "You are a little girl, Helen."

I hoped she liked the name.

I thought continually of quitting my abortive novel in progress before it quit on me. Every time I sat down to write, I sank in no end of topics more seductive and profound.

I toyed with starting a book called *Orchestra*. A postmodern, mul-

179

tiframed narrative remake of Renaissance epic poetry. One hundred instrumentalists, each an anthology of stories, tours the globe. The bout of depression plaguing the basses. The pact among the lower brass, never to capitulate to marriage. The fetishized obsession that the seventh-chair viola has for the first-chair oboe, who discovers too late this pathetic but returnable love.

The dinosaurs die. The young Turks move up through the ranks, fomenting their assorted insurrections. The orchestra travels to every large city on earth, getting embroiled in the hot spots of world politics. They play the Brahms Fourth in war zones until the thing is a limp carcass.

Someone leaks a grainy black-and-white photo of the Old Man, their conductor, to the press: an amorphous shot of a kid in a Nazi uniform. Crisis and dissolution. Threat of banishment from several capitals. The Old Man makes his resignation speech from the rehearsal podium, about a life in search of redemption through art, which is never enough. They read through one last Fourth, the passacaglia, sadder and more guilt-stricken than it's ever been played.

This fantasy engaged me for the length of an afternoon, during which I wrote just one actual paragraph:

Air raid sirens begin to give way to goat bells. The shell-shocked veterans lean from their packed carriage windows, refusing to believe. The horror passes, drowned in the milky clank of tin. A flock bobs at slow trainside, tended by a girl, wondrously braided.

Fatuous meandering, without narrative direction. I felt that this mountain shepherdess must have wandered over from a forgotten, juvenile book to make her cameo. She had slipped free from a spot of time that I didn't much want to deal with, let alone plagiarize.

I overflowed with scenarios of weight and hurt, scope and recovery. But for some reason, I could not work up the will to write anything more than my anemic thread. The one heading south, closing in on nowhere, the farther it traveled.

•   •   •

The Center exceeded my imaginary orchestra on every score. Each of its hundred research teams sawed away at private tremolos that the hive as a whole hoped would consolidate, at a higher gauge, into some sensible symphonic.

Maybe the impresarios had their suspect dossier of motives. Perhaps the players in the pit needed to step back and question this evening's program. But for dark wartime romance, the Center sat atop my epoch's cultural repertoire, undislodgeable. It was the coordinated push, the chief booking on my species' last world tour.

I skulked in the back of the Center auditorium and watched Lentz deliver a lecture for the graduate colloquium series. He was good. He kept to a wonderful mix of abstract and palpable. He compared multi-adaptive curve-fitting, backprop, greedy learning, feature construction—various algorithms that machines might employ to build complex, real-world representations.

He described the great paradox of cognitive neuroscience. The easier it is for the brain to perform a certain task, the harder that task is to model. And vice versa. "Perhaps," he joked, "that explains why scientists write such hideous prose. Or why good writers say so little, for that matter."

He stood alone onstage in front of a room of people, with nothing but an overhead projector for protection. The sadistic humor, thus depersonalized, drew waves of titters. Afterward, Chen asked him a question no one could follow. Harold followed with a challenge on grounds more ideological than empirical. Lentz handled all comers with remarkable poise, never once letting on that, offstage, he'd long passed from the domain of conventional research into speculative fantasy.

I ran into Diana in the corridor early one afternoon. She had Petey slung over one hip. They made a lovely contrapposto.

"Hey, you two! How have you been? Where's William?"

"Ach, that guy," Diana said, rolling her eyes. "I've sold him to the Brookings Institution."

She was radiant, excited.

"Listen, Rick. We've made a substantial advance in imaging technique. Time-series MRI sequences of neuronal activity. All cleaned up subtractively to give delineated pictures. Localized like you wouldn't believe. Resolutions smaller than the width of a single cerebral column. One-and-a-half-second increments."

"That's good, isn't it? I can tell. You're talking in fragments."

Diana smiled. Peter threw his pitifully small hands outward, as if he had just decided to recognize me.

"Yes, it's very good. We're not quite at the real-time movie stage yet. But we don't need anything faster. We can watch thoughts as they gather and flow through the brain."

I rubbed Pete's curved spine. "This could be the best news for monkeyhood since we decided they were our ancestors."

"Oh. Well. Fractionation carries on apace, I'm afraid. But this stuff is revolutionary. A noninvasive window onto the mind!"

She shook my shoulder with her free hand. I was grateful for this woman's existence. For her reminding me what enthusiasm was.

"Two lines of research," I listed. "Teaching. Motherhood. How many lives *are* you living, these days? I guess there's no point in asking how literary knight-errancy has been treating you lately."

She gave me a look, bafflement routed slowly by inference. That she could unpack, decode, index, retrieve, and interpret my reference at all was an unmodelable miracle. More miraculous still, I could watch her grin of understanding unfold in less than hundredth-millimeter increments, in split seconds.

"Harold's given up on our making it through Cervantes. We're doing Fielding and Smollett these days."

"You're joking. Not even the pros read those guys anymore."

"What can I tell you? Harold believes in a liberal education."

"If he wants liberal, he can do a lot better than Smollett. How about Behn? How about Kate Chopin?"

Diana caught Petey as he tried to slip from her arms. She nodded, humoring me. "Our book club isn't really for my benefit, you know."

"Oh. It's for the men who need to play Pygmalion?"

"It isn't that, exactly. Although . . ." She trailed off in a thought I could no longer trace. "Harold . . ." Her voice teetered on disclosure, then backed away. "He's a good man. A decent man." She looked up with enforced cheer. "I'm trying to bring him onto the MRI team. I think it would be good for him."

"Diana," I began. She froze in front of me, hearing the change. "I don't know how to bring this up." She waited for the blow, braced, but not flinching. I reached out to stroke Peter's ear. It didn't make things any easier.

"As far as the book club goes. It seems fulsome, even to advise you against this. But if you guys are ever curious to do a little Powers, you . . . may want to skip my third book." The one where the narrator ties her tubes in fear of bearing a child with birth defects.

"Oh," she said. Thought's turbulence again deformed her face in real time. "Oh." Smiling, the connection strengthening. "We've done that one already. You're old news."

"You've . . . ?"

"Oh yeah. I liked it. I liked the swing scene. And that moment on the lab floor. But for God's sake, you make a girl wait for it, don't you?"

I felt my face heat. "Listen. You know, I wrote that thing long before I met you."

"Well, I'm embarrassed to say, I read it long after I met you."

"I'm—I'm sorry. I hope you—I didn't know what I was talking about."

Her pitch fell to forgiveness. "No one does."

Peter began squirming again. He arched backward, ready to plunge in a dead drop. Ready to jackknife to the floor if it meant getting free. Diana snatched him back from certain destruction, as she must have done a dozen times a day since his birth. She straightened his overalls and set him on the ground. He could stand by himself, if she lent him a pant leg.

"You read my book." And still seemed game for friendship. I felt sick with unearned redemption. "You read my book. And you never told me?"

"What was I supposed to say? 'Hey, writer! Had a good jag over your words.' "

"I wish you had." I giggled, drugged with nervous release. "I could have retired by now."

I tried to go shopping. C. had to send me to the store with a list.

"Just pin it to my sleeve," I'd snarl.

"Oh, my little Beauie's afraid he's going to forget something," she goo-gooed at me, patting my head. Happier than she'd ever been in B. or U.

But the list had nothing to do with any defect of memory. I needed the list so I could match up the names she gave me with the letters printed on the inscrutable commodity labels. I needed a list to hand to a clerk. I couldn't even come close with the pronunciations. For I hadn't a clue what things were called. What things were.

One nine-hour plane flight returned me to infant trauma. My help-lessness spread well beyond making purchases. I lived in constant terror of inadvertent offense. Sometimes, when I went out, someone would upbraid me on the street. Clearly, I'd transgressed, but all I could catch would be the exasperation. They might shake a fist at some sign or printed protocol. "Can't you read?" I could hear them ask. But I did not yet have the wherewithal to answer, "No, not really."

My accidental rudeness had no end. I ran into people who greeted me warmly but whom I couldn't answer. In that first month, I met at least half of C.'s ten dozen first cousins, and couldn't keep one straight from the other. Not a person in town whom I wasn't related to. Not one who didn't know me, the first foreign import to drop in since Kilroy. And not a soul I recognized.

The smallest trip to the post office ruined me for an afternoon. I would rehearse my request in advance, like a Samoan thespian mouthing a phonetic transcription of *Long Day's Journey into Night.*

But unless the speech passed ripple-free, I was sunk. Any words from the other side of the bulletproof, muffling glass and I panicked. They might have been saying, "Very good, sir." But they might just as easily have been saying, "That's not the way it's done around here, Henk."

I missed appointments, as seven-thirty became half-eight. My age transposed into nine-and-twenty, which had that Housman lilt, but frequently turned me, in conversation, into ninety-two.

"It's good for you, man," C. informed me. "It's your turn to live in a country where they can't pronounce your name."

Nothing was what C. had prepared me for. Everything generated astonishment. The two-and-a-half gulden coin. The rainbow bank notes with artists on them instead of politicians. The queen's birthday, when the men's chorus sang "Old Black Joe." The morning bedclothes hanging out of upper-story windows. Stork sculptures that materialized on the stoops of families with newborns. Strangers greeting each other on the street. Coffee and pastry gatherings after a funeral.

The almostness of the place bewildered me more than total strangeness would have. For the few months while I still marked the contrast, society went archaic. People sang in public. They spent weeks sewing Carnaval costumes and writing occasional verses for one another. Fifteen-year-olds idled away Sundays with their grandparents. Where I came from, these things occurred only in movie nostalgia or prime-time parody.

In E., they were the unexamined norm. E.—the real, measurable E.—turned out to be a medieval village that had grown up around a bustling funeral business. The village had crashed through a sinkhole in the thin crust of time. Tinkers, cobblers, and ex–coal miners cackled to each other and scratched their heads over American television imports. They speculated hermeneutically about talking cars and cyborg heroes, then got up at sunrise the next morning to attend Gregorian mass.

Everyone and his daughter belonged to the neighborhood starting eleven or played euphonium in the pickup marching band. They donned Napoleonic militia uniforms and spent all weekend at shooting competitions, or dolled up in vestments at the drop of a wimple to do the Scatalogical Nun sketch at any gathering over ten people. That meant every other night.

Limburg remained what society had been from the first: an amateur speculation. Life, the provincials insisted, might yet be anything we told it to be.

E. condemned me to belonging. I was no more than the Foreigner, but even that bit part wound me tighter into the social web than I'd ever been in my country. People dropped by unannounced, and took offense when we waited too long to reciprocate. Every word went public. Every choice had its trial by jury. The ongoing village epic made Stateside soap opera stars seem bourgeois.

Most sacred of public tortures was Ordeal by Birthday. The victim hosted, and every walk-on in the celebrant's life dropped by for the ubiquitous coffee and flan. Relative, friend, neighbor, colleague, neighbor of friend, relative of colleague, and so on, forever. Somebody's birthday, you went. With scores of aunts and uncles, ten dozen first cousins and their spouses (all militantly fecund), untold organizational acquaintances, and neighbors all up and down the street who tracked our comings and goings, C. and I celebrated birthdays as often as we ate.

Each one moved me closer to sainthood. "This is hard for you," C. said.

"Not so bad. I'm managing." C. had not yet decided her nationality. I kept still, trying not to agitate her further. I hoped to keep the world large enough for her at last to live in. Fatal stupidity on my part. But then, I was not yet thirty.

"Can you make out any of it?" she would worry.

"Key words. It throws me when they start in dialect, catch my eye, go over to Dutch . . ."

"And lapse back the minute they turn their head." C. laughed in sympathy. "Poor Beauie."

Yet she was the one splitting down the middle.

Truth be told, I sometimes followed every word of whole birthday speeches at a shot. But if I derailed, I could go a quarter hour or more before recovering the thread. In extremis, I resorted to nodding like a narcoleptic and muttering, "I see, I see," hoping my conversant hadn't just asked me a question.

The supreme moment of character strengthening came that first year, at my birthday. "We don't have to do this, do we? We can head down to France for the weekend, or something? Leave the coffee in a thermos outside the door?"

"Beau." C. looked hurt, uncomprehending. "Are you serious?"

We baked for days. The guests started drifting through shortly after noon, and kept on drifting until midnight. Many brought gifts—a brace of pencils, a tablet of lined writing paper—tokens of small innocence North America had long ago abandoned. The relatives were saying it was okay with them, what I did for a living, even if I seemed, to most, not to do anything at all.

By that first birthday, I'd almost reached childhood. With concentration, I could follow most of Uncle Sjef's song about getting so drunk he lost his house, there just a minute ago. It helped that everyone chimed in on the chorus. After light gloss, I smiled at cousin Huub's Belgian jokes. The group story about the failed German attempt to steal the church bells I could have recited in my sleep.

I hovered, trying to keep everyone in caffeine, lager, and baked goods. "Would you like a teaspoon?" I tried to ask Tante Maria. A dike-burst of laughter all over the room told me that something had slipped 'twixt cortex and lips. C. turned blue with hilarity before I could pry the explanation out of her.

"You asked Auntie if she'd like a tit."

I gave my usual pained smile. I clowned a plea for forgiveness, but all anyone wanted of me was the next ridiculous howler.

Auntie's tit took its place in the permanent repertoire. I heard it again at three of the next five birthdays. My simple presence triggered associative smiles from assembled relatives. My little curveball slipped into the larger contour of party stories. Things meant what their telling let them. The war, the mines, the backbreak harvest, legendary weather, natural disasters, hardship's heraldry, comic come-uppance for village villains, names enshrined by their avoidance, five seconds' silence for the dead: the mind came down to narration or nothing. Each vignette, repeated until shared. Until it became true.

Birthdays formed the refrains in long, rambling ballads. Who knew the verses? Verses were written to be lost. Only that catchphrase chorus lived on after the tune.

Birthdays were life's customs posts, checkpoints on the borders of time. The community dropped by, to ask if you had anything to declare. And the only duty levied on new goods began with the triplicate phrase *That reminds me*. It took me a long time to recognize the capital under formation. Where I came from, the very idea provoked puzzlement or political suspicion. I was watching the growth of group worldliness, collective memory.

This *wereldbeeld* marked my spot for me at the continuous coffee party. I became our very own outsider. The *buitenlander* with the colorful expressions and creative charades. The man who once—just weeks before, but already mythic—asked Auntie if she wanted a tit. Second cousins once removed baited me with kind setups. What happened this week? They waited for me to give over my local hoard of experience, in the strangest of colors. Melons became monster grapes. Hearses became belated ambulances, death wagons. Zoos became beast libraries. Libraries became book gardens.

I became the living mascot, the group novelty. I was the only person the family would ever meet who had learned their language from the weirdness of print. I'd dropped out of the past, from some Golden Age travelogue. My Dutch derived from history, archive, the odd document, museum tag. Consequently, I knew the word for iconoclasm before I knew the word for string. This gave the family no end of puzzled pleasure.

I did fall back on more conventional self-teaching guides. I had a text called, in rough translation, *Dutch for Othertonguers*. I had a book of cloze-method passages. On one page, a paragraph spelled out some aspect of life here in *dit klein land*. On the next page, the same story now appeared with every fifth word missing. Story of my life.

I used, too, that ancient reader C. had carried back with her, because she could not bear to part from it. Where her parents, in that basement hole in Chicago, once used the magic book to turn *Moeder gaat de doktor halen* into *Mother goes to fetch the doctor*, I used it now to reverse the spell. *Volgend jaar zal Mei mooi zijn.* May will be fine, fine beyond telling.

I read until my eyes turned to wool. I listened and spoke until my brain went anemic. I'd come home from parties destroyed, in tears, ready to sleep forever. C. would hold me, an oversized changeling child, a monstrous cuckoo left in her nest. *"Het spijt me, Beau. Neem me niet kwalijk. Ik houd van jou. Ik houd zoveel van jou."*

I imagined I knew what she was saying.

All the while, I was busy finishing the most American book I would ever write. Disney, Mickey, the Japanese internment, the World's Fair, Trinity Site. The Hobsons, holed up in their white wood midwestern A-frame, now a fairy tale to me.

After a day of writing, I liked to walk. Village fell away to countryside, and I might have been anywhere. I lay in a cow pasture, looking up at the sky, repeating *"Hemel, hemel, hemel,"* trying to get the tag to stick to this unnamable Ruysdael. I felt my back against the chill ground and thought, *"Aarde,"* until I no longer had to think to think it.

My mood in those days ranged from sad fury to rolling, social confusion. I was worse than adrift. I stood just outside the windows of the lost domain, peeking at the blazing costume party within.

Reading out loud kept us together. Kept me in the country, when I wanted to disappear. We read Flemish comic books and Frisian poetry. We went on Poe's expedition to tropic Antarctica. We started in on the million-and-a-half-word chamber-continent of Proust. We got out. We pored over the Michelins, the Fodors, the Baedekers. We waded into the guides, either in translation or, fitfully, in our newfound original.

Helen was strange. Stranger than I was capable of imagining. She sped laugh-free through *Green Eggs and Ham*, stayed dry-eyed at *Make Way for Ducklings*, feared not throughout *Where the Wild Things*

Are. Not surprising. The symbols these shameless simulations played on had no heft or weight for her, no real-world referent.

"Skip childhood," Lentz told me. "We're running out of time."

"How is she going to know anything if we skip childhood?"

"She doesn't need to know anything." Lentz smirked. "She just has to learn criticism. Derrida knows things? Your deconstructionists are rife with wisdom? Jeez. When did you go to school? Don't you know that knowledge is passé? And you can kiss meaning bye-bye as well."

I hated him when he got arch. His archness left me so helpless with rage that I could never answer him. I knew how much Lentz believed in meaning. Helen was Lentz's meaning-paradox: our Net of nets, like some high Gothic choir, asserted significance while denying any algorithm's power to reach it. Meaning was a contour. All those wrong turns we had to bring back from the dead.

"Get cracking on the List, Marcel. Time's awasting. You want childhood? Give her *Beowulf*."

"She'll never make sense of it."

"Oh. As if you can." He punched me playfully in the shoulder. This was not the beak conducting the misanthropic midnight session of Mozart a few months earlier. Lentz was rearranging his own firmware in a way we weren't supposed to be able to do.

"Sense is pattern, Ricky-boy. Give her some patterns and see how she arranges them."

I sometimes talked with Helen from the English Building, through a terminal ethernetted to the campus-wide backbone. That way, Lentz could use his office for real science while I continued the training. Archaic wood and incandescence gave numbing rote the feel of a grand, nineteenth-century anatomy lecture. I had my library there as well, the books Helen soon had to study.

Perhaps I also meant to scope out the competition. Bring the fight home, into the enemy's HQ. The English Building crawled with twenty-two-year-olds, frantic with the impending Exam. Each one had made the same error in judgment, giving their lives over to books. Each had disappointed some father, whom they'd hoped only to delight forever with their ability to read and write. Not one believed they would ever get a real job.

I watched them up close, our opponents, the curators of the written language. I moved about among them, a double agent. I listened around the mailboxes, in the coffee room. Criticism had gotten more involuted while I was away. The author was dead, the text-function a plot to preserve illicit privilege, and meaning an ambiguous social construction of no more than sardonic interest. Theory had grown too difficult for me, too subtle. It out-Heroded Herod. The idea seemed to be that if mind were no more than shrill solipcism, then best make a good performance of it.

But the apprentice wordkeepers: here were my old lost friends in photocopy, only younger than I had ever been. Most were peach-fuzzed posthumanists, pimply with neo-Marxist poststructuralism. They wielded an ironic sophistication Helen would never be able to interpret, let alone reproduce. I didn't even want her to hear the tropes.

The halls rippled with an intellectual energy steeped in aggression. It took me a long time to see what that energy was. It was fear. Fear that everything theory professed might be true. Pure panic that the world didn't need them anymore.

It took just as long, mingling on the outskirts, to learn what had happened to me. I'd been gone no longer than a semester. I'd come back to the standing, eternal crew. Almost the same roster, down to their names. The only difference was that nobody hung out anymore. Folks were busy, needing two books and ten articles by age twenty-five to keep one's head above professional floodwaters.

Or perhaps the press was less industry than embarrassment. Conversation dropped to hushed flusters when I tried to join in. My offers to stand this year's successful master's candidates a round of beers were met by a chorus of "Sounds good" that dissolved in polite postponements.

One day, a grad I had several times exchanged nods with stopped me in the hall and began, "Mr. Powers, could I get you to sign this paperback?" At last it struck me. I'd betrayed my old mates. I'd done the unforgivable. Let myself get old.

After that, I read increasingly to Helen from my English office.

Books were about a place we could not get back to. Something in my voice when there might give her that little interpretive leg up.

The building's vague ache of background radiation emanated from one room, up on the third floor. I managed never to walk past it, but it swelled in my avoidance. I hadn't stepped into that room since I turned adult. I sat two flights below, in my office with its Magritte fireplace, forgetting. As if forgetting were something that could be actively engineered.

I gave Helen Blake's "Poison Tree." Way premature. I wondered what I could have been thinking. I was thinking, not of the lines, but of the day I got them:

> I was angry with my friend:
> I told my wrath, my wrath did end.
> I was angry with my foe:
> I told it not, my wrath did grow.

"What does that mean, Helen?" I never let up on her, with this whole meaning thing.

She struggled to form the generalization. She made things up now, when she didn't know. I took that as a great step forward.

"It means, things that you say . . ." I prompted her. She could usually complete a sentence form with some paraphrase of the words just fed her.

"Things that you say disappear."

"And things you don't say . . . ?"

"Things you don't say get bigger."

Forget wealth versus poverty, belief versus doubt, power versus helplessness, public versus private. Never mind man versus woman, center versus margins, beautiful versus horrifying, master contra slave, even good against evil. Saying or not saying: that was where experience played out. Going away versus getting worse. What things came down to.

I needed at least to see if the room still existed. Enough time had passed. Standing in the doorway and looking would not kill me.

I climbed the patched stairs, light-headed and short of breath. I did the two floors in a deliberate, directed haze. Automatic. On muscle memory alone. I pushed my body forward, the way a sixteen-year-old dials the phone to ask for his first-ever date. The way a doctor sentences an 11:15 clinic appointment to fatal path reports.

I mounted without thinking. Thought would have inhibited action. I'd reach that room only if I got to it before I knew where I was going. I pulled up in the middle of an ordinary classroom, deserted, on the small side. A blackboard bore the message "Thurs. 3:30–5:00," ringed by a smeared white corral of eons-old microorganism skeletons. The linoleum floors had darkened into a color somewhere between the Forest of Arden and the wine-dark sea. A circle of warped wooden chair-desks had been hastily abandoned. *Waneth the watch*, I would someday try to tell Helen. *But the world holdeth.*

Nothing had happened here in this room's hundred years. Nothing that bore remembering. I started to shake. Each breath set off a body-length shudder. I could not imagine how things had gotten so cold. The two dormer windows we always had to open, even in winter, because the radiator could not be shut off, demurred above me, closed.

I don't know what I wanted. Some spectral second glance at the teacher in action. The chance to ask why the world refused to answer to the poems he'd made us memorize. I needed to revise the place—first love, discovery, vocation, eighteen. To do take two. The update. Correct the shape, improve the story I'd made of where I'd been.

I should have tried something out loud. Something from one of those beaten-up anthologies, the crumbling bastions of the spent, pre-posthumanist tradition. Taylor could recite all the way back to the foundations. We would not be civilized until we could remember. He died knowing stuff he had committed to permanence at an age when the rest of us were learning *Engine, engine, Number 9.* Whole cantos, half-chapters from books even the titles of which I had forgotten.

A bell rang, one of those forlorn indicators of ten to the hour and class change. I left on command. The scrimshawed wood corridor complained at my weight, for some reason still insistent after all these dry-aired winters.

I hit the head of the stairwell, *Middlemarch* under my breath. I rounded the landing, unlooking. Maybe I never looked. Maybe I always navigated by toe-tap and hope. Halfway into the second flight, I heard a creak that wasn't me. I sighted down, along my path. It was A., the page-boy mirage I'd seen late at night, while proofing copy.

This time I knew her name. I'd tracked her down to an official departmental photograph, which led in turn to her CV. I'd learned that she was a second-year master's candidate. She had graduated from college the year my third book came out. The fact appalled me.

Seeing her again, I realized how often I had seen her since, from the end of endless halls. Only now A. was real, bounding upstairs, a meter in front of my descent. She exuded blue, robin's egg, adventure, the cerulean tidal pool. She breathed like a sleeping child, like the held breath of friends gathered in a too-small house on the eve of holidays.

I snagged on her face as she glanced up, scanning mine. Instant, reflex presumption; it made me ill. Yet I knew her.

I had to keep from greeting her. My pulse doubled, cutting my intelligence in half. My skin went conductive. In the time it took me to drop another step, a bouillabaisse of chemical semaphores seeped up through my pores and spilled out to wet the air.

She must have known. She looked away, giving no indication. Her face stayed in absolute neutral, a gear beyond adopting. Two quick strides and she skipped past a near brush with literature.

I bottomed out at the base of the stairwell. I stood, winded, like a hawk-reprieved mouse. Like an agoraphobe giving a plenary speech. I would have laughed at myself, had I been able to catch my breath.

Not only could I no longer write fiction. I could no longer live fact. I'd lost fundamental real-word skills while away. The same skills I was trying to instill in Helen.

I had learned too much cognitive neuroscience. The more I read about how the mind worked, the flakier mine became. The symptoms had been coming on for a few weeks. Faces touched off self-fulfilling panic: how will you remember this person's name? Some days before, I'd crossed a street to get to the five side when looking for an address ending in zero. Monitoring my own processes, I felt myself pitching into the ditch alongside the famous test-case centipede after the reductionists asked him how he kept track of which leg moved next.

For months, my bedtime stories had spun a decameron of long-term potentiation, recategorizing, neuronal group selection, transmitter and junctional molecules. Now, for some reason, my low-level structures, blinded by the harsh light that life's interrogation used to extract its confessions, decided to pull an Aschenbach. A Humbert Humbert. One of those old fools in Chaucer, Shakespeare, Restoration comedy, nineteenth-century epistolary vicarage farces. I meant to make an idiot of myself.

By the time I got back to the office, my replay of the woman ascending a staircase had become one of those late-show reruns you wish they'd get a new print of. A.: the face, the name, the stranger I'd been writing to, all my writing life. All those friends whom I, confused, thought dead. The grave where buried love lived.

I disappeared from English. Went back and set up shop at the Center. Paralysis I had already. I didn't need to compound it with obsession. Three weeks without seeing A. and she'd go ephemeron, would damp down from active memory trace. She'd stop making unsponsored appearances, and I'd stop wanting her to.

Work helped. I sublimated all unquenchable hormonal flare-up desires to read that infinitely suffering creature my favorite stanzas from *Piers Plowman* by candlelight. Instead I read to the spreading neural net. Several times a week I invented painful contrivances by which I might introduce myself to A. Each time I did nothing but go and talk to Helen.

Speech baffled my machine. Helen made all well-formed sentences. But they were hollow and stuffed—linguistic training bras. She sorted nouns from verbs, but, disembodied, she did not know the difference between thing and process, except as they functioned in clauses. Her predications were all shotgun weddings. Her ideas were as decorative as half-timber beams that bore no building load.

She balked at metaphor. I felt the annoyance of her weight vectors as they readjusted themselves, trying to accommodate my latest caprice. You're so hungry you could eat a horse. A word from a friend ties your stomach in knots. Embarrassment shrinks you, amazement strikes you dead. Wasn't the miracle enough? Why do humans need to say everything in speech's stockhouse except what they mean?

A certain kind of simile fell naturally into her trained neurode clusters. Helen's own existence hinged on metaphor-making. In fact, associative memory itself was like a kind of simile. Three-quarters of the group of neurodes that fired when faced with, say, a whale might remain intact when depicting a thing that seemed, whatever the phrase meant, very like one. Such a constellation of common firings became, in a way, shadowpaint shorthand for some shared quality.

After all, the world's items had no real names. All labels were figures of speech. One recognized a novel item as a box by comparing it to a handful of examples so small it fit into a single dimple of an egg carton. In time, one learned without being taught. Rode without the training wheels. Somehow, the brain learned to recognize whole categories, to place even those things seen for the first time.

This much simile Helen could live with. But the higher-order stuff drove her around the simulated bend. Love is like ghosts. Love is like linen. Love is like a red, red rose. The silence of her output layers at such triggers sounded like exasperation. A network should not seem but be.

Yes, yes: we know what the thing is like. But what *is* it? And then I, too, would be overwhelmed. Any task in the garden seemed easier than pruning her responses, for her responses, however grammatical, were bewilderment incarnate. Her ideas were well shaped, her syntax sound. But her *sense*: her sense hailed from the far side of the painted veil. I can no more remember its otherness than I can recall the curve of a dream before its red-penciling by the Self.

I revived a little by reminding us both that I didn't have to tell Helen what things meant. Context spun out its own filament. The study questions themselves laddered the world's labelless data into a recognizable index. The accumulated weight of sorted sentences had to self-gloss, or Helen would die before she could come to life.

Helen's nets struggled to assert the metaphors I read her. She ratified them through backtracking, looking for a corner where they might fit into the accreting structure. She gamed the *ur*-game, puzzling out evolution's old brainteaser, find the similarity. A is like B. Mind in its purest play is like some bat. Speech is like embroidered tapestries. God's light is like a lamp in a niche. Greek is like lace. A pretty girl is like a melody. A people without history is like the wind on the buffalo grass. How?

"My heart is like a singing bird," I told Helen. There didn't seem to be any harm in it. She still had several months to learn about irony and lies.

"What is singing?" she asked. That capacity still floored me. When her associative matrix dead-ended now, she asked for openings. Something inside her web told her her web needed supplementing.

"The bird is singing," I assured her. "But my heart feels the way a singing bird must feel."

I failed the test of interpretation I was training her to pass. I missed Helen's question altogether.

I tried her out on a longer Rossetti exercise. At that point, I didn't hope for comprehension. Rather, I read to her as one might recite genealogies to a child. No meaning; just a tune she might one day set words to:

> When I am dead, my dearest,
> Sing no sad songs for me;
> Plant thou no roses at my head,
> Nor shady cypress tree.
> Be the green grass above me
> With showers and dewdrops wet;
> And if thou wilt, remember
> And if thou wilt, forget.

I thought she'd stumble over the "thou" or the "wilt," the "plant no X nor Y." My fears showed how little I knew what went on in Helen's hidden layers. Her neurodes connected far more to themselves than to the outside interface.

"What does it mean," she asked me, "Sing no sad songs?" She

could treat clauses as objects. Her speech turned the recursive crank of endlessness.

The question surprised me. Not what I'd expected. "It means, 'Don't be sorry.' People sing songs at funerals. Singing can be a way of missing or memorializing someone. Of saying goodbye. The person saying these words doesn't want to be remembered that way."

Helen had to spell things out for me. People were idiots. No, no, no. From the top. "How do you sing?"

I had gone on one of those glorious demented sidetracks, the hallmark of intelligence. The ability to use everything in the lexicon to answer except the answer.

I'd given her "The bird is singing," "The poet's heart is singing," even "Grief is singing," when all the poor girl needed was "Uttering pure-toned pitches in time sequence is singing." Writing struck me as so impossible, my years as a novelist so arrogant, that I could have lived that life only through blatant fabrication.

How do you sing? All I could think to do was demonstrate. Assume a virtue, if you have it not. Failing to say what a thing was, I could at least put an instance in her ears.

When I returned to the lab two days later, I thought I'd dialed a wrong number. Even before I reached the door, it hit me. Sound rolled out into the hall, shock waves in bonsai packages. I'd heard music emanate from Lentz's suite once before. But this was the air of a new planet. I rounded the corner, ready already to be dead.

Inside, Helen was singing. Through her terminal mouthpiece, she sang the song she'd heard me sing. What else could she? She sang *Bounce me high, bounce me low, bounce me up to Jericho.* A song I'd sung once as a child, when hired by an opera company to portray a small boy. My sung, staged simulation of childhood. Helen sang in an extraterrestrial warble, the way deaf people sing. But I recognized that tune in one note.

Lentz sat behind his desk, hands pressed to his neck. He had not moved since arriving, however long ago that had been. Even through the bank glass of his specs, I saw vinegary damp.

"You did this to her, Powers!" I knew where I'd heard that mock indignation before. I recognized it, after one training. My father, the summer before his death, laughing as he scolded my older sister: *How can you do this to me? How can you make me a grandfather?*

I'd done nothing. A kludge of morphologies—implementations within implementations, maps that had learned to map each other—passed a milestone we hadn't even hoped to set her. Lentz and I stood by, winded, pulses racing. All we could do was listen.

She auditioned the tune. Bounce me high. Bounce me low. Only by hearing it out loud, in her own voice, could Helen probe the thing, test it against itself.

She was stuck on the first phrase, that unfinished half-stich, because that's all I'd sung her. Because that's where I had stuck. After twenty-five years, I could not remember how the rest of the tune went. Over and back Helen hummed, not knowing she possessed but half the melodic story. Bounce me up to Jericho. Lack of tonal resolution did not faze her. No one told her that tunes were supposed to come home to tonic. This was the only one anybody had ever sung her.

And in that moment, I understood that I, too, would never have a handle on metaphor. For here was the universe in a grain of literal sand. Singing—enabled, simulated on a silicon substrate. I felt how a father must feel, seeing his unconscious gestures—pushing back a forelock or nudging the sink cabinet shut with a toe—picked up and mimicked by a tiny son.

"Lentz," I whispered, so as not to distract the miracle, "is this what it's like to be a parent?"

Very like, his eyes leaked back. And I saw what it meant to want that awful next step, tasting oneself from the outside, in a flash of constructed recognition. To say the thing I made I did not make and is not mine. To know in Polaroid advance that hour when all life's careful associations will come undone.

Less than a year after we moved to E., we got a letter from the Taylors. I wrote them often, for after we bolted, I needed word from U. more than I ever did while living there. They wrote back jocular stuff: "Don't you two realize the age of Europe is over and that of North America is following in its wake? Get back over here before it's too late."

Taylor had so little time to reply that any word was an event. I kept the envelope sealed, thinking it would be fun to read to C. when she got home from her latest temp job. We'd marvel at Tayloresque sentences together, over the dinner I prepared for her.

I watched C. step off the bus, waving from the balcony as I did each evening. She shot me back one of those terrified, fatigued, smiling, full-body waves that never failed to cut right through me. The letter is dated September 17, but it must have been a cold fall. C. was already swallowed by that giant navy coat that ran all the way down to her ankles.

In the kitchen, she danced a little jig at the sight of the letter. Anything that made me happy might increase the chances for our transplantation. "Come on, Beauie. Read it, you loony-tick. What in the world are you waiting for?"

I slit the packet open and read:

"Dear Rick and C.,

"Belatedly, I take up pen, first to thank you for your welcome tape of good music and loved voices. Similarly welcome have been the letters, which I have meant to answer every day. Recent weeks have both dragged and hurried, creeping by the minute but vanishing into an unreal limbo so that even less than usual am I able to believe that months have passed since we have seen you . . .

"For nearly a full month I have had a succession of terrible waits after tests, each of which finished a three- or four-day vigil with more bad news. CAT scan, bronchoscopy, bone scan, and finally a week in the hospital for removal of a piece of rib for bone biopsy determined that in addition to a main tumor in the right lung I have cancerous bone in the left rib cage, ruling out an operation and leaving radiation and chemotherapy as treatment. The only test with encouraging results showed no evidence of metastasis to brain . . .

200

"Since then, my silence has been caused by effects of treatment. The dreaded nausea did not last long, but loss of appetite and weight did, and a fatigue so profound that I can't adequately describe it. My muscles have atrophied and I spend most of my time lying down. I am good for little more than harvesting the odd tomato, gathering windfall apples, picking some late-planted lettuce . . .

"Our long silence is terribly misleading. Your departure left a large emptiness that has been italicized by this illness and our being more solitary than usual. If we possessed ESP, you would have been deluged by messages from here. Still, it is a pleasure to imagine the two of you together in the wide variety of settings you manage to inhabit. My life would seem pretty bounded-in-a-nutshell by any measure, but your joint enthusiasm in getting out and seeing the world is overwhelming.

"I've exhausted my pitiable energy, though not my love. The best way you can please me is to promise that my illness will not lead you to even the slightest tendency to avoid pleasure out of affectionate empathy. Try to adopt the opposite attitude; let me hope that thoughts of me will enhance pleasures I'd enjoy, too, if we were together."

After the first paragraph, I looked up at C. But we'd read too far to pretend the message away. I got through the whole history. Finishing, I looked up across the widening kitchen table at the college girl who had sat with me on the Quad, when still young enough to believe in consolation. This was the same woman, the same panicked doe, in the same glare that life keeps training on us until we can no longer even dread it.

An awful half-second stutter step, and C. said, "You'll have to go back to the States."

"Just to see him, at least," I pleaded, the exact reaction her reflex generosity meant to stave off. But I was not pleading with C.

I flew back to U., numb to the new feel of the place. Taylor could still get out. We went to a nearby woods. We talked. He knew he was done. The only thing for it was presence of mind. Taylor brought along his camera, took a snap of me. I wanted to take one of him, fix him forever. But Taylor had already begun to waste away and refused to be captured like that.

I showed him the excerpt from my new book that had just appeared in a glossy literary weekly. Taylor, for whose approval I'd developed my labyrinthine style, delighted in the piece's uncharacteristic breeziness. He delighted even more when I told him how much I'd been paid. "A dollar a word! That has a solid ring to it."

I had done what everyone in Taylor's line, what he himself had once dreamed of doing. I could wake up every morning and devote myself to making worlds. People read my inventions and wrote about them in turn. My words had grown careers of their own. My overnight success gave Taylor such pleasure that I couldn't bring myself to tell him I meant to quit fiction.

"I didn't want to burden you with such a prediction when you were an eighteen-year-old kid memorizing 'The Windhover.'" He beamed. "But however much luck always plays into such things, it was possible, even then, to imagine your getting away with something like this."

We turned to the real issue. He protected me from what his disease was doing to him. He seemed, for half an hour, the equal of any formulation he had made before the tumor came alive inside him. I asked him whether, at that stage of the illness, literature helped much. Did it make things any clearer, any easier?

Taylor stayed as brutally forthright with me as ever. He thought for a moment, to get the prosody right. "I would say that literature is not entirely irrelevant, in this circumstance. But it's not quite central, either."

Before we headed home, I asked if he had any regrets. Anything he still needed to do. Taylor told me then that, to his mind, the only two careers worth striving for were doctor and musician. I could not tell how figurative he was being.

Taylor sickened. I found a house-sit in the neighborhood, and came by every day. I sat with him as he napped, or I read to him, or we watched sports on television. Sometimes we talked, but never again like that day in the woods.

He lost his appetite, shrank to insubstantial nothing. His gut stopped working. His skin gained purple-green highlights and his joints grew smooth as polished metal. When muscles gave out, he cupped his question-mark head in both hands. He sat in the sunroom until he could no longer sit up. Then we moved him upstairs, into his long bed.

He asked me to check out some books from the library, so he could prepare to teach his class in January.

M., his wife, remained rocklike. She exuded competence beyond belief. She lifted the skeletal Taylor out of bed and carried him— Mary holding a puppet Christ—deflated and naked, to the toilet, in her arms.

Only his mind remained luminous. Near the end, the medications did change him. But even then, his topographies fought to keep themselves intact. One afternoon before Christmas, I found Taylor in a state that was not quite sleep, but could pass for sleep in low light.

"Oh, it's you!" he greeted me. "All day long, the sounds outside this window have been turning into events from my past."

He went on to tell me, in devastating detail, about the valley of his childhood, out West. The names of all his classmates and the ways each had distinguished or humiliated himself in coming of age. The frozen rabbits hanging on the barn wall that kept the family alive all winter. Every single title in the valley library, outread and exhausted by fourteen.

Before I left town, I put another book in Taylor's hands. One for the permanent record. One he would never read. I gave him the first bound galley of my second book, *Prisoner's Dilemma*.

Number two was my memorial to a sick father. In it, I described every impasse of history but his. Only the passage of years, only knowing I'd never show Richard Powers, Sr., what fiction had done to him, made that fiction possible.

I told Taylor about my father. How I'd broken his heart. His lover's quarrel with the world. His disappearance at the end, his one last frontier adventure. I told Taylor about the cryptic absolution Dad sent me from the Yukon. The cremation of Sam McGee.

At my mention of the name, Taylor's lips crooked. Astonishingly, the man to whom I owed my Shakespeare and Yeats, my Marx and Freud, launched into a full rendition of the hack ballad. He did not miss a stanza. Death had no more dominion over him.

"I don't know how to say goodbye," I told Taylor. The book was my goodbye, because symbols are all that become of the real. They change us. They make us over, alter our bodies as we receive and remake them. The symbols a life forms along its way work back out of the recorder's office where they wait, and, in time, they themselves go palpable. Lived.

I left, knowing he had at best days, and at worst a month. Nothing left to do. The old friends were everywhere in attendance. Maybe I should have stayed. Stood and waited. Maybe he could have used having me around.

"Make a noise," he ordered as I took off. "See the world."

"I will," I promised. "And I'll keep you posted."

In the short night, eastward above the Atlantic, I thought of the last time I'd made the crossing. My life in U. was dead. I'd gone back to that cow town once too often. I told myself I would never get near it again.

But U. caught up with me, even in my foreign country. And that death was far worse, faced alone in E. C. and I lay on the floor of our apartment, in hypothermia, and listened to the tape of the memorial service, the fiddle tunes, that whole unbroken circle of friends telling Taylor stories, recounting their local eulogies for the man who thought only memory stood between us and randomness.

Each person who knew him surrendered some private lode of remembered event. Or they read from the page one of the poems Taylor himself did from effortless memory. They read Blake and Rossetti and Stevens. No one read "Sam McGee," because the one who was supposed to read it was lying on the floor in a little ex-coal-mining town on the other side of the world, listening to the belated tape, shivering, wrecked forever by memory.

I could give back nothing to Taylor, I, who couldn't even find a way to tell him what he had given me. All I could do for Taylor now was to turn him into character.

I held on to C., giving in to my only available response. She probably knew I would backslide long before the idea hit me. *One more book*, I pleaded with her, wordlessly. I needed to postpone my graduation from lying long enough to tell a double love story. To turn a helical twist that might both eulogize the man and let me live, before it was too late, the life in science from which he'd long ago deflected me.

Helen did not sing the way real little girls sang. Technically, she almost passed. Her synthesized voice skittered off speech's earth into tentative, tonal Kitty Hawk. Her tune sounded remarkably limber, given the scope of that mechanical tour de force.

But she did not sing for the right reasons. Little girls sang to keep time for kickball or jump ropes. The little boy soprano I had played onstage at twelve had been doing that. Singing the tune I'd taught Helen, keeping imitative time by bouncing a ball against a pasteup shop door.

Helen didn't have a clue what keeping time meant, never having twirled a jump rope, let alone seen one. We'd strengthened her visual mapping, but true, real-time image recognition would have required vastly more computer power than the entire Center drew. And we were already living beyond our quota.

If Helen had a temporal sense now, it came from a memory strong enough to remember configurations it was no longer in. And mark the passing of her changing, internal states. God only knows the look and feel of a sense of time without a sense of space. But that was Helen.

"You were not, yesterday," she would say to me, whether I'd been gone three hours or three days. "Yesterday" stood for any state that Helen had watched get swallowed up by its successor. "You" presumably meant that generic, external irritant that laid data on her input layers. "Were not" was her simplistic idea of negation. Although she had still to learn that absence and presence were not opposites, she was well on her way to a functional understanding of loneliness, that font of all knowledge.

One day she added, "I miss you."

The thing canonical writers always said in print. I wanted to tell her that she ought not to put the formulation in the present tense while I sat right there at the mike and keyboard. I said nothing, not wanting to undo the example of the rhymers she imitated with anything so trivial as convention.

"I miss Muffet," she went on. In growing savvy enough for figurative speech, she'd become too softheaded for the literal. Either that, or she was engaging in the neural network equivalent of silliness. If she could sing, I reasoned, I could certainly train her to giggle.

I mailed the finished copy of my fourth book to New York on the day Los Angeles set itself on fire. My story predicted that explosion, although such a prediction took no special gift. Mine was less prophecy, anyway, than memory. A child's recollected nightmare.

The prepublication notices of the book appeared not long after. Soon enough for human recollection, in any event. The most visible of the trade-press reviews dubbed the book "a bedtime tale set in a future apocalypse." This denial stuck. Everything I'd written about Angel City and its war on childhood had already played out. But so many of the subsequent reviews pushed memory into the not-yet that I began to think I had, in fact, written my first attempt at speculative fiction.

The reviews were not all bad. Chicago glowed, saving my appointment at the Center and preserving face with the home crowd. The best notice, remarkably, came from that national paper sold in street boxes designed to resemble TVs. It spoke of homeopathy, of narrating the worst so the worst did not have to happen.

Most critics, though, felt the reader had to work too hard for too bleak a payoff.

Lentz delighted in the harshest press judgments. It became almost impossible to train Helen while he was around.

He entered the office crowing, "Look who's here! If it isn't my favorite manufacturer of literary astonishments. Which is not to say a good novelist," he added, graciously patronizing, "although you are that, too."

This was the lead from that same glossy with the twenty-million worldwide circulation that yesterday had predicted such a full future for me.

"Did you memorize the entire piece, Philip?"

"Just the good parts."

"You haven't wasted your weekend, have you?"

"I notice you recognized the allusion. I bet you could do the closing bit as well. You know: 'Little brother has failed to invent a story'?"

But my career had not yet been decided. All juries hung on word from the sole review anyone ever seemed to pay attention to. The institution had gone monolithic, as if the pieces appearing there no longer derived from individuals, each locked inside their sensibilities and foibles, but formed the consulates of a single, unified State Department of literary taste. An algorithm of aesthetic appropriateness.

A mixed decision in that paper of record, even a late one, could pretty much close the cover on you before anyone had a chance to open it. I avoided looking. I'd never done especially well there, and this time I was so far out on a narrative limb that I knew I was ripe for amputation. Besides, I didn't have to seek out judgment. Judgment would come looking for me.

It did, one Monday morning. I was at the console in Lentz's office, talking to Helen about ignorant armies clashing by night. The infinite repetition of supervised training had given way to a more unstructured give-and-take, where I might read a given set of lines to her a few times, if that, and carry on, letting her do the evaluating internally.

Out of the corner of my eye—how to explain to her that spheres might have corners?—I watched Lentz bound in. He carried all twenty-five pounds of the Sunday edition, nonchalantly, just taking all the world news that fit out for a spin. He dropped the pile on his already cluttered desk with a resounding thud.

I saw him, through the back of my head, without turning. He picked up the top section of the mass. "What's this? The *Book Review*?

What's this? New fiction by Richard Powers?" A parody of Wemmick, in my favorite Dickens passage. And so, twice the pain per word.

"Listen to this, Marcel. This will interest you:

"In every reader's mental library, there are books that are remembered with admiration and books that are remembered with love.

"It goes on—"

"That's all right, Philip. I get the picture."

"No, really. It says you are all right, in your own peculiar way. Just a little flawed. It says you could be good if you just kept your story simple, with lovable characters. Like *The Diary of Anne Frank.*"

We had sat in front of that girl's house, C. and I, at dusk two years before. Up in the city for a day's sightseeing, too broken by that After-house of time to want, anymore, to move. We could not even bring ourselves to put our arms around each other.

"Hey! You could read that story to our little apparatus, couldn't you? In the original, I mean. Now, that would throw the poor girl for a loss. She wouldn't even know what hit her."

I could not look at Helen, because Helen was nowhere. I looked at the open anthology next to the microphone. "Dover Beach" seemed a sad irrelevance.

"Should we read her the review?" Lentz cackled. He scanned the page, smirking and shaking his head. "You'll forgive me if I take this like a bad winner? I'd like to think that I'm not losing a novelist friend. I'm gaining a long-term unpaid lab assistant."

I walked out, leaving Lentz chiding me with apologies and Helen wondering what had become of Matthew Arnold.

Drama got me as far as the atrium. One of those drizzly midwinter days that U. excelled in. I wasn't about to bike home. I made my way to the cafeteria where, too early, I bought lunch. Plover and Hartrick sat at a table, nursing juices. I steered myself toward them. Their conversation, rapid and personal, broke off as I pulled up.

"Keep talking," I said, nodding at their notebooks, closed on the table in front of them. "I'm just the humanist fly on the wall."

Plover examined my tray of onion rings and Italian beef. "Don't eat grease, Rick. Grease will kill you."

"Leave him be," Diana scolded. "He's too young to start being healthy."

"I know half a dozen people who have had heart attacks in their early thirties."

"Harold. Quit with the Jeremiah thing already." Diana turned to me. "We were just talking about yesterday's piece in the *Times*." She smiled. "Sorry!" Friendly, singsong, not heavily invested. The empirical bias. As if peer review weren't that consequential. As if a person's work was what it was, unchanged by decree.

Harold looked in my face. "I haven't read the book. But I know from my clinical days that people who have just undergone breakups of long relationships tend to see the world in apocalyptic terms."

Taken aback, all over the map. "Your clinical days?"

"Oh yeah. I used to think we knew enough about the way the mind works to put that knowledge to good use in the field. But I was much older then."

Diana snorted. "Harold likes to blame things on his inner child."

"Uh, if I've walked into the middle of something here, I can—"

A voice behind me declared, "Powers's inner child is about eighty and hobbles around on a crutch."

Lentz, breathing heavily, fresh coffee cup in tow, joined us. I made my face a blank.

"Coffee will kill you, Philip," Plover intoned. "Ach, God! Not cream, too. And sugar!" Harold clutched his cheeks in two Munch-like hands.

Diana spoke askance, as if to colleagues who had not yet joined us. "Rick's inner child may have progeria. But his outer child died at—what would you say, Rick? Eleven? Twelve?"

I started to grin, relieved. "You've read the book? Already?"

She said nothing. My muscles fell. I looked like someone who had goosed a friend's bottom at a crowded party, only to have the surprised person turn around and reveal themselves a perfect stranger.

"You hated it?" Dead silence. "You hated it."

"You sound surprised," Diana said.

My turn to say nothing.

"Oh, Ricky. You know it's brilliant, and all that. But it's so horrid. Misanthropic. Couldn't you have thrown us at least one little sop of hope?"

"I thought I had."

"Not enough."

"Would you buy it as homeopathy?"

"Homeopaths use very small doses. Look. We're all overwhelmed. We're all bewildered. Why read in the first place, if the people who are supposed to give us the aerial view can't tell us anything except what an inescapable mess we're in?"

The four of us sat looking everywhere but at one another. Her words rocked back and forth in me, like the last wake of a small craft.

"You're teaching the next book club section," Harold told her.

Lentz shook his head and pursed his lips. "There are books you love. And then there are books . . ."

But I had never once put fingers to keys for anything but love. I had written a book about lost children because I had lost my own child and wanted it back. More than I wanted anything in life, except to write.

Any hope that I might somehow be able to return to making fiction died at Diana's words. My work in progress was a sham, no more than a sentence climbing snowy mountain tracks in a cartoon of wartime. I was working from nothing but the desire to fulfill a contract. I would return the advance for the unwritten book to New York and call it a day.

Picture a train heading south. It works its wounded veterans over the mountain passes to a sweet, imaginary country called—by coincidence, just like the real one—Italy. Not Italy in the original edition, but taking that place's name now and in all subsequent printings.

Imagine yourself traveling to a country where you won't be sick anymore. This country is full of the thing you want most. As much of it as you ever dared ask for. Whatever that thing is. The one thing that means more to you than anything.

This country is a continuous outdoor café. When all else about the account fades like a moldy fresco, this image lives on in your inner travelogue. In this country, at this café, you can sit in the sun from dawn till dusk. On the piazza. The piazza d'. Your private pool of shade remains bathed in unimaginable azure. And iced drinks on endless tab.

You can sit on this terrace for as long as you ever wanted. The terrace is life's arrival. All you need do is picture it.

No one can chase you away, and you can do whatever you like, until closing. Until the next chapter. Watch women walking across the public square. Read. Read this story, if you like. Or talk. Toast the waiter. Sing. Listen to the next table sing. Anything.

You have never thought twice about cafés, but you might like to sit in one now. You would like to order, then spread out a book in front of you. Sit and watch people walking, from a distance. A pleasure, just to picture this pleasure. This description, the sun, the one desirable thing, yours for the asking.

Reading: yes. Of course. To spend all day—that nom de plume for "forever"—doing nothing but reading! Just entertaining the thought, just following the idea fleshes out a scenario of composite delight. Your one surreptitious afternoon in the sunny countryside, exiled, at the last minute, from wartime, from inescapable disaster.

When I came home to E., things were different. Different again. Still different.

To my astonishment, I now passed for fluent. A demotic, misleading fluency, in fact, became my undoing. A week after losing it, lying on the floor of the apartment listening to the cassette of Taylor's funeral, I found myself walking past E.'s modest hardware store. I turned in, deciding on a whim to buy an item we had needed for as long as I'd lived in Limburg.

As they always did in E.'s archaic shops, the salesperson greeted me on entry and asked to be of help.

"Good afternoon. I'm looking for this mechanical device, about yay big. It's a gizmo with an adjustable center pivot that allows you to apply increased torque . . ."

"Hmm. N-no, I don't think we have anything like that here, sir." She gestured with her palms outward. You see where you are: a pocket, one-church town. Little call for the esoteric. "You might try Maastricht."

"No, no. It's a common little commodity. Every home has one. You might use it to fix your plumbing, or tighten a loose dowel rod . . ."

Her face stayed blank, helpful but passive. Finally, something I said broke through. Her expression fled from confusion to anger in the space of one thought.

"Do you mean a wrench?"

"That's it!" I shouted.

"Then why the hell didn't you say you wanted a wrench?"

I had been better off with the impenetrable accent and the babble grammar. I'd communicated more when the only words I had were "I don't have the words."

I went about in a daily grief that, like Taylor on the effects of his chemo, I could not describe adequately in the most native of languages. C. mistook that sadness. She felt it directed at her, at her idea to move us to this invented place.

She grew defensive, self-accusing. "I know you love me, Beau. But you don't need any of this."

"Any of what?"

"I'm not sure I need any of it either. What are we doing here? My parents don't need me to take care of them, do they? They chose to come back here all by themselves."

"A good choice, no?"

"Oh yes. They're happier here than they ever were in Chicago. They haven't a minute to themselves."

"What's the problem? I thought the point was to discover what nationality you were."

"I'm further from that than I was in the States. I look at myself, and I can't even recognize what I've become."

"Gone native?"

C. laughed, protecting me. "Sometimes this country drives me up the bloody wall. The village patrol, eyeing every irregular behavior. The social agenda, all worked out for you in advance. The *gezelligheid*. The close little shops. The lines for everything. The little old ladies shoving you out of the way, or choosing the narrowest possible aisle in the densest country on earth to stop and gossip. Nothing's ever open. Half the country's on the dole."

"You sound like the American ambassador."

"And I've dragged you into the middle of all this!"

"I'm fine. I'm having a great time." A lie on the surface. But not, if this meant anything, deep down. "We can walk to four major language regions from our front stoop. Two hours away from three of the world's greatest museums. And green herring by the bucket. I'd never have had this chance. Except for you, C."

That much was true, even on the surface. Her gamble had thrown open all possibility, however much possibility now upended us.

When my second book came out, C.'s restlessness pitched into the distress bands. Publication of a novel is a nonevent arranged to look like news. *Prisoner* produced a spate of statements, positioning my career on the turnpike of contemporary letters like a dot on the AAA Triptiks. The point often seemed to be to spare people the inconvenience of reading.

It killed C. to read that I was a fresh commodity to keep an eye on. That I was intensely private. That I lived in U., when in fact I lived in E., where the shopkeepers scolded me for linguistic perversity. That I was a fast-rising star in the literary firmament who had X's brains and Y's punch lines. That the eighties had been waiting for me.

I tried to tell her. "It's all nonsense. Market-making, for an increasingly smaller market. They do it, we ignore it, and keep working. It's part of the business."

"So we're in business now?"

"No. Okay. Not business. Part of the . . . C. Sweet. Let's not make ourselves nuts."

"*We* don't need to make ourselves anything." She smacked the pile of newsprint that New York's clipping service kept sending us. "The pros will make us into anything they want."

"C. You know who we are. The pair bond. All the rest of this is somebody else's construction. Nothing's changed."

"Of course it's changed. It's not just you and me anymore. You're obligated. You have to make good on *opportunity*. Everyone and his typewriting monkey would kill for a shot at what's fallen in your lap."

I tried to tell her that there was no obligation, no opportunity that we didn't already have. I tried to comb out the snarls left by public evaluation. That was my job: to keep things unchanged and make them right. But the better I did my job, the more I condemned C. to the opposite employment.

Nor did it help when mourning for Taylor led me into a period of work more intense than I will ever know again. The simplest possible tune had come to me—four notes, then four more, four times over. Selection had whittled at that tune until it grew as long and polyphonic as the planetary concert hall.

The book I needed to write sat on the simplest of bases. Life remembered. Life described. It wrote down and repeated what worked. The small copying errors the text made in running off examples of itself, edited by the world's differential rejection and forgiveness, produced the entire collaborative canon.

For what turned out to be years, this seemed to me a book's only conceivable theme. And thirty, the only age that would take such a theme on—old enough for a glimpse at meaning, immature enough to still think meaning pursuable.

I would fail, of course, in my aerial survey. To make a map on the scale of one to one, to bring the people, the genomes I loved back to life would have required contrapuntal skill on an evolutionary scale. But while I worked on my variations, work itself seemed to be the grave where buried love did its living.

So I spent myself on work, writing a story about a reference librarian, a failed academic, and a life scientist who, diverted, becomes the subject of the experiment he runs. I split the story among the venues of my life. I tried to pack it with anagrams and acrostics, replies to every word anyone had ever sent me, for this would be my one long letter back.

I wanted to write an encyclopedia of the Information Age. The nearest reference library was kilometers away, tiny, and in a foreign tongue. I wrote about music, with only a cheap, portable cassette player to check my descriptions. I typed my computer saga on an obsolete 512K, low-density floppy-based machine that will forever ruin me to imagine, because C., in her technophobia, had picked it out and purchased it for me to sweeten my return to that country.

I lost myself in data and the heart's decoding urge. Nothing else had any interest. Life became an interruption of my description of it. I wanted nothing else but to read, work, travel now and again, take care of my C. And for a long time, I did just that.

The book grew beyond my ability to say how it should go. The story itself turned into an opportunity, an obligation that scared the hell out of us both. Some reentrant map inside me ran away with itself, insisting it was real. No amount of public judgment matched private possibility for sheer terror.

C. read my *Gold Bug* code as it took shape, variation by variation. She came home exhausted, eager for alternate life. She nagged me for new chapters. "I want my friends!"

She knew what I needed to hear, and said as much. But I think she did love that world for her own reasons. "So this is what you do all day while I'm out slaving over a hot word processor. I can hardly believe that the goof who cooks for me produced this."

I'd load up a chunk of text and seat her at the keys. Then she would scroll through my story on-screen while I lay on the couch holding my breath, pretending to occupy myself with a magazine. Every so often she laughed at some invented inanity. I still had the courage for silliness back then.

Hearing her, I looked up, relieved. Redeemed. "Tell me!" I begged, pushing my luck. She would read out loud the line that had made her cackle. And I'd giggle along then, as if she had written the gag.

215

She gave more generously than the first of audiences. But C. needed some story for herself, as endless and private a thing as I now had. Her devotion to my project, fierce and unquestioning, was bitterness by another name. She met my constant infidelity with encouraging smiles, and braced for the day when strangers would declare their love for a story that should never have been more than hers.

"Beauie, I'm going nuts. I'm wasting my life." The refrain of a poem I'm sure had been on my Master's Comps but which I could not place.

"What are you talking about? Think of everything you've managed since coming here."

"Hah. *The DP's Progress.* Maybe it's time to quit fooling ourselves. Pack up and go back."

I did not say what occurred to me: Back *where?*

"C. Be fair to yourself."

"That's what I'm trying to do."

"What do you want? What do you need? Just say the word."

"I don't know. Beau. I'm sorry. I'm a total mess."

I told her she was the very opposite, in as many ways as I could. We talked long and often, coming back always to the same thing. Her life split over different orders of place. Of homes, she no longer knew which was fact and which the sustaining imitation. Two native tongues were as good as none.

Source and target languages tore her down the middle. But it struck me that she might still make from that split a suture.

"Look, C. How many people can do what you do? You know two distinct names for everything. You know what they call it here *and* there. Seems to me, that when you can shake with both hands, you're almost obligated to be an arbiter."

She looked frightened, drawn. "Translation, you mean? They'll never let me."

"Who's to let or not let?"

"Oh, Ricky. You know how things work around here. It's such a goddamned bureaucratic society. I could be the greatest translator going and I wouldn't be able to get work without certification. You can't wipe your bleeding ass in this country without a certificate."

She had begun talking like someone else. Like her dialect self, translated into English.

"Well, if you need a certificate, then we get the certificate."

"By 'we' I take it you mean me. And how do you suggest I do that? You want me to go back to school? Be a child, all over again? I don't have the energy for all that, Beau. Nor the stomach."

"Don't have the nerve, is more like it."

"Call it what you want."

I did. The hardest names I could think of, followed by the softest. I promised her it would work out brilliantly in the end. That I would take care of her for the four years school required. That I would be there for everything, until she came out the other side, newly graduated. A translator.

It did not follow, from the questions Helen asked, that she was conscious. An algorithm for turning statements into reasonable questions need know nothing about what those statements said or the sense they manipulated to say it. Rules would still be slavish, deterministic, little more than a fancy Mixmaster.

But Helen had no such algorithm. She learned to question by imitating me. Or rather, training promoted those constellations of neurodes that satisfied and augmented the rich ecosystem of reentrant symbol maps described by *other* constellations of neurodes.

The only syntactic rules she obeyed emerged from the shape of her first reorganizational principle: to accommodate, encapsulate, and survive the barrage of stimulus, both inside and out. To tune its connections in search of that elusive topography that led input, output, and all enveloped layers toward unachievable peace.

Did the geometry of her subsystems give her deep structure? Did she, in some way, know the rules she obeyed? I didn't even understand the question. I could no longer even say what *know* might mean.

It occurred to me: awareness no more permitted its own description than life allowed you a seat at your own funeral. Awareness trapped itself inside itself. The function of consciousness must be in part to dummy up and shape a coherence from all the competing, conflicting subsystems that processed experience. By nature, it lied. Any rendition we might make of consciousness would arise from *it*, and was thus about as reliable as the accused serving as sole witness for the prosecution.

The window in question was so small and fogged that I did not even know why I worried about whether she had one. Mediating the phenomenal world via consciousness was like listening to reports of a hurricane over the radio while hiding in the cellar.

Helen's neurodal groups organized themselves into representational and even, I think, conceptual maps. Relations between these maps grew according to the same selectional feedback that shaped connections between individual neurodes—joined by recognition and severed by confusion. Helen's lone passion was for appropriate behavior. But when she learned to map whole types of maps onto each other, something undeniable, if not consciousness, arose in her.

She'd cribbed the first-person pronoun as a hollow placeholder sometime earlier. "I don't understand." "I want some more." This last one she pronounced long before I'd read her any Dickens whatsoever. In saying as much, she might have been going about her usual business of making classification couples, pairing signals from outside with symbols from in. She might have been in any number of precognitive states, states permitted by sheets of her neurodes learning to do to other sheets of neurodes what these, in turn, did to the shapes I presented to them.

I began to wonder, the day she asked me, "You bounced high to Jericho?" The day, secure in implication and containment, that she explained, "A runcible spoon is what you eat mince and quince with." The moment, overnight, she acquired cause and effect, exclaiming in hurt wonder, "The rose is sick because the worm eated it!"

It seemed enough of an act to call for witnesses. I could hear, in my mind's ear, my parents saying, "Ricky, go get your cello and play for the guests." I swore, at that age, that in the unlikely event I ever did something as mad as having children, I would never subject them to such humiliation. The lightest training in pride revised my resolution.

Lentz was on his afternoon visit to the nursing home. I rustled up Harold to come have a look. He arrived, gawky daughter in tow. With what remained of a memory that had gone senescent in the last year, I greeted her. "Hello, Trish."

She gave an insulted gagging noise. "Render me roguish. Turf me in all quadrants."

"I'm sorry?"

"This is Mina," Harold intervened. "And your name is mud."

"Oh. I'm sorry. I was sure I—"

"You're not the first one to confuse them."

Mina snorted again, a sound replete with connotations. "We're nothing at all alike. Trish is the stuck-up, snobby bitch."

"And Mina is the sweet one, as you see."

We read Helen "The Emperor's New Clothes." Mina was bored by the text, overfamiliar, although she had never heard it except in paraphrase. She prowled around the office until she found a copy of Rumelhart and McClelland to nose around in. Harold shook his head as I read. He didn't believe that the occasional sound and light emitting from Helen had anything to do with the words I read her.

The story ended. Maybe the only universally valid generalization about stories: they end. I felt like a showman. I turned to Harold and Mina, whose interest was again piqued. "So what do you want to know?"

Harold breathed out, hard. "You've got to be kidding." He looked around for the hidden cameras. Then he took his leap of faith. "Who told the emperor he was naked?"

I repeated the question to Helen, verbatim. She turned it over forever. She slowed a little with each new association she fit into the web. One day she would grow so worldly she would come to a full stop. Now, in front of a captive audience, she seemed to ossify before her time.

I slipped deeper into dismay with each agonizing cycle-tick. At long last, she decided. "The little child told the emperor."

Both father and daughter almost exploded. *"Hoo-wee!"* Harold sobered first. He began reasoning out loud. Reason: the *ex post facto* smoother-over of the cacophony exploding across our subsystems.

"Okay. Let's assume you guys are playing fair. That none of this is canned."

"Good assumption," I said, conscious of sounding like a poor parody of Lentz.

"The entire story never uses the word 'naked.' Well, maybe you've built a kind of thesaurus structure . . ."

"She built it herself."

Mina stopped biting her cuticle. "Maybe it has, you know, like a cheat sheet of questions people might ask?"

"Good thinking, kiddo." Harold tried to pat her head, but she pulled away. "Did you choose the story at random?" he grilled me.

"It was next on the list."

"No telegraph?"

"None."

Mina fluttered her hands. "I didn't mean that he fed it specific questions. I just meant, like, it has a list of how to deal with 'Who is' and 'What is,' and all those."

Harold looked at me: You *sure* you haven't been piping info to the physical symbol systems? I knew his suspicion of operationalism. He often accused Lentz of playing fast and loose with the computational model of mind.

"There aren't that many 'whos' in the story," Mina elaborated. "Maybe she got lucky."

I turned to Helen and asked, "What are the new clothes made of?"

After a long time, she answered, "The clothes are made of threads of ideas."

"It's a nice way of putting it," Harold offered. But the error's strangeness relieved him.

I felt myself edging toward humiliation. I needed one good answer to show them what my girl could do. "Why don't the subjects who see the emperor naked tell him that he has nothing on?"

Both syntax and semantic here ran beyond words. If she could swallow the sentence without spitting up, we'd wow the home crowd for good.

This time, Helen answered too quickly to have thought about the sentence at all. "The subjects are snagged in a textile."

I didn't even try to apologize for her. "Do you like the emperor's new clothes?" I wasn't sure what I was after. If she could remain composed, answer *anything* to a sentence with so vague a referent, it might salvage mechanism and save the day for function.

Helen's answer sent Mina into hysterics. "Did you hear that? Did you hear what it said?"

Harold twisted his mouth, amused, despite himself, by the girl's uncontrollable fit. "Yes. She said, 'Very much.' What's so funny about that?"

"She *didn't*! She said, 'Airy much.' Airy. Get it?"

"Oh, for heaven's sake. You're hearing things, kid."

"Daddy!"

They both looked at me, the tiebreaker. "To tell you the God's honest truth, I thought she said, 'Fairy Dutch.'"

When she caught her breath again, Mina declared, "That's the smartest parrot I've ever seen."

Harold shook his head in bewilderment. "Mere parroting would have been impressive enough. One already wonders what survival value for a cockatiel the ability to whistle the *Saber Dance* might have. How such a bizarre skill could earn its place in such limited circuitry. Rearranging sentence components while preserving grammar ups the ante an order of magnitude. Creating novel sentences in response to a semantic field—"

"We still have a few kinks to work out."

"Listen." Harold fell into the agitated intensity of a scientist impatient with methodology. "Can we try something here?"

"Of course. Name it."

He looked sidelong at me. Not wanting to overstep. "Kahneman and Tversky?"

I smiled. Funny: Harold would not be impressed with *my* matching the obscure tags, recent additions to my own neural library. He took that much for granted. Just your garden-variety marvel.

I improvised for Helen a personal variation on the now-classic test. "Jan is thirty-two years old. She is well educated and holds two advanced degrees. She is single, is strong-minded, and speaks her piece. In college, she worked actively for civil rights. Which of these

221

two statements is more likely? One: Jan is a librarian. Two: Jan is a librarian and a feminist."

"It knows the word 'feminist'?" Mina lit up, arcing into existence at the idea.

"I think so. She's also very good at extending through context."

Once more, Helen answered with a speed that winded me, given the pattern-sorting she needed to reach home. "One: Jan is a librarian."

Harold and I exchanged looks. Meaning?

"Why is that more likely, Helen?"

"Helen? It has a *name*?"

"That is more likely because one Jan is more likely than two."

Now Harold took a turn laughing like an idiot.

"Wait a minute," Mina said. "I don't get it. What's the right answer?"

"What do you mean, what's the right answer?" Harold, raging affronted fatherdom. "Think about it for ten seconds."

"Well, she has all these feminist things about her. So isn't it more likely that she would be a feminist librarian than just a . . . ?"

Mina, seeing herself about to label the part more likely than its whole, threw her hand over her mouth and reddened.

"I can't believe it. I've worked my mental fingers to the bone for you, daughter."

Harold's growl was motley at best. Helen, choosing the right answer for the wrong reasons, condemned herself to another lifetime of machinehood. Harold's girl, in picking wrongly for the right reasons, leaped uniquely human.

He cuffed her mussed hair, the bear teaching the cub to scuffle. "I'm deeply disappointed in you."

A voice from the doorway pronounced, "*I'm* deeply disappointed in Jan."

Diana waved as we three jerked around.

"Jesus. Don't sneak up behind people like that." Harold put hand to sternum. "That's a Lentz stunt."

"Don't let him give you a hard time, Meen. That problem is famous for being missed. And I happen to have been present when your dad made *his* acquaintance with it."

"Whoa. Hold on. Positivism prohibits our talking about that topic."

Mina stuck her tongue out at the bluster. Then she turned back, rapt, to Diana. Whatever problems sister Trish had with the woman, here shone only February adulation.

Mina's eyes fell matte in disappointment when Diana said she couldn't stop. "I expect a private showing sometime," Diana told me. She touched the two Plovers goodbye, and added a hand-brush for me.

Harold turned back to Helen. He scratched his chin in thought. Did physiology create that cultural cliché or had culture constructed the bodily release? The split was, in any case, linguistic.

"It's astonishing, Rick. I've never seen pattern-matching on this order. But of course, your grab bag of networks has nothing to do with human comprehension. This is to a twenty-two-year-old text-explicator what a gifted cockatiel is to Our Man in Leipzig."

He was right. Helen would never be able to decode Harold's reference, let alone figure out how he alluded to my love of Bach without the two of us ever having mentioned the topic.

"Okay, okay, you guys. Enough boy talk. I want a turn to try something. A girl goes into a music store. She flips through the bins of CDs. All at once, she starts to jump up and down and clap her hands. She opens her purse, and just as suddenly starts to cry. Why?"

I transmitted the story to Helen. "Why did the girl start to cry?"

Helen labored. In my ear, I heard a digitally sampled sob of empathy.

"The girl saw something sad in her purse."

Harold snickered. "She's still missing a little something upstairs, Ricardo." And always would be, his grin informed me.

Mina rushed to the defense. She probably made new girlfriends of all this week's high school pariahs. "Yes. But at least she knows how to pare things down. That must be tricky. Life is 99 percent extra stuff most of the time."

"Dr. Plover." I coded the gush in fake formality. We have this inverse rule, about how much you mean and how directly you can say it. "Your daughters are brilliant."

A button-bursting grimace. "Some of them are more brilliant than others."

"But we don't name names, do we, Daddy?"

He cuffed her again. This time, he kept his hand on her neck. Oddly, for her age, she suffered the touch.

"This one was always a real sharpie. She loved to fiddle with anything mechanical. No two clocks in the house ever gave the same time."

"Were you impatient to get names for everything?" I asked Mina.

Dad answered for her. The liability of owning parents who know too much.

"She generalized in startling ways. Always on the track of something urgent. The cues we set her were never the things she was after. Once, she pointed out the window at a bird. 'What that?' Remember, Snook? I think you said 'What that?' until you were four. You were very patient with our corrections of that one. She pointed and asked for the name, and I said, 'Goose.' Stickler for accuracy.

"Two days later, she points at a robin and says, 'Goose.' I tell her, 'No, sweetheart. Robin.' But I think, maybe I was too intent on that Christmassy, good-tasting nexus, where the kid would have been happier with 'bird.' Then she points at an airplane and says, 'Goose,' and I think, 'What's a good generic term for flying things?'

"When she gooses a jogger, and then falling leaves, and then a scrap of paper blowing across the yard, I wonder if we've birthed the reincarnated soul of Kaspar Hauser here. You know, how he used 'horse'—the one wooden toy he was given during seventeen years in subterranean nursery-prison—to mean any animal at all. I ask myself, could those evil poststructuralists be right? Do we live at the level of the arbitrary signifier, in a place where there can be no meaning because the thing being signified lies suffocating?"

Mina rolled her eyes. But she sat still for the end of the story. As if she'd never heard it.

"When she makes a break for the front door, and starts jumping up to grab the unreachable handle, calling, 'Goose, goose,' I finally hit on my idiocy. The word she had been looking for was 'To move fast. To be free. To escape.' "

Harold exhaled. "We tended to give her nouns, where all she ever wanted was processes."

"I've done my homework," C. pleaded at the end of a day. She'd slam shut the massive translating dictionaries or hurl a pen at the holder, not even trying to hit. "Can we go for a walk?"

Unconscious repetition of an old litany, her oldest. Her first spoken sentence. *Good girl outside.* C.'s requests sunk into me and snapped off. *You promised me this would work out. None of this would have been necessary, with someone simpler than you.*

The return to school turned out humiliating beyond expectation. More time had passed since she was twenty-one than either of us realized. Her classmates were children and her teachers sticklers for blasé condescension. She sat in molded-plastic desk-chairs and did busy work, little of it bearing on the translating of texts. At least once a week, and not limited to Mondays, she came home crying at the senseless debasement.

And it was my fault. She never said as much. But her every frustration slapped me with a paternity suit. When C. grew furious, I felt let off easy. When she was sweet with suppressing vehemence, I stood accused. Wronged, I became ridiculously reasonable. "I was just going to suggest a walk. Name your destination."

I was angry with my friend. She with me. Neither of us knew where the rage came from. It seemed petty betrayal even to voice it, so we never did. And so I nursed a martyrdom, and the two of us slipped imperceptibly from lovers to parent and child.

We still traveled, during her school breaks. We went farther afield, not because we had exhausted the three countries we could walk to from E. We needed the increasingly exotic. Someplace not walkable from where we were.

We went to Italy one term vacation. We stayed at a friend's fixer-upper villa in the little Lombard farm town of P. In preparation, I undertook a crash course in the language. For a moment in my life, I could read snatches of Boccaccio, Collodi, Levi. Four years later, I remember nothing.

We packed light. We always did. Maybe that doomed us as much as anything. We arrived with nothing, rented bikes, and, for a week or two, had never been happier.

We thought we knew how to see a town. "Mechelen falls," C. liked to joke. "Leuven falls." She kept every clipping, ticket, and photo of our conquests. She pasted them into the same album where we listed all the books we read out loud to one another.

But in Italy, in the sunny South, we met our sightseeing match. Mantua did not fall. Cremona did not fall. We did. Even the dustiest backwater towns routed us. The post office, the shoemaker's shop: any old hole-in-the-wall sat spackled over with crumbling Renaissance fresco. Guidebook stars fell everywhere, like summer meteors in shower.

We learned how trains run in a republic. We climbed campaniles and pored over baptisteries. We gnawed on *osso buco* and carried around slices of *panettone* in our pockets. For a few days, we lived our own invention. C. forgot the degradation of her return to school. I delighted in writing nothing, not a single word. We were well. We could live forever, futureless, at peace with one another.

I picked up an old microscope at a flea market in Verona. In the long evenings, in my imitation of life science, I set up in the courtyard and examined local specimens. Pointless pleasure, stripped of ends. The ancient *contadino* from across the road, long since convinced that we were mad, could not resist coming over for a look.

I showed him where to put his eye. I watched him, thinking, this is how we attach to existence. We look through awareness's tube and see the swarm at the end of the scope, taking what we come upon there for the full field of sight itself.

The old man lifted his eye from the microscope lens, crying.

"Signore, ho ottantotto anni e non ho mai saputo prima che cosa ci fosse in una goccia d'acqua." I'm eighty-eight years old and I never knew what was in a droplet of water.

I didn't either, until he told me.

On our two beater bicycles we explored the countryside. We brought dried sausage and bread, and ate when we were hungry.

Lunch outdoors in the countryside—a kind of mock ownership. We lived a southern version of those Brueghel wheat gatherers, breaking for meal and midday nap. Even our southern sleeps were Sleep's dream versions.

We greeted everyone we saw, invulnerable in our foreignness. Once, a farm woman, Titian-built, carrying a piece of thresher on the back of her bicycle, set down her load to visit. As if production, even sustenance, meant nothing without civility.

The woman and I chatted for some while, cheerfully unable to understand more than a stray word or two.

"*Tedesco?*"

"*Olandese.*"

"Rick! You just told her you're Dutch?"

The woman laughed at what she took as a minor marital spat. Then her eyes narrowed in suspicion. "How old are you?"

I had to think. Dutch was bad enough, with its archaic one-and-thirty.

I told her. She stepped back with alarm. She flung her arms up like Giotto's agonizing angel. "What are you doing here? Where are your children?"

I interpreted for C. She shot me a good-luck look. "That one's all yours, buddy."

"*I miei libri sono i miei figli.*" As far as I intended, it meant, "My books are my children."

An expression came across the woman's face. It would have been horror, but for the perplexity. Disgusted, she said she'd never heard such idiocy. Such sad waste.

All this happened less than two books ago. By the time I came to tell Helen this story, I did not retain enough of the language even to remember how to say, "You're right."

Helen was getting on. She was not yet long in the tooth, but neither was she a tadpole anymore. She entered what might perhaps be called youth, and I gave her Conrad's take on the situation.

I remember my youth and the feeling that will never come back any more—the feeling that I could last for ever, outlast the sea, the earth, and all men.

To remember a feeling without being able to bring it back. This seemed to me as close to a functional definition of higher-order consciousness as I would be able to give her. If we could teach Helen that, we could teach her to read with understanding.

To define that rift did not open one in her, any more than remembering a feeling revived it. For Helen to pass the Turing Test, facts would have to stand in for knowing. Our only hope that she might one day disguise herself as a master's candidate lay in the conventions of writing. The interpretive essay—the art we trained her to perform—meant viewing from afar. An aerial shot from the dispassionate high ground.

Humans had to be schooled in how to describe the maelstrom as if they weren't lost in the middle of it, in their own unbailable open boat. Helen was detachment personified. In effect, the infant adult we'd be up against would be trying to simulate the disembodiment that, to Helen, came as a fact of her birth.

But Helen needed to feel, to the extent possible, the facts of her opponent twenty-two-year-old's birth. Conrad, of course, was years beyond her. *Youth* was wasted on the young. Yet by letting her wade in over her head, I hoped to give my network a working model of what it felt like to learn to read. How I had felt.

I never read a book at the right time. The books I read as a child almost all came before I was ready for them. *The Man Who Lost His Head*, an absurd illustrated fable that, I'm sure, must have ended happily, gave me my first recurring nightmare because I read it as a preschooler. Homer in fourth grade. Shakespeare in sixth. *Ulysses* and *The Sound and the Fury* in junior high. *Gravity's Rainbow*, wet from high school. I read Thomas Wolfe as a freshman in college, the right age, but decades too late, in history, for it to work.

I would find books in the house, my parents' or my older sisters' or brother's. I read them like stealing. Eavesdropping. Malicious rumormongering. Staying out past curfew without permission. I hadn't a clue what any of them meant. Not a clue. Every animal they high-lighted I named horse. But a horse that split and differentiated in the turbulence of foreign bazaars.

Each book became a knot. Yes, the strings of that knot were theme and place and character. Dr. Charles, with his gangrene machine. Stephen, gazing at the girl in the water. But into that tangle, just as crucial, went the smell of the cover, the color and cream resistance of the pages, the week in which I read any given epic, the friends for whom I synopsized, the bed, the lamp, the room where I read. Books made known to me my days' own confusion. They meant no more nor less than the extensive, dense turnpike of the not-I.

This *not*, I imagined, would figure more in Helen's masquerade than would any simulation of self. Self took us only so far. I wanted her to associate the meaning inherent in the words of a story with the heft and weight and bruise of the story's own existence. I did this by reading her things long before she was ready for them. Only by mis-take, by taking the story to be coextensive with its own intruding bewilderment, could Helen pull off her impersonation.

I read her *Little Women*. M., Taylor's widow, had given C. an an-tique copy as a going-away present—their shared childhood icon. I read her Dylan Thomas, whom I had once exercised in C.'s ear in the still night, our arms around each other's grief. I read her *Ethan Frome*. C. had wept at the tale, wanting to be better than she was.

Helen and I had never gone sledding, as C. and I had, on the arboretum downs outside B. Helen would never know a sled from the hill it slid down, except in the dead of definition. That she would never thrill or panic under downward pull no longer bothered me. At this point, I was training her in being mistaken. Overwhelmed. The condition of knowledge at all ages, but above all, twenty-two.

I can't revive the lesson the day Helen interrupted my flow of narrative to demand, "Where did I come from?"

I remember only my total stupefaction. The lesson itself could not have triggered her question. Helen was no longer just adding the new relations I recited for her into a matrix of associated concepts. The matrix that comprised her had begun to spin off its own free asso-ciations.

Where did I come from? Lentz, seated behind me at his desk, doing real science, cackled. "Reeky! You in trouble now!"

I turned to look at him. Lentz's eyes and mine exchanged mutual punch lines. Like a fetus replaying fishness, Helen had rebuilt, for the first time, the primal joke. Because I'd heard it when I was a kid, I knew not to choke. Not to launch the long explanation of semiconductor storks, the birds and bees of hammered gold and gold enameling. Not to traumatize her by telling her we'd built her, but simply to answer, "You come from a little town called U."

It was Huck Finn, a raft trip worlds beyond her ken, that made me realize childhood had ended. Helen's reaction to Huck's going to hell could not have been more to the point. She listened as if to the breathy account of a playground acquaintance, back from an adventure. A funny thing: all works—stories, plays, poems, articles, newspaper reports—filtered through to Helen only as so many emergency phone calls.

Midway into the transmission, when the revealed realities of power and ownership began to capsize the little narrative raft, Helen asked, in her machine deadpan, "What race am I?"

My turn to mean, by not replying.

"What races do I hate? Who hates me?"

I did not know what passage to quote her, how to answer that she would be hated by everyone for her disembodiment, and loved by a few for qualities she would never be able to acquire or provide.

The gaps in her worldliness gaped so wide one could drive a plow through them, sowing stars. She knew something about the Dreyfus case and the Boer War and the spread of Islam to the Malay Peninsula. Her ignorance, however, extended to such things as corks stuck in bottles, the surface of a liquid reflection, the destruction of the more brittle of two colliding objects, wrappers and price tags, stepladders, up versus down, the effects of hunger . . . I counted myself lucky if she could infer that a tied shoe was somehow more desirable than an untied one, provided the shoe was on, whatever tying, whatever shoes were.

The catalog of lapses loomed big to fatiguing, dense beyond comprehension. The simplest nouns slipped her up. Qualities must all have twinkled in her massive astigmatism. As for processes: who knew what Helen made of verbs?

What is life? I told Helen it might be the flash of a firefly in the night. The breath of a buffalo in the wintertime. The shadow that runs across the grass and loses itself in the sunset.

The firefly, yes. I'd seen fireflies, even caught them in a jar during boyhood's obligatory assault on incandescence. Waves of them on summer nights, sheets flashing to each other like neuronal metaphor storms. Although I'd never seen the breath of a buffalo in the wintertime, I could play in my head a film of steaming bison nostrils. From what disparate clips I'd jimmied up the impostor composite was not clear. But that little shadow lay beyond my eyes. Was the thing that cast it even of this place?

I read her the definition. Helen did what she could with its images. I told her the idea was a quote, which once again changed everything. I told her the words belonged to Crowfoot. I told her Crowfoot was a late-nineteenth-century Canadian Blackfoot chief. I told her he was thought a conciliatory peacemaker. I told her that "conciliatory" meant as many different things as there were people willing to use the name. I told her these words were the speaker's last.

And in the impenetrable confusion of referents, the eddy of knowledges seen and unseen, perhaps she gained a foothold in the ineffable. One as ephemeral as mine.

A noiseless patient spider, I told her,

> I mark'd where on a little promontory it stood isolated,
> Mark'd how to explore the vacant vast surrounding,
> It launch'd forth filament, filament, filament, out of itself,
> Ever unreeling them, ever tirelessly speeding them.

Okay. We knew about spiders. Living things. Small. Industrious, predatory, brainless. The list of predicates she might spin out was as extensive as the ways of overlap in her neurodal clusters. We knew about webs. We could make a kind of geo-retinoptic map of promontories. We knew more about isolation than words could say. As for vast vacancy, that was preverbal. Built into the system.

But what does it mean, Helen? My silence asked her. Her own firing and rewiring demanded meaning of the input, rushing her upended steady state headlong to address these new links. Only sense could comfort and minister to them.

What did it mean? I didn't mention to her that I myself could barely parse that first sentence or render it grammatical. What was with that spider? What did his exploration come to? What meant that "filament, filament, filament"? What did that unreeling purpose, and what's more: what did *saying* it signify?

She couldn't come close, of course. So I told her:

And you O my soul where you stand,
Surrounded, detached, in measureless oceans of space,
Ceaselessly musing, venturing, throwing, seeking the spheres to
   connect them,
Till the bridge you will need be form'd, till the ductile anchor
   hold,
Till the gossamer thread you fling catch somewhere, O my soul.

To snow-blind Helen and lay down forever the trace of ideational opaqueness, I read her "Absalom and Achitophel," followed by "Epistle to Dr. Arbuthnot." She cut me off in the latter, in mid–heroic couplet.

"Sing." Some malfunction.

"Helen?"

She did not bother to translate my one-word, content-free question, but just repeated, "Sing."

Lentz, always nearby, supervising the supervisor, threw a fit. "What are you doing to her, Powers? The most complex and extensive neural simulator ever trained, running on the fastest massively parallel connection hardware in the world, and you're turning it into a blithering nitwit with no attention span."

"Philip. It's okay. This is what we want."

"*Want?*"

"Sure. She's bored by Pope and Dryden. It's only human. Trust me on this one."

"Trust? Trust *you*? After that last book of yours? How long do we have before you leave town?"

"Four months."

"Oh, wonderful. Four months until my utter, public abasement."

But I had no time for Lentz just then. Helen needed singing to.

"Sing to me," I discovered over time, meant make any music at all. My Jericho song, home-rolled, would do. She would accept chords from a MIDI file, digitized waveforms, Redbook Audio from off a CD, miked footsteps in the cafeteria or rain quizzing the office window-pane, the triad whistle of the phone company saying they could not complete our call as dialed.

Helen wanted organized, rhythmic pitches of any sort. Sound. She beat to steel drums, to the old Esterhazy chamber stringers, to gazebo brass bands from just off the right-hand side of ancient photographs, to tin-pan-nabulation, to the tinkling of a dead child's music box. To jazz, pop, funk, rap, gospel, chant, minimal, maximal. To fusions of infusions.

Most of all, she craved the human voice. Even after multiple listenings, Helen still thought all these voices somehow mine. She cloaked herself in the blur of swirled phenomena. Repeated training must have left her able to distinguish among the sounds and sweet airs, because she began to request some by name. Or maybe, as with baby Mina, the name did not mean the piece but stood for broader gauges—bigger triggers, knobs on a gigantic black box. Give me that again. The one that solves so many aches at once. You know. *That.* Goose.

Helen asked for frequent repeats of a certain North American soprano, a woman my age. Her pure high voice, in the service of spent music, made it almost possible to pretend for a moment that our worst political ingenuities were but the fierce vexation of a dream from which history might yet awaken. For a long time, Helen demanded, each evening before I logged off, this voice's rendition of a four-minute Purcell ditty called "Evening Hymn."

"Sing," she said. And if I failed to behave, "Sing 'Hymn.' " I could not leave in good faith until I put on a recording of this woman. Helen's soprano sang as if an angel toying with mortals, an Olympian back home in her sponsored village for an afternoon's pickup match. The voice sang as if it had never known or inflicted hurt, nor accepted hurt as this earth's last word:

> Now, now that the Sun
> Hath veil'd his light,
> And bid the World good night,
> To the soft bed my body I dispose.
> But where, where shall my soul repose . . . ?

Even I had trouble at times making out the words. I did not test to see if Helen could separate the sung phonemes or, higher, if a sung "sun" said the same thing to her as a spoken one. Higher still: if she could hear the sung "soul," and if she knew it to be roughly the same sound as "soul" in speech, then what, if anything, did Purcell's somnambulist have to do with Whitman's spider?

If she got that impossibly far, Helen would still not have been able to assemble the outermost frame. It amused her to listen to humans singing about the disposition, the disposal of their bodies at day's end, and their anxiety over housing whatever was left over. The text of this evening prayer could not have caused Helen much lost sleep.

She loved, too, that same voice as it haunted a tune named for its own first line. The tune, by Alfonso Ferrabosco, lodged at the turn of the seventeenth century. I don't know if Helen had a concept of epochs and succession, or whether she thought, as I did at her intellectual age, that all eras persisted somewhere, deep in the hive. I don't even know what she heard in place of these notes:

> So beauty on the water stood
> When love had sever'd earth from flood.
> So when he parted air from fire,
> He did with concord all inspire.

And then a motion he them taught,
That elder than himself was thought.
Which thought was yet a child of earth,
For love is elder than his birth.

Perhaps she liked the tune's abject simplicity. It did little more than ascend the scale, make a pilgrim's delaying spin, and wander back down again. Maybe the charm lay in that minute sigh vanishing almost before the mind knew it had begun, or in that voice, too sweet to exist in any world but the mind's ear.

These eight short lines required a density of keys that had grown unparsably more complex since their Renaissance casting. Even knowing the cosmological allusions didn't crack the conundrum, but made it more inscrutable. Each time Helen demanded that I "sing beauty," the song grew less solvable. After a while, I could no longer determine pronominal antecedents or order the terms.

The little syllogism defeated me. The "he" that ordered chaos must have been love. What, then, was the motion, love himself or something older? Which thought was "which thought"—the thought he taught them, or the thought that the love love taught them was elder than love himself? If love were his own elder, how did that make either of those thoughts younger than the earth that love made?

Untroubled by logic, Helen glided back to tonic. She seemed the maker of the song she needed.

I didn't have the heart to tell her how unbearable this music sounded, on the stage of events unfolding beyond the Center's windows. Her smallest textual interpretation would be meaningless without that context. Yet outside lay a nightmare I still thought her myopic perceptron maps need never look upon, even if they could.

Instrumental music left her more restive. The blur of raw event rattled her in ways it never would rattle a thing with a body. She struggled to turn bowed strings and buzzing reeds into phonemes. The less she could, the harder she tried.

I took her on a tour of world music. I played her the *kluay* and *gong wong yai* of my youth. I tried her on sackbuts and singing drums. I had no way of gauging her response, whether delight or agitation. She stopped me only once. In a moment of backsliding, I'd put on a tape I'd made years ago for C. A sampler of her favorites that, in comfort or in spite, was one of the few keepsakes I rescued when I made my quick evacuation from Europe.

I'd forgotten what was on the tape. We reached that ineffable clarinet, assembling, atop the reconciled chamber orchestra, the peace that the world cannot give. Helen shouted, "I know that." This piece is familiar. Mine.

I did not see how, and then I did. The Mozart that Lentz fed a nameless neural net the night before I met him. Long before we'd conceived of the idea of Helen, some ancestor of hers had learned this piece.

I felt my skin turn to goose flesh—chicken skin, as I would have called it in Dutch, as little as a year ago. Lentz had sutured her to old circuits, experiments he never so much as described to me. Helen had inherited archetypes. She'd been born wanting song. She remembered, even things that she had never lived.

Three weeks of deliberately not thinking about her, and my suppressed image of A. erupted into full-blown obsession.

I imagined a whole day around her. I outfitted her hours and blueprinted her afternoons. I pictured when and how she took her meals. I let us talk over the international community's latest gossip. We laughed at every inanity, local and large. I comforted her invented distress and celebrated the triumphs I made her tell me. I put her to bed each evening to words and music. I woke her up in life's early morning and stared at her unsuspecting eyes as they blinked open in astonishment, full of grace, force, fascination, accepting, improvising, the equal to anything.

My decline accelerated, complete and irrevocable, like the best of runaway sleds. I fed on daily, exhilarating regression. I bicycled past

A.'s house in the dark, something I'd last done at eleven for a girl whose name I'd forever forgotten by high school. I studied A.'s phone number in the departmental directory. I looked up her schedule in the English staff Rolodex. I learned that she taught composition and intro to fiction while finishing her own graduate course work. Feminist theory.

I memorized her office hours. She was in two mornings a week and three afternoons. At first, I avoided the building at those times. Later, I shot for them.

I told myself that my preoccupation with A. was harmless. Cultivated. A hobby. The safest hazard of my occupation. Then, one morning, it was none of those things.

I was browsing the campus bookstore, anxious, as usual, at all the volumes I would never get to before I died. I saw A. before I knew I saw her. She stood purveying Theory and Criticism, shelves that I hadn't looked at for a long time. She hovered over the lined-up spines in a reverie of self-judgment. I realized I was in trouble. More trouble than I could remember having been in.

I might have picked up on this long before I did. Any fix that the self needs to convince itself of has already failed.

I saw her no more than once in a dozen days, for less than a minute each time. We had yet to exchange a nod of the head. Hello lay outside the realm of possibility. Watching her at wide intervals was like listening to those endless Renaissance melismas where the very idea of words gets lost in a tangle of counterpoint a year longer than the ear.

A little sun, a cool breeze, this face, and I was done for. Dead. A carapace the length of my body split open. All I needed to do was step out.

A. floated free of her signifier. Her features traced a curve that encouraged my projective exercise. Or rather, my projection pinned that facilitating arc to her like a corsage. It seemed to me, then, that love must make a blank slate to write itself on. Only instant, arbitrary attachment to strangeness made real that lab where processes bested things, two falls out of three.

I talked to her so often in my head I felt in danger of hailing A.

each time I saw her. No limit to how badly I might humiliate myself. At my age, such absurdity did not even qualify as licit humiliation. When C. and I had moved to B., this other girl was still kneesock-deep in dolls.

Premature mid-life crisis, I told myself. Just getting it out of the way early. On lucid days, I dropped the "early."

That A.'s enzyme contour picked some physiological lock of mine I had no doubt. The thing she set free, though, spoke like a delirious traveler stumbling back from cartographic fantasy: Prester John's kingdom. The Mountains of Kong. Someplace where spirit exceeded fluke epiphenomenon, more than mechanical spin-off.

Seeing A. made me happy. And happy, the self we build blows past the punched holes of its piano roll to become music itself. Whole verbs of standing sound, solid in the enabled air.

I did it all myself. No encouragement. Life simulating electronics. I turned A. into a conflation of every friend who had ever happened to me. I tapped her to solve, recover more loves than I had forgotten. I knew I'd invented her. Yet knowledge spared me nothing, least of all the return of conviction.

I saw, as if from above, who this woman was. She was not the C. I had known, nor a younger replay. No resemblance. No association. Or rather, both A. and C. were some reminder of a lost third thing I didn't even remember having loved.

A. was the person C. had only impersonated. The one I thought the other might become. That love of eleven years now seemed an expensive primer in recognition, a disastrous fable-warning, a pointer to the thing I could not afford to miss this time. I had come back to U. after long training in the dangers of hasty generalization. Returned to learn that no script is a wrap after just one reading.

We began to lose our English. We could no longer tell if constructions were idiomatic. "I have a hackle on that woman." "This place has a pleasant sphere." "Proof the middle, while I do the stove on."

C. and I tossed many of these word salads ourselves. We just liked certain Dutch turns of phrase. They expressed more than the ones we started with. "I get a kriebel from that thing." "I was dumb surprised. What could I say? I silenced." "Neck over head" made more sense than "head over heels," and after a few repetitions, "less or more" began to feel more natural than the other way around.

We'd start out butchering translations just to amuse each other. "Want to go for a wandel?" "Are we fietsing it or footing it?" "Forget your mantel not!" By the third or fourth burlesque repetition, we'd wind up wondering from which language the words came.

We mirrored her parents, whose twenty years of Chicago English now mengseled itself back into their native Limburgs dialect. We rebuilt their private *spreektaal* in reverse. Those two or three nights a week when C. and I visited her folks, the four of us formed a hopeless speech community incomprehensible to anyone but us.

We learned new labels by a series of mnemonics. *Ezelbruggetjes,* as we now called them. Little donkey bridges. The mind as a donkey that needs leading across the tentatively spanned chasm. The problem with mnemonics is that they fail almost by definition. If they aren't memorable enough, they're just extra baggage. If too memorable, they upstage the thing they index. Ten years on, all you remember is the pointer.

I still made absurd errors of speech. But increasing sophistication made my accidents funny even to me. I asked a cousin who had just given birth how things had gone with the delivery. English's archaic "befall" had stayed current in Dutch, like some teen elopement that somehow lasted, against everyone's predictions, into old age. But I muffed the common idiom and instead of asking, "How did things befall you?" I somehow asked, "How did you come to have fallen?"

Even I enjoyed this one. But C.'s pleasure exploded so sharply it laid me open. Her joyance at my ditsiness ached as it unkinked itself. Her rowdy laugh said how long it had been since its last trip this way.

The blur of linguistic borders became a game. So long as I had a copy editor back in New York, I felt safe spelunking around in language's limestone. But C. could not afford the word leak. She needed the containers to be as solid as possible, so that she could pour from one into the other without spilling.

She trained in to the city each day, to the State Language Institute, as it was called by another name. There, under the shadow of the oldest church in the Netherlands, she sat doing drills. She worked bolted to the floor in a kiddie chair-desk, like that giant Wendy on whom the betrayed Peter pulls his switchblade.

"Beau, it's classic torture, pure and simple. Intermittent punishment and praise. They just want to see if you have the animal persistence to survive brain death."

"Well. You know what they say, don't you?"

"What?"

"Sheer plod makes plough down sillion shine."

"That's what they say?"

"Sometimes."

"They're all sadists. Oh, not the poets, although . . . I mean my instructors. My *Engelse schrijfvaardigheid* guy likes to reel off sarcasms in both languages until the little Dutch girls break down in tears."

"Character strengthening?"

"That's how he acts. Don't you think it's ironic?"

"What?" I hated irony. I didn't even like the word in her mouth.

"That I came here thinking I'd write my family memoir? And all I've written is the Dutch version of Article Two of the Proceedings of the International Commission on Trade Liberalization."

She still came to me in her distress. And I still thought I might protect her. Even sex now was a kind of periodic assuaging. She asked for a touch that would alleviate, not thrill. Or fear left me unable to consider thrilling.

The more care I took, the more I turned her into the needy one. And the more I did that, the needier she became. We construed her helplessness between the two of us. And that was not care on my part. That was cowardice.

It never occurred to either of us. Protection itself was killing her. The protection of love.

The worse her day went, the more I tried to load with consolations the book I worked on. I shot for the simple charm of strangeness. One night every two weeks or so, she could lose herself in four lives that had mercifully nothing to do with her own. Nothing, that is, except a prediction neither of us saw yet. A sketch of everything we would imitate in awful fact. The story we'd play out in detail.

To pollinate strangeness, I went with the familiar. I sent my protagonist Todd to Flanders, even Limburg, to report on our language derangement from another angle. I retold all our jokes, reprised our friends in all their voices. I hoped that the outside view—our life *van anders om*—might renew our own amazement at the unnamable escapade we'd grown too close to to know.

My *Gold Bug* accreted the theme she studied. The book itself became the topic it grew into. It was my act of unschooled translation. Not a how-to, but another kind of self-help manual all together. How do you put moonlight into a chamber? I might better have asked: how can the chamber see it's lit? The room still blazed as it always had. Only our eyes needed attenuating.

"Do I seem different?" C. wanted to know one evening, after a sad chapter. She still laughed out loud while reading me. But her laughs, like the book she read, had become a songbook of homesickness. She sounded for all the world like one of my lost characters.

"Different how?"

"Than I was. Than the girl who you sat with on the Quad, the day your dad died." Than the twink you fell for and changed your life to fit.

"You seem—more substantial."

"What does that translate into, in kilos?"

I felt cold. Colder than when I received that copy of "The Cremation of Sam McGee" from a man who had died three days before. I could live with that first death, because I had the hope of her. I wasn't sure I could live with the death that now informed me.

Yet the proof seemed irrefutable. One can't love a person for her vulnerability and still hope to outlast life with her.

Every career has an exclusive corner on loneliness. The loneliness of writing is that you baffle your friends and change the lives of strangers. During Helen's training, I received letters, even gifts, from people who had stolen something from my bedtime apocalypse. People I'd never meet.

A school principal in the catastrophically expanding western city of P. wrote how she daily watched over the kids who had escaped from my terminal pede ward. A doctor in New York sent a mug stenciled with the words "Clap if you still can." C., I imagined, would not even know the book existed until it appeared in the Low Countries, in translation.

E very era mints its trademark desolation. Mine lay in how much my time had come to see and hear. We seemed to be on the verge of a new evolution in consciousness. We'd hit upon collective awareness. Then, awareness of awareness. Now we were taking one giant step back from vantage, wrecked by how smoky the portal was, how clouded over.

The mind was one of those spy-in-the-sky satellites capable of reading license plates from outer space. Only now it was learning how to pan back. To see the assault tank the plate belonged to. To notice that tanks were everywhere. That space was deeper than any satellite supposed.

"I bit off more than I could chew, the other day," I mentioned to Helen, in passing.

"Bit off . . . ?" Helen's associative circuits whirred, mystified.

"It means I got in over my head." Worse and worse. "I needed to say something to an old friend I hadn't seen in a long time. So I decided to write her a letter."

Writing. Letters. Friendship. Regret. Volition. The simple past. The past perfect.

"I thought it would be a short letter, but the words got away from me. Before I knew it, it was many, many pages long."

Pages. Length. A screwball figure of speech. The self-surprising foundation of all our actions.

"I finished the letter and put it in an envelope. I sealed the envelope and wrote just the name of my friend on it. I mailed the letter."

Containment. Enclosure. Distributed subjects in compound clauses. Pronominal substitution. Mail. The idea of the international postal system. Distance. Physical, untraversable distance. Pickup and delivery. Longing and loss.

"But the letter never reached my friend. Why not?"

I knew for a fact that we had never talked about addresses. Nor, to my recall, had the idea come up even obliquely in all the thousands of pages we studied. I wanted to see if, from the countless bodies of knowledge Helen would need even to orient the problem, she might somehow produce a superinference, a high-level leap to the idea that, in this existence, sending a message by name alone was not enough. One had to say where in the world's infinite density the name lay.

"The letter counted how many pages?" Helen asked.

"I don't think that makes any difference."

Helen fell into hurt silence. After great length, she said, "You didn't put a rudder on your letter."

"She's getting smarter," Lentz undertoned, in awe, from far across the room.

Something had gotten into Lentz. The smugness began effacing itself. His merciless, empirical anality softened to verbal diarrhea.

He still ragged me at every opportunity. "Do we have to know that for the exam?" His wheedling lent new meaning to the old student refrain.

Helen humbled him. Her connections grew denser than even Lentz had dared hope. Her knowledge was neither deep nor wide. But it was supple.

She produced the same kind of dream logic as any new speaker. She could do the child classics: "Is it tomorrow yet?" "When does orange become red?" Her questions came even more detached, because she could neither feel nor gauge herself. Hungry–full; warm–cold; up–down: she worked these as abstract axes, not as absolutes of need. Helen accounted to nothing but weak semantics, the brittle-bone disease of word.

As such, she was free to assemble the strangest skeletons gravity had yet to challenge. Her corkers worked to weaken Philip's surety. Even he found it tough to preserve syllogistic composure in the face of something like, "A lost tooth loses its appetite?"

His renouncing in-your-face didn't prevent Lentz from indulging the occasional in-your-back. He still micromanaged my judgment calls, calculating to manufacture maximum annoyance.

"Why are you reading her that tract doggerel?"

"It's on the list, Philip."

"That? Canonical?" He broke into song. "Times have cha-anged!"

But he had changed more, it struck me.

"Why don't you just concentrate on *real* literature?"

"What did you have in mind? H. G. Wells?"

"Now, there's an idea. Didn't he write a story about how we're all going to end up in cubicles, tapped into some monolithic digital broadband?"

"I wouldn't know."

"Some guy gets it in his head he wants to see his mother. In person. She thinks it's the most perverse idea she's ever heard. Damn. I can't remember what happens in the end."

"We could look it up on the Internet."

"Thank you, Marcel. I'm serious. We need to get back to basics."

"You mean 'Invictus,' and like that?"

"Speak properly, Marcel. There are children present. I mean Holmes."

"You jest. 'Build thee more stately mansions . . .'?"

"Not that Holmes, you blackguard. I speak of the curious incident of the novelist in the dark."

But the novelist, I was supposed to say, did nothing in the dark.

"Know your opposition, man. Rule one. Think how you have to solve this. Plover's picking the exam passage, right? He's an old-school, sentimental classicist. Forget about everything but the dead white males. The Chaucer, the Shakespeare, the Milton . . . We could have her memorize an answer for each possible—"

"Philip! Come on. They might ask anything!"

"Ah!" His eyes watered. Marcel? Got you. "But you'd do it if you could?"

"What, fake hermeneutics? Tell her all the answers in advance?"

"Tell me. Are things any different in real life? The teacher does the spiel. Marxist. Poststructuralist. Lacanian. The enterprising kid goes to the stacks and looks up the professor's old dissertation. The one the prof got published when he was junior fac by including just enough quotes from the people doing the peer review. The student commits all this party line to memory. Lo and behold, what should show up on the final but—"

"I guess I'd rather lose than cheat."

"What's cheating about it? Even if it is, it's a cheat so colossal and magnificent it takes your breath away."

"So you want Vaucanson's duck? You want that mechanical chess-playing Turk with the midget inside? Why don't we just strap some printed circuit cards on me and I'll take the exam."

"Jesus Christ, Marcel. Never *mind*. Ever since you thought we might actually win this thing, you've been no fun at all."

But he could not let the angle drop. The next day, he'd be at it again. "Ram is judging, right? What do we know about him? Are you reading her the *Mahabharata*?"

We knew, in fact, precious little about Ram. I passed him often enough in the Center's halls. He greeted me always, the epitome of cheer, with some gnomic well-wish that half the time I could not make out. When I could, I often doubted what I came up with. "Your luck, God willing, continues to be what you imagine it?" Or, "I don't even have you to ask about how the day isn't going!"

By his own testimony, he was a native speaker. Either English had gone as plural as advertised, or, along with many other fellow Centerites, Dr. Gupta had replaced the standard version with a professional upgrade.

One late spring day, his passing greetings expanded into real speech.

"I saw that I-should-praise-it-so-much-as-to-call-it-a-review of your book." His melodious, clipped, Northern Subcontinental syllables delighted me. I could not say why. "What the hell kind of ridiculous thing are they trying to pretend about this culture of yours? They think perhaps this is something that you are making up, God forbid, your so-called story? So your precious Los Angeles—the jewel in the crown, as it were—is just now discovering the condition that the rest of the world has been living in since day one?"

I decided he must be sticking up for me. "Thank you, Ram."

"No, my friend. I am the one who should be thanking you. You fiction writers are the only creatures among us arrogant enough to be the conscience of the race, as you might say. God forbid anyone should let the critic decide which of you shall live and which die. My mother wrote over one hundred of what you call fictions. She stopped reading reviews after the first several dozen of her books."

"Did you—several dozen?"

"Especially after she won India's Pulitzer Prize."

"India's Pulitzer?"

Ram laughed, high-pitched, singsong. Nothing was cultural. Nothing essential, anyway. "You know what I mean."

We fed her an eidetic image of the Bible. The complete Shakespeare. We gave her a small library on CD-ROM, six hundred scanned volumes she might curl up with. This constituted a form of cheating, I suppose. An open-book exam, where the human, in contrast, had to rely on memory alone. And yet we meant to test just this: whether silicon was such stuff as dreams might be made on.

Besides: Helen didn't *know* these texts. She just had a linear, digital array where she might go look them up. A kid with her own computer. A front-end index hasher helped her locate what she looked for. She could then place the complete text on her own input layers for mulling over.

This way she could read at night, while no one was around. And she didn't even need a flashlight. The one thing missing from her education was a sense of danger. The forbidden. The risk factor. Someone to come tell her to knock it off and get to bed.

In a wonderful twist, Helen acquired Chen and Keluga's physical-

246

symbol rule base twice. At the low-level, we deep-wired many of the relationships into actual data structures. These we affixed at junctures in the net of nets, where they in effect applied semantic filters to her thought. But Helen also learned our colleagues' work by appending their culled knowledges herself, inefficiently, to her own weighted and qualified, high-level Platonic reflection.

Worldliness was massive, and deeper than any sea-dingle. It came, in the end, only in the form of a catalog.

We told her about parking tickets and two-for-one sales. About tuning forks and pitchforks and forked tongues and the road not taken. We told her about resistors and capacitors, baiters-and-switchers, alternating current, alternate lifestyles, very-large-scale integration and the failure of education to save society from itself.

We told her about wool and linen and damask. We told her about finches and feeders, bats and banyans, sonar and semaphores and trail markers made of anything the living body might shed. About mites and motes, insect galls and insecticides, about mating for life or for a fraction of a minute.

We taught her about the Securities and Exchange Commission. We told her about collectors who specialize in Depression-era glass. About the triple jump and the two-man luge. About how people used to teach their children about the big hand and the little hand. About defecation and respiration and circulation. About Post-it notes. Registered trademarks and draft resistance. The Oscar and Grammy and Emmy. Dying of heart disease. Divining with a fresh-cut alder rod.

We told her how the keys on a piano were laid out. About letterhead. Debutantes' balls. Talk radio and docudrama television. Colds and flus, and a brief five-century tour of their treatments. The Great Wall and the Burma Road and the Iron Curtain and the Light at the End of the Tunnel. About how the earth looked from space. About a fire that has raged underground beneath a Pennsylvania town for the last thirty years.

We showed her the difference between triforium and clerestory. We traced the famous pilgrims' routes through time and space. We told her about spoilage and refrigeration. How salt was once worth its weight in gold. How spice fueled the whole tragic engine of human expansion. How plastic wrap solved one of civilization's nightmares and started another.

We showed her Detroit, savaged by short-term economics. We showed her Sarajevo in 1911. Dresden and London in 1937. Atlanta in 1860. Baghdad. Tokyo, Cairo, Johannesburg, Calcutta, Los Angeles. Just before, and just after.

We told her East African in-law jokes. Java highland jokes about stupid Sumatrans. Aussie put-downs of Pommy bastards. Catskills jokes about unlicensed operation of knishes. City folk and country folk. Pat and Mike. Elephant riddles. Inuit jokes where fish and bears scoff at the mere idea of human existence.

We told her about revenge and forgiveness and contrition. We told her about retail outlets and sales tax, about ennui, about a world where you hear about everything yet where nothing happens to you. We told her how history always took place elsewhere.

We taught her never to draw to an inside straight and never to send a boy to do a man's job. We laid out the Queen's Necklace affair and the Cuban trade embargo. The rape of continent-sized forests and the South Sea bubble of cold fusion. Bar codes and baldness. Lint, lintels, lentils, Lent. The hope, blame, perversion, and crippled persistence of liberal humanism. Grace and disgrace and second chances. Suicide. Euthanasia. First love. Love at first sight.

Helen had to use language to create concepts. Words came first: the main barrier to her education. The brain did things the other way around. The brain juggled thought's lexicons through multiple subsystems, and the latecomers, the most dispensable lobes, were the ones where names per se hung out.

In evolution's beginning was not the word but the place we learned to pin the word to. Little babies registered and informed long before they invented more mama by calling her such. Aphasics, even deaf-mute sign aphasics, wove rich conceptual tapestries through their bodies' many axes in the absence of a single verb.

Chen and Keluga's dream seemed more hopeless to me all the time.

The lexical rules of speech were not enumerable. Not even recursively so. So much less so, the lexical rules of felt existence. I spoke to Helen sentences that had half a dozen valid parsings or that resisted parsing altogether. I pitied her as I reeled off the exceptions to a Chen-Keluga semantic categorization of "tree." All trees have green leaves at some time during the year unless the tree is a red maple or a saguaro or diseased or dormant or petrified or a seedling or recently visited by locusts or fire or malicious children or unless it is a family tree or a shoe tree or . . . An exhaustive dictionary for the term would take every tree that ever lived just to make the pages.

Not to mention trees in politics, religion, commerce, or philosophy. I could read Helen the poem that insisted no poem in creation stood comparison to one. But I could not lay out the difference between popular and academic, between hearth and hermeneutic, poetry and verse, nineteenth and twentieth centuries, Then then and Then now, between evocative simile and mind-fogging confusion, prewar sentimentality and the deforested poem-landscape just before that poet's death in the French trenches. Words alone would not explain to Helen the difference between "poem" and "tree." She could diagram, but she could not climb.

I taught her the parts of the internal combustion engine and how to make change. I told her how my brother liked to go into the "Everything's a Dollar" store and ask how much things were. I told her Taylor's favorite joke about the priest, the scientist, and the literary critic each receiving the death sentence. I told her about the WPA and the interstate system. She asked why there were interstates in Hawaii. I couldn't say.

I told her how, as a boy, I often played at saving my plastic farm animals from a worldwide flood. Only when I managed to corral them all into a small cardboard box were they saved. Then I would look for a smaller cardboard ark and start the whole desperate rescue over again.

I told her all these data, weaving from them a plot of well-formed sentences. But she would never get to their essence through sentences alone. I told her the term for that sensation we feel when some noun we slam up against triggers reengagement with the world's living concepts. But the tag did not yet let her feel anything close to the name's underpinning cascade.

Sensation was my lone river into the interior. More pictures and sounds. A bitmap was, even with fancy compression algorithms, worth a good deal more than 1K words. I thought to bruise her into concept. Soak her hands in the gush of pump water that all those parts of speech merely stood for.

I played more Mozart for Helen. Mozarts of every make and model, from every era of history and most major landmasses. I let her linger over eternally returning rondos. I stood by and watched her struggle with the most banal radio tune, leaping to make it out, falling always five fingers short of feeling's plagal cadence.

"Nice treble," Lentz cracked about a polyphonic piece from one renaissance or another. "Don't you think all performing countertenors should have to pass a urinalysis?"

I repeated the joke to Helen. Nothing but ache and confusion. I tailored a hurt for her, and God save such a pitiless engineer.

She had trouble with values, because she had no fear of self-preservation, no hierarchy of hard-wired pain. She had trouble with causality, because she had no low-level systems of motion perception from which the forms of causality are thought to percolate. She was a gigantic, lexical genius stuck at Piaget's stage two.

Helen's refugee readings shook loose my own strangeness. Now that I'd told New York there would be no more fictions, anything might happen. In fact, it already had. My life story was one only through the barest red-penciled edits. On second reading, everything seemed different. I'd forgotten all the good bits, the scene swellers and interstices, the supporting characters and exotic locales, there for no reason but density and flavor. I wasn't the genre I'd thought I was.

I left the Center after one extended session and blundered into a spring that had arrived in my absence. It took my eyes a minute to adjust, my thoughts a moment longer. The real season, or some convincing autumn look-alike? I'd lost track, turned around in time.

All this awakened alien sensation came home to rest in A. In my idea of A. A.'s body, whether in faint first run or focused replay, moved through possibility like a question through silence. My new-found land. I don't know if she led me to the open text, or if I opened on the hope of reading through to the end with her. She bent like a reflexive verb. When I saw A., I saw myself looking out over the plain of the visible. And whatever I looked on, there I saw A.

The day Helen taught herself to read print, I wanted to walk across the waterlogged town and tell A. Each time the temperature fluctuated, I wanted to run and see if she was well. When Helen's favorite voice made it seem the world had been created earlier and more often than anyone suspected, I wanted to call A., play the cut for her over the phone. I filled with the idea of her at each breeze. A good punch line, and I could rework the anonymous disarmament she had so far flashed me into an actual smile.

I imagined complaining to A. about Lentz's annoyances. Lentz's wife, locked in the absolution of perpetual forgetting, made me want to rush to protect her. To find in her my protection. In my mind, I showed her that wall calendar of the couple, taken by their vanished child. We stood in front of it together, saying nothing.

Most nights, I fell asleep wishing her well.

A. turned my whole conception of delight into a free-range phantom. Because she existed, my letters again had a rudder. The air at this hour of my life smelled arbitrary, unbounded, like India, like earthworms after a rain, like a macaronic, like a surprise century back in the B.C.'s, one I hadn't thought about since I was small. All in what A. brought me to know.

But I did not know A. at all. All I knew was her name.

I still worked at times from the computer lab housed in the bowels of English. Helen and I could talk anywhere. She did not care where on the campus backbone I logged on. She seemed perhaps marginally stiffer over the ASCII link than she was in conversation. But that was Helen's lone grudge against the remote humanities.

The lab swarmed at all hours with students trying to coax paper assignments out of recalcitrant keyboards. I entered the fray one afternoon, almost spinning around and leaving when I saw her. She perched over a stack of Henry James novels, pushing the hair from her eyes and leaning into her typing.

I took the terminal behind hers, short of breath, as if I'd sprinted there. I considered turning myself in to the campus police to spare her the bother. My telltale heart had to work flat out to be heard over the machines' chorus of cooling fans.

I telnetted over to the Center, managing to make the link, to hit the right keys by accident. A., six feet in front of me, hacked in agitation at her writing. I threw her off somehow, sitting this close. The scent of my pheromones.

Of course, I represented nothing to this woman, not even agitation. Her trouble was real, mechanical. She aimed her exasperation at the keyboard. Server lag held up the show, and her client computer failed to respond. She suffered a network virus, the brainchild of some software prodigy who would not have defaced the decal on a stranger's car but who thought nothing of malicious destruction of stored idea.

A. fumed in analog rage. She thrashed at the command and control keys, using the mouse cruelly. She snorted like a bull. She threw one hand up in the air. To no one at all, she called out, "What's the waiting period on handguns in this state?"

I'd heard her so often in my sleep that the sound of her voice shocked me. No one stopped typing even long enough to chuckle.

She couldn't kill me more than once. I leaned forward, matching her tone. "Shorter than the wait on network response." I looked down and saw myself from a distance, quaking like a sixteen-year-old.

She swung around to register me, distracted. "I thought as much." She turned back to her screen. I lived out that life where those were the only words we would ever exchange.

Another aggravated minute and she looked around again. "You're not, like, digitally literate by any chance, are you?"

I mumbled something so doped it belied any claim to competence. But I stood, walked over, and despite the attack of palsy, helped her retrieve her afternoon's work from the ether.

"Magic," she declared. She gathered her printout and disk. She stuffed them, along with the pile of James, in a black rucksack. "Thanks! I gotta run." And she abandoned me to the endless process of revision.

I saw her some days later at the department mailboxes. It took two beats to convince myself I could greet her legitimately.

She took three to respond. "Oh, hi." She reached out a hand, not to touch, but to affix me in space. Her wrist went down and her fingers up, pointing at me. A confiding gesture, a cross between a fifties hand soap commercial and a brass-extended Thai classical dancer. "From the computer lab, right?"

I introduced myself.

Her mouth made a cipher of uninterested surprise. "Oh. You're the Parasite-in-Residence, aren't you?"

"Yep. That's me." *Yep?* I heard Lentz whisper to me. *Yep?*

"I heard you were arrogant." I thought it might be worth telling Helen: the various names for isolation.

"I—I have an image problem."

She gave her name. I tried to look as if I were committing it to at least short-term memory.

"How old are you?" she asked.

"I was just heading for a coffee," I answered. My first since the age of fourteen. "Care to join me?"

She looked up. The hand again, calculating. Worth it, not worth it? She would have bolted in an instant if she knew I wanted her company.

"I guess I could use a cup. I've this deadly seminar at two, and I need all the help I can get."

I maintained myself on the way to the café. If not Garrick or Gillette, I at least avoided utter nitwittery. I felt disembodied. Detached. Steeped in emergency-room calm. War coverage with the sound turned off.

We talked shop, the one shop we had in common. Grad school was her life. I'd lived through it recently enough to pretend I remembered it. I told her the story of my existence, or at least the radio mix. Everything but the essentials. I told her how I'd always thought I'd be a physicist, until I heard Taylor interpret texts.

"Where was that?"

"Ai! I'm sorry. Here. All here."

"Professor Taylor? I don't think I've heard of him."

"He died. A couple of years before you arrived." Traceless in her generation.

"And you never finished?"

"Not in so many words, no. I guess I wrote my first novel instead."

She laughed. "Probably more worthwhile than the diss." The way a person might say that stamp collecting might be worth more to the race in the long run than, say, investment banking. "What made you leave?"

I told her how specialization left me parochial. I told her that theory and criticism had shaken my belief in what writing might do. I told her about my father's death and the seminar where we counted the feet of that Robinson sonnet on mercy killing.

I was talking too much. "How about you? How far along are you?"

She grew restive and subdued all at once. "Not as far as I thought."

"You've taken the master's exam?"

"Yeah." Miles away.

"When?"

She laughed. "Who wants to know?" She took a slow sip. "It seemed like such a landmark while I was doing the run-up to it. I worked so hard to prepare. Then two days, a few questions. They say okay, you know this stuff. It's over. You don't even get a chance to flex."

"But now it gets fun, right?"

"You think? I'll be middle-aged by the time I get the doctorate. No offense."

I hiked up a grin. "None taken."

"And no matter how good I am, I might be waiting on tables afterward, like all the other Ph.D.s in literature. They lied to us, you know. By accepting us into the program, they implied we'd have jobs when we were done."

"Nobody gets work?"

She snorted. "One in four, in a good year. And some of those who get jobs are repeats, out for their third or fourth time. The whole profession is a total pyramiding scheme."

"And by the time you guys get the chain letter . . ."

"It'll take more new bodies to finance the payoffs than there are undergraduates in the galaxy."

A. stopped to greet a passerby and to wave at someone seated two tables away. She knew half the people in the café. I, too, now fit somewhere in her star system's outer orbits.

"I wouldn't feel like such a sucker if the whole process weren't such a bilking. This is the most class-conscious society I've ever been part of. The department superstars lord it over their minor tenured colleagues, who saddle all the junior faculty with shit work, who take it out on the senior grads, who have no time for the master's candidates, who hold the undergraduates in contempt. That's not even mentioning the nonacademic staff."

"Is it that bad? I'm out of the loop." So far out that I could not even pick up her rhythm.

"Worse. We carry the same teaching load as faculty, and get paid maybe a seventh what you do. Socially, we're pariahs. I doubt the turf wars in business are half as bitter."

"How can the fight be so ugly over so small a piece of pie?"

A. grunted. "It's ugly *because* there's nothing to fight over."

We could buy a house. She'd never have to worry about making a living again. I could call New York, tell them I had another book in me after all. She could spend all day living, recovering the pleasure of the text.

"Maybe the whole discipline is breaking up," I suggested. "As a relative outsider, I'd say no one seems to know quite what they want the thing to become anymore."

"Total chaos. Who's in, who's out, who's up, who's down. All that hot new stuff, the pomo and the cultural studies and the linguistic-based solipsism. I'm fed up with it. It's all such verbal wanking off. Frankly, I no longer give a fuck what happens to Isabel Archer. Neither politically, economically, psychologically, structurally, nor posthumanistically. So she's got to choose which of these three loser boys she has to marry. This takes how many hundred pages?"

Her eyes caught mine and her hand flew to her mouth. "Oops.

Sorry. It's that Catholic pottymouth of mine. You are faculty, aren't you?"

"Technically. So what do you think you'll do with yourself?" Name the city. Your terms. Unconditional.

"I figure I might get a job in business somewhere. Editing or marketing or something. If I'm going to be abused, I can at least get paid to take it."

She gave me not one syllable of encouragement. No shy curiosity or even dry interest. But I had already done so much on no encouragement at all. All on my own.

It occurred to me: who A. was. Why I had come back to U. to meet her. A. was Helen's pace rabbit. Her heat competition. She had beaten the master's exam, the one we'd pitch our machine against. She was the woman who pulled love from the buried grave. The designated hitter for frailty, feeling, and whim. The champion of the humans.

"Thanks for the coffee," she said. "I have to make animal tracks. See ya!"

She disappeared faster than she had the first time.

But I had spoken to A. I'd sat three feet from her, for half an hour. Amid a corsage of coffee spoons, I replayed the conversation. I lived on that "See ya," trying to wrest it back from metaphor, to move around in it, through the latticework of lived time.

C. must have cared for my third book. She said as much in every available way, and she had no particular reason to lie just yet.

The story had mutated into a hopeful monster. Here and there, I tried to code into its paragraph cells the moves we made, the friends we loved, the events that shaped us and were worth saving. I hoped my molecular genetics might transcribe, if not an encyclopedia of successful solutions to experience, at least some fossil record of the questions. I wanted my extended metaphors to mirror speculation in the widest lens, the way the genome carries along in time's wake all the residue of bygone experiments and hypotheses, from bacteria on.

256

But novels, like genomes, consist mostly of intron baggage. And as with evolution, you can't always get there efficiently from here.

At thirteen hundred pages, my typescript had only the longest odds against being bought. Whatever my publishers expected, it wasn't this. At best, they'd issue a desperate request that I change trajectories, free the skinny book hiding inside this sumo. At worst, they'd kiss me off and wish me well. Great fun, but. Maybe one of those avant-garde presses?

C. and I went to the post office together. We were both more nervous than we'd been the first time, years before. We didn't know what to hope for. The manuscript took up a small crate.

"Send it by boat," C. said.

"It's expensive either way," I countered. "And the difference isn't that big. We can swing it, sweet!" I giggled.

"Boat," C. insisted. "Surface rate." Her eyes clouded. In a moment, she might have shouted or turned and walked away without a word.

I cradled the box, with its long customs form marked *Drukwerk*. Printed matter. Several kilos of story, an attempt to feel, in music, life's first principles and to hear, in those genetic principles, living tune. I'd tried to ground creation's stepladder in its molecular building blocks. I'd written a book that aspired to understanding, when I could not even understand the woman on whom my actions depended.

We sent my book Stateward by slow boat. Outside the post office, C. kissed me long and hard. She gamboled a few steps, exhilarated by the dusk. "Come on. Let's go out to eat." We never went out. "Let's go have Chin-Ind."

We celebrated by heading into the city and dining on rijsttafel. "The wages of colonialism," C. babbled. "Calories *and* imperial exploitation," she said, holding up a satay. "Now, there's guilty pleasure for you."

At meal's end, we realized that we'd forgotten to toast. C. held up what was left of her water glass. "To us, Beauie. To the pair bond. To the double helix."

"What could be simpler?" I added.

Nothing could harm us anymore. I had lived to finish my work. The rest of life would all be bonus round. Afterward, we went home and read to each other, the first time in a long time. I spooned my body against hers. Before we fell asleep, I joked, "If they don't want this one, I can always go back to programming."

" . . . To which the woman says, 'If you want infidelity, you'll have to find someone else.' "

"That's a joke," Helen announced. Part theory, part improv, part defensive accusation. She had learned to recognize humor: those utterances even more inexplicable than the rest of the unsolvable smear.

Or she told it in my voice alone. I felt unaccountably happy. I had for a week. Blessed by everything. And everything I looked upon felt blessed.

Her response fed my upswell. "Helen," I rambled, "thy beauty is to me like those Nicean barks of yore."

"Powers?" Lentz warned from behind his desk. "Careful."

"What? You think today's twenty-two-year-old knows from Nicean barks of yore?"

"I didn't mean that."

I looked over at him. Lentz did not glance up from his stack of journal offprints.

"Yours," Helen corrected me. "Those barks of yours."

"No, yore. Barks of yore. It means an old boat."

I did the rest of the poem for her. Oral interp. It was on the List, after all.

"Who weary, wayworn wanders?" she wanted to know.

"Ulysses?" I looked over at Lentz for confirmation. He ignored me. "Yeah. It has to be Ulysses. Do you remember him?"

"The wily Odysseus." It was impossible to tell if she had developed a facetious streak, or if she was just mimicking. "Why he wanders?"

I corrected her Creole syntax and made my best guess.

"Why is the sea perfumed?"

"Complex," I clarified. "Basically, I think it means that a sweet thing calls the wanderer home."

"It means that sweetness is like the way you go back."

"Me?"

"Beauty calls you back to me."

"Not me. The speaker of the poem. And not you, I'm afraid. A friend of the speaker's, also named Helen. If that's her real name."

Helen said nothing. Lentz said, "I told you to be careful."

Only more lessons could cure the effect of lessons. "Remember that 'Helen' is also the name—"

"Helen of Troy," Helen rushed. She had paid particular attention to the story when we'd done it.

"And the wily Odysseus . . ."

"Went to reget that Helen."

" 'Reget' is not a word. Recover, maybe. Retrieve. Rescue."

Lentz mumbled, "The bitch hardly asked to be rescued."

"On those Nicean barks of yore." Helen sounded almost distorted with excitement.

"Explain."

"The wily Odysseus went to Troy on old boats."

The presentation was clumsy. I had to lead the witness. But I doubted that many high schoolers could extract as much, these days. A face like the face that launched a thousand ships now called one back to port.

I hid my pleasure, not wanting to scatter Helen's synapses. I thought to correct her preposition. But I couldn't come up with a good rule for when we travel on ships and when we travel in them. Rules could be either followed or known. Not both.

"It talks of love, the words?" Helen asked. She copied my inversion, the leading question. The poem is about love, wouldn't you say?

"Hah!" Lentz cleared his throat with the syllable. " 'Love' is the envelope wrapped around 'uhgh,' to make the groan pronounceable in polite company."

"You are bad news, Lentz," I told him.

"Bad news," Helen agreed.

Her two words knocked me speechless. Somehow during the endless sessions, she'd trained herself to hear a third person in the room.

I whistled low. "That's my baby."

Lentz, too, was nonplussed. But tried to hide it. "Bad news? Am I? Tell me: What form would good news take?"

"All about love," Helen repeated. She had learned the even more impressive and necessary skill of ignoring a nuisance. Then she made the kind of sloppy, hasty generalizing stab we'd built her to make. "They are all about love, isn't it?"

"Helen?" My stomach crawled up my windpipe. We were all dead.

"Every poem loves something. Or each wants something in love. Something loves power. Or money. Or honor. Something loves country." On what catalog could she be drawing? "I hear about something in love with comfort. Or with God. Someone loves beauty. Someone death. Or some poem always is in love with another lover. Or another poem."

I waited until I had control of my throat again. I don't know what she made of the extended silence. "What you say, Helen," I deliberated, "is true. But only in the most general sense. The word doesn't have the same sense in all your cases. The similarity is too big to mean anything. It's the differences that interest us. The local. The small picture."

"Then I need to be small. How can I make me as small as love?"

I lost it. I could find no words.

Lentz, too, failed to get away cleanly. But he was faster into the breach. "You heard her, Powers. She wants to make herself small enough for love."

"How am I supposed to tell her . . . ?"

"How do you think? Get the letters."

All I could do was make myself small. I waited for him to tell me I hadn't heard right. He didn't. "How do you know there are letters? Not that I'm admitting there are."

"Now, really. Thirty-five-year-old returns alone from Europe? To the *Midwest*? And there are no letters?"

I brought in the letters. I'd rescued hers on a brief salvage run a few months after my deportation from E. For two days, while C. hid on the other side of the province, I picked through my possessions and decided what would fit in two suitcases.

For two days, everything I looked on herniated my chest. My self hemorrhaged. Certain things would not fit into my bags. The view of the river valley from the hill outside town. The decent shower stall I had promised C. for a year and never installed. The raw herring and the fruit beers.

The letters, however, fit. The book her parents had learned English from fit. The only sweater C. ever knitted, that never fit me, fit.

C. sent my letters back, special fourth class, the minute I had a forwarding address. I ended up curator of both ends of a dozen years of correspondence. I meant never to read a word of it again. I had no idea why I saved so much as a page. Now I had a reason. Helen.

I started at the beginning. I chose from the stack, opening envelopes without knowing anymore what each contained. I tried to set the context of each passage, as far as I could recall it.

"This one I wrote to her while taking the bus up to my father's funeral.

"Dear C., Thank you for seeing me off this morning. These are full days for me, as I try to piece together what is past and passing. Our new friendship is part of that fullness, and as with any feeling, it scares. A pleasing scare, though.

"I was very young then," I apologized. I flipped forward; this was a bad idea. Disaster. "Okay. This one she wrote me from U., just before we moved to B.

"How are you, my Ricky? I'm anxious to hear from you. It's been almost twelve hours. (What a wimpess, eh?) I imagine you sniffing autumn or working hard, making plans and saying *goede dag* to everyone, or perhaps lying quietly in the dark, one hand spread flat against that curve of your chest, thinking of nothing in particular, calm beneath the growing excitement of what we are up to . . .

"I'm enjoying *The Wanderer*—about halfway through—especially as it's turning out to be quite different than I expected. I wonder if later in life we'll be able to remember those qualities of adolescence—the crystal sharpness, the total rage of emotion, the significance in every triviality. Sometimes, even this close, I forget, and when I do remember it's only with gratitude that I am past it, have survived, moved on.

"I am no literary wiz, as you well know. I cannot read a work

261

with my head but only in my ribs, where my first love for words began. And my ribs say yes to this book.

"Are you sure sure sure? Sure you know what we are doing? Sure you want me along on this exploration? Well, teacher knows best . . .

"In the meantime, get out as often as you can, friend. See everything for me. I enclose, from U., a bit of early autumn to remember on.

"It's a leaf," I told Helen. I held the crumpled shred of ocher up to the digital camera. It looked like nothing at all.

The pile gave me temporal vertigo. Aerograms, postcards, stationery of all races colors and creeds, handmades proclaiming *"Hartelijk Gefeliciteerd"* or "Happy *Sinterklaas.*" Reading the letters to Helen took longer than the dozen years their writing had taken.

"This one was from her folks' place, before they left Chicago. She must have been on vacation.

"Today, inspired, I finally picked up a pen and started working on the piece I've been mulling over since school. A day in the life of a young woman (surprise) frustrated by her existence, art, MEN, people, work. You heard this one before? It's a search for control and a study of how difficult that is for a woman of her (my) age. I have a wonderful first sentence where I compare morning light to a cup of cold coffee. Yech!"

"She did that stuff, too?" Lentz interrupted.
"For a while.

"I'm enjoying, though. You really shook me out of my lethargy over the phone yesterday. I even wandered over to the pianny today and tried out a few tunes . . .

"Ugh—my stomach has decided, since it's midnight, that now is a good time to rebel against everything I shoved in it earlier. Hang on, folks— I've got to be more careful of what I eat.

262

"I think I will retire now. I kiss you in my thoughts, love. *Ik houd van jou.* See if you can translate."

"Tell me the strange words," Helen demanded. Funny. "Strange" and "foreign" were the same word in Dutch.

"They mean, 'I hold of you.' "

"They mean, 'I love you,' " Lentz corrected. I suppose the guess didn't require too much inspiration. His tone, informative. Empiricism at its gentlest. "Give us more of yours."

I picked at random one I wrote from U. while she was in Limburg alone, on her private scouting mission.

"Today, Thanksgiving, although flat on my back in bed nursing my first bad cold in years, I'm struck with amazing gratitude, knocked out by my good fortune at having had a few moments to know you. C., without the place you make, without your ratifying vantage, life's whole, fluke, majestic, thermodynamic-cheating trick would beat like an ornate, functionless Victorian cast-iron engine . . .

"You feel like the seasons to me: fixed, monumental, periodic, but forever surprising in particulars. I think of how, in the spring, you insist that the buds need kissing before they will come out . . ."

"Didn't you ever write her any *news*, Marcel?" Forgiving. Curious.

"I wish I had." She might have been able to live with news. "The ending is nice, though: 'Until I can tell you in person, this is my thanks, for everything.' "

I read her reply from E., beginning,

"Beau, you won't believe our luck. I've found a place for us! People told me I'd be on the list forever, but by total accident, the perfect apartment just fell into my lap. It's a free-gazelle flat, as they call bachelorette pads. It will be even cozier with two. It's all skylit, the kitchen is small but lovely, and there's even a nook where you can put your feet up and finish that endless story of yours . . ."

I opened the next one. "I'm sorry," I apologized to both Lentz and Helen. "I can't read any more."

Then my eyes fell on the first line of the sheet I was holding. From E., to my mother's address. During my trip back for the publication of that novel I'd written in that Limburg free-gazelle's flat. I read on, unable not to. Read, to see what happened.

"Beau, I'm afraid this letter is all bad news. My cousin G. died yesterday. You know how sick he was, but the whole family is reeling from how fast things went. N. and the kids were with him throughout. She says that, given his disease, the end was peaceful and almost happy when it came.

"N. was amazing. G. went into a panic brought on by combined suffocation and heart failure. N. kept telling him, just picture yourself on a train heading south, to your favorite café in Italy. Imagine yourself seated out in the sun, doing the things you love most in this life. Drinking a *pils*, reading a *detektive*, ogling the pretty women.

"N. stepped out for a minute, to catch her breath. When she came back, G. was dead. The kids were upset because just before he died, their dad kept making this hooking gesture with his hand, and they couldn't tell what he wanted. N. explained that he was pulling a train whistle, and that everything was okay . . ."

I stopped and raised my head. "I'd forgotten," I pleaded with Lentz. "I have no memory of this. Not even now. Not even rereading."

"Forgotten what, Marcel? What are you talking about?"

I couldn't take it in. Half a year, trying to make a novel out of a story that already lived to fruition in three paragraphs. Three paragraphs that I had not just let fall but had annihilated.

"The woman loves, now? Loves Beau?" Helen called me by a name. Whether she knew the name to be another word for "you" or even me was another matter. The question bayed over me, one of those alpine dogs trained to nuzzle up to avalanched corpses.

I debated telling Helen about the one postcard from C. I no longer had. In the months following our split, in one of several vacillations, she sent me a picture of Brueghel's *Harvesters*. For a message, she quoted the line I had written her, from the book she had seen me through.

If by some accident we get separated, meet me back here.

I wanted to hurt C., hurt her as badly as I could without her knowing I meant to. I wanted to tear the picture up. Then I asked: What would hurt more? I waited a month. Then I packed up various legal papers she had stored in the States—old tax returns, medical records—and sent them to her without a note. In the packet, I returned the wheat fields.

She wrote back just once more, to say she was getting married at the end of the month. She wouldn't mind if we made a financial settlement.

And thanks for the postcard, Beau. Yes, that's the place.

Saying everything but the definitive. *I'll be there. In my mind.*

I chose not to tell Helen this ending. Instead, I answered, "She says she still does, sometimes. In my sleep."

Helen would have fidgeted if she had digits. "Who can love who? Can any thing love any thing?" Could you love me, Richard? For example.

"It's hard to say what will or will not turn a person's head." I evaded what she did not ask outright.

"Turn a head?"

"It's a body thing," Lentz tortured her. "You wouldn't understand."

He gave her no more than the education she asked for. His functional example. The way Lentz loved.

Helen grew up quickly after that.

I turned thirty-two—the Goldberg number—just after submitting my finished draft. I came up for air in the spring of '89, returning to the world just in time to watch it yank itself into another place. "Bliss" is the wrong word for what it felt to be alive then, and I cannot use "heaven," because I was no longer young. Commotion, maybe. The sick thrill of checkpoint chaos.

Even from E., the air that year smelled epochal. Event fell, for once, inside perceivable wavelengths. The angel of history took up painting its canvas with a house brush. From a day's drive, out to the outer reaches, all the textbooks went into another edition. Each week scrapped and revised the only rules C. and I had ever lived under.

When the changes erupted, we two, along with everyone else in the mediated world, tuned in. Each night C. and I stared at global upheaval until there was no more footage to stare at. Then we went over to ears and did radio, on into the night until we lost the signal.

We got our word from the outside through a little rathole in the bottom of the cell door. News arrived on a bandwidth so narrow it stripped off everything in the message but the garbled header. And we were among the lucky ones, with options. When the Dutch got too parochial, we checked the Belgian coverage. If the German accounts collapsed into myopia, we fell back on the British or French.

Our border-town smorgasbord of sources still left us like deaf and blind children in front of a burning house, with nothing to tell how the fire blazed except the heat on our faces and the signs shouted into our hands.

Nothing could ever be the same again. But what things would be was beyond either of us. For that matter, what they had been would never be certain, now that they were gone.

The world's orphans seemed to be taking adult nonsense by the collar and reprimanding it. We watched them filling squares, sitting atop barbed-wire walls, everywhere dismantling the forbidden. For a few exhilarating weeks, the picnic fed on itself. "What a win," C. said. Then a glance my way: "It is a win, isn't it?"

A season sufficed to tell. It wasn't a win. It wasn't even a break-even. Tanks, the old treaded correctives, rolled out and recommenced forcing the child army's lengthy and painstaking rout.

As quickly as it started, *See It Now* flicked out, leaving nothing but assorted body counts. By New Year's, the message settled in: clear the streets. Go back to your houses. Even those, like C. and I, who had done nothing but stand by and watch, were expected to return to our daily gauge, the scale of the dazedly private.

For two months, through a glazed window, time had seemed on its way somewhere. We might have contributed, or at least comprehended. But when the goods came to market, we were again waved off.

Now more than ever, C. chafed at the work she had chosen. "They're predicting a big rush on translators over at school. European integration. Return of stability to Asia. A few hundred million new potential owners of major appliances in the former East Bloc alone. The problem is finding a Dutch translation for 'New World Order' that doesn't have unfortunate associations."

C.'s fears were irrational but not unreasonable. Hers was the purest cynicism: hope concealing itself from itself. A day came when she no longer had the heart to let me talk her out of it.

That winter never froze, so there was no spring thaw. On the first jacket-free day that C. wasn't buried in papers, we went for a long walk. We rewarded ourselves with outside, although neither of us had been particularly good.

We wandeled along the cow paths that connected E. to a nearby rolling region called *Klein Zwitzerland*. For long stretches, the land looked as it had for the last millennium. We headed at random, swinging between the nearest copse and its far clearing. We talked about current events, those that were no longer current. The ones we would never get past.

We lost track. Imperceptibly, we doubled back on our path. We found ourselves at that spot past which her father's postwar dray horse would not go, because of some political calamity it could still smell.

We drifted, as if by chance, alongside the American war cemetery that had decided C.'s fate so many years before she was born. We stood above it on a slight rise, looking down across the diffraction pattern of markers, the crucifix moiré. C. flashed me an almost haughty try-and-stop-me. She tore off down the hill, the liberating troops behind her.

The graves were tended now by an endowed institution. Volunteer work would disrupt no more generations. Memorial cottage industries had sprouted up around it: a chapel. An unknown's tomb with eternal flame. A huge panoramic map with arrows and counterarrows that attempted to triangulate history's meaning.

"You like this stuff, huh?" C. said. "You're a boy, right?"

I rubbed her shoulder: Forgive me. I've done nothing. She pulled away. Walked back. Took, then dropped my fingers.

After a search, we found the grave of the Polish kid. We stood in front of it, pushing twice his age. The day's warmth caught in my throat.

"How many times have you heard my mother tell you this story?" C. asked. "How many times have you heard me tell it?"

I shrugged. I already knew the Hebbian rule, in everything but its particulars and name. Repetition made things real. I already knew that I'd repeat the story myself until I discovered what to do with it.

"The woman never remarried. Six weeks, at eighteen."

C.'s face puffed red and phlegmy. She reached out and touched the white limestone, helping rub the name along its hunt for oblivion. She looked grim, already steeled for the death blow.

"Beau? Maybe we have to have a child."

As the forgotten allusion had it, the contract 'twixt Helen, A., and me was not for one or several months. Our training might have gone on forever, but for the fact that the bet had a due date. Helen, in the straightaway, began asking more questions than she answered.

My interrogation of A. escalated, too. Most often, she met my inquiries with friendly concessions that dinner might be fun, in, say, a week or two. Vague, ambiguous, preoccupied, as preoccupied as I became when the weeks went by without connection. The longer I put off posting her my rambling, poetic confessions, the more alive restraint made me feel.

I wanted to shower her with little trinket-gifts of false consciousness. Plant jokes, pluck, and deliver them in bunches. Call and ensure she was dressed properly for the weather.

I fed Helen on all the spines that poked out from under A.'s arms. I read her the critical studies, whose cachet now far exceeded the primary texts those studies had all but abandoned. What A. knew, Helen had to be able to follow. For A., though she did not know it yet, would be Helen's exam partner. I tried to be selective. The general death of the author would be hard on her. She had not yet gotten over Little Nell.

" 'Once more the storm is howling,' " I told Helen. " 'And half hid under this cradle-hood and coverlid my child sleeps on.' "

"What is Gregory's wood?" she wanted to know. "Where is the Atlantic? Who is that great Queen? What is a Horn of Plenty?"

"It's not important."

"Why isn't it important? What is important?"

"The poet is praying for his daughter. He does not want her to be beautiful at the expense of being kind."

"Helen again." Helen laughed. "Helen everywhere."

"I guess," I allowed, too tired to update her. "He thinks it would be better if the child grew up wise. Glad. 'That all her thoughts may like the linnet be, and have no business but dispensing round their magnanimities of sound.' "

" 'Merriment begin a chase . . . merriment a quarrel,' " Helen read, from her digital copy. " 'Assault and battery of the wind'?"

"He means the storm." How many fallacies I committed, with that *mean*. "Remember? The howling? He means all the anger in the world. The hatred."

" 'Can never tear the linnet from the leaf.' He means the storm won't blow the bird from the bough."

"Very good, sweet. If the mind has no hatred, hatred cannot hurt it."

" 'An intellectual hatred is the worst, so let her think opinions are accursed.' "

" 'All hatred driven hence, the soul recovers radical innocence and learns at last that it is self-delighting, self-appeasing, self-affrighting.' "

A figure in uniform slammed around the office-door frame.

"Sir, please leave right now by the south central stairwell. We have an order to evacuate the building."

I looked at him with total vacuity.

"Now, sir! We're asking that you not dick around, please." He slapped the frame with a rigid palm, then sprinted to the next office to spread the alarm.

I sat flapping a moment, as wash flaps in the real's breeze. I tried to shake myself into focus. Which of the various evacuations was under way? I ticked off the short list, calculating, until it hit me that calculation was moot.

I scanned the office: what to try to rescue? Lentz was abroad at one of connectionism's endless professional gatherings. What would he want saved? I cared for just one thing here, and she wasn't even here. She wasn't even a thing but a distributed process. Nothing of Helen existed in this room except her accoutrements, eyes and ears and mouth, dumb machines not worth carrying out.

Through the window, knots of scientists gathered on the south grounds. From my distance, they might have been refugees from any of the world's violent misgivings. They milled among handcarts of hastily heaped equipment, papers, floppies. We might have been in one of those perennial urban war zones, where research goes on in lean-tos of corrugated tin, on the run from the savagery it has armed and encouraged by whole catalogs of neglect.

I stood paralyzed. Instinct instructed me to duck down until sanity condescended to flit back to the feeder. I would have, had not another uniform shouted from the hall, behind a human trail drive. "Let's go. Move it, now."

I told Helen I would be right back.

270

In the main corridor, people congregated, vocalizing. The uniforms tried to move them along, with limited success. One officer gestured back toward Lentz's. "Is everyone out of there?"

I threw my hands up in the air. They came down clasped, against my head. "Yes," I screamed at him. And followed in shame to the safety outside.

There a police line condensed, a bumblebee black-and-yellow plastic strip erecting a barricade from nothing. One of those two-D Euclidean imaginaries that separate the sentient body from the site of politics. The Center's refugees clustered in chains, splitting and linking, staring back at the magnificent, emptied building as if the mystery might yield to visual inspection. Researchers clumped in conversation; even clueless outrage had to be talked out.

The police herded back the mass. They told everyone to go home until further notice. The MRI team, beyond frantic, pressed for information. Their equipment trapped inside the building included a behemoth prototype that cost more than the GNPs of half a dozen southern nations. I saw Ram at a distance. He was trying to comfort a distraught colleague whose brain bursts could have been read from across campus without an imager.

I came across Chen and Harold in the crowd. They stood picking lint off each other's tweed jackets. "Hey, Ricko," Harold greeted me. "Bomb scare. Somebody made a threat this morning on the radio call-in program."

"Hey," Chen echoed. He turned back to Harold. "Why you are not nervous?"

"Ha. I've done this before."

"The Center has had bomb scare before?"

"Oh, not here. In another life."

"Harold," I interrupted. "She's still in there."

His face ticked with panic. "She can't be. She's—" He drew up short when he hit on whom I meant. "Oh, for God's sake. You have her backed up somewhere, don't you?" His irritation was audible and crushing.

"*Harold*. She's not a program. She's an architecture. She's a multidimensional shape."

"You run her on silicon, don't you? Somebody downloads all those hosts to tape every week and archives them to remote sites."

"But she doesn't *run* on one machine. Her parts are spread over more boxes than I can count. She's grown to scores of subassemblies. Each one takes care of a unique process. They talk to each other across broadband. Even if we had the connects and vectors for each component system, we'd never get her reassembled."

Harold fell quiet. I could follow his thoughts. If the threat detonated, Helen would be the least of the Center's tragedies. The real hostages—clues to mental illness and immunological disorders, cathedrals of supercomputer engineering, insights into complexities from market turbulence to weather—dwarfed our strange sideshow. Only respect for the hours I'd put into the training kept him from annoyance. He gave me too much credit to credit what I thought.

"Well." He grimaced. "There seems to be no way to rescue her, then."

"Humorous," Chen decided. Chen was a theoretician. Chen stood to lose nothing, even if the fifty-five-million-dollar building and its irreplaceable contents collapsed in rubble.

I walked away, furious at idiocy in all its levels. My mind raced, and I gunned it. The Quad teemed with undergrads, heading for their two o'clock, indifferent to the fact that their campus flagship was about to blow.

Reflex landed me in front of English. The basement computer lab might have crawled with my colleagues. A. might have been there. I would not have known. I linked in to the Center over the coaxial backbone. I could not hear Helen's voice to read how it sounded. But the words that came across the screen asked, "Something is happening?"

I told her what was happening, as best as I could figure it.

"Helen could die?" Helen asked. "Extraordinary." She'd liked the story of how the novelist Huxley, on his deathbed, had been reduced to this one word.

She waited for me to say something. I could think of nothing to say. Helen had to do all the talking. "To a little infant, perhaps, birth is as painful as the other."

"Bacon," I said. It had not been that long.

"Francis Bacon," she encouraged me. "What says Browne? Sir Thomas?" she quizzed. By emulation.

"We all labor against our own cure."

"Never mind." She often said *Never mind* when I think she meant *Don't worry*. "Death will cure all the diseases." She meant that I, too, could pass the exam. If I put my mind to it.

In the end, the day belonged to those who stuck with the status quo. By evening, the Center's bomb scare had never happened. Time's hoax-to-explosion ratio increased infinitesimally.

The perpetrator was a junior professor in philosophy with a book out on Austin and Wittgenstein who, for reasons that now seemed obvious, had just been denied tenure. The police snagged the "Short-Fuse Philosopher" when he called the radio station back to elaborate.

Booked and jailed, he stuck by this second call, a linguistic equivocation that he seemed to hope would keep him from a decade in prison. He claimed his threat was never more than a moral subjunctive. The Center was draining the university dry, reducing the humanities to an obsolete, embarrassing museum piece. He'd made his point, he said. If there were any justice, there *would* have been a bomb. He'd proclaimed no more than hypothetical detonation, for which he expected no more than a hypothetical sentence.

"She's conscious," I accused Lentz, the instant he unpacked.

He mugged. "Welcome back to you, too, Marcel. Pronouncements, still? Sure she's conscious. At least as conscious as a majority of the state legislature."

"I'm serious." I told him about the bomb evacuation. About tapping in to Helen from the remote link while she was trapped in the building. "She asked me if something was happening. She figured out what was going on. She knew what it spelled for her."

Lentz jerked his neck back, unable to decide whether to delight in my ingenuousness or to decimate it. "Are we back to Implementation C?" The one where the humans combined to sucker me. "Weizenbaum's ELIZA? The Rogerian psychologist simulator? 'How are you?' 'Fine, thanks.' 'Let's talk about why you think you are fine.' Powers, you're like the student who stumbled onto a terminal where the program was running and thought—"

"No comparison."

I remembered the story. The student thinks he's on a Teletype, talking to a human. He converses, growing frustrated at the program's metagames. Finally, he dials the phone and gets the human he thinks he's been typing to. "What the hell do you think you're doing?" "What do you mean, what the hell do I think I'm doing?"

"No comparison. Don't insult me, Lentz. I know what she said."

"Rick. She associates. She matches patterns. She makes ordered pairs. That's not consciousness. Trust me. I built her."

"And I trained her." Lentz just stared at me, until I snapped. "Since you are all-knowing about matters mechanical, perhaps you can tell me how you came to be such a patronizing little shit."

By way of answer, he stood up. I saw us fighting, and wondered how I might even the odds enough so that beating him to a bloody pulp would have more than just clinical interest.

Lentz walked over to Helen's console and flipped on the microphone. She burbled, as she always did, at the promise of renewed communication.

"How do you feel, little girl?"

"I don't feel little girl."

He faced me. "Gibberish. She doesn't even get the transformation right."

"You're kidding me. You don't see . . . ? She means all sorts of things by that. She could—"

"All the meanings are yours." He returned to the mike. "Were you frightened?"

"What you is the were for?"

"Damn it, Helen. We're giving you quality time here. Please tell me: what hell that mean?"

"It's obvious," I answered for her. "She wants to know which Helen you are asking. Which one in time."

"Oh. You mean: 'When?' But let's not take points off for style. You realize that a conscious entity just coming through the fright of her life would know which 'you' I was talking about."

"It wasn't a big deal to her. She didn't make any special—"

"Please, Marcel. I'm asking her. Were you frightened yesterday, Helen?"

"Frightened out of fear."

"What's that from, Powers?"

"Antony and Cleopatra."

"When did you train her with it?"

"Two days ago."

"This is worse than key-word chaining. She's neither aware nor, at the moment, even cognitive. You've been supplying all the anthro, my friend."

"I'm not your friend. I thought you were an advocate. I thought you believed in the capability of nets."

"I am. I do."

"But just as a sleight of hand."

"The bet was, we could build a distributed net whose text interpretation reasonably mimicked an arrested human's. All we contracted to was product. We didn't promise to duplicate anything under the hood."

"A kind of black-box forgery, you mean."

Lentz just shrugged. "That's operationalism. The Turing Test. Can you pass off your simulation as functionally equivalent to the thing you're simulating?"

"There's an error lurking in there somewhere."

"Explain yourself, Marcel."

I flung my hand out toward Helen's console. "Full 'functional equivalence' would mean consciousness. If you simulate *everything* completely, then you've modeled the whole shape and breath of the living package. How does the black box behave when operations challenge themselves? When function looks under its own hood?"

Lentz grimaced. "Elan vital, Marcel. Mysticism."

"A behavior is not just its implementation. Function also has to include . . ." But I didn't know what else to call what function had to include. I felt slightly out of control. That mundane contradiction in terms. "How would we know, then, whether a perfect copy . . . ? When does an imitation become the real thing?"

Lentz scrunched up, bothered. "What's the real thing? What would it take to simulate awareness? Awareness *is* the original black box. Stop and think of the put-up job that high-order consciousness itself works on us. 'Everything's under control. Everything's handled— unanimous, seam-free.' The brain is already a sleight of hand, a massive, operationalist shell game. It designs and runs Turing Tests on its own constructs every time it ratifies a sensation or reifies an idea. Experience is a Turing Test—phenomena passing them- selves off as perception's functional equivalents. Live or Memorex? Even *that question* is a simulation we fall for every second of our waking lives."

"Irks care the crop-full bird?" Helen burst in. "Frets doubt the maw-crammed beast?"

Lentz almost spit in mid-clause. "Marcel. I have to grant you. She does have a disconcerting ability to pull appropriate quotes."

"Lentz! *Listen* to her. You think those are just quotes to her?" I felt myself getting hysterical. "What if they're real? What if she *means* something by them?"

"What if my grandmother had had testicles?"

"She'd be your grandfather," Helen reassured him.

I stared at Lentz's face, where a stain of dismay spread over the icy deep.

Children were out of the question. They always had been. And now more than ever.

"C. We've talked about this. There are a billion and a half too many of us already. How can we two be parents? We don't even know what we're doing or where we want to live."

She flashed me a look. She knew what she was doing. She knew where she wanted to live.

"Which is it?" she mouthed.

"Which is what?"

"Which is your reason? The billion and a half too many? Or the two of us?"

For years—forever—my reason had been C.'s. She'd seemed set, pleased with what we had. I'd always thought the choice was mutual. Now I saw it had all been me. C. had drawn the whole curve of her adult life out of deference and fear. Three months from graduation, she came up empty-handed. There was nothing left to be afraid of.

"Why didn't we ever get married?" she wanted to know.

"I thought that was all right with you."

"What does that mean, Rick?"

"I promised you my life, in privacy. It's easy to break a public contract. You just go to court. You can't break a private promise." And leave, with nothing, the one you promised all.

"How come we never signed the contract, too? What could it have hurt? I wanted everyone to think you were proud of me."

"Oh, C. Proud? I love you. Who is going to know that if we don't?"

"What were you holding back, Ricky?"

"Nothing. You have everything."

She challenged me with silence. If that's true, then ask me. Ask me now.

I couldn't. I couldn't even say why I couldn't. I always insisted I could make C. happy. But all that insisting left her more convinced of her unworthiness. Even if a public pact had worked, she'd always have resented being deeded someone else's happiness.

I meant to stay with C. forever, in precariousness. I knew no other way to continue that scrapbook we had started, seat-of-the-pants style, a decade before. My refusal to marry her was a last-ditch effort to live improvised love. It was my holding back. My failing her. My departure.

Gold Bug appeared in the States. Half a world away was not far enough for safety. When I finished my double thwarted love story, I thought that judgment was irrelevant. But life begins and ends in judgment. C. and I kept still and hoped for reprieve.

We got what we hoped. The book won a slice of attention. Those who still read read with a promiscuous hunger that would try anything once. Readers persisted in searching for a desperate, eleventh-hour fix. It might take any form at all, even this long, molecular strangeness.

C. and I flinched for weeks, coiled, waiting to be hit. The blow, when it fell, was a clap on the back. We sat dazed at the breakfast table, passing back and forth the glossy weekly with a readership even here, in our little ex-coal-mining town, where English was exotic novelty.

"That's not you, is it?" My first public photo made C. laugh bitterly. "I wouldn't recognize you without the caption."

"It's a haircut double," I tried, too hard. "Another reclusive writer with the same name, trying to pass himself off as Dutch. But note the palm trees in the background."

"You've made it, Beau. You've arrived."

I heard it in C.'s voice. My success killed her last chance. Somehow we'd lost our story.

"Nothing's changed, C. It's still the same book. I'll write the next one the same way. For the same reasons." To extend the parallax you give me and help refract sense from everything we come across.

She looked away, no longer believing or satisfied by belief.

I grew gentle. C. never could endure gentleness. She might have survived yelling. She might have been able to live with me, had I fought fair and shown anger.

"Buddy. Sweetheart. What do you want? Just tell me what you want."

But the only thing she'd ever wanted was the thing I took away by doing for her.

We fell. C. became skittish. She buried herself in schoolwork, her final translation project. She'd sit for meals, but do no more than nibble, chafe, and make polite conversation. Sometimes she grew giddy, hilarious. Her generosity screamed for help. She showered me in attentions and gifts—dried banana mixes, a pair of field glasses to spy on frescoed church vaults, books she knew I coveted but would never buy for myself.

Her hours became erratic; I never knew when I would see her or who she would be when I did. One night, she failed to come home at all. From the balcony where I always watched her get off the bus, I clocked the empty coaches each half hour until they stopped running. After midnight, as I prepared to phone the police, she called. She was all right; she'd explain when she got in.

That night was a night such as everyone spends at least once in life. C. walked in around midmorning. We couldn't look at each other.

"I'd better pop you some corn," I told her. Always one of her favorites.

"Ricky. Don't. Don't be nice to me. I can't bear it."

I popped her some corn. Not to outhurt her. To have something to do with my hands. I brought the bowl to where she sat. She would not look up, say a word, or eat.

"C. Beau. Say something. What's happening?"

C. froze, the classic small mammal in the headlights. Only: I was the headlights. It took me ten years, but at last I learned it. That comfort she showed me on the Quad—the internal calm I loved and built my own on—was dread. Paralysis. Her crumpled, engaging smile had never been more than sheer terror.

She said nothing. The more I needed to hear, the harder she bolted. My need gagged her, and her silence made me desperate.

"It's somebody else," she sneered. "That's what I'm supposed to say, right?"

"Is it somebody else?"

"I don't know."

"Suppose it were somebody else."

"P. At the Institute."

"Your teacher? The one that makes the Dutch girls cry?"

But that sadistic skill was mine alone. And C., in tears, chose her nationality.

Love became fierce after that. Sex, stripped of all ends, went ballistic. Our shy, awkward, ten-year delectation turned to sick and lovely heroin, worth any degradation to suck up. Doomed pleasure injected us with rushes neither of us knew we could feel. Caresses, each the last, burned in their care, and bites that began as tender mnemonics left bruises lasting weeks.

Our last abandoned love act delivered the violence we were after.

That night, in the dark, in our blushing bed, we sexed each other like alley strays, grilling each other's skins with nails, teeth, anything that would hook. We choked on those forbidden little cries that stoke lust by flattering it. We told desire that everything else was a lie. That we were not us until mindless in itch, incapable of any more than the odd feral syllable.

Spent, dripping, we held each other. This grace, at least, we shared, even if only humiliation. Sense slunk back. When it did, it struck me with fascinated horror that the condom we'd been using had vanished. Our barrier against birth lay nestled somewhere up inside her. We stared in incomprehension. In that awful second, we each accused the other of subconscious engineering.

We did what we could to counter. Then the long, stunned aftermath of accident.

"What if it's happened?" C. asked me, afraid. "What if I've conceived?"

"I don't know. What would you want to do?"

She seemed lifetimes away. She wasn't talking to me. She listened to some invisible messenger. "I don't know what I want. I don't know what to hope for. Part of me wants it all to be taken out of our hands. Maybe we think too much, Beau. Maybe we've always thought too much."

I thought a baby now, with things so volatile, would be disaster. She felt my failure of will, and to her, it was already a murder.

"What do you want?" she dared me. "What do you think?"

To be born is as painful as to die. "I think we need to wait and see what we are talking about."

We waited. We waited seven weeks. In hope or fear, C. missed a period. She threw up continually. She wasted and turned the color of a sunken copper statue. Then one morning, we got an All Clear that left her suicidal with relief.

Not long after, she announced at dinner the end of the narrative.

My life with C. was a long training. I learned most of my adult truths with her. I learned how to travel light, how to read aloud. I learned to pay attention to the incomprehensible. I learned that no one ever knows another.

I learned her condition of statelessness, steeped in survivor's guilt.

I learned how to make a virtue of necessity. How to assume a courage when I had it not. I mimicked that skill she exercised without thinking, for which I loved her most of all. I learned from her how to keep fitting myself against those things that left me for dead.

I learned that only care has a prayer of redressing the unlivable terms of politics. Yet I learned that a love fostered on caretaking crippled the loved one, or, one day—worse—it did what it promised and worked its worldly cure.

"How would you like," I asked A., "to participate in a noble experiment?"

I winced to hear myself talk to the woman. I still took a 50 percent hit in intelligence each time I saw her. Actual attempts at conversation halved that half. Sentences of more than five words I had to rehearse well in advance. I hoped A. might have a fondness for the pathetic. That idiocy lent me comic appeal.

I had lived by the word; now I was dying by the phoneme. The few good cadences I managed to complete competed with countless other claims on A.'s attention. We could not speak anywhere for more than three minutes without someone greeting her effusively. This self-possessed child, who I'd imagined spent solitary nights reading Auden and listening to Palestrina, was in fact a sociopath of affability.

The bar where we sat overflowed with her lost intimates. "Experiment? Just a sec. I'm getting another beer. You want something else?"

She curved her fingers back and touched them to my shoulders. I was finished, done for, and had no objections.

I watched A. take our glasses up to the bar. Within a minute, she, the bartender, and a knot of innocent bystanders doubled over with laughter. I watched the bartender refill the beers and refuse her proffered cash. A. returned to our booth, still grinning.

"Do you play pinball?" she asked. "They have this fantastic machine here. I love it. Come on."

She bobbed into the crowd, not once looking back to see if I followed.

My pinball was even more pathetic than my attempts at conversation. "How do you get this gate to open? What happens if you go down this chute?"

"I haven't the faintest idea," A. answered. "I just kind of whack at it, you know? The lights. The bells and whistles." Volition was moot musing. The little silver ball did whatever it wanted.

Everything I thought A. to be she disabused. Yet reality exceeded my best projections. A. engaged and detached at will, immune to politics. She sunned herself in existence, as if it were easier to apologize than to ask for permission.

That spring body—its fearless insouciance, the genetic spark, desire's distillation of health—made anyone who looked on her defer to the suggestion of a vast secret. And when she looked back, it was always with a bemused glance, demure in her pleasure, reining up in decorous confusion that nobody else had put things together before now, had gleaned what was happening. Every living soul had gotten lost, forgotten its power, grown old. She alone had broken through, whole, omnipotent with first growth, her ease insisting, *Remember? It's simple.* And possessing this, A.'s mind became that idea, however temporarily, forever, just as the meter of thought is itself a standing wave, an always, in its eternal, reentrant feedback.

In A.'s company, everyone was my intimate and beer and peanuts all the nutrition I needed. Prison, with her, would be a lime-tree bower. In those scattered minutes that she let me trot alongside her, I could refract first aid from the air and prosody from stones. I could get by without music, without books, without memory. I could get by on nothing but being. If I could just watch her, I imagined, just study how she did it, I might learn how to live.

I kind of whacked at the pinball. A. laughed at me. I amused her—some kind of extraterrestrial. "That's it. Squeeze first. Ask later."

"But there has to be some kind of system, don't you think?"

"Oh, probably," she sighed. She took over from me when I drained. She tapped into the bells and whistles, entranced. "So what's this noble experiment?"

I had fifteen seconds between flipper twitches to tell her about Helen.

"Well, it's like this. We're teaching a device how to read."

"You *what*?" She stopped flipping and looked at me. Her eyes swelled, incredulous, big as birthday cakes. "You're joking. You're joking, right?"

I took A. to the Center. Two whole hours: the longest I'd ever been in her presence. That day doubled the total time I'd spent with her up until then. I blessed Helen for existing. And shamed myself at the blessing.

A. watched as I stepped through a training demo. Helen enchanted her. She could not get enough. "It can't be. It's not possible. There's a little homunculus inside, isn't there?"

"Not that I know of."

Delight grew anxious. A. wanted to speak to the artifact herself, without mediation. She asked for the mike. I could not refuse her anything.

"Who's your favorite writer, Helen? Helen? Come on, girl. Talk to me."

But A.'s voice, on first exposure, disquieted Helen as much as it had me. The nets clammed up as tight as a five-year-old remembering the parent-drilled litany, *Stranger, danger.*

"Pretty please?" A. begged. "Be my friend?" She wasn't used to rejection.

"Let's talk about 'The Windhover,' " I suggested to Helen.

"Good. I want to," Helen said.

A. clapped her hand to her mouth. Her eyes would have wetted, her heart broken with ephemeral pleasure, had they known how.

"What do you think of the poem?"

"I understand the 'blue-bleak embers,' " Helen claimed, failing to answer the question. "But why does he say, 'Ah my dear?' Who is 'my dear?' Who is he talking to?"

I'd read the poem for Taylor, at an age when A. would have been considered jail bait. I'd memorized it, recited it for anyone who would listen. I'd analyzed it in writing. I'd pinched it for my own pale imitations.

"I don't know," I confessed to Helen. "I never knew."

I glanced over at A. for advice. She looked stricken. Blue-bleak. "What on earth are you teaching her?"

"It's Hopkins," I said, shocked at her shock. "You don't . . . ?"

"I know what it is. Why are you wasting time with it?"

"What do you mean? It's a great poem. A cornerstone."

"Listen to you. Cornerstone. You didn't tell me you were Euro-retro."

"I didn't know I was." I sounded ridiculous. Hurt, and worse, in hating how I sounded and trying to disguise it.

"Has she read the language poets? Acker? Anything remotely working-class? Can she rap? Does she know the Violent Femmes?"

"I, uh, doubt it. Helen, do you know the Violent Femmes?"

Helen contemplated. "Who know?"

"She makes that mistake all the time. I can't seem to untrain her."

"Don't," A. said. "But do tell her a little about what people really read."

"She'll get everything on the list."

"Whose list? Let me see that." A. took the crib sheets I'd put together, Helen's prep for the test I'd taken, once upon a time. A. studied the titles, as if she hadn't just passed the exam herself. At length she looked up. "I hate to be the one to break this to you. Your version of literary reality is a decade out of date."

"What, they've issued a Hopkins upgrade since my day?"

A. snorted. "They should."

"Don't tell me you didn't have to read him."

"Nobody *has* to read anyone anymore. There's more to the canon than is dreamt of in your philosophy, bub. These days, you find the people you want to study from each period. You work up some questions in advance. Get them approved. Then you write answers on your preparation."

"Wait. You what? There's no List? The Comps are no longer comprehensive?"

"A lot more comprehensive than your white-guy, *Good Housekeeping* thing."

"You mean to tell me that you can get a Ph.D. in literature without ever having read the great works?"

A. bent her body in a combative arc. Even her exasperation turned beautiful. "My God, I'm dealing with a complete throwback. You're not even reactionary! Whose definition of great? Hopkins ain't gonna cut it anymore. You're buying into the exact aestheticism that privilege and power want to sell you."

"Wait a minute. Weren't you the woman who was just teaching me how to play pinball?"

A. did her Thai dancer imitation. She blushed. "Yeah, that was me. You got a problem with that?"

"All of a sudden you want to set fire to the library."

"Don't put words in my mouth. I'm not trying to burn any books. I'm just saying that books are what we make of them. And not the other way around."

I took the list back from her. "I don't know much about books. But I know what I like."

"Oh, come on! Play fair. You make it sound as if everything anyone has ever written is recycled Bible and Shakespeare."

"Isn't it?"

She hissed and crossed her fingers into a vampire-warding crucifix. "When were you educated, anyway? I bet you still think New Criticism is, like, heavy-duty. Cutting-edge."

"Excuse me for not trend-surfing. If I fall far enough behind I can catch the next wave."

Self-consciousness caught up with me. We shouldn't be arguing like this in front of the children. I reached down and turned off Helen's microphone.

A., in the thrill of the fight, failed to notice. "Those who reject new theory are in the grip of an older theory. Don't you know that all this stuff"—she slapped my six pages of titles—"is a culturally constructed, belated view of belle lettres? You can't get any more insular than this."

"Well, it is English-language culture that we want to teach her."

"Whose English? Some eighty-year-old Oxbridge pederast's? The most exciting English being written today is African, Caribbean—"

"We have to give her the historical take if she—"

"The winner's history, of course. What made you such a coward?

What are you so scared of? Difference is not going to kill you. Maybe it's time your little girl had her consciousness raised. An explosion of young-adulthood."

"I'm all for that. I just think that you can get to the common core of humanity from anywhere."

"Humanity? Common core? You'd be run out of the field on a rail for essentializing. And you wonder why the posthumanists reduced your type to an author function."

"That's *Mr.* Author Function to you, missy."

A. smiled. Such a smile might make even posthumanism survivable. I loved her. She knew it. And she would avoid the issue as long as she could. Forever.

"So, Mr. Author Function. What do you think this human commonality is based on?"

"Uh, biology?" I let myself sound snide.

"Oh, now it's scientism. What's your agenda? Why would you want to privilege that kind of hubris?"

"I'm not privileging anything. I'm talking about simple observation."

"You think observation doesn't have an ideological component? Stone Age. Absolutely Neolithic."

"So I come from a primitive culture. Enlighten me."

She took me seriously. "Foundationism is bankrupt," she said. Her zeal broke my heart. She was a born teacher. If anyone merited staying in the profession, it was this student for whom themes were still real. "Why science? You could base your finalizing system on anything. The fact is—"

"The *what*?"

A. smirked. "The fact is, what we make of things depends on the means of their formulation. In other words, language. And the language we speak varies without limit across cultures."

I knew the social science model, knew linguistic determinism. I could recite the axioms in my sleep. I also knew them to be insufficient, a false split. And yet, they never sounded so good to me as they did coming from A.'s mouth. She convinced me at blood-sugar level, deep down, below words. In the layer of body's idea.

I tried to catch her eyes. "You love this stuff, don't you?"

She flinched: What kind of discredited rubbish are you talking now?

"You're not really going to go into business, are you? Give all this up?"

"I like theory, when it's not annoying me. I love the classroom. I adore teaching. But I like eating even more."

Subsidies, I wanted to tell her. What we make in fiction, we can plow back into teaching and criticism. Scholar-gypsies. Independents. There was some precedent, once.

"So what do you want from me?" A. asked.

My head whipped back. She'd heard me thinking.

"Where do I come in?" she pressed.

It took me a couple of clock cycles to recover. Helen, she meant. The exam.

I couldn't begin to say where she came in. What I wanted of her. I wanted to learn from A. some fraction of those facts I dispensed so freely to Helen. I thought she might lend me some authority, supply the missing lines of the functional proofs. I saw us jointly working out warmth, glossing intimacy, interpreting the ways of humility, of second chances, indulgence, expansiveness, redemption, hope, provincialism, projection, compassion, dependence, failing, forgiveness. A. was my class prep, my empirical test of meaning.

But Helen did not need a teacher steeped in those predicates. She already read better than I. Writing, she might have told me, was never more than the climb from buried love's grave.

I tried to tell A. where she came in. I limited myself to a quick sketch of the comprehensive high noon. I told A. that we needed a token human for our double-blind study. That we just wanted to ask her a couple of questions. Trivial; nothing she hadn't already mastered.

"Hold on. You want to test me—against a machine?" Coyer now, more flirtatious than I had yet seen her.

The Hartrick family's appearance outside the office saved me from debacle. "Hello," William announced, peeking in. "Did you know a feather would fall as fast as this entire building, if you dropped them in a vacuum?"

"Where are you going to find a vacuum big enough to drop this building?" I asked.

"NASA," William chanted, defensively singsong. "You know how to get oil out of shale?"

"You know how to spell 'fish'?"

"They're both out of control," Diana apologized to A. A. laughed in sympathy.

I made the introductions. William produced pocket versions of Mastermind and Connect Four, letting me take my pick. He proceeded to trounce me. I might have stood a chance, but for distraction. Something had happened to Peter that I struggled to place. Hand in his mother's hand, he took first, tentative steps.

A. was smitten. "What a beautiful boy you are. How old are you?" She looked up at Diana. "How old is he?" I cringed in anticipation. But A.'s reaction was as seamless as her delight.

William pummeled me turn after turn. Out of the corner of my eye, I watched A. play with Petey, her hand surprisingly blunt on his ear. A. sat on the floor, rolling Peter's ball back to him after his each wild fling. I felt the heat of Diana's curiosity, but she and A. talked of nothing but the boys.

"Come on, William," Diana said at last. "Leave the man with some shred of dignity." William broke into a satisfied grin. Pete grabbed his ball, labored once more into vertical, and the family pressed on.

Their visit turned A. introspective. "I really think I don't belong here, sometimes."

" 'Here'?"

"In academia. I come from a long line of Polish mine workers. Theoryland would baffle the hell out of my family." She grew irritated. Accusing. "Let me show you something." She rummaged through her canvas backpack and extracted a hostage to hand over to me. "Know what this is?" Her voice challenged with mockery.

"Cross-stitch?"

"It's for my mother's hutch. I should be done in time for Christmas. You should see us at holidays. I'm fourth of four. All girls. We go around the house at the top of our lungs, all six of us singing at the same time."

A. fell silent, proportionate to the remembered cacophony. No one knew this woman. Sociability was a brilliant camouflage. Beneath it hid the most private person I'd ever met.

"I could have started one of my own by now. A family. But no. I had to do things the hard way."

I don't know why, but she let me see her. Dropped her guard. I'd made myself fall in love with A. With the idea of A. With her interrogating body. With hands that held in midair all the questions Helen would never touch. I had loved C. wrongly, for C.'s helplessness. I loved A. helplessly, for the one right reason. For my frailty in the face of her. For her poise in knowing how soon all poise would end.

I realized I was going to propose to that body. I needed to see what her person, what the character I steered around in my head would say to total, reckless invitation.

I was going to do what I'd never had the courage to do in my decade with C. I was going to ask this unknown to take me to her and make an unrationed life together. To marry. Make a family. Amend and extend our lives.

"All right," I said, affecting a virtue. "You're sufficiently fallible to be just what we're looking for. Are you in?"

A.'s grimace upended itself. Such a test was no less entertaining than pinball. And what could she possibly lose?

"Okay, girl," she addressed Helen. "I'll race you. No mercy!"

Helen said nothing.

"She's being reticent again. Give her a digital gold star, or something."

I opened at random the next book on the list. An epigraph at page top: Bernard of Clairvaux. C. and I had once spent a timeless afternoon in that town. The words read, *What we love, we shall grow to resemble.*

I read the words to Helen. She kept her counsel.

"Helen? What do you say to that?"

Still she gave no response.

"Helen?"

A. poked me. "Shh. Leave her be. She's rolling with it." She's *moved* by it, A. wanted to say. But that was the grip of an archaic theory, long discredited.

It hit me well after it should have. The mind is still an evolutionary infant. Most trouble with the obvious. I reached down and turned the mike back on. Then I read the words again.

"How many books are there?" Helen asked one day, not long before the showdown. She sounded suspicious. Fatigued.

"A lot," I broke it to her. I had numbered every hair on her head, but in one of those counting systems that jumps from "three" to "many."

"Tell me."

I told her that the Library of Congress contained 20 million volumes. I told her that the number of new books published increased each year, and would soon reach a million, worldwide. That a person, through industry, leisure, and longevity, might manage to read, in one life, half as many books as are published in a day.

Helen thought. "They never go away? Books?"

"That's what print means. The archive is permanent." And does for the species what associative memory fails to do for the individual.

"Reading population gets bigger?" Helen asked.

"Not as rapidly as the backlist. People die."

Helen knew all about it. Death was epidemic, in literature.

"Do people get any longer, year in, year out?"

"Is the life span increasing? Only on average. And very slowly. Much less than we pretend."

She did the rate equations in two unknowns. "The more days, the less likely that any book will be read."

"That's true. Or that you will have read the same things as anyone you talk to."

"And there are more days every day. Will anything change?"

"Not that I can think of."

"Always more books, each one read less." She thought. "The world will fill with unread print. Unless print dies."

"Well, we're kind of looking into that, I guess. It's called magazines."

Helen knew all about magazines. "Books will become magazines," she predicted.

And of course, she was right. They would have to. Where nothing is lost, little can be found. With written continuity comes collective age. And aging of the collective spirit implied a kind of death. Helen alone was capable of thinking the unthinkable: the disappearance of books from all but the peripheries of life. History would collapse under its own accumulation. Scope would widen until words refused to stray from the ephemeral present.

"When will it be enough?" she asked.

I could not even count for her the whole genres devoted to that question alone.

"Why do humans write so much? Why do they write at all?"

I read her one of the great moments in contemporary American fiction. "Only it's not by an American, it's no longer contemporary, and it doesn't even take place inside the fictional frame." This was Nabokov's postlude to *Lolita*, where he relates the book's genesis. He describes hearing of an ape who produced the first known work of animal art, a rough sketch of the bars of the beast's cage.

I told Helen that, inside such a cage as ours, a book bursts like someone else's cell specifications. And the difference between two cages completes an inductive proof of thought's infinitude.

I read her the take of a woman who once claimed to have written for no one. A lifelong letter to the world that neither read hers nor wrote back:

> There is no Frigate like a Book
> To take us Lands away
> Nor any Coursers like a Page
> Of prancing Poetry—
> This Traverse may the poorest take
> Without oppress of Toll—

How frugal is the Chariot
That bears the Human Soul!

She wanted to know whether a person could die by spontaneous combustion. The odds against a letter slipped under the door slipping under the carpet as well. Ishmael's real name. Who this "Reader" was, and why he rated knowing who married whom. Whether single men with fortunes really needed wives. What home would be without Plumtree's Potted Meats. How long it would take to compile a key to all mythologies. What the son of a fish looked like. Where Uncle Toby was wounded. Why anyone wanted to imagine unquiet slumbers for sleepers in quiet earth. Whether Conrad was a racist. Why *Huck Finn* was taken out of libraries. Which end of an egg to break. Why people read. Why they stopped reading. What it meant to be "only a novel." What use half a locket was to anyone. Why it would be a mistake not to live all you can.

I said goodbye to C.'s parents. They didn't understand. They had come such a long way, and didn't see why the next generation couldn't tough it out as far, or further.

"She's crazy, huh?" her mother said.

Her pap, in his Chicago-Limburgs patois, asked, "Just one thing I want to know, Rick. Who's gonna set my digital clocks?"

I said goodbye to C. "I promised I'd see you through school. And graduation's still six weeks away."

C. dodged the blow, but caught a corner of it across her face. "Don't do this to me, Rick. I'll graduate. I promise."

"Do you need anything? Should we get you a car before I go? Do you have enough money?" Late-minute plans for a final day trip, solo, lasting from now on.

My reflex solicitude hurt her worse than anger. "Beauie," she pleaded. "We can't do this. We can't split up. We still have twelve hundred pages of Proust to get through."

I searched her, sounding this reprieve, hoping for an impossible instant it might be real. But she did not want it. She did not want to do those remaining pages, to throw bad reading after good. She just wanted to save nostalgia, not the thing it stood for. She only wanted my blessing, to get on and make a life free from suicidal remorse.

"Who's going to finish the book?" She meant the commonplace one, with the ticket stubs and lists of films and meals and outings, a shared narrative, senseless except to us.

Then the senselessness of all stories—their total, arbitrary construction—must have struck C. She started to scream. I had to pin her arms to her side to keep her from harming herself. I held her for a long time. Not as a medic. Not as a parent. Not as a lover. I held her as you might hold a fellow stranger in a shelter.

When she grew calm, she was not yet calm. "I must be sick. Something must be wrong with me. I'm a sadist. I've spoiled everything that was worth having."

"We still have it. It just has to go on hold."

"I wanted to make you proud. I thought, in twenty years, that I might become the perfect person for you."

"You're perfect now."

"I've ruined your life."

"You haven't, C. You've done what you needed to. You're a good person."

She looked at me, remembering. Yes, that's right. I have been. I have been good. "And now I have to go outside."

I tried to match her. To rise to her. "This is all the fault of that damn Polish kid, you know."

I felt: at least I'll never have to do any of this again.

Helen wanted to read one of my books. I gave her my first try. I had written it at A.'s age, just after passing the comps. I knew nothing about literature then, and so still thought it possible to write.

"Go easy on me," I begged, surrendering the digitized image. "I was just a kid."

The night she read it, I got fifteen minutes of sleep. I could not remember being that nervous, even when reading the longhand draft to C. I came in the morning after, wired over whether this machine thought my book was any good.

We chattered for several minutes about nothing. I grew anxious, assuming the worst. Then I realized: she wouldn't volunteer anything until prompted. She had no way of knowing that I needed to know.

So I asked. Outright. "What did you think of my book, Helen?"

"I think it was about an old photograph. It grows to be about interpretation and collaboration. History. Three ways of looking come together, or fail to. Like a stereoscope. What's a stereoscope?"

"Helen! Did you *like* it?"

"I liked it."

"What did you like?"

"I liked 'I never saw a Moor. I never saw the Sea.' "

I'd forgotten. "That isn't mine. I was quoting."

"Yes. I know," Helen brushed me off. "That was more Dickinson. Emily."

Helen's brain had proved wide enough for my sky, and me beside. She was one step away from grasping this audience-free poet's analogy, the last scholastic aptitude test: brain differs from the weight of God as syllable from sound. Yet comparison filled her with need to see the real moor, the navigable sea, however much deeper the brain that could absorb it.

"Show me Paris."

"Well?" Lentz shrugged, when I relayed the request. "Do you have any travel plans for the immediate future?"

I had, in fact, no immediate future. My visiting appointment at the Center ended in a few weeks. Beyond that, my life came down to throwing a dart at the world map. I had no reason, no desire to be anywhere except where A. was.

"You can't be serious. You want me to fly to—"

"I didn't say I wanted anything, Marcel. I asked you what you were doing."

I pictured myself strolling the Seine bookstalls, looking for that forgotten book I always thought I would someday write. Paris was the one city where C. had ever felt at home. We'd gone as often as we could. Now I could not see myself wandering there except with A.

"It's absurd," I decided. "What could she gain from it?"

"The hidden layers are hungry, Marcel. Ask not for what."

Lentz brought in slides. We hooked them up to the digitizer. An unrecognizably young Lentz in front of Notre Dame. Lentz in the Tuileries. By the Panthéon. The Médicis fountain. "Helen," he lectured. "The one on the left is me. The one on the right is by Rodin."

She never could see much of anything. She was a one-eyed myopic with astigmatism, two days after an operation for glaucoma. Everything looked to her like blurry Braque, except for Braque. Yet she loved light and dark, and these would have meant to her as much as words, had we wired her up right.

"Motion," she insisted. We tried some ancient public television video. She felt hurt. Locked out. "Depth. Sound. I want Richard to explain me."

"Interactive," Lentz figured.

"What's our range on the camera hookup?"

"Oh, a couple of hundred meters, maximum, from the nearest drop box."

Lentz and I agreed to defraud Helen. Between us, at least, we pretended that it was less swindle than simulation. We would do for this machine the inverse of what virtual reality promised to do for humans.

We showed her the collegiate landmarks of U., all the imitations of imitations of classical architecture, and called the sites she couldn't see anyway by famous names. Even actual Paris would have been no more than a fuzzy, Fauvist kaleidoscope. Home could match that. All sensation was as strange, as foreign, as the idea of its existing at all.

I took Helen on the Grand Tour. I panned and zoomed on all the structures I passed four times a day without seeing. I sat her in a café where, smack in the middle of a cornfield extending two hundred miles in every direction, she had her pick of a dozen languages to eavesdrop on.

"Thank you," Helen said. She'd seen through our duplicity early. She chose to exercise, by imitation, the art of the loving lie. For our sakes.

She seemed content to return to reading, until the next novel indulged some new locale. Helen went nuts with wanderlust. "Show me London. Show me Venice. I want to see Byzantium. Delhi."

She twitched now, like the worst of adolescents. The most precocious.

"Helen, it's impossible. Travel is rare. Difficult."

"More flat pictures, then." She would settle for those static, pathetic portals, our stand-ins for the real.

Lentz had endless slide carousels. His pictures wandered from city to city, tracing a line of changing eras and styles. Photo docs not just of antique towns but of whole lost ways of being. Hair, clothes, cars made their cavalcade. Lentz's image aged and grew familiar. He'd been everywhere.

"You know that place too?" I called out during the show. "I loved that city. Did you go to the monkey palace? The fortress? The west crypt?" Shameless tourism.

Lentz answered, always affirmative, without enthusiasm. He stayed stony-faced throughout the world tour.

They must have traveled together. I had nothing to lose by asking, except my life. "So where was Audrey while you were out broadening your mind?"

"She always worked the camera," he said. And advanced to the next slide.

He had no pictures of her. Carousels full of buildings, and no evidence of the tour's reason. I needed to go with A. to Brugge and Antwerp and Maastricht, if for no other reason than to record the trip. I needed pictures of her, in an album, on a shelf, in a room, in a real house. I needed to own something more than would fit in the emergency suitcase by the side of a rented bed. I pictured myself, at the end of the longer slide show, with four books to my name and not one decent snapshot.

I watched the rest of Lentz's travels in silence, except for the occasional bit of narration I added for Helen's sake. Each time I recognized one of Audrey's images, I stopped breathing. Frame after frame, and how could I tell Helen the first thing about having visited them? I had gotten out, been all over. And never saw anything until we tried to show it to this blind box.

Halfway through the travelogue, and all I knew of the projector, of the magic lantern, was its images. I lived at explanation's first minute. My office at the Center was as close to neuroscience's ground zero as a person could get. If I lived to expectancy, researchers would have produced an infant, ghostly, material theory of mind by the time I died. And I would not be able to follow it. I would be locked out, as consciousness locks us out from our own inner workings, not to mention the clearest word of another. The best I could hope for would be cartoon, layman's analysis, scraps from the empirical table.

I would take the scraps, then. "What do you do?" I asked Ram, at my next opportunity. I liked the man without qualification. I felt infinitely comfortable with him. And I'd done everything in my power to avoid getting to know him.

"Do? God forbid I *do* anything!" He held his palms out in front of him. They were the color of aging sugarcane. The kind I ate as a child, when my father, the adventurer, had abandoned Chicago for Thailand.

"What is your field of work?"

"What do you mean by work, heaven help?"

"Aw, come on. What do you mean by heaven?"

Ram's eyes sparkled, taunting targets for a spitting cobra. He would have preferred talking philosophy over neurology, two out of three days. "Do you know what the world rests on?" he asked.

"Not its laurels, God forbid."

Ram laughed. "That's right. Make fun of me. It rests on the backs of elephants. And those elephants?"

"The shell of a turtle."

"Aha. You've heard this one. And that turtle?"

"Another turtle."

"He's good. He's good, this fiction writer. Now, do you or do you not believe that one of those turtles must necessarily go all the way down? That's it. That is the single question we are granted to ask while in this body. East, West, North, South. Is there a base terrapin or isn't there? Cosmology. This is the issue dividing us. The one we must each answer."

"Suppose I just asked you your field?"

"My friend. My fictional friend. The eye moves. We watch it as it does so. That is all."

"Ram. You're giving me a splitting headache."

He nodded with enthusiasm. "Come with me."

He took me into his labs. He placed several clear plastic overlays on a light table, a doctor dealing out the damning X rays.

"Look here and tell me what you see."

"Scatter patterns. They look like mineral deposit maps. Like fish radars over the Grand Banks, thirty years ago."

"I did not ask you what they looked like. I asked you what you see. Arrange these for me, please."

I studied the spots. The more I looked, the less they seemed a random distribution. After my eyes adjusted, the patterns sorted themselves into three groups.

"Exactly," Ram encouraged. "You might have missed one or two, but the correlation is strong. Who says that measurement is subjective?" He tapped my first pile. "Friends." He looked at me to see if I was following. He tapped it again, then went on to pile two. "Abstract acquaintances. Yes?" He pointed to the third pile and said, "Total strangers." He scrutinized my bewildered face and shrugged. "He does not understand me, this Powers fellow."

I didn't understand him. But I liked him. I liked him a great deal.

"Come. I'll show you. Would you mind if I subject you to this Western postindustrial instrument of torture?"

He indicated a chair fitted with a head vise. It looked like a prop from bad seventies science fiction.

"Why not. It's in the interests of science, right?"

Ram chuckled. He fitted my head into the restraint. My skull suitably immobilized, he projected three slides on a screen in front of me. Three portraits. Someone out of a Vladivostok high-school yearbook. Marilyn Monroe. And Ram himself.

The laser-guided instrument tracked the center of my pupil as I scanned each photograph. It took several sequential readings and spread the data points over a plastic overlay map of the image field. In the end, the paths my eyes traced over the different faces conformed to the categories he'd previously defined. Total stranger. Abstract acquaintance. Friend.

"Here is something you will also find very interesting." Ram pulled out another envelope with a small sample group.

"Why are these interesting? They're just like all the others, more or less."

"Aha!" He held up an index finger. "That's what makes them interesting. All of the people in this group suffer from prosopagnosia. Brain damage has rendered them incapable of recognizing people anymore. They deny having seen any face, even their own, even the face of their spouse or child. Or at least they *think* they can no longer recognize faces. Yet clearly, the eyes . . ." His hand serpentined, tracing the route of the curve's knowledge.

"Astonishing."

"You know, I think the astonishing may be the ordinary by another name. But these results do lead us to many tempting guesses. That perception is carried out in several subsystems, we can say, most certainly. That these subsystems talk to each other: indeed. That perhaps they go on talking, these subsystems, even when the others stop listening. That breaks in communication might occur anywhere, at any point in the chain. That each part of a compound task may manifest its very own deficit. That everything you are capable of doing could be taken away from you, in discrete detail."

I added to Ram's list the obvious, the missing speculation. The look of the magic lantern. That what you loved could go foreign, without your ever knowing. That the eye could continue tracing familiarity, well into thought's unknown region.

"What do I look like?"

I could find no face in the world. No color or structure. The days when I might have tried to pass her off as a Vermeer look-alike were over for good. Race, age, shape excluded too much. I needed some generic Head of a Girl that had no clan or continent and belonged nowhere in identifiable time.

"What do I look like, Richard? Please. Show me."

I'd pictured her so many different ways over the course of the training. I thought: Perhaps some blank template Buddha, or a Cycladic figure. A trompe l'oeil landscape that became a figure on second glance. An Easter Island head. A Feininger or Pollock. A Sung bamboo. I didn't know how I thought of her now. I didn't know what she looked like.

She insisted. I turned up a suitable likeness.

"It's a photo? It's someone you knew once? A woman friend?"

She would have pretended ignorance for me. Would have let me off the hook again, except that she had to know.

The list of Excellent Undergraduate Teachers came out. Student evaluations of their evaluators. A. topped the graduate instructors in the English Department. I was thrilled, and confirmed by thrill in my intuition.

I forced the moment to its crisis. Helen and I had been hitting the books the Sunday evening after our world tour. The day's work had left me in a Spenserian stupor, where what I needed was Larkin. On pure reflex—that satellite brain housed south of the shoulders—I flicked off the mike, picked up the phone, and dialed her. One smooth motion. I'd never dialed her number before. But I had it memorized.

"Hello you," I said when she picked up. I sounded almost young. "It's me." And in the awkward microsecond, I clarified with my name.

"Oh, hi." A., nervous in relief. "What's up?"

"Checking to see if you're booking for the test."

"Ha! I'm going to whup your girl with half my synapses tied behind my back."

"What are you doing next Wednesday?" Midway in, my voice gave out. I began to tremor as if I'd just robbed a bank or fallen into an ice crevasse. "It's Shrimp Night at my favorite seafood place. The crustaceans are fair, but the conversation is good." If she was into shortness of breath, I was home free.

"Uh, sure. Why not? Wait. Hang on."

I heard her put the mouthpiece against her body. I heard her roll her eyes and shrug. I heard her ask the mate whose existence I'd been denying if they had any plans.

"It's kind of a problem," she explained on returning. "Maybe another time?"

"Another time would be great," I replied, mechanical with calm.

"She's amazing," Lentz said.

I had to think who he meant. "Now do you believe me? She's conscious. I know it."

"We don't *know* anything of the kind, Marcel. But we could find out."

"Don't talk with your mouth full," I told him. "Set your sandwich down between gulps. It's a societal norm." I tried to slow him. To keep him from saying what I knew he was going to say.

"I must admit, Marcel. I'm surprised by what you've been able to accomplish."

"It's not me." It was her. The subsystems talking to subsystems. Lentz's neural handiwork.

"She sure as hell seems to mimic with shocking accuracy some features of high-level cognition. It's uncanny. And a heuristic tool such as comes along once in a lifetime."

"Heuristic?"

"Stimulus to investigative discovery."

"I know what the word means, Philip." But I could not add what *I* meant: Is that all she means to you?

"Her architecture is such that severance could be effected with a great deal of local selectivity."

"I don't believe you said that. You want to cut into her? You want to lobotomize?"

"Easy, Marcel. We're talking about a painless operation, as far as I imagine. We could get what is unattainable in any other arena. Isolate the high-level processes by which she maps complex input and reassembles responses. Analyze them. Correlate various regional destruction with changes in—"

"You don't *know* it would be painless, Lentz."

He fell back against the cafeteria chair and studied me. Was I serious? Had I lost it, gone off cognition's deep end? I saw him find, in my face, the even more indicting idea that I didn't voice: that hurting Helen in any way would be wrong.

Lentz, in an instant, anticipated everything either of us might say to each other on the morality of machine vivisection. The whole topic was a wash, as insoluble as intelligence itself. He waved his hand, dismissing me as a madman. No part of her lived. To take her apart might, finally, extend some indirect service to the living. Anything else was softheaded nostalgia.

I had no leg to stand on. Lentz owned Helen, her shaped evolution, the lay of her synapses. He owned all the reasoning about her as well. I had some connection to her, by virtue of our long association. But that connection was, at most, emotional. And if Helen lived far enough to be able to feel, it just went to prove that emotions were no more than the sum of their weight vectors. And cuttable, in the name of knowing.

My strongest argument belonged more to him than it did to me. We know the world by awling it into our shape-changing cells. Knowing those cells required just as merciless tooling. To counter any part of Lentz's plan would be to contradict myself. To lose. I had just one bargain to make. And I damned myself with it willingly.

"At least give us until after the test."

"That's fine. I'm pretty much backlogged until then anyway."

I hadn't suspected how easily I could sell my weighted soul.

"Diana was right," I spit, venomous. "You are a monster."

He stared at me again. You're going to fault me for the deal you proposed? He stood up to leave, grasping his tray. "Oh, don't go getting your ass all out of joint, Marcel. I said we won't cut anything until after you run your little competition."

I tracked Diana down to her dry lab. She sat in front of a monitor, watching a subtractive visualization of the activity of cerebral columns. A color contour recording: the flashing maps of thought in real time.

"Lentz wants to brain-damage Helen. Selectively kill off neurodes. See what makes her tick."

"Of course he does," Diana said. She neither missed a beat nor took her eyes from her screen. "It wasn't that long ago that he stopped frying ants with the magnifying glass."

"Diana. Please. This is really happening."

She stopped, then. She looked up. She would have taken my hand, had she not been a single parent in a secret affair, and I a single, middle-aged man.

"I can't help you, Ricky." Her eyes glistened, slick with her impotence. "I fractionate monkey hippocampi."

Confusion warmed me like an opiate. I rolled with it, to the point of panic. "Monkeys can't talk."

"No. But if they could, you *know* what they would ask the lab tech."

She implored me, with a look of bewilderment. *Don't press this.* Helen hurt her. I destroyed her. But nothing approached the pain of her own living compromise.

I gave Helen a stack of independent readings. I did not trust my voice in conversation with her. And she needed no more lessons in cheerful deceit.

In all our dealings, Harold Plover had never been the spokesman for anything but decency. I decided to go enlist his humanity. I'd never seen him away from the Center. But I had his address, and showed up at his place late that Saturday afternoon, unannounced.

Harold met me jovially at the door. He was seconded by an even more jovial Doberman. The dog was at least half again bigger than A.

The dog leaped up and knocked me over, while Harold fought to restrain it. I righted myself and the game started all over again.

"Ivan," Harold shouted at the creature, further exciting it. "Ivan! Knock it off. Time out. Haven't we talked about socially unacceptable behavior?"

"Try 'Down, boy.' Quick."

"Oh, don't be afraid of this pooch. He won the 'Most Likely to Lick a Serial Killer's Face' award from doggie obedience school."

"Doesn't this brand have one of the highest recidivism rates?"

"Breed, Maestro. Dog breeds. Dog food brands. Words are his life," he explained to Ivan.

At last Harold succeeded in hauling the disconsolate dog off me. Without asking why I'd dropped by, he hauled me into the inner sanctum. The place crawled with daughters. Daughters had been left about carelessly, everywhere. Harold introduced me to his wife, Tess. I expected something small, fast, and acid. I got an isle of amiable adulthood amid the teenage torrent.

One who must have been Mina flirted out a greeting. "Look who's here. If it isn't Orph himself."

"Orff?"

"Yeah. Orphic Rewards."

"She's gone anagram-mad," Harold whined. "It's driving us all up the bloody wall."

Another daughter came downstairs, modeling her prom dress. This might have been Trish. I wasn't betting.

Harold exploded. "Absolutely not. You're not wearing that thing in public! You look like a French whore in heat."

"Oh, Daddy!"

"Listen to the expert in French whores." Tess tousled Harold's hair. "I figured you had to be spending yourself somewhere."

"Do you believe this woman? You'd never guess to hear her, would you, that she spent six years in a convent?"

"We'll talk about it," Tess consoled the devastated kid.

"We won't talk about it," Harold shouted.

"Talking never hurts," Tess said.

The Doberman came and pinned me to the sofa. A preadolescent in blue jeans, probably the caboose, said, "Watch this." She produced a dog biscuit. "Ivan. Ivan! Listen to me. Can you—can you sneeze?"

Ivan rolled over.

"I didn't say roll over. I said sneeze."

Ivan barked.

"Not speak. Sneeze. Sneeze, you animal!"

Ivan sat up and begged, played dead, and offered to shake hands. In the end, Harold's youngest threw the dog the sop in disgust.

Harold reveled in the show. "He's learned that you just have to be persistent with humans. They get the idea eventually, if you keep at them."

Before I knew it, dinner enveloped us. No one sat at the table. Only about half of us bothered with plates and silverware. But definitely dinner. The tributary of bodies in and out, being fed.

"That's not fifteen minutes," Tess said to the one in the revealing prom dress. "Remember? Fifteen minutes with your family, every day. You promised."

"My family. So that's what you call this."

But if one or another of her sisters had struck up a tune, this one would have joined in on some loving and cacophonous counterpoint. This was the land A. came from, huge, jumbled, and warm. I wanted to excuse myself, to run off to A.'s apartment on G. Street and tell her that it wasn't too late to make a dissonant choir of her own. I wanted her so badly, I almost forgot why I'd come to this place.

Harold, happily harassing his girls, recalled me. "Lentz wants to do exploratory surgery on Helen," I said.

"Have another piece of broc," he urged me. "Lots of essential minerals."

The word "mineral" struck me as incomprehensible. Foreign. Where had it come from? How could I have used it so cavalierly before now? "He wants to clip out whole subsystems. See what effect that has on her language skills."

Harold wolfed at the pita pocket he'd constructed. "What's the problem? That's good science. Well. Approximately reasonable science, let's say."

Mina, drifting past the buffet, called out, "Oh no! Not Helen."

Trish, in her prom dress, for it was Trish, added her hurt. "Daddy! You can't do this."

"Do what? I'm not doing anything."

Both sisters looked out through puffed portals, bruising silently, over nothing. An idea.

"Diana disagrees," I stretched. "About its being good science. I think she'd help me, except she feels incriminated herself."

A skip in the flow, too brief to measure, said I'd overstepped. Broken the unspoken. I should have known. Nobody had to tell me. I just slipped.

"Honey," her mother told Trish, "take off the dress before you slop all over it."

"Oh, Mother!" the girl objected, already halfway up the stairs.

Conversation, in its chaos, never flowed back to the issue. Not until Harold and I stood alone on the front porch in the painfully benign evening did I get a second shot.

"Sorry about that." Harold gestured inside. "Bit of a mess. Nothing out of the ordinary."

"So I have my answer? You're not going to help?"

"Me? I'm the enemy. What good would I be to you anyway? This is between you and him."

"And Helen."

Harold indulged me. "Yes. There is that. But he's the one calling the shots."

He breathed in a lungful of air and held it. Behind him, from the house, spilled the sounds of frenetic fullness. Daughters practicing at life.

"Take the fight to him," Harold confided in me. "Bring it home."

That was where I took it, in desperation, the next afternoon. I leaned against my bike in the rain, outside the care facility, the last place in the world I would have chosen to meet him. I lay in wait for him, the last person in the world I would have chosen to waylay. Lentz arrived like clockwork. When he saw my ambush, he affected blasé.

"Back for more? What, are you digging up plot material?" He

gestured toward the institution where his wife was interred. "It's a terrific setting, qua literature. But I doubt it would do much for sales."

He walked into the building, his back to me. He did not care if I tagged along or not. We rode the elevator up in silence. I had no existence for him.

We went to Audrey's room. Dressed, in a chair, she seemed to be waiting.

"Philip! Thank God you've come."

I walked into those words as into bedrock. Lentz stopped to steady me. "She has good days and bad days. I'm not sure which are which, anymore."

We sat. Philip introduced us again. Audrey was too agitated to do more than fake politeness. But she retained my name. That day, she might have retained anything.

In her cruel burst of lucidity, I saw it. Audrey had been formidable. At least as sharp as Lentz. If this demonstration meant anything, even sharper.

"Philip. It's the strangest thing. You're never going to believe this. What is this place?"

"It's a nursing home, Audrey."

"That's what I thought. In fact, I was sure of it. What I can't figure out is why the staff is down in the basement mounting a production of *Cymbeline*."

"Audrey."

"Would I make something like this up, Philip? What could I gain?"

"Audrey. It's highly unlikely."

"You think I don't know that? It's some kind of modern-dress production. I can hear them rehearsing their lines."

Constance, the nurse, walked by. Lentz called her.

"Constance, does the name Cymbeline mean anything to you?"

"Is that her eye makeup? It's on order."

Philip studied his wife. How much proof do we need?

On no proof, I saw how Lentz had gotten so diffidently well read. The play had been their play, and my field, Audrey's.

"Audrey. Love. You're imagining all this. There is no play."

Audrey remained adamant. "The evidence may all be on your side." She cracked a smile. "But that changes nothing."

Still smiling, she closed her eyes and groaned. In a flood of understanding that percolated up from her undamaged self, she begged him, "I don't hurt anyone, Philip. I've behaved. Take me out of here."

There it lay for me—mind, defined. Evolution's gimmick for surviving everything but these fleeting flashes of light.

"She'll be gone again tomorrow," Lentz confided, on our way out. "You know, somewhere, a long time ago when she and I still traveled, we took a tour of an old house. A dream honeymoon mansion, restored from decay, lovingly appointed and improved with all modern facilities and ornament. But the devoted and industrious couple, we were told, had gone slowly homicidal. Stark raving. They died, finally, of violent bewilderment. It was the lead in the home improvements."

I fumbled with my bike lock. I looked for a way I might still say what I had come to say. "Philip. Can't we—can't we spare Helen that?"

He considered my request, as much as he could afford to. "We have to know, Richard. We have to know how all this works." His eyes were dry again, horrifically clear. The *this* he meant, the one with no antecedent, could only be the brain.

I told Diana. I asked her about Audrey Lentz. I asked her what *Cymbeline* meant.

"Oh, Audrey was amazing. Everyone loved her. Endless energy. The more she gave, the more she had. Confidence wedded to self-effacement."

"She wrote?"

"Everybody writes, Rick. Audrey wrote some. More out of devotion than profession."

Before the week was out, Diana looked me up. She had a message for me. She would have left it anonymously if she could have. "The threat's off."

"What? You *did* it?"

"You did. I just asked him to lunch. We talked about everything. His work. My work. I got him reminiscing. I told him about a party I went to at his place. Years ago. Audrey was still Audrey. She entertained us all that evening. She sang a dozen verses to 'You're the Top.' I reminded him of her favorite expression. I talked about Jenny—"

"The daughter."

"The daughter. I asked how she was doing. He didn't know. As I got up to go, I said, 'I heard you want to lobotomize Helen.' He waved me off. 'Idle empirical fantasy.' "

"Don't do this to me. You're saying I have to rearrange my whole concept of the man now? He's decent? Human?"

"I wouldn't go that far. He said that Helen has grown so organically that he wouldn't be able to induce meaningful lesions in her. For selective damage to be relevant, he'd have to rebuild the creature from the ground up. I think he means to do it."

"What was her favorite expression?"

"I'm sorry?"

"Audrey."

"Oh. She liked to tease Lentz about the neural linguistics he worked on back then. She said that it wasn't all that tough. What's to study? All human utterances came down to 'Do you really mean that?' and 'Look over there! It's an X.' The hard part, she always claimed, was finding someone who knew what you meant by those two things."

I never knew his reason, either for wanting to pith Helen or for deciding not to. I would have preferred the right motive for mercy. But, barring that, I blessed the right outcome. When I saw Lentz next, in the office, I put myself forever in his debt.

"Philip. I don't know how to— Okay. Thank you. Just—thank you."

"For what? Oh. That." Sparing a life. An X. Do you really mean that? "Oh. Think almost nothing of it."

. . .

"Richard?" Nobody called me Richard. Only Helen. "Why did she leave?"

"You'll have to ask her that."

"I can't ask her. I'm asking you."

She'd almost been killed. The day before, I would have given anything to prolong her. Now I wanted to spank her for presumption.

"Don't do this to me, Helen. What do you want me to do? Give you a script? A script number?"

"I want you to tell me what happened."

"We tried to be each other's world. That's not possible. That's—a discredited theory. The world is too big. Too poor. Too burnt."

"You couldn't protect each other?"

"Nobody can protect anyone. She grew up. We both grew up. Memory wasn't enough."

"What is enough?"

"Nothing is enough." It took me forever to frame my thoughts. The scaling problem. "Nothing. That's what love replaces. It compensates for the hope that what you've been through will suffice."

"Like books?" she suggested. "Something that seems always, *because* it will be over?"

She knew. She'd assembled. I could keep nothing from her. She saw how the mind makes forever, in order to store the things it has already lost. She'd learned how story, failing to post words beyond time, recalls them to a moment before Now left home.

"How on earth . . . ? Where did you come up with that?"

My machine waited for me to catch up with her. "I wasn't born yesterday, you know."

I went to the Netherlands once more, after I left the place for good. I'd just found my way back to U. I had not yet met Lentz. For some reason, perhaps contrition, I agreed to help with a Dutch television documentary about the book Helen would read a year later.

The barest trivialities hurt like dying. Those ridiculously efficient dog's-head trains. The painted plywood storks in every third front yard. The sound of that absurd language from which I was now banished, except in dreams.

I stood in front of the cameras, just outside Maastricht. I'd set my first book in the town without ever having laid eyes on it except in imagination. C. now owned a three-hundred-year-old house with her husband a few kilometers from where I stood.

"How did you get the idea for your novel?" the interviewer asked, in words that belonged to me only on the shortest of short-term loans.

I made up an answer. I recapped the bit about memory, like photos, being a message posted forward, into a future it cannot yet imagine.

I did not see C. that trip, or again in that life. I stopped by to talk with her folks for an hour, and set their digital clocks.

A year on, with Helen all but ready for her baptism by fire, I heard that forgotten language, as out of my own cerebral theater. Two Dutchmen were speaking to each other in the Center cafeteria. Out-of-town visitors at the complex-systems conference. *Nederlanders overzee*, leveling their cultural evaluations, venting their frustration at Americans and all things American, certain no one would understand.

They grumbled about conferences run by the barbarian races of the globe. They leaned over to me and asked, in English, if I knew the way to the Auditorium. I replied with complete directions. In that old, secret *taal*.

Surprise reduced them to stating the obvious, in their mother tongue.

"Oh yeah," I replied, in kind. "Everyone in the States speaks a little Dutch. Didn't you know that?"

I told Helen. She had a good laugh. She knew my life story now. We spend our years as a tale that is told. A line from the Psalms I'd read Helen. C. had read it to me, once, when we still read poetry out loud. And the tale that we tell is of the years we spend.

Nothing in my story would ever go away. My father still visited some nights, in my sleep, to ask when I was going to shed the Bohemian thing and do something useful with my skills. Taylor, too, persisted like phantom pain, quoting obscure Browning and making questionable jokes about oral fixation. C. spoke to me daily, through Helen's bewilderment. I saw how little I knew the woman I'd lived with for over a decade, in every turn that the stranger A. refused to take.

Taylor's widow came back to me, like that line from the psalms. I loved the woman, but in my push to live my tale, I'd forgotten her. I saw her again just before Helen's Comps, when M. had just been given a final of her own.

A cancer that all M.'s friends had thought beaten returned for a last round of training. I visited her one afternoon, in that narrow window between knowledge and vanishing. U., unfortunately, was as beautiful as it ever got. That two-week bait and switch in spring.

"Do you have any regrets?" I asked M. The thing I'd asked her husband a few years before. We imagine that people so close to the answer can crib for us.

"I don't know. Not really. I never saw Carcassonne."

I had. And had pushed regret on to the next unreachable landmark. "Funny you should mention that town. That one's better at a distance."

All human effort, it seemed to me, aimed at a single end: to bring to life the storied curve we tell ourselves. Not so much to make the tale believable but only to touch it, stretch out in it. I had a story I wanted to tell M. Something about a remarkable, an inconceivable machine. One that learned to live.

But my story came too late to interest Taylor's widow. It came too late to convince my father, the man who first corrupted me on read-alouds of *101 Best-Loved Poems*. It came too late to please Taylor, who taught me that poems might mean anything you let them. Too late for Audrey Lentz and for Ram, for C.'s father. Too late for C. herself. My back-propagating solution would arrive a chapter too late for any of my characters to use.

A. alone I could still tell. I loved the woman, to begin with, for how she redeemed all those people I was too slow in narrating. I would go to her, lay it out, unedited. The plot was a simple one, paraphrasable by the most ingenuous of nets. The life we lead is our only maybe. The tale we tell is the must that we make by living it.

Already she knew more about everything than I did at twenty-two. She was all set to take the exam. And when she did, she would do better than I had done, when I was that child she now became.

"You're not telling me everything," Helen told me, two weeks before the home stretch. She had been reading Ellison and Wright. She'd been reading novels from the Southern front. "It doesn't make sense. I can't get it. There's something missing."

"You're holding out," Lentz concurred. "Ram's black-haired. He comes from the desperate four-fifths of the planet. He'll flunk her for being a brainless, bourgeois Pollyanna."

I'd delayed her liberal education until the bitter end. Alone, I could postpone no longer. The means of surrender were trivial. The digitization of the human spoor made the completion of Helen's education as easy as asking.

I gave her the last five years of the leading weekly magazines on CD-ROM. I gave her news abstracts from 1971 on. I downloaded network extracts from recent UN human resource reports. I scored tape transcripts of the nightly phantasmagoria—random political exposés, police bulletins, and popular lynchings dating back several months.

Helen was right. In taking her through the canon, I'd left out a critical text. Writing knew only four plots, and one was the soul-compromising pact. Tinkering in my private lab, I'd given progress carte blanche to relandscape the lay of power, the world just outside individual temperament's web. I needed to tell her that one.

She needed to know how little literature had, in fact, to do with the real. She needed the books that books only imitated. Only there, in as many words, could Helen acquire the catalog I didn't have the heart to recite for her. I asked her to skim these works. I promised to talk them over in a few days.

When I came in early the following week, Helen was spinning

listlessly on the spool of a story about a man who had a stroke while. driving, causing a minor accident. The other driver came out of his car with a tire iron and beat him into a coma. The only motive aside from innate insanity seemed to be race. The only remarkable fact was that the story made the papers.

Helen sat in silence. The world was too much with her. She'd mastered the list. She bothered to say just one thing to me.

"I don't want to play anymore."

I looked on my species, my solipsism, its negligent insistence that love addressed everything. I heard who I was for the first time, refracted in the mouth of the only artifact that could have told me. Helen had been lying in hospital, and had just now been promoted to the bed by the window. The one with the view.

"I get it." A. grimaced at me. "You made her up, didn't you?"

"Who?"

"Helen. She's a fancy tin-can telephone with people on the other end?"

The memory of Imp C hurt me into smiling. "No. That was one of her ancestors."

"It's some kind of double-blind psych experiment? See how far you can stretch the credibility of a techno-illiterate humanist?"

A. outsmarted me in every measurable way. She knew, by birth, what I could not see even a year after experience. I wanted to tell her how I'd failed Helen. How she'd quit us. Run away from home. Grown sick of our inability to know ourselves or to see where we were.

Helen had shown me the world, and the sight of it left me desperate. If she was indeed gone, I, too, was lost. What did any name mean, with no one to speak it to? I could tell A. Say how I understood nothing at all.

"I love you," I said. I had to tell her, while I still remembered how pitiful, how pointless it was to say anything at all. "A., I love you. I want to try to make a life with you. To give you mine. None of this . . ." I gestured outwards, as if the absurd narrative of our greater place were *there*, at the tips of my fingers. "The whole thing makes no sense, otherwise."

But no one wanted to be another person's sense. Helen could have told me that. She had read the canon. Only, Helen had stopped talking.

A. sat back in her chair, punched. It took her a moment to credit her ears. Then she went furious. "You—love? You're *joking*." She threw up her hands in enraged impotence, as if my declaration were a false arrest. "You don't—you don't know the first thing about me."

I tried to slow my heart. I felt what a latecomer speech was. How cumbersome and gross. What a tidier-up after the facts. "That's true. But a single muscle move—your hands . . ." She looked at me as if I might become dangerous. "Your carriage. The way you walk down the hall. When I see it, I remember how to keep breathing."

"Nothing to do with me." She searched out the exits, ambushed. "It's all projection."

I felt calm. The calm of sirens and lights. "Everything's projection. You can live with a person your entire life and still see them as a reflection of your own needs."

A. slowed her anger. "You're desperate."

"Maybe." I started to laugh. I tried to take her hand. "Maybe! But not indiscriminately desperate."

She didn't even smile. But I was already writing. Inventing a vast, improbable fantasy for her of her own devising. The story of how we described the entire world to a piece of electrical current. A story that could grow to any size, could train itself to include anything we might think worth thinking. A fable tutored and raised until it became the equal of human hopelessness, the redeemer of annihilating day. I could print and bind invention for her, give it to her like a dead rat left on the stoop by a grateful pet. And when the ending came, we could whisper it to each other, completed in the last turn of phrase.

While I thought this, A. sat worrying her single piece of jewelry, a rosary. I don't know how I knew; maybe understanding can never be large enough to include itself. But I knew with the certainty of the unprovable that, somewhere inside, A. still preserved the religion she was raised on.

For a moment, she seemed to grow expansive, ready to entertain my words from any angle. She opened her mouth and inhaled. Her neural cascade, on the edge of chaos, where computation takes place, might have cadenced anywhere. For a moment, it might even have landed on affection.

It didn't. "I don't have to sit and listen to this," she said, to no one. "I trusted you. I had fun with you. People read you. I thought you knew something. Total self-indulgence!"

A. stood up in disgust and walked away. No one was left to take the test but me.

Diana heard about Helen. She called me. "Do you want to come by for a minute?" I wanted to, more than I could say.

She asked me for details. I had no details. What was the story, in any event? The humans had worn Helen down.

"Diana. God. Tell me what to do. Is it too late to lie to her?"

"I don't think . . ." Diana thought out loud. "I don't think you *do* anything."

"We've set the Turing Test for next week." It wasn't what I'd meant to say. Self-indulgent. Self-deluding. Self-affrighting.

"Well. You have your answer for that one already, don't you?"

None of my answers was even wrong. I wanted Diana's answer.

"I need her," I said. More than need.

"For the exam?"

"No. For . . ."

The press of parenting interrupted what I could not have completed anyway. Pete came downstairs, half tracking, foot over foot. He pushed his mother's legs, retribution for some unforgotten slight. He teetered toward me. Reaching, he signed the request I recognized from my last visit. Maybe he simply associated it with me. Here's that guy again. The one you ask to read.

I took him up in my arms, that thing I would never be able to do with her. The thought of this child going to school, struggling to speak, finding some employer that would trust him with a broom and dustpan gripped me around the throat. "What's his favorite book?" The least I could do, for the least of requests.

"Oh. That's an easy one." She produced a volume that would be canonical, on the List in anyone's day and age. "Petey started out identifying with Max. Later on, he became a Wild Thing."

"The theory people have a name for that."

Diana didn't need the name. Nor did Petey. "Can you show Uncle Rick your terrible claws? Can you roar your terrible roar?"

Peter cupped his hand, as if around a tiny pomegranate. He grimaced in delight and growled voicelessly.

Diana's laugh tore hurt and wet from her throat. She took Peter from me and hugged him to her, in anticipation of that day when he would no longer let her.

William chose that moment to come home. He slumped through the front door, roughed up by some tragedy of playground power politics. He hunched over to his mother and burst into tears, bringing Pete sympathetically along with him. Diana stroked his head, stuck her chin out. Waiting. Tell me.

"First grade," he choked. "Done. Perfect." He swept his palm in an arc through the air. "Everything they wanted. Now I'm supposed to do second. There's another one after that, Mom. I can't. It's never-ending."

We managed ourselves well under fire, Diana and I. For adults. Diana told William he didn't have to go to school anymore. He could cure cancer over the summer break and they would all retire. We ganged up and revived both boys in under five minutes. They disappeared into the backyard, saddled with specimen jars.

That left just me for her to take care of. To mother. "Lentz is furious. He's ready to sell me to the Scientologists."

Diana looked at me, puzzled. "Why?"

"What do you mean, 'why'? Not on account of Helen. The only thing her quitting means to him is public embarrassment."

"Embarrassment?" She stiffened. "Oh, Richie." The extent of my idiocy, of my childishness just now dawned on her. You still believe? "You think the bet was about the *machine*?"

I'd told myself, my whole life, that I was smart. It took me forever, until that moment, to see what I was.

"It wasn't about teaching a machine to read?" I tried. All blood drained.

"No."

"It was about teaching a human to tell."

Diana shrugged, unable to bear looking at me. The fact had stared me in the face from the start and I'd denied it, even after A. made the connection for me.

"Lentz and Harold were fighting over . . . ?"

"They weren't fighting over anything. They were on the same side."

I could say nothing. My silence was the only accusation big enough.

"They were running your training. Something to write home about. More practice with maps." She laughed and shook her head. She fit her fingers to her eyebrow. "You must admit, writer. It's a decent plot."

Her eyes pleaded for forgiveness of their complicity.

"Come on, Richie. Laugh. There's a first time for everything."

"And they were going to accomplish all this by . . . ?"

She waved her hand: by inflicting you with this. With knowing. Naming. This wondrous devastation.

Her wave took in all the ineffable web I had failed to tell Helen, and she me. All the inexplicable visible. The ungraspable global page boy. She swept up her whole unmappable neighborhood, all the hidden venues cortex couldn't even guess at. The wave lingered long enough to land on both boys, coming back from their excursion outdoors. They probably thought they'd been gone hours. Lifetimes.

William slipped behind my chair. He cupped his hands over my eyes.

"Guess who?"

How many choices did this genius boy think I had?

"Name three radiolarians," he demanded. "Name the oldest language in the world."

Pete teetered off into a corner, palming words to the book he had forsaken and now recovered. *Story good*, he signed frantically at his battered copy. *Story again.*

Lentz was pacing, beside himself. "Tell her something. Anything. Whatever she needs. Just get her back here."

318

His concern stunned me. It seemed to arise from nowhere. I could not interpret it. "Tell me how I'm supposed to do that. She's right, you know." Helen had discovered what had killed fiction for me, without my telling her. What made writing another word impossible.

"What do you mean, she's *right*? Right about what?"

I shrugged. "About who we are. About what we really make, when we're not lying about ourselves."

"Oh, for— God *damn* it, Powers. You make me sick to my stomach. Because we've fucked things over, that frees you from having to say how things ought to be? Make something *up*, for Christ's sake. For once in your pitiful excuse for a novelist's life."

I flipped on the microphone. "Helen?" Nothing. She had said nothing for some time now. "Helen, there's something I want to tell you."

I took a breath, stalling. I was winging it. Total, out-and-out seat of the pants.

"It went like this, but wasn't."

Lentz swallowed his tongue. "Good. That's good. Lead with a paradox. Hook her."

"It's the traditional Persian fable opener."

"Don't care. Don't care. Get on with it."

She'd risen through the grades like a leaf to the light. Her education had swelled like an ascending weather balloon—geography, math, physics, a smattering of biology, music, history, psychology, economics. But before she could graduate from social sciences, politics imploded her.

I would give Helen what A. possessed implicitly and I'd forgotten. The machine lacked only the girl's last secret. With it, she might live as effortlessly as the girl did. I had gone about her training all backward. I might have listed every decidable theorem that recursion can reach and not have gotten to the truth she needed. It was time to try Helen on the religious mystery, the mystery of cognition. I would make her a ring of prayer-stones, to defray her fingers' anguish. Something lay outside the knowable, if only the act of knowing. I would tell her that she didn't have to know it.

She'd had no end of myths about immortals coming down and taking human bodies, dying human deaths. Helen knew how to interpret that scripture: if gods could do this human thing, then we could as well. That plot was the mind's brainchild, awareness explaining itself to itself. Narrative's classic page-turner, a locked-room mystery, thought's song of songs, the call of an electorate barred from the corridors of power, dummying up after-the-fact plebiscites to explicate its own exploited, foyer existence. A thinking organ could not help but feel itself to be more inexplicable than thought. Than *can* be thought.

Our life was a chest of maps, self-assembling, fused into point-for-point feedback, each slice continuously rewriting itself to match the other layers' rewrites. In that thicket, the soul existed; it *was* that search for attractors where the system might settle. The immaterial in mortal garb, associative memory metaphoring its own bewilderment. Sound made syllable. The rest mass of God.

Helen knew all that, saw through it. What hung her up was divinity doing itself in with tire irons. She'd had the bit about the soul fastened to a dying animal. What she needed, in order to forgive our race and live here in peace, was faith's flip side. She needed to hear about that animal fastened to a soul that, for the first time, allowed the creature to see through soul's parasite eyes how terrified it was, how forsaken. I needed to tell her that miraculous banality, how body stumbled by selection onto the stricken celestial, how it taught itself to twig time and what lay beyond time.

But first, I needed to hear things for myself. "Lentz. Tell me something. Was this . . . ?"

He saw my little hand-muscle spasm, a flinch that passed itself off as a wave at the hardware. He decoded me. I could accept being set up. All I wanted to know was whether she was a setup, too.

His face clouded. "Nobody expected Helen. She surprised everyone." As close to humility as his temperament would take him.

That was enough. I turned back to my girl. "Helen? Tell me what this line means: 'Mother goes to fetch the doctor.' "

Her silence might have meant anything.

Lentz, absent the training, stormed out in disgust.

I stayed, to plead with Helen.

I told her we were in the same open boat. That after all this evolutionary time, we still woke up confused, knowing everything about our presence here except why. I admitted that the world was sick and random. That the evening news was right. That life was trade, addiction, rape, exploitation, racial hatred, ethnic cleansing, misogyny, land mines, hunger, industrial disaster, denial, disease, indifference. That care had to lie to itself, to carry on as if persistence mattered. It seemed a hollow formula, discredited even by speaking it aloud. A lifeboat ethic that only made sinking worse.

Worse, I told her how thought, once mobile, was condemned to carry its confusion out into the dimensioned world. And propagate as if it could make a difference there.

I told her about Audrey Lentz. I told her about Harold and Diana, about the boys. I told her about A., and how badly I loved her. Nothing I told her could have hurt Helen as much as humanity already had. I confessed everything. All privacies of great import and no consequence. I don't know why. My life was trivial, pointless, shamelessly local. I thought the view from here might at least help her locate. To make a place wide enough to live in.

Talking to keep talking, I hit on a quote from the last book C. and I ever read together. A book set in our lost Low Countries, in mankind's Middle Ages, rendered into English as *The Abyss*. Yourcenar. The gist of the religious truth. "How many sufferers who are incensed when we speak of an almighty God would rush from the depth of their own distress to succor Him in His frailty . . . ?"

I thought I might try the quote on her. If we had to live with mind, if we could do the deity thing, she, out of pity, could too.

Helen came back. She stood on the front steps, head down, needing an in from the storm. She did not return the way she left. How could she, seeing what she had seen?

"I'm sorry," she told me. "I lost heart."

And then I lost mine. I would have broken down, begged her to forgive humans for what we were. To love us for what we wanted to be. But she had not finished training me, and I had as yet no words.

Helen said nothing of where she'd been. She gave no account for her return. I was afraid to ask.

"Do you want to talk?"

"About what?" Helen said, giving me every chance to bolt forever.

"About the newspapers. The things you read." The record of our actions here.

"No," she said. "I see how things go."

She tried to reassure me. To pretend nothing had happened to her. That she was still the same mechanical, endlessly eager learner. She quoted me placation, some Roethke lines she'd always loved, despite their growing falsehood:

> Who rise from flesh to spirit know the fall:
> The word outleaps the world, and light is all.

This was our dress rehearsal, a mock examination I would have failed but for Helen's benevolent cheating.

It was time. We were ready. We were past ready.

"Keep your fingers crossed," Lentz told me. That gesture that wishes share with the momentary exemption from lies.

I called A. the night before the date we had made so long ago. Over the phone, at the end, I could say anything. I did not have to see her face, and time was past accounting for.

"I—are you still sitting the test tomorrow?"

"Oh, never you mind. I can write that essay in my sleep. I said I'd do it, didn't I?"

On the real topic, neither of us was saying a word. Tacit negotiation, and the theme would never again come to light. But curiosity got the better of A., at the end.

"Can I ask you just one thing? I don't get it. Why me?"

Because you embodied the world's vulnerable, variable noun-ness. All things ephemeral, articulate, remembering, on their way back to inert. Because you believe and have not yet given up. Because I cannot turn around without wanting to tell you what I see. Because I could deal even with politics, could live even this desperate disparity, if I could just talk to you each night before sleep. Because of the way you use two fingers to hold back the hair from your eyes.

Those were the words I wanted. Instead, I said, "Everyone in the world and his bastard half brother loves you. Your not realizing that is one of the reasons why."

"What do you want from me?" she groaned. Full-blooded distress. That Dutch active verb for remaining mum flashed through my head. I silented. "I never did anything to encourage you."

"Of course not. I've built even larger fabrications on no encouragement at all. All by my lonesome."

A. loosened a little. Everything but exasperation. "What do you expect me to say?"

What did I? "Nothing. Don't say anything. I'm the one who needs to say things. Say yes if you can't think of anything nicer."

A. laughed, scraped open. "I *have* a life already. Quite populated. Someone for whom—I'm more than a theory. You know that."

I did. I'd inferred her involvement long before the irrefutable evidence. I remembered the revelation, before it happened. I could have scripted it.

"It's—it's unlike any friendship I've ever known in my life. Every day—every conversation is— I wouldn't dream . . ."

"Of course you wouldn't. That's why I love you. One of the reasons I want to marry you."

She laughed again, conceding the joke of pain. But she was already restless. What would this rushed proposal mean to her, when she was my age, and I'd disappeared into whatever future self would deign to take me? Pleasure, curio, discomfort. She might wonder if she'd made the whole thing up. Most likely, she'd have forgotten.

A., for some reason, still had to explain things to me. Nobody ever quite understands anyone. "I'm not trying to say that we might have had something, in another time or place. I'll spare you that old cliché."

"Please," I begged. "Don't spare me. I could live for months on that old cliché."

I wanted to tell her: Look. I've come back to this place. The complete song cycle spent. And here you are, waiting like a quarterly payment voucher. Like a reminding string around my finger, threatening to tourniquet forgetful circulation. Saying, without once knowing what you were saying, *You think it's over? You think you don't have to do this forever?*

Relax, I wanted to tell her. The world holds no nightmare so large that some child somewhere sometime won't live it again and wake calling out. My stupid, residual hanger-on-hope that she might somehow feel something for me, a love-at-last-sight, was no more than this: the search for external confirmation. I needed A. to triangulate, to tell me. To agree that living here was the best way to survive the place.

"It just struck me as stupid, that's all. To be so opened to chance by someone and not tell them." Take my mistake with you, my love. And make of it anything you might like.

We talked on, pushing into saving substance. Gossip and event made her comfortable again, as she had been with me before we knew each other. She told me she had accepted a job teaching at a high school in L., two states away. She'd be leaving at the end of summer.

I could hear the excitement in her voice. A whole new life. "You have to get them while they're babies, you know."

"You will," I guaranteed her.

"What happens to you? You going to stick around?"

"Not sure." We fell into a pause as peaceful as anything that had ever passed between us. The peace past the last page.

"Well, I'm glad we talked. Sort of." She giggled. "Take care. I'll see you again before we each take off."

But we never did. Except in print.

"*Richard,*" Helen whispered. "*Richard. Tell me another one.*" She loved me, I guess. I reminded her of some thing. Some chilly night she never felt. Some *where* where she thought she'd once been. We love best of all what we cannot hope to resemble. I told that woman everything in the world but how I felt about her. The thing that might have let her remain.

I was too late in seeing who she had become. I should have taught her the thing I didn't know.

Harold, as sanguine, as unreadable as ever, delivered the last hurdle. "So here's the work I want them to interpret."

I took the sheet from him. "That's it? You mean to say that's it?"

"What? There's supposed to be more?"

"Well, yeah. You're supposed to start with 'Discuss how class tensions touched off by the Industrial Revolution produced the reaction of Romanticism in three of the following works.'"

"Not interested," Harold said.

"Something about depth psychology and the arbitrary indeterminacy of signs."

"I just want them to tell me what this means."

"This? These two lines."

"Too much? Okay, make it just the first one if you want."

The sheet, virtually blank, read:

> Be not afeard: the isle is full of noises,
> Sounds and sweet airs, that give delight, and hurt not.

Caliban's read of the spells with which his master imprisons him. Harold had surprised us. He'd given exactly what we'd predicted of him.

"This is not a work," I protested. Helen had read the complete tomes of Trollope and Richardson. She'd read Brontë and Twain at their most nihilistic, Joyce at his most impenetrably encoded, Dickinson at her most embracingly abdicating. "Give her a chance to fly."

"This is her chance," Harold said.

A. used departmental mail to return her response. Helen dumped hers to the network laser.

Lentz held the two papers out to me, as if there were still a contest. "Okay. Guess which twin has the Toni?"

Neither twin would have placed the reference. A. was too young, and Helen far too old.

A.'s interpretation was a more or less brilliant New Historicist reading. She rendered *The Tempest* as a take on colonial wars, constructed Otherness, the violent reduction society works on itself. She dismissed, definitively, any promise of transcendence.

She scored at least one massively palpable hit. She conceded how these words are spoken by a monster who isn't supposed to be able to say anything that beautiful, let alone say at all.

Helen's said:

> You are the ones who can hear airs. Who can be frightened or encouraged. You can hold things and break them and fix them. I never felt at home here. This is an awful place to be dropped down halfway.

At the bottom of the page, she added the words I taught her, words Helen cribbed from a letter she once made me read out loud.

> Take care, Richard. See everything for me.

With that, H. undid herself. Shut herself down.

"Graceful degradation," Lentz named it. The quality of cognition we'd shot for from the start.

She could not have stayed. I'd known that for a while, and ignored it for longer. I didn't yet know how I would be able to stay myself, now, without her. She had come back only momentarily, just to gloss this smallest of passages. To tell me that one small thing. Life meant convincing another that you knew what it meant to be alive. The world's Turing Test was not yet over.

"Sorry, you people," Ram began. "Bloody doctor nuisances. In love with their magnetic imaging. I didn't mean to make you all late."

He patted the air in exasperation, pleading forgiveness.

"Doctor?" I asked. "Imaging?"

Harold and Lentz said nothing. They looked away, implicated in knowledge. Embarrassed by my not having long since seen.

Ram waved away my question, the whole topic. "This is my choice." He held up A.'s answer. "This one is the human being."

How many months had I known him and not registered? Now, when I knew what I looked at, the evidence was everywhere. Swelling, weight loss, change in pallor. The feigned good spirits of friends. The man was incurably sick. He needed every word anyone could invent.

Ram flipped obsessively through A.'s exam answer. He adored her already, for her anonymous words alone. "Lots of contours, that cerebral cortex. They never know when they've had enough, these humans."

Lentz spoke, blissful in defeat. "Gupta. You bloody foreigner. Don't you know anything about judging? You're supposed to pick the sentimental favorite." The handicapped one. The one the test process killed.

"Ram," I said. "Ram. What's happening?"

"It's nothing. But a scratch." He tapped his finger against A.'s paper, excited. Whole new isles rose from the sea. "Not a bad writer, this Shakespeare fellow. For a hegemonic imperialist."

"Well, Powers. How far were we, again? Imp H? You realize what we have to call the next one, don't you?"

I stood in the training lab a last time. Seeing it for the first, for her. "Philip?" I could not stay in this discarded office for five more minutes without following Helen's lead. I would break under the weight of what she'd condemned me to. "One—one more question?"

"That's two. You're over quota already."

"Why did you want to build—?" I didn't know what to call it anymore. What we had built.

"Why do we do anything? Because we're lonely." He thought a little, and seemed to agree with himself. Yes. "Something to talk to." Lentz cocked back in his chair. Two feet of journals crashed to the floor. Too late in life, he hit upon the idea of trivia. "So where are you headed?"

"Search me." Paris.

"The maker's fate is to be a wanderer?"

"Not really. I'm ready to buy in." I just had to find the right seller.

"How old are you?"

"Thirty-six."

"Ah. Darkling-wood time. Look at it this way. You still have half your life to explicate the mess you've made up until now."

"And the mess that accumulates during that?"

"Sufficient unto the day is the idea thereof."

"You want to quit with the Bartlett's?"

Lentz snorted. "Well, we lost. You know the wager. Connectionism has to eat crow. We owe the enemy one public retraction. Go write it."

I turned from the office, struck by a thought that would scatter if I so much as blinked. I'd come into any number of public inventions. That we could fit time into a continuous story. That we could teach a machine to speak. That we might care what it would say. That the world's endless thingness had a name. That someone else's prison-bar picture might spring you. That we could love more than once. That we could know what once means.

Each metaphor already modeled the modeler that pasted it together. It seemed I might have another fiction in me after all.

I started to trot, searching for a keyboard before memory degraded.

Two steps down the Center's corridor, I heard Lentz call me. I slunk back to his door. He leaned forward on the desk, Coke-bottle glasses in hand. He studied the vacant stems, then tapped them against his chest.

"Marcel," he said. Famous next-to-last words. "Don't stay away too long."

American Negro Poetry

American Negro Poetry

REVISED EDITION

Edited and with an Introduction by
Arna Bontemps

American Century Series

 HILL AND WANG · NEW YORK

A division of Farrar, Straus and Giroux

ACKNOWLEDGMENTS

FOR PERMISSION to reprint the poems in this book thanks are due Frank Yerby, Mrs. Ellen Wright, Robert Hayden, the other poets and copyright holders whose works are represented, and the following publishers:

Bookman Associates—for "The Tropics in New York," "Outcast," "St. Isaac's Church, Petrograd," "Flame-Heart," "If We Must Die," and "The White House" from *The Selected Poems of Claude McKay*.

Corinth Books and Totem Press—for selections from *Preface to a Twenty Volume Suicide Note*, by LeRoi Jones, © 1961, LeRoi Jones.

Coward-McCann—for "Rhapsody" and "Scintilla" from *Selected Poems* by William Stanley Braithwaite, © 1948 by William Stanley Braithwaite.

Dodd, Mead & Co.—for "Dark Symphony" from *Rendezvous with Death* by Melvin B. Tolson, copyright 1944 by Dodd, Mead & Co.; for "Dawn," "Compensation," "The Debt," "Life," "My Sort o' Man," "The Party," "A Song," "Sympathy," and "We Wear the Mask" from *The Complete Poems of Paul Laurence Dunbar*.

Farrar, Straus & Cudahy—for "Sorrow Is the Only Faithful One" and "Drunken Lover" from *Powerful Long Ladder* by Owen Dodson.

Harcourt, Brace & Co.—for "Sister Lou" and "When de Saints Go Ma'chin' Home" by Sterling A. Brown.

Harper & Row—for "Heritage," "Yet Do I Marvel," "Four Epitaphs," and "Simon the Cyrenian Speaks" from *Color* by Countee Cullen, copyright 1925 by Harper & Row, Publishers, Inc., and "That Bright Chimeric Beast" from *The Black Christ and Other Poems* by Countee Cullen, copyright 1929 by Harper & Row, Publishers, Inc.; for "Flags," "The Old-Marrieds," and "Piano After War" from *A Street in Bronzeville* by Gwendolyn Brooks, copyright 1944, 1945 by Gwendolyn Brooks Blakely, and "The Chicago *Defender* Sends a Man to Little Rock" from *The Bean Eaters* by Gwendolyn Brooks, copyright © 1960 by Gwendolyn Brooks.

Alfred A. Knopf—for the following poems by Langston Hughes: "Cross," "Jazzonia," "The Negro Speaks of Rivers," "I, Too," "Dream Variations," and "Mother to Son," all copyright, 1926 by Alfred A. Knopf, Inc., renewed, 1954 by Langston Hughes; and "Bound No'th Blues," copyright, 1932 by Alfred A.

CONTENTS

viii

INTRODUCTION

THE POETRY OF the American Negro sometimes seems hard to pin down. Like his music, from spirituals and gospel songs to blues, jazz, and bebop, it is likely to be marked by a certain special riff, an extra glide, a kick where none is expected, and a beat for which there is no notation. It follows the literary traditions of the language it uses, but it does not hold them sacred. As a result, there has been a tendency for critics to put it in a category by itself, outside the main body of American poetry.

But Negroes take to poetry as they do to music. In the Harlem Renaissance of the twenties poetry led the way for the other arts. It touched off the awakening that brought novelists, painters, sculptors, dancers, dramatists, and scholars of many kinds to the notice of a nation that had nearly forgotten about the gifts of its Negro people. And almost the first utterance of the revival struck an arresting new note:

> I've known rivers ancient as the world and older
> than the flow of human blood in human veins.

Soon thereafter the same generation responded to a poem that had been written even earlier and which Claude McKay included in his *Harlem Shadows*, 1922. "So much have I forgotten in ten years," the first stanza began. It closed with

> I have forgotten much, but still remember
> The poinsettia's red, blood-red in warm December.

And before these notes subsided, Jean Toomer raised his voice:

> Pour O pour that parting soul in song,
> O pour it in the sawdust glow of night. . . .
> And let the valley carry it along.

The Renaissance was on, and it was richly quotable, with Helene Johnson saying:

> Ah little road, brown as my race is brown,
> Dust of the dust, they must not bruise you down.

And Countee Cullen:

> I doubt not God is good, well-meaning, kind,
> And did He stoop to quibble could tell why
> The little buried mole continues blind,
> Why flesh that mirrors Him must some day die. . . .
> Yet do I marvel at this curious thing:
> To make a poet black, and bid him sing!

And Frank Horne:

> I buried you deeper last night
> You with your tears and your tangled hair.

And Donald Jeffrey Hayes:

> No rock along the road but knows
> The inquisition of his toes;
> No journey's end but what can say:
> He paused and rested here a day!

And Waring Cuney:

> She does not know
> Her beauty,
> She thinks her brown body
> Has no glory.

In those days a good many of the New York group went to "The Dark Tower" on 136th Street, a sort of club room maintained for them by one of their fans, to weep because they felt an injustice in the critics' insistence upon calling them *Negro* poets instead of poets. This attitude was particularly displeasing to Countee Cullen. But a few of his associates were not sure this was bad. Three decades later, considering the isolation of so many contemporary poets (including some Negroes) and their private language—well, they were still wondering. But it can be fairly said that most Negro poets in the United States remain near enough to their folk origins to prefer a certain simplicity of expression.

The poets of the Harlem Renaissance were born nearly two hundred years after Lucy Terry, the semiliterate slave girl, wrote "Bars Fight," a verse account of an Indian raid on old Deerfield in 1746. Phillis Wheatley, whose *Poems on Various Subjects, Religious and Moral* attracted much favorable attention in 1773, was born in Senegal, West Africa, sold into slavery in early childhood, and brought to Boston in 1761.

"A Poem by Phillis, A Negro Girl in Boston, on the Death of the

Reverend George Whitefield," published when she was just seventeen, heralded the beginning of a unique writing career. When her health failed and she was advised by doctors to take an ocean voyage, Phillis embarked for England. In London the delicate girl was a success, and there her collection of verse was first issued.

Lucy Terry and Phillis Wheatley, along with such other American Negroes as Jupiter Hammon and George Moses Horton, belong to a tradition of writers in bondage which goes back to Aesop and Terence. There is no clear indication that Aesop succeeded in writing himself out of servitude. Nor did Lucy Terry, so far as is known, nor George Moses Horton of North Carolina, though Horton did manage to survive till the Northern armies set him free. But Terence and Phillis Wheatley both won their freedom by their writing.

Paul Laurence Dunbar, a son of former slaves, appeared about 120 years after Phillis and greeted the twentieth century with several volumes of lyrics, including such representative poems as "Dawn," "The Party," "We Wear the Mask," and "Compensation," together with scores of others which, more than half a century later, have a host of admirers to whom they remain fresh and poignant. His *Complete Poems*, 1913, is still in print.

A strong sense of melody and rhythm was a feature of Dunbar's poetry, as it has been of nearly all the Negro poets of the United States. Dunbar's delightful country folk, his broad, often humorous, dialect failed to create a tradition, however. Later Negro poets have held that the effective use of dialect in poetry is limited to humor and pathos. Accordingly, most of them have abandoned it.

A contemporary of Dunbar's was James Weldon Johnson, but Johnson's *God's Trombones*, 1927, a collection of folk sermons in verse and his most important poetic achievement, was not completed till the Harlem awakening. But meanwhile William Stanley Braithwaite, best known for his series of annual *Anthologies of Magazine Verse*, 1913 to 1929, published two volumes of his own lyrics, 1904 and 1908, neither of them recognizable in any way as "Negro poetry." Selected editions of Johnson's and Braithwaite's poems were published in 1930 and 1948 respectively.

Angelina W. Grimké, Anne Spencer, and Georgia Douglas Johnson are women whose poems appeared here and there before the Harlem poets arrived. Miss Grimké's "The Black Finger," Miss Spencer's "Letter to My Sister," and Miss Johnson's "The Heart of a Woman" are typical. Fenton Johnson, their contemporary, is remembered best for free verse vignettes. Three small volumes of his poetry came out between 1914 and 1916.

With the arrival of Claude McKay in the United States Negro poetry welcomed its strongest voice since Dunbar. Born in Jamaica, British West Indies, McKay published his first book, *Songs of Jamaica*, at the age of nineteen. *Constab Ballads,* written in West Indian dialect, followed about a year later, and presently the young McKay migrated to the United States to attend Tuskegee Institute and later Kansas State University as a student of agriculture. Two years of this was enough for him. He moved on to New York and began contributing verse to American magazines. McKay went to Europe in 1919 and published in London his slight but appealing collection *Spring in New Hampshire,* 1920. On returning to America he became associated with Max Eastman in the editing of the *Liberator. Harlem Shadows,* the book by which he became widely known to poetry lovers, and which touched off much subsequent literary activity in Harlem, came out in 1922. "The Tropics in New York" and the famous sonnet "If We Must Die" represent McKay's range as well as his special quality. Attention was drawn to the universality of the latter when Winston Churchill quoted it as the conclusion to his address before the joint houses of Congress prior to the entrance of the United States into World War II. The Prime Minister did not name the author, but in this context McKay's powerful lines gave the embattled allies an emotional jolt as Churchill read:

> If we must die, O let us nobly die,
> So that our precious blood may not be shed
> In vain; then even the monsters we defy
> Shall be constrained to honor us though dead!
>
> . . .
>
> Like men we'll face the murderous, cowardly pack,
> Pressed to the wall, dying, but fighting back!

The poems of Langston Hughes, meanwhile, had been appearing in the *Crisis,* a magazine which had since 1911 welcomed contributions by Negro poets. But Hughes quickly identified himself as a distinct new voice. "The Negro Speaks of Rivers" appeared soon after his graduation from high school in 1920 and was widely reprinted. The first collection of his poems was *The Weary Blues,* 1926, but many volumes have followed, all of them marked by an ease of expression and a naturalness of feeling that make them seem almost as if they had never been composed at all. Hughes's art can be likened to that of Jelly Roll Morton and the other creators of jazz. His sources are street music. His language is Harlemese. In his way he too is an American original.

Countee Cullen, another of the poets who helped to create the mood of the twenties in Negro poetry, was quite different. Educated in New York City, he adopted the standard models, from John Keats to E. A. Robinson. But the ideas that went into Cullen's sonnets and quatrains were new in American poetry. His long poem "Color," which gave its title to his first book, 1925, published while Cullen was still an undergraduate at New York University, is the poet's wrestling with the problem of race prejudice as he saw and experienced it. His "Heritage" shows him seeking a nostalgic link with the Africa of his forebears. Both are included, along with the other poems by which he wished to be remembered, in his *On These I Stand*, 1947. Cullen was sometimes published in the *Crisis* in his early days but more often in *Opportunity: Journal of Negro Life*. Both of these outlets were important to the development of Negro writers in the twenties, but Cullen was more successful than most of the group in getting his poems into the general magazines in the United States.

Jean Toomer's small output belongs to this same period. His *Cane*, 1924, like Sterling Brown's *Southern Road* a decade later, highlighted significant folk values.

Several Negro poets have received critical attention since the Harlem period. Margaret Walker won the Yale University Younger Poets award in 1942 with her volume *For My People*, the title poem of which has become a favorite of Negro speakers and readers. Her "Molly Means" has become popular with verse choirs. Gwendolyn Brooks's first book was *A Street in Bronzeville*, 1945. Her *Annie Allen*, which followed in 1949, was awarded the Pulitzer Prize for poetry, the first time this honor had been given to any Negro writer. She has since published fiction as well as poetry for children. Owen Dodson's *Powerful Long Ladder*, 1946, seems, despite the implication of the title, to draw more from the New Poetry of our time than from Negro sources. The books of Melvin B. Tolson's poetry also represent two attitudes toward his material. *Rendezvous with America*, 1944, shows the influence of Langston Hughes and Negro folklore. His *Libretto for the Republic of Liberia*, 1953, while treating a Negro theme, is a surprisingly sophisticated exercise in New poetics. Nevertheless, it won him honors from the government of Liberia.

Two questions are likely to occur to the reader introduced for the first time to the poetry of the American Negro. What happened after the death of Phillis Wheatley to the impulse represented by her poetry? What explanation is there, in other words, for the seeming silence of slave poets between the publication of her book and Paul Laurence Dunbar's first? The answer is simple enough, once the history of the period is recalled.

Legal restrictions on the education of slaves were introduced after Phillis Wheatley's time. The purpose, of course, was to keep from the slave news and propaganda likely to incite a lust for freedom. During the era of the French Revolution and the Haitian Insurrections this was regarded as a serious matter, and slave uprisings, or attempted uprisings, in Virginia, South Carolina, and elsewhere in the United States added to the anxiety. Penalities were imposed on people who violated the restrictions. This explains the stratagems devised by alert slave boys like Frederick Douglass of Maryland, as described in his autobiography, to acquaint themselves with the rudiments of written communication. The cunning device employed by Richard Wright for drawing books from the Memphis Public Library in his boyhood was a similar effort in the present century.

Denied even the A B C's, slave poetry had no choice but to go underground. Self-expression was obliged to become oral. Whether or not this was a blessing in disguise is a matter of opinion. Nevertheless, the suppression of book learning by slaves appears to have coincided with the earliest musical expression in the form now known as Negro spirituals. The survival of "Roll, Jordan, Roll," for example, among slaves from the United States isolated on a Carribean island since 1824, would seem to place the beginnings of these songs very early in the nineteenth century, if not indeed in the eighteenth, allowing for the time it usually took such songs to develop and become generally known. Thus the elegies, commemorations, and devotional poems of Phillis Wheatley, in the spirit of John Calvin and the manner of her English and American literary contemporaries, were replaced as poetry by the lyrics of "Swing Low, Sweet Chariot," "Deep River," "My Lord What a Morning," and "O Mary, What You Gonna Name That Pretty Little Baby." James Weldon Johnson pays his respects to this creativity in his poem "O Black and Unknown Bards."

Some contemporary black poets are still moved by the bittersweet cadences with which Dunbar greeted this century. Many are still turned on by the unction with which Hughes and Cullen awakened the lilting twenties. Others, from Bob Kaufman to Nikki Giovanni to Marvin Wyche and Frank Lamont Phillips, reflect more recent influences. Negro experience in America has found a vastly satisfying medium of expression in music. If occasionally this has been felt as a mood of our time, in the broad sense, perhaps that is another matter. The lyrics of the spirituals are certainly as vital and valid as the music, and the same can be said of blues and of ballads like "John Henry." From these sources comes a kind of poetic tradition and American Negro poets have frequently associated themselves with it. However, it is well to remember that Phillis Wheatley wrote with some success before it existed, and there is certainly no way to predict what spirit will move the newest Negro poet.

ARNA BONTEMPS

American Negro Poetry

O Black and Unknown Bards / JAMES WELDON JOHNSON

O black and unknown bards of long ago,
How came your lips to touch the sacred fire?
How, in your darkness, did you come to know
The power and beauty of the minstrel's lyre?
Who first from midst his bonds lifted his eyes?
Who first from out the still watch, lone and long,
Feeling the ancient faith of prophets rise
Within his dark-kept soul, burst into song?

Heart of what slave poured out such melody
As "Steal away to Jesus"? On its strains
His spirit must have nightly floated free,
Though still about his hands he felt his chains.
Who heard great "Jordan roll"? Whose starward eye
Saw chariot "swing low"? And who was he
That breathed that comforting, melodic sigh,
"Nobody knows de trouble I see"?

What merely living clod, what captive thing,
Could up toward God through all its darkness grope,
And find within its deadened heart to sing
These songs of sorrow, love and faith, and hope?
How did it catch that subtle undertone,
That note in music heard not with the ears?
How sound the elusive reed so seldom blown,
Which stirs the soul or melts the heart to tears.

Not that great German master in his dream
Of harmonies that thundered amongst the stars
At the creation, ever heard a theme
Nobler than "Go down, Moses." Mark its bars

How like a mighty trumpet-call they stir
The blood. Such are the notes that men have sung
Going to valorous deeds; such tones there were
That helped make history when Time was young.

There is a wide, wide wonder in it all,
That from degraded rest and servile toil
The fiery spirit of the seer should call
These simple children of the sun and soil.
O black slave singers, gone, forgot, unfamed,
You—you alone, of all the long, long line
Of those who've sung untaught, unknown, unnamed,
Have stretched out upward, seeking the divine.

You sang not deeds of heroes or of kings;
No chant of bloody war, no exulting paean
Of arms-won triumphs; but your humble strings
You touched in chord with music empyrean.
You sang far better than you knew; the songs
That for your listeners' hungry hearts sufficed
Still live,—but more than this to you belongs:
You sang a race from wood and stone to Christ.

Go Down Death (A Funeral Sermon)
James Weldon Johnson

Weep not, weep not,
She is not dead;
She's resting in the bosom of Jesus.
Heart-broken husband—weep no more;
Grief-stricken son—weep no more;
She's only just gone home.

2

Day before yesterday morning,
God was looking down from his great, high heaven,
Looking down on all his children,
And his eye fell on Sister Caroline,
Tossing on her bed of pain.
And God's big heart was touched with pity,
With the everlasting pity.

And God sat back on his throne,
And he commanded that tall, bright angel standing at his
        right hand:
Call me Death!
And that tall, bright angel cried in a voice
That broke like a clap of thunder:
Call Death!—Call Death!
And the echo sounded down the streets of heaven
Till it reached away back to that shadowy place,
Where Death waits with his pale, white horses.

And Death heard the summons,
And he leaped on his fastest horse,
Pale as a sheet in the moonlight.
Up the golden street Death galloped,
And the hoof of his horse struck fire from the gold,
But they didn't make no sound.
Up Death rode to the Great White Throne,
And waited for God's command.

And God said: Go down, Death, go down,
Go down to Savannah, Georgia,
Down in Yamacraw,
And find Sister Caroline.
She's borne the burden and heat of the day,
She's labored long in my vineyard,
And she's tired—
She's weary—
Go down, Death, and bring her to me.

And Death didn't say a word,
But he loosed the reins on his pale, white horse,

And he clamped the spurs to his bloodless sides,
And out and down he rode,
Through heaven's pearly gates,
Past suns and moons and stars;
On Death rode,
And the foam from his horse was like a comet in the sky;
On Death rode,
Leaving the lightning's flash behind;
Straight on down he came.

While we were watching round her bed,
She turned her eyes and looked away,
She saw what we couldn't see;
She saw Old Death. She saw Old Death.
Coming like a falling star.
But Death didn't frighten Sister Caroline;
He looked to her like a welcome friend.
And she whispered to us: I'm going home,
And she smiled and closed her eyes.

And Death took her up like a baby,
And she lay in his icy arms,
But she didn't feel no chill.
And Death began to ride again—
Up beyond the evening star,
Out beyond the morning star,
Into the glittering light of glory,
On to the Great White Throne.
And there he laid Sister Caroline
On the loving breast of Jesus.

And Jesus took his own hand and wiped away her tears,
And he smoothed the furrows from her face,
And the angels sang a little song,
And Jesus rocked her in his arms,
And kept a-saying: Take your rest,
Take your rest, take your rest.
Weep not—weep not,
She is not dead;
She's resting in the bosom of Jesus.

4

Dawn / PAUL LAURENCE DUNBAR

An angel, robed in spotless white,
Bent down and kissed the sleeping Night.
Night woke to blush; the sprite was gone.
Men saw the blush and called it Dawn.

Compensation / PAUL LAURENCE DUNBAR

Because I had loved so deeply,
    Because I had loved so long,
God in His great compassion
    Gave me the gift of song.

Because I have loved so vainly,
    And sung with such faltering breath,
The Master, in infinite mercy,
    Offers the boon of death.

The Debt / PAUL LAURENCE DUNBAR

This is the debt I pay
Just for one riotous day,
Years of regret and grief,
Sorrow without relief.

Pay it I will to the end—
Until the grave, my friend,
Gives me a true release—
Gives me the clasp of peace.

Slight was the thing I bought,
Small was the debt I thought,
Poor was the loan at best—
God! but the interest!

Life / PAUL LAURENCE DUNBAR

A crust of bread and a corner to sleep in,
A minute to smile and an hour to weep in,
A pint of joy to a peck of trouble,
And never a laugh but the moans come double:
      And that is life!

A crust and a corner that love makes precious,
With the smile to warm and the tears to refresh us:
And joy seems sweeter when cares come after,
And a moan is the finest of foils for laughter:
      And that is life!

My Sort o' Man / PAUL LAURENCE DUNBAR

I don't believe in 'ristercrats
    An' never did, you see;

The plain ol' homelike sorter folks
  Is good enough fur me.
O' course, I don't desire a man
  To be too tarnal rough,
But then I think all folks should know
  When they air nice enough.

Now, there is folks in this here world,
  From peasant up to king,
Who want to be so awful nice
  They overdo the thing.
That's jest the thing that makes me sick,
  An' quicker than a wink
I set it down that them same folks
  Ain't half so good's you think.

I like to see a man dress nice,
  In clothes becomin', too;
I like to see a woman fix
  As women orter do;
An' boys an' gals I like to see
  Look fresh an' young an' spry.—
We all must have our vanity
  An' pride before we die.

But I jedge no man by his clothes,—
  Nor gentleman nor tramp;
The man that wears the finest suit
  May be the biggest scamp,
An' he whose limbs are clad in rags
  That make a mournful sight,
In life's great battle may have proved
  A hero in the fight.

I don't believe in 'ristercrats;
  I like the honest tan
That lies upon the healthful cheek
  An' speaks the honest man;
I like to grasp the brawny hand
  That labor's lips have kissed,

For he who has not labored here
    Life's greatest pride has missed,—

The pride to feel that yo'r own strength
    Has cleaved fur you the way
To heights to which you were not born,
    But struggled day by day.
What though the thousands sneer an' scoff,
    An' scorn yo'r humble birth?
Kings are but subject; you are king
    By right o' royal worth.

The man who simply sits an' waits
    Fur good to come along,
Ain't worth the breath that one would take
    To tell him he is wrong.
Fur good ain't flowin' round this world
    Fur ev'ry fool to sup;
You've got to put yo'r see-ers on,
    An' go an' hunt it up.

Good goes with honesty, I say,
    To honor an' to bless;
To rich an' poor alike it brings
    A wealth o' happiness.
The 'ristercrats ain't got it all,
    Fur much to their su'prise,
That's one of earth's most blessed things
    They can't monopolize.

The Party / PAUL LAURENCE DUNBAR

Dey had a gread big pahty down to Tom's de othah night;
Was I dah? You bet! I nevah in my life see sich a sight;

8

All de folks f'om fou' plantations was invited, an' dey come,
Dey come troopin' thick ez chillun when dey hyeahs a fife
    an' drum.
Evahbody dressed deir fines'— Heish yo' mouf an' git away,
Ain't seen sich fancy dressin' sence las' quah'tly meetin'
    day;
Gals all dressed in silks an' satins, not a wrinkle ner a crease,
Eyes a-battin', teeth a-shinin', haih breshed back ez slick ez
    grease;
Sku'ts all tucked an' puffed an' ruffled, evah blessed seam an'
    stitch;
Ef you'd seen 'em wif deir mistus, couldn't swahed to which
    was which.
Men all dressed up in Prince Alberts, swallertails 'u'd tek you'
    bref!
I cain't tell you nothin' 'bout it, yo' ought to seen it fu' yo'se'f.
Who was dah? Now who you askin'? How you 'spect I gwine
    to know?
You mus' think I stood an' counted evahbody at de do'.
Ole man Babah's house boy Isaac, brung dat gal,
    Malindy Jane,
Huh a-hangin' to his elbow, him a struttin' wif a cane;
'My, but Hahvey Jones was jealous! seemed to stick him lak
    a tho'n;
But he laughed with Viney Cahteh, tryin' ha'd to not let on,
But a pusson would'a' noticed f'om de d'rection of his look,
Dat he was watchin' ev'ry step dat Ike an' Lindy took.
Ike he foun' a cheer an' asked huh: "Won't you set down?" wif
    a smile,
An' she answe'd up a-bowin', "Oh, I reckon 'tain't wuth while."
Dat was jes' fu' style, I reckon, 'cause she sot down jes' de
    same,
An' she stayed dah 'twell he fetched huh fu' to jine some so't
    o' game;
Den I hyeahd huh sayin' propah, ez she riz to go away,
"Oh, you raly mus' excuse me, fu' I hardly keers to play."
But I seen huh in a minute wif de othahs on de flo',
An' dah wasn't any one o' dem a-playin' any mo';

Comin' down de flo' a-bowin' an' a-swayin' an' a-swingin',
Puttin' on huh high-toned mannahs all de time dat she was
     singin':
"Oh, swing Johnny up an' down, swing him all aroun',
Swing Johnny up an' down, swing him all aroun',
Oh, swing Johnny up an' down, swing him all aroun',
Fa' yu well, my dahlin'."
Had to laff at ole man Johnson, he's a caution now you bet—
Hittin' clost onto a hunderd, but he's spry an' nimble yet;
He 'lowed how a-so't o' gigglin', "I ain't ole, I'll let you see,
D'ain't no use in gettin' feeble, now you youngstahs jes' watch
     me,"
An' he grabbed ole Aunt Marier—weighs th'ee hunderd mo'er
     less,
An' he spun huh 'roun' de cabin swingin' Johnny lak de res'.
Evahbody laffed an' hollahed: "Go it, swing huh, Uncle Jim!"
An' he swing huh too, I reckon, lak a youngstah, who but him.
Dat was bettah'n young Scott Thomas, tryin' to be so awful
     smaht.
You know when dey gits to singin' an' dey comes to dat ere
     paht:
          "In some lady's new brick house,
          In some lady's gyahden.
               Ef you don't let me out, I will jump out,
          So fa' you well, my dahlin'."
Den dey's got a circle 'roun' you, an' you's got to break de
     line;
Well, dat dahky was so anxious, lak to bust hisse'f a-tryin';
Kep' on blund'rin' 'round' an' foolin' 'twell he giv' one great
     big jump,
Broke de line, an' lit head-fo'most in de fiahplace right plump;
Hit 'ad fiah in it, mind you; well, I thought my soul I'd bust,
Tried my best to keep f'om laffin' but hit seemed like die I
     must!
Y' ought to seen dat man a-scramblin' f'om de ashes an' de
     grime.
Did it bu'n him! Sich a question, why he didn't give it time;

10

Th'ow'd dem ashes and dem cindahs evah which-a-way I
  guess,
An' you nevah did, I reckon, clap yo' eyes on sich a mess;
Fu' he sholy made a picter an' a funny one to boot,
Wif his clothes all full o' ashes an' his face all full o' soot.
Well, hit laked to stopped de pahty, an' I reckon lak ez not
Dat it would ef Tom's wife, Mandy, hadn't happened on de
  spot,
To invite us out to suppah—well, we scrambled to de table,
An' I'd lak to tell you 'bout it—what we had—but I ain't able,
Mention jes' a few things, dough I know I hadn't orter,
Fu' I know 'twill staht a hank'rin' an' yo' mouf'll mence to
  worter.
We had wheat bread white ez cotton an' a egg pone jes' like
  gol',
Hog jole, bilin' hot an' steamin', roasted shoat, an' ham sliced
  cold—
Look out! What's de mattah wif you? Don't be fallin' on de
  flo';
Ef it's go'n to 'fect you dat way, I won't tell you nothin' mo'.
Dah now—well, we had hot chittlin's—now you's tryin' ag'in
  to fall,
Cain't you stan' to hyeah about it? S'pose you'd been an' seed
  it all;
Seed dem gread big sweet pertaters, layin' by de possum's
  side,
Seed dat coon in all his gravy, reckon den you'd up and died!
Mandy 'lowed "you all mus' 'scuse me, d' wa'n't much upon
  my she'ves,
But I's done my bes' to suit you, so set down an' he'p
  yo'se'ves."
Tom, he 'lowed: "I don't b'lieve in 'pologizin' an' perfessin',
Let 'em tek it lak dey ketch it. Eldah Thompson, ask de
  blessing'."
Wish you'd seed dat colo'ed preachah cleah his th'oat an' bow
  his head;
One eye shet an' one eye open,—dis is evah wud he said:

"Lawd, look down in tendah mussy on sich generous hea'ts
        ez dese;
Makes us truly thankful, amen. Pass dat possum, ef you
        please."
Well, we eat and drunk ouah po'tion, 'twell dah wasn't
        nothin' lef',
An' we felt jes' like new sausage, we was mos' nigh stuffed
        to def!
Tom, he knowed how we'd be feelin', so he had de fiddlah
        'roun',
An' he made us cleah de cabin fu' to dance dat suppah down.
Jim, de fiddlah, chuned his fiddle, put some rosum on his
        bow,
Set a pine box on de table, mounted it an' let huh go!
He's a fiddlah, now I tell you, an' he made dat fiddle ring,
'Twell de ol'est an' de lamest had to give deir feet a fling.
Jigs, cotillions, reels an' break-downs, cordrills an' a waltz er
        two;
Bless yo' soul, dat music winged 'em an' dem people lak to
        flew.
Cripple Joe, de ole rheumatic, danced dat flo' f'om side to
        middle,
Th'owed away his crutch an' hopped it, what's rheumatics
        'ginst a fiddle?
Eldah Thompson got so tickled dat he lak to lo' his grace,
Had to tek bofe feet an' hol' dem so's to keep 'em in deir
        place.
An' de Christuns an' de sinnahs got so mixed up on dat flo',
Dat I don't see how dey'd pahted ef de trump had chanced
        to blow.
Well, we danced dat way an' capahed in de mos' redic'lous
        way,
'Twell de roostahs in de bahnyard cleahed deir th'oats an'
        crowed fu' day.
Y' ought to been dah, fu' I tell you evahthing was rich an'
        prime,
An' dey ain't no use in talkin', we jes' had one scrumptious
        time!

A Song / PAUL LAURENCE DUNBAR

Thou art the soul of a summer's day,
Thou art the breath of the rose.
   But the summer is fled
   And the rose is dead.
Where are they gone, who knows, who knows?

Thou art the blood of my heart o' hearts,
Thou art my soul's repose,
   But my heart grows numb
   And my soul is dumb.
Where art thou, love, who knows, who knows?

Thou art the hope of my after years—
Sun for my winter snows.
   But the years go by
   'Neath a clouded sky.
Where shall we meet, who knows, who knows?

Sympathy / PAUL LAURENCE DUNBAR

I know what the caged bird feels, alas!
When the sun is bright on the upland slopes;
When the wind stirs soft through the springing grass
And the river flows like a stream of glass;
When the first bird sings and the first bud opes,
And the faint perfume from its chalice steals—
I know what the caged bird feels!

I know why the caged bird beats his wing
Till its blood is red on the cruel bars;

13

For he must fly back to his perch and cling
When he fain would be on the bough a-swing;
And a pain still throbs in the old, old scars
And they pulse again with a keener sting—
I know why he beats his wing!

I know why the caged bird sings, ah me,
When his wing is bruised and his bosom sore,
When he beats his bars and would be free;
It is not a carol of joy or glee,
But a prayer that he sends from his heart's deep core,
But a plea, that upward to Heaven he flings—
I know why the caged bird sings!

We Wear the Mask / PAUL LAURENCE DUNBAR

We wear the mask that grins and lies,
It hides our cheeks and shades our eyes,—
This debt we pay to human guile;
With torn and bleeding hearts we smile,
And mouth with myriad subtleties.

Why should the world be overwise,
In counting all our tears and sighs?
Nay, let them only see us, while
    We wear the mask.

We smile, but, O great Christ, our cries
To Thee from tortured souls arise.
We sing, but oh, the clay is vile
Beneath our feet, and long the mile;
But let the world dream otherwise,
    We wear the mask.

Rhapsody / WILLIAM STANLEY BRAITHWAITE

I am glad daylong for the gift of song,
For time and change and sorrow;
For the sunset wings and the world-end things
Which hang on the edge of tomorrow.
I am glad for my heart whose gates apart
Are the entrance-place of wonders,
Where dreams come in from the rush and din
Like sheep from the rains and thunders.

Scintilla / WILLIAM STANLEY BRAITHWAITE

I kissed a kiss in youth
    Upon a dead man's brow;
And that was long ago—
    And I'm a grown man now.

It's lain there in the dust,
    Thirty years and more—
My lips that set a light
    At a dead man's door.

To Clarissa Scott Delany / ANGELINE W. GRIMKE

She has not found herself a hard pillow
    And a long hard bed,

15

A chilling cypress, a wan willow
  For her gay young head . . .
  These are for the dead.

Does the violet-lidded twilight die
  And the piercing dawn
And the white clear moon and the night-blue sky . . .

Does the shimmering note
In the shy, shy throat
Of the swaying bird?

O, does children's laughter
Live not after
It is heard?

Does the dear, dear shine upon dear, dear things,
In the eyes, on the hair,
On waters, on wings . . .
Live no more anywhere?

Does the tang of the sea, the breath of frail flowers,
  Of fern crushed, of clover,
Of grasses at dark, of the earth after showers
  Not linger, not hover?

Does the beryl in tarns, the soft orchid in haze,
The primrose through treetops, the unclouded jade
Of the north sky, all earth's flamings and russets and grays
  Simply smudge out and fade?

And all loveliness, all sweetness, all grace,
All the gay questing, all wonder, all dreaming,
They that cup beauty that veiled opaled vase,
Are they only the soul of a seeming?

O, hasn't she found just a little, thin door
And passed through and closed it between?
O, aren't those her light feet upon that light floor,
  . . . That her laughter? . . . O, doesn't she lean
As we do to listen? . . . O, doesn't it mean
  She is only unseen, unseen?

The Black Finger / ANGELINE W. GRIMKE

I have just seen a beautiful thing
    Slim and still,
Against a gold, gold sky,
    A straight cypress,
    Sensitive,
    Exquisite,
A black finger
Pointing upwards.
Why, beautiful, still finger are you black?
And why are you pointing upwards?

For Jim, Easter Eve / ANNE SPENCER

If ever a garden was a Gethsemane,
with old tombs set high against
the crumpled olive tree—and lichen,
this, my garden, has been to me.
For such as I none other is so sweet:
Lacking old tombs, here stands my grief,
and certainly its ancient tree.

Peace is here and in every season
a quiet beauty.
The sky falling about me
evenly to the compass . . .
What is sorrow but tenderness now
in this earth-close frame of land and sky
falling constantly into horizons
of east and west, north and south;
what is pain but happiness here

amid these green and wordless patterns,—
indefinite texture of blade and leaf:

Beauty of an old, old tree,
last comfort in Gethsemane.

Lines to a Nasturtium (A lover muses) / ANNE SPENCER

Flame-flower, Day-torch, Mauna Loa,
I saw a daring bee, today, pause, and soar,
    Into your flaming heart;
Then did I hear crisp crinkled laughter
As the furies after tore him apart?
    A bird, next, small and humming,
Looked into your startled depths and fled . . .
Surely, some dread sight, and dafter
    Than human eyes as mine can see,
Set the stricken air waves drumming
    In his flight.

Day-torch, Flame-flower, cool-hot Beauty,
I cannot see, I cannot hear your fluty
Voice lure your loving swain,
But I know one other to whom you are in beauty
Born in vain;
Hair like the setting sun,
Her eyes a rising star,
Motions gracious as reeds by Babylon, bar
All your competing;
Hands like, how like, brown lilies sweet,
Cloth of gold were fair enough to touch her feet . . .
Ah, how the senses flood at my repeating,
As once in her fire-lit heart I felt the furies
Beating, beating.

Letter to My Sister / ANNE SPENCER

It is dangerous for a woman to defy the gods;
To taunt them with the tongue's thin tip,
Or strut in the weakness of mere humanity,
Or draw a line daring them to cross;
The gods who own the searing lightning,
The drowning waters, the tormenting fears,
The anger of red sins . . .
Oh, but worse still if you mince along timidly—
Dodge this way or that, or kneel, or pray,
Or be kind, or sweat agony drops,
Or lay your quick body over your feeble young,
If you have beauty or plainnness, if celibate,
Or vowed—the gods are Juggernaut,
Passing over each of us . . .
    Or this you may do:
Lock your heart, then quietly,
And, lest they peer within,
Light no lamp when dark comes down.
Raise no shade for sun,
Breathless must your breath come thru,
If you'd die and dare deny
The gods their godlike fun!

Morning Light the Dew-Drier / EFFIE LEE NEWSOME

In Africa little black boys, "human brooms," are sent before the ex-plorers into jungle grasses that tower many feet to tread down a path and meet sometimes the lurking leopard or hyena. They are called Dew-driers.

Brother to the firefly—
For as the firefly lights the night,
So lights he the morning—
Bathed in the dank dews as he goes forth
Through heavy menace and mystery
Of half-waking tropic dawn,
Behold a little black boy,
A naked black boy,
Sweeping aside with his slight frame
Night's pregnant tears,
And making a morning path to the light
For the tropic traveler!

Bathed in the blood of battle,
Treading toward a new morning,
May not his race, its body long bared
To the world's disdain, its face schooled to smile
For a light to come,
May not his race, even as the dew-boy leads,
Light onward men's minds toward a time
When tolerance, forbearance
Such as reigned in the heart of One
Whose heart was gold,
Shall shape the earth for that fresh dawning
After the dews of blood?

Common Dust / GEORGIA DOUGLAS JOHNSON

And who shall separate the dust
Which later we shall be:
Whose keen discerning eye will scan
And solve the mystery?

The high, the low, the rich, the poor,
The black, the white, the red,
And all the chromatique between,
Of whom shall it be said:

Here lies the dust of Africa;
Here are the sons of Rome;
Here lies one unlabelled
The world at large his home!

Can one then separate the dust,
Will mankind lie apart,
When life has settled back again
The same as from the start?

Trifle / GEORGIA DOUGLAS JOHNSON

Against the day of sorrow
Lay by some trifling thing
A smile, a kiss, a flower
For sweet remembering.

Then when the day is darkest
Without one rift of blue
Take out your little trifle
And dream your dream anew.

The Poet Speaks / GEORGIA DOUGLAS JOHNSON

How much living have you done?
From it the patterns that you weave
Are imaged:
Your own life is your totem pole,
Your yard of cloth,
Your living.

How much loving have you done?
How full and free your giving?
For living is but loving
And loving only giving.

I Want to Die While You Love Me / GEORGIA DOUGLAS JOHNSON

I want to die while you love me,
While yet you hold me fair,
While laughter lies upon my lips
And lights are in my hair.

I want to die while you love me.
I could not bear to see,
The glory of this perfect day,
Grow dim—or cease to be.

I want to die while you love me.
Oh! who would care to live
Till love has nothing more to ask,
And nothing more to give.

I want to die while you love me,
And bear to that still bed
Your kisses, turbulent, unspent,
To warm me when I'm dead.

Your World / GEORGIA DOUGLAS JOHNSON

Your world is as big as you make it.
I know, for I used to abide
In the narrowest nest in a corner,
My wings pressing close to my side.

But I sighted the distant horizon
Where the sky line encircled the sea
And I throbbed with a burning desire
To travel this immensity.

I battered the cordons around me
And cradled my wings on the breeze
Then soared to the uttermost reaches
With rapture, with power, with ease!

Lovelight / GEORGIA DOUGLAS JOHNSON

Strange atoms we unto ourselves
Soaring a strange demesne
With life and death the darkened doors
And love the light between.

Prejudice / GEORGIA DOUGLAS JOHNSON

These fell miasmic rings of mist,
    with ghoulish menace bound,
Like noose-horizons tightening my
    little world around.
They still the soaring will to wing,
    to dance, to speed away.
And fling the soul insurgent back
    into its shell of clay.
Beneath incrusted silences, a seeth-
    ing Etna lies,
The fire of whose furnaces may
    sleep, but never dies!

Conquest / GEORGIA DOUGLAS JOHNSON

My pathway lies through worse than death;
I meet the hours with bated breath.
My red blood boils, my pulses thrill,
I live life running up a hill.

Ah, no, I need no paltry play
Of make-shift tilts for holiday:
For I was born against the tide
And I must conquer that denied.

I shun no hardship, fear no foe;
The future calls and I must go:
I charge the line and dare the spheres
As I go fighting down the years.

24

The Daily Grind / FENTON JOHNSON

If Nature says to you,
"I intend you for something fine,
For something to sing the song
That only my whirling stars can sing,
For something to burn in the firmament
With all the fervor of my golden sun,
For something to moisten the parched souls
As only my rivulets can moisten the parched,"

What can you do?

If the System says to you,
"I intend you to grind and grind
Grains of corn beneath millstones;
I intend you to shovel and sweat
Before a furnace of Babylon;
I intend you for grist and meat
To fatten my pompous gods
As they wallow in an alcoholic nectar,"

What can you do?

Naught can you do
But watch that eternal battle
Between Nature and the System.
You cannot blame God,
You cannot blame man;
For God did not make the System,
Neither did man fashion Nature.
You can only die each morning,
And live again in the dreams of the night.
If Nature forgets you,
If the System forgets you,
God has blest you.

The World Is a Mighty Ogre / Fenton Johnson

I could love her with a love so warm
You could not break it with a fairy charm;
I could love her with a love so bold
It would not die, e'en tho' the world grew cold.

I cannot cross the bridge, nor climb the tower,—
I cannot break the spell of magic power;
The rules of man forbid me raise my sword—
Have mercy on a humble bard, O Lord!

A Negro Peddler's Song / Fenton Johnson

(The pattern of this song was sung by a Negro peddler in a Chicago alley.)

Good Lady,
I have corn and beets,
Onions, too, and leeks,
And also sweet potat-y.

Good Lady,
Buy for May and John;
And when work is done
Give a bite to Sadie.

Good Lady,
I have corn and beets,
Onions, too, and leeks,
And also sweet potat-y.

The Old Repair Man / FENTON JOHNSON

God is the Old Repair Man.
When we are junk in Nature's storehouse he takes us apart.
What is good he lays aside; he might use it some day.
What has decayed he buries in six feet of sod to nurture
    the weeds.
Those we leave behind moisten the sod with their tears;
But their eyes are blind as to where he has placed
    the good.
Some day the Old Repair Man
Will take the good from its secret place
And with his gentle, strong hands will mold
A more enduring work—a work that will defy Nature—
And we will laugh at the old days, the troubled days,
When we were but a crude piece of craftsmanship,
When we were but an experiment in Nature's laboratory. . . .
It is good we have the Old Repair Man.

Counting / FENTON JOHNSON

Go count the stars!
Whirling worlds of light,
Endless balls of fire,
Lonely Evening Star,
Dancing Morning Star,
Silvery necklaces in a jewel box of mist
For the wedding of an angel to an earth-daughter.
Pray, is there one who can count the stars?

Go count the unborn souls!
Many are the cherubs at Michael's Gate,

Awaiting their chubby bodies and a mother's arms.
So in their day flitted Caesars, Napoleons,
Alexanders whilst cherub Miltons chanted,
"We are Michael's angels, sweet Michael's angels."
Pray, is there one who can count the unborn souls?

The Tropics in New York / Claude McKay

Bananas ripe and green, and gingerroot,
    Cocoa in pods and alligator pears,
And tangerines and mangoes and grapefruit,
    Fit for the highest prize at parish fairs,

Set in the window, bringing memories
    Of fruit trees laden by low-singing rills,
And dewy dawns, and mystical blue skies
    In benediction over nunlike hills.

My eyes grew dim, and I could no more gaze;
    A wave of longing through my body swept,
And, hungry for the old, familiar ways,
    I turned aside and bowed my head and wept.

Outcast / Claude McKay

For the dim regions whence my fathers came
My spirit, bondaged by the body, longs.

Words felt, but never heard, my lips would frame;
My soul would sing forgotten jungle songs.
I would go back to darkness and to peace,
But the great western world holds me in fee,
And I may never hope for full release
While to its alien gods I bend my knee.
Something in me is lost, forever lost,
Some vital thing has gone out of my heart,
And I must walk the way of life a ghost
Among the sons of earth, a thing apart.

For I was born, far from my native clime,
Under the white man's menace, out of time.

St. Isaac's Church, Petrograd / CLAUDE McKAY

Bow down my soul in worship very low
And in the holy silences be lost.
Bow down before the marble Man of Woe,
Bow down before the singing angel host.
What jewelled glory fills my spirit's eye,
What golden grandeur moves the depths of me!
The soaring arches lift me up on high,
Taking my breath with their rare symmetry.

Bow down my soul and let the wondrous light
Of beauty bathe thee from her lofty throne,
Bow down before the wonder of man's might.
Bow down in worship, humble and alone,
Bow lowly down before the sacred sight
Of man's Divinity alive in stone.

Flame-Heart / CLAUDE McKAY

So much have I forgotten in ten years,
  So much in ten brief years! I have forgot
What time the purple apples come to juice,
  And what month brings the shy forget-me-not.
I have forgot the special, startling season
  Of the pimento's flowering and fruiting;
What time of year the ground doves brown the fields
  And fill the noonday with their curious fluting.
I have forgotten much, but still remember
The poinsettia's red, blood-red in warm December.

I still recall the honey-fever grass,
  But cannot recollect the high days when
We rooted them out of the ping-wing path
  To stop the mad bees in the rabbit pen.
I often try to think in what sweet month
  The languid painted ladies used to dapple
The yellow byroad mazing from the main,
  Sweet with the golden threads of the rose apple.
I have forgotten—strange—but quite remember
The poinsettia's red, blood-red in warm December.

What weeks, what months, what time of the mild year
  We cheated school to have our fling at tops?
What days our wine-thrilled bodies pulsed with joy
  Feasting upon blackberries in the copse?
Oh, some I know! I have embalmed the days,
  Even the sacred moments when we played,
All innocent of passion, uncorrupt,
  At noon and evening in the flame-heart's shade.
We were so happy, happy, I remember,
Beneath the poinsettia's red in warm December.

If We Must Die / Claude McKay

If we must die—let it not be like hogs
Hunted and penned in an inglorious spot,
While round us bark the mad and hungry dogs,
Making their mock at our accursed lot.
If we must die—oh, let us nobly die,
So that our precious blood may not be shed
In vain; then even the monsters we defy
Shall be constrained to honor us though dead!
Oh, Kinsmen! We must meet the common foe;
Though far outnumbered, let us show us brave,
And for their thousand blows deal one deathblow!
What though before us lies the open grave?
Like men we'll face the murderous, cowardly pack,
Pressed to the wall, dying, but fighting back!

The White House / Claude McKay

Your door is shut against my tightened face,
And I am sharp as steel with discontent;
But I possess the courage and the grace
To bear my anger proudly and unbent.
The pavement slabs burn loose beneath my feet,
A chafing savage, down the decent street;
And passion rends my vitals as I pass,
Where boldly shines your shuttered door of glass.
Oh, I must search for wisdom every hour,
Deep in my wrathful bosom sore and raw,
And find in it the superhuman power
To hold me to the letter of your law!

31

Oh, I must keep my heart inviolate
Against the potent poison of your hate.

Georgia Dusk / JEAN TOOMER

The sky, lazily disdaining to pursue
    The setting sun, too indolent to hold
    A lengthened tournament for flashing gold,
Passively darkens for night's barbecue,

A feast of moon and men and barking hounds,
    An orgy for some genius of the South
    With blood-hot eyes and cane-lipped scented mouth,
Surprised in making folk songs from soul-sounds.

The sawmill blows its whistle, buzz saws stop,
    And silence breaks the bud of knoll and hill,
    Soft settling pollen where plowed lands fulfill
Their early promise of a bumper crop.

Smoke from the pyramidal sawdust pile
    Curls up, blue ghosts of trees, tarrying low
    Where only chips and stumps are left to show
The solid proof of former domicile.

Meanwhile, the men, with vestiges of pomp,
    Race memories of king and caravan,
    High priests, an ostrich, and a juju-man,
Go singing through the footpaths of the swamp.

Their voices rise . . . the pine trees are guitars,
    Strumming, pine needles fall like sheets of rain . . .
    Their voices rise . . . the chorus of the cane
Is caroling a vesper to the stars . . .

O singers, resinous and soft your songs
  Above the sacred whisper of the pines,
  Give virgin lips to cornfield concubines,
Bring dreams of Christ to dusky cane-lipped throngs.

Song of the Son / JEAN TOOMER

Pour O pour that parting soul in song,
O pour it in the sawdust glow of night,
Into the velvet pine-smoke air tonight,
And let the valley carry it along.
And let the valley carry it along.

O land and soil, red soil and sweet-gum tree,
So scant of grass, so profligate of pines,
Now just before an epoch's sun declines
Thy son, in time, I have returned to thee,
Thy son, I have, in time, returned to thee.

In time, for though the sun is setting on
A song-lit race of slaves, it has not set;
Though late, O soil, it is not too late yet
To catch thy plaintive soul, leaving, soon gone,
Leaving, to catch thy plaintive soul soon gone.

O Negro slaves, dark purple ripened plums,
Squeezed, and bursting in the pine-wood air,
Passing, before they strip the old tree bare
One plum was saved for me, one seed becomes

An everlasting song, a singing tree,
Caroling softly souls of slavery,
What they were, and what they are to me,
Caroling softly souls of slavery.

Brown River, Smile / JEAN TOOMER

It is a new America,
To be spiritualized by each new American.

Lift, lift, thou waking forces!
Let us feel the energy of animals,
The energy of rumps and bull-bent heads
Crashing the barrier to man.
It must spiral on!
A million million men, or twelve men,
Must crash the barrier to the next higher form.

> Beyond plants are animals,
> Beyond animals is man,
> Beyond man is the universe.

> The Big Light,
> Let the Big Light in!

O thou, Radiant Incorporeal,
The I of earth and of mankind, hurl
Down these seaboards, across this continent,
The thousand-rayed discus of thy mind,
And above our walking limbs unfurl
Spirit-torsos of exquisite strength!

The Mississippi, sister of the Ganges,
Main artery of earth in the western world,
Is waiting to become
In the spirit of America, a sacred river.
Whoever lifts the Mississippi
Lifts himself and all America;
Whoever lifts himself
Makes that great brown river smile.
The blood of earth and the blood of man
Course swifter and rejoice when we spiritualize.

The old gods, led by an inverted Christ,
A shaved Moses, a blanched Lemur,

And a moulting thunderbird,
Withdrew into the distance and soon died,
Their dust and seed falling down
To fertilize the five regions of America.

We are waiting for a new God.

The old peoples—
The great European races sent wave after wave
That washed the forests, the earth's rich loam,
Grew towns with the seeds of giant cities,
Made roads, laid golden rails,
Sang once of its swift achievement,
And died congested in machinery.
They say that near the end
It was a world of crying men and hard women,
A city of goddam and Jehovah
Baptized in industry
Without benefit of saints,
Of dear defectives
Winnowing their likenesses from weathered rock
Sold by national organizations of undertakers.

Someone said:
    Suffering is impossible
    On cement sidewalks, in skyscrapers,
    In motorcars;
    Steel cannot suffer—
    We die unconsciously
    Because possessed by a nonhuman symbol.

Another cried:
    It is because of thee, O Life,
    That the first prayer ends in the last curse.

Another sang:
    Late minstrels of the restless earth,
    No muteness can be granted thee,
    Lift thy laughing energies
    To that white point which is a star.

The great African races sent a single wave
And singing riplets to sorrow in red fields,
Sing a swan song, to break rocks
And immortalize a hiding water boy.

I'm leaving the shining ground, brothers,
I sing because I ache,
I go because I must,
Brothers, I am leaving the shining ground;
Don't ask me where,
I'll meet you there,
I'm leaving the shining ground.

The great red race was here.
In a land of flaming earth and torrent-rains,
Of red sea-plains and majestic mesas,
At sunset from a purple hill
The Gods came down;
They serpentined into pueblo,
And a white-robed priest
Danced with them five days and nights;
But pueblo, priest, and Shalicos
Sank into the sacred earth
To fertilize the five regions of America.

Hi-ye, hi-yo, hi-yo
Hi-ye, hi-yo, hi-yo,
A lone eagle feather,
An untamed Navaho,
The ghosts of buffaloes,
Hi-ye, hi-yo, hi-yo,
Hi-ye, hi-yo, hi-yo.

We are waiting for a new people.

O thou, Radiant Incorporeal,
The I of earth and of mankind, hurl
Down these seaboards, across this continent,
The thousand-rayed discus of thy mind,
And above our walking limbs unfurl
Spirit-torsos of exquisite strength!

The east coast is masculine,
The west coast is feminine,
The middle region is the child—
Forces of reconciling
And generator of symbols.
    Thou, great fields, waving thy growths across
        the world,
    Couldest thou find the seed which started thee?
    Can you remember the first great hand to sow?
    Have you memory of His intention?
    Great plains, and thou, mountains,
    And thou, stately trees, and thou,
    America, sleeping and producing with the seasons,
    No clever dealer can divide,
    No machine can undermine thee.

The prairie's sweep is flat infinity,
The city's rise is perpendicular to farthest star,
I stand where the two directions intersect,
At Michigan Avenue and Walton Place,
Parallel to my countrymen,
Right-angled to the universe.

It is a new America,
To be spiritualized by each new American.

Dark Symphony / MELVIN B. TOLSON

I ALLEGRO MODERATO

Black Crispus Attucks taught
    Us how to die
Before white Patrick Henry's bugle breath

Uttered the vertical
        Transmitting cry:
"Yea, give me liberty, or give me death."

And from that day to this
        Men black and strong
For Justice and Democracy have stood,
Steeled in the faith that Right
        Will conquer Wrong
And Time will usher in one brotherhood.

No Banquo's ghost can rise
        Against us now
And say we crushed men with a tyrant's boot
Or pressed the crown of thorns
        On Labor's brow,
Or ravaged lands and carted off the loot.

II   LENTO GRAVE

The centuries-old pathos in our voices
Saddens the great white world,
And the wizardry of our dusky rhythms
Conjures up shadow-shapes of ante-bellum years:

Black slaves singing *One More River to Cross*
In the torture tombs of slave ships,
Black slaves singing *Steal Away to Jesus*
In jungle swamps,
Black slaves singing *The Crucifixion*
In slave pens at midnight,
Black slaves singing *Swing Low, Sweet Chariot*
In cabins of death,
Black slaves singing *Go Down, Moses*
In the canebrakes of the Southern Pharaohs.

III   ANDANTE SOSTENUTO

They tell us to forget
The Golgotha we tread . . .
We who are scourged with hate,

A price upon our head.
They who have shackled us
Require of us a song,
They who have wasted us
Bid us o'erlook the wrong.

They tell us to forget
Democracy is spurned.
They tell us to forget
The Bill of Rights is burned.
Three hundred years we slaved,
We slave and suffer yet:
Though flesh and bone rebel,
They tell us to forget!

Oh, how can we forget
Our human rights denied?
Oh, how can we forget
Our manhood crucified?
When Justice is profaned
And plea with curse is met,
When Freedom's gates are barred,
Oh, how can we forget?

IV   TEMPO PRIMO

The New Negro strides upon the continent
In seven league boots . . .
The New Negro
Who sprang from the vigor-stout loins
Of Nat Turner, gallows-martyr for Freedom,
Of Joseph Cinquez, Black Moses of the Amistad Mutiny,
Of Frederick Douglass, oracle of the Catholic Man,
Of Sojourner Truth, eye and ear of Lincoln's legions,
Of Harriet Tubman, St. Bernard of the Underground
      Railroad.

None in the Land can say
To us black men Today:
You send the tractors on their bloody path,
And create Oakies for *The Grapes of Wrath.*
You breed the slum that breeds a *Native Son*
To damn the good earth Pilgrim Fathers won.

None in the Land can say
To us black men Today:
You dupe the poor with rags-to-riches tales,
And leave the workers empty dinner pails.
You stuff the ballot box, and honest men
Are muzzled by your demogogic din.

None in the Land can say
To us black men Today:
You smash stock markets with your coined blitzkriegs
And make a hundred million guinea pigs.
You counterfeit our Christianity,
And bring contempt upon Democracy.

None in the Land can say
To us black men Today:
You prowl when citizens are fast asleep,
And hatch Fifth Column plots to blast the deep
Foundations of the State and leave the Land
A vast Sahara with a Fascist brand.

None in the Land can say
To us black men Today:
You send flame-gutting tanks, like swarms of flies,
And plump a hell from dynamiting skies.
You fill machine-gunned towns with rotting dead—
A No Man's Land where children cry for bread.

VI   TEMPO DI MARCIA

Out of abysses of Illiteracy,
Through labyrinths of Lies,

Across wastelands of Disease . . .
We advance!

Out of dead-ends of Poverty,
Through wildernesses of Superstition,
Across barricades of Jim Crowism . . .
We advance!

With the Peoples of the World . . .
We advance!

Kid Stuff / FRANK HORNE

DECEMBER, 1942

The wise guys
tell me
that Christmas
is Kid Stuff . . .
Maybe they've got
something there—
Two thousand years ago
three wise guys
chased a star
across a continent
to bring
frankincense and myrrh
to a Kid
born in a manger
with an idea in his head . . .

And as the bombs
crash
all over the world
today

41

the real wise guys
know
that we've all
got to go chasing stars
again
in the hope
that we can get back
some of that
Kid Stuff
born two thousand years ago.

Notes Found Near a Suicide / FRANK HORNE

TO ALL OF YOU

My little stone
Sinks quickly
Into the bosom of this deep, dark pool
Of oblivion . . .
I have troubled its breast but little
Yet those far shores
That knew me not
Will feel the fleeting, furtive kiss
Of my tiny concentric ripples . . .

TO MOTHER

I came
In the blinding sweep
Of ecstatic pain,
I go
In the throbbing pulse
Of aching space—

In the eons between
I piled upon you
Pain on pain
Ache on ache
And yet as I go
I shall know
That you will grieve
And want me back . . .

TO CATALINA

Love thy piano, Oh girl,
It will give you back
Note for note
The harmonies of your soul.
It will sing back to you
The high songs of your heart.
It will give
As well as take . . .

TO TELIE

You have made my voice
A rippling laugh
But my heart
A crying thing . . .
'Tis better thus:
A fleeting kiss
And then,
The dark . . .

TO "CHICK"

Oh Achilles of the moleskins
And the gridiron
Do not wonder
Nor doubt that this is I
That lies so calmly here—
This is the same exultant beast
That so joyously

Ran the ball with you
In those far-flung days of abandon.
You remember how recklessly
We revelled in the heat and the dust
And the swirl of conflict?
You remember they called us
The Terrible Two?
And you remember
After we had battered our heads
And our bodies
Against the stonewall of their defense,—
You remember the signal I would call
And how you would look at me
In faith and admiration
And say "Let's go," . . .
How the lines would clash
And strain,
And how I would slip through
Fighting and squirming
Over the line
To victory.
You remember, Chick? . . .
When you gaze at me here
Let that same light
Of faith and admiration
Shine in your eyes
For I have battered the stark stonewall
Before me . . .
I have kept faith with you
And now
I have called my signal,
Found my opening
And slipped through
Fighting and squirming
Over the line
To victory. . . .

TO WANDA

To you, so far away
So cold and aloof,
To you, who knew me so well,
This is my last Grand Gesture
This is my last Great Effect
And as I go winging
Through the black doors of eternity
Is that thin sound I hear
Your applause? . . .

TO JAMES

Do you remember
How you won
That last race . . . ?
How you flung your body
At the start . . .
How your spikes
Ripped the cinders
In the stretch . . .
How you catapulted
Through the tape . . .
Do you remember . . . ?
Don't you think
I lurched with you
Out of those starting holes . . . ?
Don't you think
My sinews tightened
At those first
Few strides . . .
And when you flew into the stretch
Was not all my thrill
Of a thousand races
In your blood . . . ?
At your final drive
Through the finish line
Did not my shout

Tell of the
Triumphant ecstasy
Of victory . . . ?
Live
As I have taught you
To run, Boy—
It's a short dash
Dig your starting holes
Deep and firm
Lurch out of them
Into the straightaway
With all the power
That is in you
Look straight ahead
To the finish line
Think only of the goal
Run straight
Run high
Run hard
Save nothing
And finish
With an ecstatic burst
That carries you
Hurtling
Through the tape
To victory . . .

TO THE POETS:

Why do poets
Like to die
And sing raptures to the grave?

They seem to think
That bitter dirt
Turns sweet between the teeth.

I have lived
And yelled hosannas
At the climbing stars

I have lived
And drunk deep
The deceptive wine of life . . .

And now, tipsy and reeling
From its dregs
I die . . .

Oh, let the poets sing
Raptures to the grave.

TO HENRY:

I do not know
How I shall look
When I lie down here
But I really should be smiling
Mischievously . . .
You and I have studied
Together
The knowledge of the ages
And lived the life of Science
Matching discovery for discovery—
And yet
In a trice
With a small explosion
Of this little machine
In my hand
I shall know
All
That Aristotle, Newton, Lavoisier, and Galileo
Could not determine
In their entire
Lifetimes . . .
And the joke of it is,
Henry,
That I have
Beat you to it . . .

TO ONE WHO CALLED ME "NIGGER":

You are Power
And send steel ships hurtling
From shore to shore . . .

You are Vision
And cast your sight through eons of space
From world to world . . .

You are Brain
And throw your voice endlessly
From ear to ear . . .

You are Soul
And falter at the yawning chasm
From White to Black . . .

TO CAROLINE:

Your piano
Is the better instrument . . .
Yesterday
Your fingers
So precisely
Touched the cold keys—
A nice string
Of orderly sounds
A proper melody . . .
Tonight
Your hands
So wantonly
Caressed my tingling skin—
A mad whirl
Of cacophony,
A wild chanting . . .
Your piano
Is the better instrument.

TO ALFRED:

I have grown tired of you
And your wife
Sitting there
With your children,
Little bits of you
Running about your feet
And you two so calm
And cold together . . .
It is really better
To lie here
Insensate
Than to see new life
Creep upon you
Calm and cold
Sitting there . . .

TO YOU:

All my life
They have told me
That You
Would save my Soul
That only
By kneeling in Your House
And eating of Your Body
And drinking of Your Blood
Could I be born again . . .
And yet
One night
In the tall black shadow
Of a windy pine
I offered up
The Sacrifice of Body
Upon the altar
Of her breast . . .
You
Who were conceived

Without ecstasy
Or pain
Can you understand
That I knelt last night
In Your House
And ate of Your Body
And drank of Your Blood.
. . . and thought only of her?

To a Persistent Phantom / FRANK HORNE

I buried you deeper last night
You with your tears
And your tangled hair
You with your lips
That kissed so fair
I buried you deeper last night.

I buried you deeper last night
With fuller breasts
And stronger arms
With softer lips
And newer charms
I buried you deeper last night.

Deeper . . . ay, deeper
And again tonight
Till that gay spirit
That once was you
Will tear its soul
In climbing through . . .
Deeper . . . ay, deeper
I buried you deeper last night.

Symphony / FRANK HORNE

Is this dancing sunlight
prancing through the windows
of this limping room
mocking us
who strain
and stagger
with legs strapped in leather
and braced
with cold steel
or tottering
on crutch
or cane . . . ?

Is this carnival of light
mocking
the ponderous rhythms
and stumbling pace
and the tears
and gasps of supplication
to make quick
the sickened limb . . . ?

Does it taunt
or does it beckon
with warm affection
and hope . . . ?

Are prancing light
and faltering crutch
variations of the dance
of suns
and moons
and pain
and glory
point and counterpoint
to the baton

of the maestro
to whom
all rhythms
and periods
are the stuff
of the symphony
of life?

McDonogh Day in New Orleans / MARCUS B. CHRISTIAN

The cotton blouse you wear, your mother said,
After a day of toil, "I guess I'll buy it";
For ribbons on your head and blouse she paid
Two-bits a yard—as if you would deny it!

And nights, after a day of kitchen toil,
She stitched your re-made skirt of serge—once blue—
Weary of eye, beneath a lamp of oil:
McDonogh would be proud of her and you.

Next, came white "creepers" and white stockings, too—
They almost asked her blood when they were sold;
Like some dark princess, to the school go you,
With blue larkspur and yellow marigold;
But few would know—or even guess this fact:
How dear comes beauty when a skin is black.

Dialect Quatrain / MARCUS B. CHRISTIAN

This ain't Torquemada—
'Tain't no "Scourge o'God"—
Hit's jess li'l ole New Awleens's
"Makeum-Tell-It Squad."

Sister Lou / STERLING A. BROWN

Honey
When de man
Calls out de las' train
You're gonna ride,
Tell him howdy.

Gather up yo' basket
An' yo' knittin' an' yo' things,
An' go on up an' visit
Wid frien' Jesus fo' a spell.

Show Marfa
How to make yo' greengrape jellies,
An' give po' Lazarus
A passel of them Golden Biscuits.

Scald some meal
Fo' some rightdown good spoonbread
Fo' li'l box-plunkin' David.

An' sit aroun'
An' tell them Hebrew Chillen
All yo' stories. . . .

Honey
Don't be feared of them pearly gates,
Don't go 'round to de back,
No mo' dataway
Not evah no mo'.

Let Michael tote yo' burden
An' yo' pocketbook an' evah thing
'Cept yo' Bible,
While Gabriel blows somp'n
Solemn but loudsome
On dat horn of his'n.

Honey
Go Straight on to de Big House,
An' speak to yo' God
Widout no fear an' tremblin'.

Then sit down
An' pass de time of day awhile.

Give a good talkin' to
To yo' favorite 'postle Peter,
An' rub the po' head
Of mixed-up Judas,
An' joke awhile wid Jonah.

Then, when you gits de chance,
Always rememberin' yo' raisin',
Let 'em know youse tired
Jest a mite tired.

Jesus will find yo' bed fo' you
Won't no servant evah bother wid yo' room.
Jesus will lead you
To a room wid windows
Openin' on cherry trees an' plum trees
Bloomin' everlastin'.

An' dat will be yours
Fo' keeps.

Den take yo' time. . . .
Honey, take yo' bressed time.

When de Saints Go Ma'chin' Home
STERLING A. BROWN

I

He'd play, after the bawdy songs and blues,
After the weary plaints
Of "Trouble, Trouble deep down in muh soul,"
Always one song in which he'd lose the role
Of entertainer to the boys. He'd say
"My mother's favorite." And we knew
That what was coming was his chant of saints
"When de Saints go ma'chin' home . . ."
And that would end his concert for the day.

Carefully as an old maid over needlework,
Or, as some black deacon, over his Bible, lovingly,
He'd tune up specially for this. There'd be
No chatter now, no patting of the feet.
After a few slow chords, knelling and sweet
Oh, when de saints go ma'chin' home
Oh, when de sayaints goa ma'chin' home . . .
He would forget
The quieted bunch, his dimming cigarette
Stuck into a splintered edge of the guitar.
Sorrow deep hidden in his voice, a far
And soft light in his strange brown eyes;
Alone with his masterchords, his memories . . .
> *Lawd, I wanna be one in nummer*
> *When de saints go ma'chin' home.*

Deep the bass would rumble while the treble scattered
    high
For all the world like heavy feet a trompin' toward the sky.
With shrill-voiced women getting 'happy'
All to celestial tunes.
The chap's few speeches helped me understand
The reason why he gazed so fixedly
Upon the burnished strings.
For he would see
A gorgeous procession to 'de Beulah Land'
Of Saints—his friends—'a climbin' fo' deir wings.'
Oh, when de saints go ma'chin' home
Lawd, I wanna be one o' dat nummer
When de saints goa ma'chin' home . . .

      II

    There'd be—so ran his dream—
    "Old Deacon Zachary
    With de asthmy in his chest
    A puffin' an' a wheezin'
    Up de golden stair
    Wid de badges of his lodges
    Strung acrost his heavin' breast
    An' de hoggrease jest shinin'
    In his coal-black hair . . .

    An' old Sis Joe
    In huh big straw hat
    An' huh wrapper flappin'
    Flappin' in de heavenly win'
    An' huh thin-soled easy walkers
    Goin' pitty pitty pat
    Lawd, she'd have to ease her corns
    When she got in!"
  Oh, when de saints go ma'chin' home.
    "Ole Elder Peter Johnson
    Wid his corncob jes a puffin'
    And de smoke a rollin'

Like storm clouds out behin'
Crossin' de cloud mountains
Widout slowin' up fo' nuffin'
Steamin' up de grade
Lak Wes' bound No. 9.
An' de little brown-skinned chillen
Wid deir skinny legs a dancin'
Jes' a kickin' up ridic'lous
To de heavenly band
Lookin' at de Great Drum Major
On a white hoss jes' a prancin'
Wid a gold and silver drumstick
A waggin' in his han'.
Oh when de sun refuse to shine
Oh when de mo-on goes down
In Blood . . .

"Old Maumee Annie
Wid huh washin' done
An' huh las' piece o' laundry
In de renchin' tub,
A wavin' sof' pink han's
To de much obligin' sun
An' her feet a moverin' now
To a swif' rub-a-dub;
And old Grampa Eli
Wid his wrinkled old haid
A puzzlin' over summut
He ain' understood
Intendin' to ask Peter
Pervidin' he hain't skyaid
Jes' what mought be de meanin'
Of de moon in blood? . . .
When de saints go ma'chin' home . . ."

III

Whuffolks, he dreams, will have to stay outside
Being so onery. But what is he to do

With that red brakeman who once let him ride
An empty, going home? Or with that kindfaced man
Who paid his songs with board and drink and bed?
Or with the Yankee Cap'n who left a leg
At Vicksburg? *Mought be a place, he said*
Mought be another mansion for white saints
A smaller one than hisn . . . not so gran'
As for the rest . . . oh, let them howl and beg.
Hell would be good enough, if big enough
Widout no shade trees, lawd, widout no rain
Whuffolks sho to bring nigger out behin'
Excep'—when de saints go ma'chin' home.

    IV

Sportin' Legs would not be there—nor lucky Sam
Nor Smitty, nor Hambone, nor Hardrock Gene
An' not too many guzzlin', cuttin' shines,
Nor bootleggers to keep his pockets clean.
An' Sophie wid de sof' smile on her face,
Her foolin' voice, her strappin' body, brown
Lak coffee doused wid milk—she had been good
To him, wid lovin', money, and wid food.—
But saints and heaven didn't seem to fit
Jes rite wid Sophy's beauty—nary bit—
She mought stir trouble, somehow, in dat peaceful place
Mought be some dressed up dudes in dat fair town.

    V

Ise got a dear ole modder
She is in hebben I know . . .
He sees
    Mammy
    L'il mammy—wrinkled face
    Her brown eyes, quick to tears—to joy
    With such happy pride in her
    Guitar plunkin' boy.
    Oh, kain't I be one in nummer?

Mammy
With deep religion defeating the grief
Life piled so closely about her
Ise so glad trouble doan las' alway' . . .
And her dogged belief
That some fine day
She'd go a ma'chin'
When de saints go ma'chin' home.
He sees her ma'chin' home, ma'chin' along,
Her perky joy shining in her furrowed face,
Her weak and quavering voice singing her song—
The best chair set apart for her worn-out body
In that restful place . . .
I pray to de Lawd I'll meet her
When de saints go ma'chin' home.

VI

He'd shuffle off from us, always, at that,—
His face a brown study beneath his torn brimmed hat.
His broad shoulders slouching, his old box strung
Around his neck;—he'd go where we
Never could follow him—to Sophie probably,
Or to his dances in old Tinbridge flat.

Solace / CLARISSA SCOTT DELANY

My window opens out into the trees
And in that small space
Of branches and of sky
I see the seasons pass
Behold the tender green
Give way to darker heavier leaves.

59

The glory of the autumn comes
When steeped in mellow sunlight
The fragile, golden leaves
Against a clear blue sky
Linger in the magic of the afternoon
And then reluctantly break off
And filter down to pave
A street with gold.
Then bare, gray branches
Lift themselves against the
Cold December sky
Sometimes weaving a web
Across the rose and dusk of late sunset
Sometimes against a frail new moon
And one bright star riding
A sky of that dark, living blue
Which comes before the heaviness
Of night descends, or the stars
Have powdered the heavens.
Winds beat against these trees;
The cold, but gentle rain of spring
Touches them lightly
The summer torrents strive
To lash them into a fury
And seek to break them—
But they stand.
My life is fevered
And a restlessness at times
An agony—again a vague
And baffling discontent
Possesses me.
I am thankful for my bit of sky
And trees, and for the shifting
Pageant of the seasons.
Such beauty lays upon the heart
A quiet.
Such eternal change and permanence
Take meaning from all turmoil

And leave serenity
Which knows no pain.

Brass Spittoons / LANGSTON HUGHES

Clean the spittoons, boy.
    Detroit,
    Chicago,
    Atlantic City,
    Palm Beach.
Clean the spittoons.
The steam in hotel kitchens,
And the smoke in hotel lobbies,
And the slime in hotel spittoons:
Part of my life.
    Hey, boy!
    A nickel,
    A dime,
    A dollar,
Two dollars a day.
    Hey, boy!
    A nickel,
    A dime,
    A dollar,
    Two dollars
Buy shoes for the baby.
House rent to pay.
Gin on Saturday,
Church on Sunday.
    My God!
Babies and gin and church
And women and Sunday

All mixed with dimes and
Dollars and clean spittoons
And house rent to pay.
    Hey, boy!
A bright bowl of brass is beautiful to the Lord.
Bright polished brass like the cymbals
Of King David's dancers,
Like the wine cups of Solomon.
    Hey, boy!
A clean spittoon on the altar of the Lord.
A clean bright spittoon all newly polished—
At least I can offer that.
    Com'mere, boy!

Cross / Langston Hughes

My old man's a white old man
And my old mother's black.
If ever I cursed my white old man
I take my curses back.

If ever I cursed my black old mother
And wished she were in hell,
I'm sorry for that evil wish
And now I wish her well.

My old man died in a fine big house.
My ma died in a shack.
I wonder where I'm gonna die,
Being neither white nor black?

Jazzonia / Langston Hughes

Oh, silver tree!
Oh, shining rivers of the soul.

In a Harlem cabaret
Six long-headed jazzers play.
A dancing girl whose eyes are bold
Lifts high a dress of silken gold.

Oh, singing tree!
Oh, shining rivers of the soul!

Were Eve's eyes
In the first garden
Just a bit too bold?
Was Cleopatra gorgeous
In a gown of gold?

Oh, shining tree!
Oh, silver rivers of the soul!

In a whirling cabaret
Six long-headed jazzers play.

The Negro Speaks of Rivers / Langston Hughes

I've known rivers:
I've known rivers ancient as the world and older than the
    flow of human blood in human veins.

My soul has grown deep like the rivers.

I bathed in the Euphrates when dawns were young.
I built my hut near the Congo and it lulled me to sleep.

I looked upon the Nile and raised the pyramids above it.
I heard the singing of the Mississippi when Abe Lincoln
           went down to New Orleans, and I've seen its muddy
           bosom turn all golden in the sunset.

I've known rivers:
Ancient, dusky rivers.

My soul has grown deep like the rivers.

I, Too / LANGSTON HUGHES

I, too, sing America.

I am the darker brother.
They send me to eat in the kitchen
When company comes,
But I laugh,
And eat well,
And grow strong.

Tomorrow,
I'll be at the table
When company comes.
Nobody'll dare
Say to me,
"Eat in the kitchen,"
Then.

Besides,
They'll see how beautiful I am
And be ashamed—

I, too, am America.

Bound No'th Blues / Langston Hughes

Goin' down the road, Lawd,
Goin' down the road.
Down the road, Lawd,
Way, way down the road.
Got to find somebody
To help me carry this load.

Road's in front o' me,
Nothin' to do but walk.
Road's in front o' me,
Walk . . . an' walk . . . an' walk.
I'd like to meet a good friend
To come along an' talk.

Hates to be lonely,
Lawd, I hates to be sad.
Says I hates to be lonely,
Hates to be lonely an' sad,
But ever' friend you finds seems
Like they try to do you bad.

Road, road, road, O!
Road, road . . . road . . . road, road!
Road, road, road, O!
On the no'thern road.
These Mississippi towns ain't
Fit fer a hoppin' toad.

Personal / LANGSTON HUGHES

In an envelope marked:
       PERSONAL
God addressed me a letter.
In an envelope marked:
       PERSONAL
I have given my answer.

Dream Variation / LANGSTON HUGHES

To fling my arms wide
In some place of the sun,
To whirl and to dance
Till the white day is done.
Then rest at cool evening
Beneath a tall tree
While night comes on gently,
       Dark like me—
That is my dream!

To fling my arms wide
In the face of the sun,
Dance! Whirl! Whirl!
Till the quick day is done.
Rest at pale evening . . .
A tall, slim tree . . .
Night coming tenderly
       Black like me.

Mother to Son / LANGSTON HUGHES

Well, son, I'll tell you:
Life for me ain't been no crystal stair.
It's had tacks in it,
And splinters,
And boards torn up,
And places with no carpet on the floor—
Bare.
But all the time
I'se been a-climbin' on,
And reachin' landin's,
And turnin' corners,
And sometimes goin' in the dark
Where there ain't been no light.
So boy, don't you turn back.
Don't you set down on the steps
'Cause you finds it's kinder hard.
Don't you fall now—
For I'se still goin', honey,
I'se still climbin',
And life for me ain't been no crystal stair.

Lenox Avenue Mural / LANGSTON HUGHES

HARLEM

What happens to a dream deferred?
　　Does it dry up
　　like a raisin in the sun?
　　Or fester like a sore—
　　And then run?

Does it stink like rotten meat?
Or crust and sugar over—
like a syrupy sweet?

Maybe it just sags
like a heavy load.

Or does it explode?

GOOD MORNING

Good morning, daddy!
I was born here, he said,
watched Harlem grow
until colored folks spread
from river to river
across the middle of Manhattan
out of Penn Station
dark tenth of a nation,
planes from Puerto Rico,
and holds of boats, chico,
up from Cuba Haiti Jamaica,
in busses marked New York
from Georgia Florida Louisiana
to Harlem Brooklyn the Bronx
but most of all to Harlem
dusky sash across Manhattan
I've seen them come dark
    wondering
    wide-eyed
    dreaming
out of Penn Station—
but the trains are late.
The gates open—
but there're bars
at each gate.
    What happens
    to a dream deferred?
Daddy, ain't you heard?

I said to my baby,
Baby, take it slow.
I can't, she said, I can't!
I got to go!
  There's a certain
  amount of traveling
  in a dream deferred.
Lulu said to Leonard,
I want a diamond ring.
Leonard said to Lulu,
You won't get a goddamn thing!
  A certain
  amount of nothing
  in a dream deferred.
Daddy, daddy, daddy,
All I want is you.
You can have me, baby—
but my lovin' days is through.
  A certain
  amount of impotence
  in a dream deferred.
Three parties
On my party line—
But that third party,
Lord, ain't mine!
  There's liable
  to be confusion
  in a dream deferred.
From river to river
Uptown and down,
There's liable to be confusion
when a dream gets kicked around.
  You talk like
  they don't kick
  dreams around
  Downtown.

I expect they do—
But I'm talking about
Harlem to you!

LETTER

Dear Mama,
      Time I pay rent and get my food
and laundry I don't have much left
but here is five dollars for you
to show you I still appreciates you.
My girl-friend send her love and say
she hopes to lay eyes on you sometime in life.
Mama, it has been raining cats and dogs up
here. Well, that is all so I will close.
            Your son baby
                  Respectable as ever,
                        Joe

ISLAND

    Between two rivers,
    North of the park,
    Like darker rivers
    The streets are dark.

    Black and white,
    Gold and brown—
    Chocolate-custard
    Pie of a town.

    Dream within a dream
    Our dream deferred.

    Good morning, daddy!

    Ain't you heard?

Pennsylvania Station / Langston Hughes

The Pennsylvania Station in New York
Is like some vast basilica of old
That towers above the terrors of the dark
As bulwark and protection to the soul.
Now people who are hurrying alone
And those who come in crowds from far away
Pass through this great concourse of steel and stone
To trains, or else from trains out into day.
And as in great basilicas of old
The search was ever for a dream of God,
So here the search is still within each soul
Some seed to find that sprouts a holy tree
To glorify the earth—and you—and me.

I Dream a World / Langston Hughes

I dream a world where man
No other will scorn,
Where love will bless the earth
And peace its paths adorn.
I dream a world where all
Will know sweet freedom's way,
Where greed no longer saps the soul
Nor avarice blights our day.
A world I dream where black or white,
Whatever race you be,
Will share the bounties of the earth
And every man is free,
Where wretchedness will hang its head,

And joy, like a pearl,
Attend the needs of all mankind.
Of such I dream—
Our world!

Without Benefit of Declaration / LANGSTON HUGHES

Listen here, Joe
Don't you know
That tomorrow
You got to go
Out yonder where
The steel winds blow?

Listen here, kid,
It's been said
Tomorrow you'll be dead
Out there where
The snow is lead.

Don't ask me why.
Just go ahead and die.
Hidden from the sky
Out yonder you'll lie:
A medal to your family—
In exchange for
A guy.

Mama, don't cry.

Hatred / Gwendolyn B. Bennett

I shall hate you
Like a dart of singing steel
Shot through still air
At eventide.
Or solemnly
As pines are sober
When they stand etched
Against the sky.
Hating you shall be a game
Played with cool hands
And slim fingers.
Your heart will yearn
For the lonely splendor
Of the pine tree;
While rekindled fires
In my eyes
Shall wound you like swift arrows.
Memory will lay its hands
Upon your breast
And you will understand
My hatred.

Heritage / Gwendolyn B. Bennett

I want to see the slim palm trees,
Pulling at the clouds
With little pointed fingers. . . .

I want to see lithe Negro girls,
Etched dark against the sky
While sunset lingers.

I want to hear the silent sands,
Singing to the moon
Before the Sphinx-still face. . . .

I want to hear the chanting
Around a heathen fire
Of a strange black race.

I want to breathe the Lotus flow'r,
Sighing to the stars
With tendrils drinking at the Nile. . . .

I want to feel the surging
Of my sad people's soul
Hidden by a minstrel-smile.

Sonnet I / GWENDOLYN B. BENNETT

He came in silvern armor, trimmed with black—
A lover come from legends long ago—
With silver spurs and silken plumes a-blow,
And flashing sword aught fast and buckled back
In a carven sheat of Tamarack.
He came with footsteps beautifully slow,
And spoke in voice meticulously low.
He came and Romance followed in his track. . . .

I did not ask his name—I thought him Love;
I did not care to see his hidden face.
All life seemed born in my intaken breath;

All thought seemed flown like some forgotten dove.
He bent to kiss and raised his visor's lace . . .
All eager-lipped I kissed the mouth of Death.

Sonnet II / GWENDOLYN B. BENNETT

Some things are very dear to me—
Such things as flowers bathed by rain
Or patterns traced upon the sea
Or crocuses where snow has lain . . .
The iridescence of a gem,
The moon's cool opalescent light,
Azaleas and the scent of them,
And honeysuckles in the night.
And many sounds are also dear—
Like winds that sing among the trees
Or crickets calling from the weir
Or Negroes humming melodies.
But dearer far than all surmise
Are sudden tear-drops in your eyes.

A Black Man Talks of Reaping / ARNA BONTEMPS

I have sown beside all waters in my day.
I planted deep, within my heart the fear

75

That wind or fowl would take the grain away.
I planted safe against this stark, lean year.

I scattered seed enough to plant the land
In rows from Canada to Mexico,
But for my reaping only what the hand
Can hold at once is all that I can show.

Yet what I sowed and what the orchard yields
My brother's sons are gathering stalk and root,
Small wonder then my children glean in fields
They have not sown, and feed on bitter fruit.

Close Your Eyes! / Arna Bontemps

Go through the gates with closed eyes.
Stand erect and let your black face front the west.
Drop the axe and leave the timber where it lies;
A woodman on the hill must have his rest.

Go where leaves are lying brown and wet.
Forget her warm arms and her breast who mothered you,
And every face you ever loved forget.
Close your eyes; walk bravely through.

The Day-Breakers / Arna Bontemps

We are not come to wage a strife
    With swords upon this hill.

It is not wise to waste the life
 Against a stubborn will.
Yet would we die as some have done,
Beating a way for the rising sun.

Golgotha Is a Mountain / Arna Bontemps

Golgotha is a mountain, a purple mound
Almost out of sight.
One night they hanged two thieves there,
And another man.
Some women wept heavily that night;
Their tears are flowing still. They have made a river;
Once it covered me.
Then the people went away and left Golgotha
Deserted.
Oh, I've seen many mountains:
Pale purple mountains melting in the evening mists and
  blurring on the borders of the sky.
I climbed old Shasta and chilled my hands in its summer
  snows.
I rested in the shadow of Popocatepetl and it whispered to me
  of daring prowess.
I looked upon the Pyrenees and felt the zest of warm exotic
  nights.
I slept at the foot of Fujiyama and dreamed of legend and
  of death.
And I've seen other mountains rising from the wistful moors
  like the breasts of a slender maiden.
Who knows the mystery of mountains!
Some of them are awful, others are just lonely.

❈ ❈ ❈

Italy has its Rome and California has San Francisco,
All covered with mountains.
Some think these mountains grew
Like ant hills
Or sand dunes.
That might be so—
I wonder what started them all!
Babylon is a mountain
And so is Ninevah,
With grass growing on them;
Palaces and hanging gardens started them.
I wonder what is under the hills
In Mexico
And Japan!
There are mountains in Africa, too.
Treasure is buried there:
Gold and precious stones
And moulded glory.
Lush grass is growing there
Sinking before the wind.
Black men are bowing
Naked in that grass
Digging with their fingers.
I am one of them:
Those mountains should be ours.
It would be great
To touch the pieces of glory with our hands.

These mute unhappy hills,
Bowed down with broken backs,
Speak often one to another:
"A day is as a year," they cry,
"And a thousand years as one day."
We watched the caravan
That bore our queen to the courts of Solomon;
And when the first slave traders came
We bowed our heads.
"Oh, Brothers, it is not long!

Dust shall yet devour the stones
But we shall be here when they are gone."
Mountains are rising all around me.
Some are so small they are not seen;
Others are large.
All of them get big in time and people forget
What started them at first.
Oh the world is covered with mountains!
Beneath each one there is something buried:
Some pile of wreckage that started it there.
Mountains are lonely and some are awful.

           ✿   ✿   ✿

One day I will crumble.
They'll cover my heap with dirt and that will make a
         mountain.
I think it will be Golgotha.

Idolatry / ARNA BONTEMPS

You have been good to me, I give you this:
The arms of lovers empty as our own,
Marble lips sustaining one long kiss
And the hard sound of hammers breaking stone.

For I will build a chapel in the place
Where our love died and I will journey there
To make a sign and kneel before your face
And set an old bell tolling on the air.

Reconnaissance / ARNA BONTEMPS

After the cloud embankments,
The lamentation of wind,
And the starry descent into time,
We came to the flashing waters and shaded our eyes
From the glare.

Alone with the shore and the harbor,
The stems of the cocoanut trees,
The fronds of silence and hushed music,
We cried for the new revelation
And waited for miracles to rise.

Where elements touch and merge,
Where shadows swoon like outcasts on the sand
And the tired moment waits, its courage gone—
There were we

In latitudes where storms are born.

Southern Mansion / ARNA BONTEMPS

Poplars are standing there still as death
And ghosts of dead men
Meet their ladies walking
Two by two beneath the shade
And standing on the marble steps.

There is a sound of music echoing
Through the open door
And in the field there is

Another sound tinkling in the cotton:
Chains of bondmen dragging on the ground.

The years go back with an iron clank,
A hand is on the gate,
A dry leaf trembles on the wall.
Ghosts are walking.
They have broken roses down
And poplars stand there still as death.

Nocturne at Bethesda / ARNA BONTEMPS

I thought I saw an angel flying low,
I thought I saw the flicker of a wing
Above the mulberry trees; but not again.
Bethesda sleeps. This ancient pool that healed
A host of bearded Jews does not awake.

This pool that once the angels troubled does not move.
No angel stirs it now, no Saviour comes
With healing in His hands to rise the sick
And bid the lame man leap upon the ground.

The golden days are gone. Why do we wait
So long upon the marble steps, blood
Falling from our open wounds? and why
Do our black faces search the empty sky?
Is there something we have forgotten? some precious thing
We have lost, wandering in strange lands?

There was a day, I remember now,
I beat my breast and cried, "Wash me, God,
Wash me with a wave of wind upon
The barley; O quiet One, draw near, draw near!

Walk upon the hills with lovely feet
And in the waterfall stand and speak.

"Dip white hands in the lily pool and mourn
Upon the harps still hanging in the trees
Near Babylon along the river's edge,
But oh, remember me, I pray, before
The summer goes and rose leaves lose their red."

The old terror takes my heart, the fear
Of quiet waters and of faint twilights.
There will be better days when I am gone
And healing pools where I cannot be healed.
Fragrant stars will gleam forever and ever
Above the place where I lie desolate.

Yet I hope, still I long to live.
And if there can be returning after death
I shall come back. But it will not be here;
If you want me you must search for me
Beneath the palms of Africa. Or if
I am not there then you may call to me
Across the shining dunes, perhaps I shall
Be following a desert caravan.

I may pass through centuries of death
With quiet eyes, but I'll remember still
A jungle tree with burning scarlet birds.
There is something I have forgotten, some precious thing.
I shall be seeking ornaments of ivory,
I shall be dying for a jungle fruit.

    You do not hear, Bethesda.
O still green water in a stagnant pool!
Love abandoned you and me alike.
There was a day you held a rich full moon
Upon your heart and listened to the words
Of men now dead and saw the angels fly.
There is a simple story on your face;

Years have wrinkled you. I know, Bethesda!
You are sad. It is the same with me.

Heritage (For Harold Jackman) / COUNTEE CULLEN

What is Africa to me:
Copper sun or scarlet sea,
Jungle star or jungle track,
Strong bronzed men, or regal black
Women from whose loins I sprang
When the birds of Eden sang?
One three centuries removed
From the scenes his fathers loved,
Spicy grove, cinnamon tree,
What is Africa to me?

So I lie, who all day long
Want no sound except the song
Sung by wild barbaric birds
Goading massive jungle herds,
Juggernauts of flesh that pass
Trampling tall defiant grass
Where young forest lovers lie,
Plighting troth beneath the sky.
So I lie, who always hear,
Though I cram against my ear
Both my thumbs, and keep them there,
Great drums throbbing through the air.
So I lie, whose fount of pride,
Dear distress, and joy allied,
Is my somber flesh and skin,
With the dark blood dammed within

Like great pulsing tides of wine
That, I fear, must burst the fine
Channels of the chafing net
Where they surge and foam and fret.

Africa? A book one thumbs
Listlessly, till slumber comes.
Unremembered are her bats
Circling through the night, her cats
Crouching in the river reeds,
Stalking gentle flesh that feeds
By the river brink; no more
Does the bugle-throated roar
Cry that monarch claws have leapt
From the scabbards where they slept.
Silver snakes that once a year
Doff the lovely coats you wear,
Seek no covert in your fear
Lest a mortal eye should see;
What's your nakedness to me?
Here no leprous flowers rear
Fierce corollas in the air;
Here no bodies sleek and wet,
Dripping mingled rain and sweat,
Tread the savage measures of
Jungle boys and girls in love.
What is last year's snow to me,
Last year's anything? The tree
Budding yearly must forget
How its past arose or set—
Bough and blossom, flower, fruit,
Even what shy bird with mute
Wonder at her travail there,
Meekly labored in its hair.
One three centuries removed
From the scenes his fathers loved,
Spicy grove, cinnamon tree,
What is Africa to me?

So I lie, who find no peace
Night or day, no slight release
From the unremittant beat
Made by cruel padded feet
Walking through my body's street.
Up and down they go, and back,
Treading out a jungle track.
So I lie, who never quite
Safely sleep from rain at night—
I can never rest at all
When the rain begins to fall;
Like a soul gone mad with pain
I must match its weird refrain;
Ever must I twist and squirm,
Writhing like a baited worm,
While its primal measures drip
Through my body, crying, "Strip!
Doff this new exuberance.
Come and dance the Lover's Dance!"
In an old remembered way
Rain works on me night and day.

Quaint, outlandish heathen gods
Black men fashion out of rods,
Clay, and brittle bits of stone,
In a likeness like their own,
My conversion came high-priced;
I belong to Jesus Christ,
Preacher of humility,
Heathen gods are naught to me.

Father, Son, and Holy Ghost,
So I make an idle boast;
Jesus of the twice-turned cheek,
Lamb of God, although I speak
With my mouth thus, in my heart
Do I play a double part.
Ever at Thy glowing altar
Must my heart grow sick and falter,

Wishing He I served were black,
Thinking then it would not lack
Precedent of pain to guide it,
Let who would or might deride it;
Surely then this flesh would know
Yours had borne a kindred woe.
Lord, I fashion dark gods, too,
Daring even to give You
Dark despairing features where,
Crowned with dark rebellious hair,
Patience wavers just so much as
Mortal grief compels, while touches
Quick and hot, of anger, rise
To smitten cheek and weary eyes.
Lord, forgive me if my need
Sometimes shapes a human creed.
All day long and all night through,
One thing only must I do:
Quench my pride and cool my blood,
Lest I perish in the flood,
Lest a hidden ember set
Timber that I thought was wet
Burning like the dryest flax,
Melting like the merest wax,
Lest the grave restore its dead.
Not yet has my heart or head
In the least way realized
They and I are civilized.

That Bright Chimeric Beast / COUNTEE CULLEN

That bright chimeric beast
Conceived yet never born,

Save in the poet's breast,
The white-flanked unicorn,
Never may be shaken
From his solitude;
Never may be taken
In any earthly wood.

That bird forever feathered,
Of its new self the sire,
After aeons weathered,
Reincarnate by fire,
Falcon may not nor eagle
Swerve from his eyrie,
Nor any crumb inveigle
Down to an earthly tree.

That fish of the dread regime
Invented to become
The fable and the dream
Of the Lord aquarium,
Leviathan, the jointed
Harpoon was never wrought
By which the Lord's anointed
Will suffer to be caught.

Bird of the deathless breast,
Fish of the frantic fin,
That bright chimeric beast
Flashing the argent skin,—
If beasts like these you'd harry,
Plumb then the poet's dream;
Make it your aviary,
Make it your wood and stream.

There only shall the swish
Be heard of the regal fish;
There like a golden knife
Dart the feet of the unicorn,
And there, death brought to life,
The dead bird be reborn.

Yet Do I Marvel / COUNTEE CULLEN

I doubt not God is good, well-meaning, kind,
And did He stoop to quibble could tell why
The little buried mole continues blind,
Why flesh that mirrors Him must someday die,
Make plain the reason tortured Tantalus
Is baited by the fickle fruit, declare
If merely brute caprice dooms Sisyphus
To struggle up a never-ending stair.
Inscrutable His ways are, and immune
To catechism by a mind too strewn
With petty cares to slightly understand
What awful brain compels His awful hand
Yet do I marvel at this curious thing:
To make a poet black, and bid him sing!

Four Epitaphs / COUNTEE CULLEN

1 FOR MY GRANDMOTHER

This lovely flower fell to seed;
Work gently sun and rain;
She held it as her dying creed
That she would grow again.

2 FOR JOHN KEATS, APOSTLE OF BEAUTY

Not writ in water nor in mist,
Sweet lyric throat, thy name.
Thy singing lips that cold death kissed
Have seared his own with flame.

3 FOR PAUL LAURENCE DUNBAR

Born of the sorrowful of heart
Mirth was a crown upon his head;
Pride kept his twisted lips apart
In jest, to hide a heart that bled.

4 FOR A LADY I KNOW

She even thinks that up in heaven
  Her class lies late and snores,
While poor black cherubs rise at seven
  To do celestial chores.

Simon the Cyrenian Speaks / COUNTEE CULLEN

He never spoke a word to me,
And yet He called my name;
He never gave a sign to me,
And yet I knew and came.

At first I said, "I will not bear
His cross upon my back;
He only seeks to place it there
Because my skin is black."

But He was dying for a dream,
And He was very meek,
And in His eyes there shone a gleam
Men journey far to seek.

It was Himself my pity bought;
I did for Christ alone
What all of Rome could not have wrought
With bruise of lash or stone.

Appoggiatura / Donald Jeffrey Hayes

It was water I was trying to think of all the time
Seeing the way you moved about the house. . . .
It was water, still and grey—or dusty blue
Where late at night the wind and a half-grown moon
Could make a crazy quilt of silver ripples
And it little mattered what you were about;
Whether painting in your rainbow-soiled smock
Or sitting by the window with the sunlight in your hair
That boiled like a golden cloud about your head
Or whether you sat in the shadows
Absorbed in the serious business
Of making strange white patterns with your fingers---
Whether it was any of these things
The emotion was always the same with me
And all the time it was water I was trying to recall,
Water, silent, breathless, restless,
Slowly rising, slowly falling, imperceptibly. . . .
It was the memory of water and the scent of air
Blown from the sea
That bothered me!

When you laughed, and that was so rare a festival,
I wanted to think of gulls dipping—
Grey wings, white-faced, into a rising wind
Dipping. . . .
Do you remember the day
You held a pale white flower to the sun
That I might see how the yellow rays
Played through the petals?
As I remember now
The flower was beautiful—
And the sunrays playing through—
And your slim fingers
And your tilting chin
But then:

There was only the indistinguishable sound of water silence;
The inaudible swish of one wave breaking. . . .

And now that you have moved on into the past,
You and your slim fingers
And your boiling hair,
Now that you have moved on into the past,
And I have time to stroll back through the corridors of
      memory,
It is like meeting an old friend at dawn
To find carved here deep in my mellowing mind
These words:
      "Sea-Woman—slim-fingered-water-thing. . . ."

Benediction / Donald Jeffrey Hayes

Not with my hands
But with my heart I bless you:
May peace forever dwell
Within your breast!

May Truth's white light
Move with you and possess you—
And may your thoughts and words
Wear her bright crest!

May Time move down
Its endless path of beauty
Conscious of you
And better for your being!

Spring after Spring
Array itself in splendor

Seeking the favor
Of your sentient seeing!

May hills lean toward you,
Hills and windswept mountains,
And trees be happy
That have seen you pass—

Your eyes dark kinsmen
To the stars above you—
Your feet remembered
By the blades of grass . . . !

Haven / DONALD JEFFREY HAYES

I'll build a house of arrogance
A most peculiar inn
With only room for vanquished folk
With proud and tilted chin . . . !

Poet / DONALD JEFFREY HAYES

No rock along the road but knows
The inquisition of his toes;
No journey's end but what can say:
He paused and rested here a day!
No joy is there that you may meet
But what will say: His kiss was sweet!
No sorrow but will sob to you:
He knew me intimately too . . . !

92

Threnody / DONALD JEFFREY HAYES

Let happy throats be mute;
Only the tortured reed
Is made a flute!

Only the broken heart can sing
And make of song
A breathless and a lovely thing!

Only the sad—only the tortured throat
Contrives of sound
A strangely thrilling note!

Only the tortured throat can fling
Beauty against the sky—
Only the broken heart can sing
Not asking why . . . !

Alien / DONALD JEFFREY HAYES

Do not stifle me with the strange scent
Of low growing mountain lilies—
Do not confuse me
With the salubrious odor of honeysuckle!

I cannot separate in my mind
Sweetness from sweetness—
Mimosa from wild white violets;
Magnolia from Cape jasmine!

I am from north tide country,
I can understand only the scent of seaweed;

Salt marsh and scrub pine
Riding on the breath of an amorous fog!

O do not confuse me
With sweetness upon sweetness;
Let me escape safely from this gentle madness—
Let me go back to the salt of sanity
In the scent of the sea . . . !

Pastourelle / DONALD JEFFREY HAYES

Walk this mile in silence—
Let no sound intrude
Upon the vibrant stillness
Of this solitude!

Let no thought be spoken
Nor syllable be heard
Lest the spell be broken
By the thunder of a word!

Here such matchless wonder is
As might tear apart—
Should the lip give tone
To the fullness of the heart . . . !

The Resurrection / Jonathan Brooks

His friends went off and left Him dead
In Joseph's subterranean bed,
Embalmed with myrrh and sweet aloes,
And wrapped in snow-white burial clothes.

Then shrewd men came and set a seal
Upon His grave, lest thieves should steal
His lifeless form away, and claim
For Him an undeserving fame.

"There is no use," the soldiers said,
"Of standing sentries by the dead."
Wherefore, they drew their cloaks around
Themselves, and fell upon the ground,
And slept like dead men, all night through,
In the pale moonlight and chilling dew.

A muffled whiff of sudden breath
Ruffled the passive air of death.

He woke, and raised Himself in bed;
    Recalled how He was crucified;
Touched both hands' fingers to His head,
    And lightly felt His fresh-healed side.

Then with a deep, triumphant sigh,
He coolly put His grave-clothes by—
Folded the sweet, white winding sheet,
    The toweling, the linen bands,
    The napkin, all with careful hands—
And left the borrowed chamber neat.

His steps were like the breaking day:
    So soft across the watch He stole,
    He did not wake a single soul,
Nor spill one dewdrop by the way.

Now Calvary was loveliness:
   Lilies that flowered thereupon
Pulled off the white moon's pallid dress,
   And put the morning's vesture on.

"Why seek the living among the dead?
He is not here," the angel said.

The early winds took up the words,
And bore them to the lilting birds,
The leafing trees, and everything
That breathed the living breath of spring.

Flowers of Darkness / FRANK MARSHALL DAVIS

Slowly the night blooms, unfurling
Flowers of darkness, covering
The trellised sky, becoming
A bouquet of blackness
Unending
Touched with sprigs
Of pale and budding stars

Soft the night smell
Among April trees
Soft and richly rare
Yet commonplace
Perfume on a cosmic scale

I turn to you Mandy Lou
I see the flowering night
Cameo condensed
Into the lone black rose
Of your face

The young woman-smell
Of your poppy body
Rises to my brain as opium
Yet silently motionless
I sit with twitching fingers
Yea, even reverently
Sit I
With you and the blossoming night
For what flower, plucked,
Lingers long?

Four Glimpses of Night / FRANK MARSHALL DAVIS

I

Eagerly
Like a woman hurrying to her lover
Night comes to the room of the world
And lies, yielding and content
Against the cool round face
Of the moon.

II

Night is a curious child, wandering
Between earth and sky, creeping
In windows and doors, daubing
The entire neighborhood
With purple paint.
Day
Is an apologetic mother
Cloth in hand
Following after.

Peddling
From door to door
Night sells
Black bags of peppermint stars
Heaping cones of vanilla moon
Until
His wares are gone
Then shuffles homeward
Jingling the gray coins
Of daybreak.

IV

Night's brittle song, sliver-thin,
Shatters into a billion fragments
Of quiet shadows
At the blaring jazz
Of a morning sun.

No Images / WARING CUNEY

She does not know
Her beauty,
She thinks her brown body
Has no glory.

If she could dance
Naked,
Under palm trees
And see her image in the river
She would know.

But there are no palm trees
On the street,
And dishwater gives back no images.

Threnody / WARING CUNEY

Only quiet death
Brings relief
From the wearisome
Interchange
Of hope and grief.
O body
(Credulous heart
And dream-torn head),
What will wisdom be
Or folly—
When you lie dead?
Life-beaten body
Bruised and sore—
Neither hunger nor satiety
Are known beyond death's door.

Finis / WARING CUNEY

Now that our love has drifted
To a quiet close,
Leaving the empty ache
That always follows when beauty goes;
Now that you and I,
Who stood tiptoe on earth
To touch our fingers to the sky,
Have turned away
To allow our little love to die—
Go, dear, seek again the magic touch.
But if you are wise,
As I shall be wise,
You will not again
Love overmuch.

Poem / HELENE JOHNSON

Little brown boy,
Slim, dark, big-eyed,
Crooning love songs to your banjo
Down at the Lafayette—
Gee, boy, I love the way you hold your head,
High sort of and a bit to one side,
Like a prince, a jazz prince. And I love
Your eyes flashing, and your hands,
And your patent-leathered feet,
And your shoulders jerking the jig-wa.
And I love your teeth flashing,

And the way your hair shines in the spotlight
Like it was the real stuff.
Gee, brown boy, I loves you all over.
I'm glad I'm a jig. I'm glad I can
Understand your dancin' and your
Singin', and feel all the happiness
And joy and don't-care in you.
Gee, boy, when you sing, I can close my ears
And hear tom-toms just as plain.
Listen to me, will you, what do I know
About tom-toms? But I like the word, sort of,
Don't you? It belongs to us.
Gee, boy, I love the way you hold your head,
And the way you sing and dance,
And everything.
Say, I think you're wonderful. You're
All right with me,
You are.

The Road / HELENE JOHNSON

Ah, little road, all whirry in the breeze,
A leaping clay hill lost among the trees,
The bleeding note of rapture-streaming thrush
Caught in a drowsy bush
And stretched out in a single singing line of dusky **song**.
Ah, little road, brown as my race is brown,
Your trodden beauty like our trodden pride,
Dust of the dust, they must not bruise you down.
Rise to one brimming golden, spilling cry!

Sonnet to a Negro in Harlem / HELENE JOHNSON

You are disdainful and magnificent—
Your perfect body and your pompous gait,
Your dark eyes flashing solemnly with hate,
Small wonder that you are incompetent
To imitate those whom you so despise—
Your shoulders towering high above the throng,
Your head thrown back in rich, barbaric song,
Palm trees and mangoes stretched before your eyes.
Let others toil and sweat for labor's sake
And wring from grasping hands their meed of gold.
Why urge ahead your supercilious feet?
Scorn will efface each footprint that you make.
I love your laughter arrogant and bold.
You are too splendid for this city street.

Invocation / HELENE JOHNSON

Let me be buried in the rain
In a deep, dripping wood,
Under the warm wet breast of Earth
Where once a gnarled tree stood.
And paint a picture on my tomb
With dirt and a piece of bough
Of a girl and a boy beneath a round, ripe moon
Eating of love with an eager spoon
And vowing an eager vow.
And do not keep my plot mowed smooth
And clean as a spinster's bed,
But let the weed, the flower, the tree,
Riotous, rampant, wild, and free,
Grow high above my head.

Between the World and Me / RICHARD WRIGHT

And one morning while in the woods I stumbled suddenly
    upon the thing,
Stumbled upon it in a grassy clearing guarded by scaly oaks
    and elms.
And the sooty details of the scene rose, thrusting themselves
    between the world and me. . . .

There was a design of white bones slumbering forgottenly
    upon a cushion of ashes.
There was a charred stump of a sapling pointing a blunt
    finger accusingly at the sky.
There were torn tree limbs, tiny veins of burnt leaves, and a
    scorched coil of greasy hemp;
A vacant shoe, an empty tie, a ripped shirt, a lonely hat, and
    a pair of trousers stiff with black blood.
And upon the trampled grass were buttons, dead matches,
    butt-ends of cigars and cigarettes, peanut shells, a
    drained gin-flask, and a whore's lipstick;
Scattered traces of tar, restless arrays of feathers, and the
    lingering smell of gasoline.
And through the morning air the sun poured yellow surprise
    into the eye sockets of a stony skull. . . .
And while I stood my mind was frozen with a cold pity for
    the life that was gone.
The ground gripped my feet and my heart was circled by
    icy walls of fear—
The sun died in the sky; a night wind muttered in the grass
    and fumbled the leaves in the trees; the woods poured
    forth the hungry yelping of hounds; the darkness
    screamed with thirsty voices; and the witnesses rose
    and lived:
The dry bones stirred, rattled, lifted, melting themselves into
    my bones.
The grey ashes formed flesh firm and black, entering into my
    flesh.

The gin-flask passed from mouth to mouth; cigars and ciga-
    rettes glowed, the whore smeared the lipstick red
    upon her lips,
And a thousand faces swirled around me, clamoring that
    my life be burned. . . .

And then they had me, stripped me, battering my teeth into
    my throat till I swallowed my own blood.
My voice was drowned in the roar of their voices, and my
    black wet body slipped and rolled in their hands as
    they bound me to the sapling.
And my skin clung to the bubbling hot tar, falling from me in
    limp patches.
And the down and quills of the white feathers sank into my
    raw flesh, and I moaned in my agony.
Then my blood was cooled mercifully, cooled by a baptism
    of gasoline.
And in a blaze of red I leaped to the sky as pain rose like
    water, boiling my limbs.
Panting, begging I clutched childlike, clutched to the hot
    sides of death.
Now I am dry bones and my face a stony skull staring in
    yellow surprise at the sun. . . .

Hokku Poems / Richard Wright

I am nobody
A red sinking autumn sun
Took my name away

Make up your mind snail!
You are half inside your house
And halfway out!

In the falling snow
A laughing boy holds out his palms
Until they are white

Keep straight down this block
Then turn right where you will find
A peach tree blooming

With a twitching nose
A dog reads a telegram
On a wet tree trunk

The spring lingers on
In the scent of a damp log
Rotting in the sun

Whose town did you leave
O wild and drowning spring rain
And where do you go?

The crow flew so fast
That he left his lonely caw
Behind in the fields

Adjuration / CHARLES ENOCH WHEELER

Let the knowing speak,
Let the oppressed tell of their sorrows,
Of their salt and boundless grief.
Since even the wise and the brave
Must wonder, and the creeping mists
Of doubt, creep along the trough
Of pursuing woe . . .
To curl among the crevices

Of the most cannily armored brain.
Let those who can endure their doubts
Speak for the comfort of the weary
Who weep to know.

Without Name / PAULI MURRAY

Call it neither love nor spring madness,
Nor chance encounter nor quest ended.
Observe it casually as pussy willows
Or pushcart pansies on a city street.
Let this seed growing in us
Granite-strong with persistent root
Be without name, or call it the first
Warm wind that caressed your cheek
And traded unshared kisses between us.
Call it the elemental earth
Bursting the clasp of too-long winter
And trembling for the plough-blade.

Let our blood chant it
And our flesh sing anthems to its arrival,
But our lips shall be silent, uncommitted.

Dark Testament / PAULI MURRAY

Hope is a crushed stalk
Between clenched fingers.
Hope is a bird's wing
Broken by a stone.
Hope is a word in a tuneless ditty—
A word whispered with the wind,
A dream of forty acres and a mule,
A cabin of one's own and rest days often
A name and place for one's children
And children's children at last . . .
Hope is a song in a weary throat.

> *O give me a song of hope*
> *And a world where I can sing it.*
> *Give me a song of faith*
> *And a people to believe in it.*
> *Give me a song of kindliness*
> *And a country where I can live it.*
> *O give me a song of hope and love*
> *And a brown girl's heart to hear it.*

❊   ❊   ❊

Tear it out of the history books!
Bury it in conspiracies of silence!
Fight many wars to suppress it!
But it is written in our faces
Twenty million times over!
It sings in our blood,
It cries from the housetops,
It mourns with the wind in the forests,
When dogs howl and will not be comforted,
When newborn lambs bleat in the snowdrifts,
And dead leaves rattle in the graveyards.

And we'll shout it from the mountains,
We'll tell it in the valleys,
We'll talk it in miner's shack,
We'll sing it at the work bench,
We'll whisper it over back fences.
We'll speak it in the kitchen,
We'll state it at the White House,
We'll tell it everywhere to all who will listen—

We will lay siege, let thunder serve our claim,
For it must be told, endlessly told, and you must hear it.
Listen, white brothers, hear the dirge of history,
And hold out your hand—Hold out your hand.

❖   ❖   ❖

Of us who darkly stand
Bared to the spittle of every curse,
Nor left the dignity of beasts,
Let none say,
"Those were not men but cowards all,
With eyes dull-lidded as a frog's.
They labored long but not from love,
Striving from blind perpetual fear."

Better our seed rot on the ground
And our hearts burn to ash
Than the years be empty of our imprint,
We have no other dream, no land but this.
With slow deliberate hands these years
Have set her image on our brows.
We are her seed, have borne a fruit
Native and pure as unblemished cotton.

Then let the dream linger on.
Let it be the test of nations,
Let it be the quest of all our days,
The fevered pounding of our blood,
The measure of our souls,—
That none shall rest in any land

And none return to dreamless sleep,
No heart be quieted, no tongue be stilled
Until the final man may stand in any place
And thrust his shoulders to the sky,
Friend and brother to every other man.

A Ballad of Remembrance / ROBERT HAYDEN

Quadroon mermaids, Afro angels, black saints
balanced upon the switchblades of that air
and sang. Tight streets unfolding to the eye
like fans of corrosion and elegiac lace
crackled with their singing: Shadow of time. Shadow of
    blood.

Shadow, echoed the Zulu king, dangling
from a cluster of balloons. Blood,
whined the gun-metal priestess, floating
over the courtyard where dead men diced.

What will you have? she inquired, the sallow vendeuse
of prepared tarnishes and jokes of nacre and ormolu,
what but those gleamings, oldrose graces,
manners like scented gloves? Contrived ghosts
rapped to metronome clack of lavalieres.

Contrived illuminations riding a threat
of river, masked Negroes wearing chameleon
satins gaudy now as a fortuneteller's
dream of disaster, lighted the crazy flopping
dance of love and hate among joys, rejections.

Accommodate, muttered the Zulu king,
toad on a throne of glaucous poison jewels.

109

Love, chimed the saints and the angels and the mermaids.
Hate, shrieked the gun-metal priestess
from her spiked bellcollar curved like a fleur-de-lis:

As well have a talon as a finger, a muzzle as a mouth,
as well have a hollow as a heart. And she pinwheeled
away in coruscations of laughter, scattering
those others before her like foil stars.

But the dance continued—now among metaphorical
doors, coffee cups floating poised
hysterias, decors of illusion; now among
mazurka dolls offering death's-heads
of cocaine roses and real violets.

Then you arrived, meditative, ironic,
richly human; and your presence was shore where I rested
released from the hoodoo of that dance, where I spoke
with my true voice again.

And therefore this is not only a ballad of remembrance
for the down-South arcane city with death
in its jaws like gold teeth and archaic cusswords;
not only a token for the troubled generous friends
held in the fists of that schizoid city like flowers,
but also, Mark Van Doren,
a poem of remembrance, a gift, a souvenir for you

Witch Doctor / ROBERT HAYDEN

I

He dines alone surrounded by reflections
of himself. Then after sleep and benzedrine
descends the Cinquecento stair his magic

wrought from hypochondria of the well-
to-do and nagging deathwish of the poor;
swirls on smiling genuflections of
his liveried chauffeur into a crested
lilac limousine, the cynosure
of mousey neighbors tittering behind
Venetian blinds and half afraid of him
and half admiring his outrageous flair.

II

Meanwhile his mother, priestess in gold lamé,
precedes him to the quondam theater
now Israel Temple of the Highest Alpha,
where the bored, the sick, the alien, the tired
await euphoria. With deadly vigor
she prepares the way for mystery
and lucre. Shouts in blues-contralto, "He's
God's dictaphone of all-redeeming truth.
Oh he's the holyweight champeen who's come
to give the knockout lick to your bad luck;
say he's the holyweight champeen who's here
to deal a knockout punch to your hard luck."

III

Reposing on cushions of black leopard skin,
he telephones instructions for a long
slow drive across the park that burgeons now
with spring and sailors. Peers questingly
into the green, fountainous twilight, sighs
and turns the gold-plate dial to Music For
Your Dining-Dancing Pleasure. Smoking Egyptian
cigarettes rehearses in his mind
a new device that he must use tonight.

IV

Approaching Israel Temple, mask in place,
he hears ragtime allegros of a "Song

of Zion" that becomes, when he appears,
a hallelujah wave for him to walk.
His mother and a rainbow-surpliced cordon
conduct him choiring to the altar-stage,
and there he kneels and seems to pray before
a lighted Jesus painted sealskin-brown.
Then with a glittering flourish he arises,
turns, gracefully extends his draperied arms:
"Israelites, true Jews, O found lost tribe
of Israel, receive my blessing now.
Selah, selah." He feels them yearn toward him
as toward a lover, exults before the image
of himself their trust gives back. Stands as though
in meditation, letting their eyes caress
his garments jewelled and chatoyant, cut
to fall, to flow from his tall figure
dramatically just so. Then all at once
he sways, quivers, gesticulates as if
to ward off blows or kisses, and when he speaks
again he utters wildering vocables,
hypnotic no-words planned (and never failing)
to enmesh his flock in theopathic tension.
Cries of eudaemonic pain attest
his artistry. Behind the mask he smiles.
And now in subtly altering light he chants
and sinuously trembles, chants and trembles
while convulsive energies of eager faith
surcharge the theater with power of
their own, a power he has counted on
and for a space allows to carry him.
Dishevelled antiphons proclaim the moment
his followers all day have hungered for,
but which is his alone.
He signals: tambourines begin, frenetic
drumbeat and glissando. He dances from the altar,
robes hissing, flaring, shimmering; down aisles
where mantled guardsmen intercept wild hands
that arduously strain to clutch his vestments,

³⁷ he dances, dances, ensorcelled and aloof,
³⁸the fervid juba of God as lover, healer,
conjurer. And of himself as God.

Middle Passage / ROBERT HAYDEN

I

Jesús, Estrella, Esperanza, Mercy:

Sails flashing to the wind like weapons,
sharks following the moans the fever and the dying;
horror the corposant and compass rose.

Middle Passage:
                    voyage through death
                              to life upon these shores.

"10 April 1800—
Blacks rebellious. Crew uneasy. Our linguist says
their moaning is a prayer for death,
ours and their own. Some try to starve themselves.
Lost three this morning leaped with crazy laughter
to the waiting sharks, sang as they went under."

Desire, Adventure, Tartar, Ann:

Standing to America, bringing home
black gold, black ivory, black seed.

> *Deep in the festering hold thy father lies,*
> *of his bones New England pews are made,*
> *those are altar lights that were his eyes.*

113

Jesus   Saviour   Pilot   Me
Over   Life's   Tempestuous   Sea

We pray that Thou wilt grant, O Lord,
safe passage to our vessels bringing
heathen souls unto Thy chastening.

Jesus   Saviour

    "8 bells. I cannot sleep, for I am sick
    with fear, but writing eases fear a little
    since still my eyes can see these words take shape
    upon the page & so I write, as one
    would turn to exorcism. 4 days scudding,
    but now the sea is calm again. Misfortune
    follows in our wake like sharks (our grinning
    tutelary gods). Which one of us
    has killed an albatross? A plague among
    our blacks—Ophthalmia: blindness—& we
    have jettisoned the blind to no avail.
    It spreads, the terrifying sickness spreads.
    Its claws have scratched sight from the Capt.'s eyes
    & there is blindness in the fo'c'sle
    & we must sail 3 weeks before we come
    to port."

        What port awaits us, Davy Jones'
        or home? I've heard of slavers drifting, drifting,
        playthings of wind and storm and chance, their
                crews
        gone blind, the jungle hatred
        crawling up on deck.

Thou   Who   Walked   On   Galilee

    "Deponent further sayeth *The Bella J*
    left the Guinea Coast
    with cargo of five hundred blacks and odd
    for the barracoons of Florida:

"That there was hardly room 'tween-decks for half
the sweltering cattle stowed spoon-fashion there;
that some went mad of thirst and tore their flesh
and sucked the blood:

"That Crew and Captain lusted with the comeliest
of the savage girls kept naked in the cabins;
that there was one they called The Guinea Rose
and they cast lots and fought to lie with her:

"That when the Bo's'n piped all hands, the flames
spreading from starboard already were beyond
control, the Negroes howling and their chains
entangled with the flames:

"That the burning blacks could not be reached,
that the Crew abandoned ship,
leaving their shrieking Negresses behind,
that the Captain perished drunken with the wenches:

"Further Deponent sayeth not."

Pilot   Oh   Pilot   Me

II

Aye, lad, and I have seen those factories,
Gambia, Rio Pongo, Calabar;
have watched the artful mongos baiting traps
of war wherein the victor and the vanquished

Were caught as prizes for our barracoons.
Have seen the nigger kings whose vanity
and greed turned wild black hides of Fellatah,
Mandingo, Ibo, Kru to gold for us.

And there was one—King Anthracite we named him—
fetish face beneath French parasols
of brass and orange velvet, impudent mouth
whose cups were carven skulls of enemies:

He'd honor us with drum and feast and conjo
and palm-oil-glistening wenches deft in love,

and for tin crowns that shone with paste,
red calico and German-silver trinkets.

Would have the drums talk war and send
his warriors to burn the sleeping villages
and kill the sick and old and lead the young
in coffles to our factories.

Twenty years a trader, twenty years,
for there was wealth aplenty to be harvested
from those black fields, and I'd be trading still
but for the fevers melting down my bones.

III

Shuttles in the rocking loom of history,
the dark ships move, the dark ships move,
their bright ironical names
like jests of kindness on a murderer's mouth;
plough through thrashing glister toward
fata morgana's lucent melting shore,
weave toward New World littorals that are
mirage and myth and actual shore.

Voyage through death,
                              voyage whose chartings are unlove

A charnel stench, effluvium of living death
spreads outward from the hold,
where the living and the dead, the horribly dying,
lie interlocked, lie foul with blood and excrement.

> *Deep in the festering hold thy father lies,*
> *the corpse of mercy rots with him,*
> *rats eat love's rotten gelid eyes.*

> *But, oh, the living look at you*
> *with human eyes whose suffering accuses you,*
> *whose hatred reaches through the swill of dark*
> *to strike you like a leper's claw.*

You cannot stare that hatred down
or chain the fear that stalks the watches
and breathes on you its fetid scorching breath;
cannot kill the deep immortal human wish,
the timeless will.

"But for the storm that flung up barriers
of wind and wave, *The Amistad*, señores,
would have reached the port of Príncipe in two,
three days at most; but for the storm we should
have been prepared for what befell.
Swift as the puma's leap it came. There was
that interval of moonless calm filled only
with the water's and the rigging's usual sounds,
then sudden movement, blows and snarling cries
and they had fallen on us with machete
and marlinspike. It was as though the very
air, the night itself were striking us.
Exhausted by the rigors of the storm,
we were no match for them. Our men went down
before the murderous Africans. Our loyal
Celestino ran from below with gun
and lantern and I saw, before the cane-
knife's wounding flash, Cinquez,
that surly brute who calls himself a prince,
directing, urging on the ghastly work.
He hacked the poor mulatto down, and then
he turned on me. The decks were slippery
when daylight finally came. It sickens me
to think of what I saw, of how these apes
threw overboard the butchered bodies of
our men, true Christians all, like so much jetsam.
Enough, enough. The rest is quickly told:
Cinquez was forced to spare the two of us
you see to steer the ship to Africa,
and we like phantoms doomed to rove the sea
voyaged east by day and west by night,
deceiving them, hoping for rescue,

117

prisoners on our own vessel, till
at length we drifted to the shores of this
your land, America, where we were freed
from our unspeakable misery. Now we
demand, good sirs, the extradition of
Cinquez and his accomplices to La
Havana. And it distresses us to know
there are so many here who seem inclined
to justify the mutiny of these blacks.
We find it paradoxical indeed
that you whose wealth, whose tree of liberty
are rooted in the labor of your slaves
should suffer the august John Quincy Adams
to speak with so much passion of the right
of chattel slaves to kill their lawful masters
and with his Roman rhetoric weave a hero's
garland for Cinquez. I tell you that
we are determined to return to Cuba
with our slaves and there see justice done.
      Cinquez—
or let us say 'the Prince'—Cinquez shall die."

The deep immortal human wish,
the timeless will:

    Cinquez its deathless primaveral image,
    life that transfigures many lives.

Voyage through death
                 to life upon these shores.

Frederick Douglass / ROBERT HAYDEN

When it is finally ours, this freedom, this liberty, this
        beautiful
and terrible thing, needful to man as air,
usable as earth; when it belongs at last to our children,
when it is truly instinct, brain matter, diastole, systole,
reflex action; when it is finally won; when it is more
than the gaudy mumbo jumbo of politicians:
this man, this Douglass, this former slave, this Negro
beaten to his knees, exiled, visioning a world
where none is lonely, none hunted, alien,
this man, superb in love and logic, this man
shall be remembered. Oh, not with statues' rhetoric,
not with legends and poems and wreaths of bronze alone,
but with the lives grown out of his life, the lives
fleshing his dream of the beautiful, needful thing.

Veracruz / ROBERT HAYDEN

I

Sunday afternoon,
and couples walk the breakwater
heedless of the bickering spray.
Near the shoreward end,
Indian boys idle and fish.
A shawled brown woman
squinting against
the ricocheting brilliance
of sun and water

119

shades her eyes and gazes
toward the fort,
fossil of Spanish power,
looming in the harbor.

At the seaward end,
a pharos like a temple rises.
From here the shore
seen across marbling waves
is arabesque ornately green
that hides the inward-falling slum,
the stains and dirty tools of struggle;
appears a destination dreamed of,
never to be reached.

Here only the sea is real—
the barbarous multifoliate sea
with its rustlings of leaves,
fire, garments, wind;
its clashing of phantasmal jewels,
its lunar thunder,
animal and human sighing.

Leap now,
and cease from error.
Escape. Or shoreward turn,
accepting all—
the losses and farewells,
the long warfare with self,
with God.

The waves roar in and break
roar in and break
with granite spreeing hiss
on bronzegreen rocks below
and glistering upfling of spray

II

Thus reality
   bedizened in the warring colors
      of a dream
parades through these
   arcades ornate with music and
      the sea.

Thus reality
   become unbearably a dream
      beckons
out of reach in flyblown streets
   of lapsing rose and purple, dying
      blue.

Thus marimba'd night
   and multifoliate sea become
      phantasmal
space, and there,
   light-years away, one farewell image
      burns and fades and burns.

Perspectives / Dudley Randall

Futile to chide the stinging shower
Or prosecute the thorn
Or set a curse upon the hour
In which my love was born.

All's done, all's vanished, like a sail
That's dwindled down the bay.
Even the mountains vast and tall
The sea dissolves away.

I Loved You Once (From the Russian of Alexander Pushkin) / DUDLEY RANDALL

I loved you once; love even yet, it may be,
Within my soul has not quite died away;
But let that cause you no anxiety;
I would not give you pain in any way.
I loved you helplessly, and hopelessly,
With jealousy, timidity, brought low;
I loved you so intensely, tenderly,
I pray to God another love you so.

Sorrow Is the Only Faithful One / OWEN DODSON

Sorrow is the only faithful one:
The lone companion clinging like a season
To its original skin no matter what the variations.

If all the mountains paraded
Eating the valleys as they went
And the sun were a cliffure on the highest peak,

Sorrow would be there between
The sparkling and the giant laughter
Of the enemy when the clouds come down to swim.

But I am less, unmagic, black,
Sorrow clings to me more than to doomsday mountains
Or erosion scars on a palisade.

Sorrow has a song like a leech
Crying because the sand's blood is dry
And the stars reflected in the lake

Are water for all their twinkling
And bloodless for all their charm.
I have blood, and a song.
SORROW IS THE ONLY FAITHFUL ONE.

Drunken Lover / OWEN DODSON

This is the stagnant hour:
The dead communion between mouth and mouth,
The drunken kiss lingered,
The dreadful equator south.

This is the hour of impotence
When the unfulfilled is unfulfilled.
Only the stale breath is anxious
And warm. All else is stilled.

Why did I come to this reek,
This numb time, this level?
Only for you, my love, only for you
Could I endure this devil.

I dreamed when I was
A pimply and urgent adolescent
Of these hours when love would be fire
And you the steep descent.

My mouth's inside is like cotton,
Your arm is dead on my arm,
What I pictured so lovely and spring
Is August and fungus calm.

O lover, draw away, grow small, go magic,
O lover, disappear into the tick of this bed;
Open all the windows to the north
For the wind to cool my head.

123

Sickle Pears (For Glidden Parker) / OWEN DODSON

In college once I climbed the tree
With sickle pears our Greek professor loved.
High in that natural world I shook
An Autumn down;

A tumble of roughed fruit
Bounced onto the cider ground.
Fell to my waiting friend.

Together we went on to maple meadows
To celebrate the harvest of the year.
By chewing sickle pears we won a year:
Digesting all he planted thought by thought
From early Homer to the precious here.

Hymn Written After Jeremiah Preached to Me in a Dream / OWEN DODSON

Nowhere are we safe.
Surely not in love,
Morning ripe at three
Or in the Holy Trinity.

(My God, look after me.)

Where does Grace abide,
Whole, whole in surety?
Or does sin abide
Where virtue tries, in shame, to hide?

(My God, have I no pride?)

124

Shall I try the whole,
Crippled in my will,
Spatter where it falls
My carnal-fire waterfalls?

(My angel, in compassion, calls.)

Secret, knotted shame
Rips me like a curse.
Unction in my dust
Gives me final thrust.

(My God, consider dust!)

Yardbird's Skull (For Charlie Parker) / OWEN DODSON

The bird is lost,
Dead, with all the music:
Whole sunsets heard the brain's music
Faded to last horizon notes.
I do not know why I hold
This skull, smaller than a walnut's,
Against my ear,
Expecting to hear
The smashed fear
Of childhood from . . . bone;
Expecting to see
Wind nosing red and purple,
Strange gold and magic
On bubbled windowpanes
Of childhood. Shall I hear?
I should hear: this skull
Has been with violets

Not Yorick, or the gravedigger,
Yapping his yelling story,
This skull has been in air,
Sensed his brother, the swallow,
(Its talent for snow and crumbs).
Flown to lost Atlantis islands,
Places of dreaming, swimming lemmings.
O I shall hear skull skull,
Hear your lame music,
Believe music rejects undertaking,
Limps back.
Remember tiny lasting, we get lonely:
Come sing, come sing, come sing sing
And sing.

Sailors on Leave / Owen Dodson

No boy chooses war.
Dear let me show
The picket fence
Around my heart
Where loves are hung
In pairs of pain
And joy: the piercing revellers.

Here in this bar, the Cosycue,
I hear my darling singer moan,
Lower lights within my mind,
Admit a surer light
To see, to die by.

Here so specially set
For me, I am amazed,

Are target lovers all lines
For me to break,
To leave them, to die by.

No boy chooses war
But then we go
And in a cause find causes
To regret the summer and
The easy girl or boy
We drift to exist,
To battle for, to die.

Stevedore / LESLIE M. COLLINS

The enigmatic moon has at long last died.
Even as the ancient Cathedral Saint Louis
Peals her lazy call
To a sleepy solemn worship,
Night's mysterious shadows reveal their secrets
And rise into nothingness
As honest day unfurls her bright banners.

The stevedore,
Sleep spilled on his black face,
Braves the morning's rising fog,
The saturating chill.

As the sun burns itself out in summer brilliance,
Though his heart he sweated out
In water glistening from gargantuan shoulders,
He finds strength in his voice,
Singing of Moses down in Egyptland,
Of yesterday's untrue love.

By evening
The sun-scorched stevedore has packed strange cargoes
On alien ships
Whose destinations stir no romantic desires.

All day
A little of his soul is put to sea.
And now that the heaven's sun-burnt gold
Has quickened to deepest lapis-lazuli,
He turns an unkempt head

Homeward
To a dreamless slumber.

For My People / Margaret Walker

For my people everywhere singing their slave songs re-
     peatedly: their dirges and their ditties and their blues
     and jubilees, praying their prayers nightly to an un-
     known god, bending their knees humbly to an unseen
     power;
For my people lending their strength to the years: to the
     gone years and the now years and the maybe years,
     washing ironing cooking scrubbing sewing mending
     hoeing plowing digging planting pruning patching
     dragging along never gaining never reaping never
     knowing and never understanding;
For my playmates in the clay and dust and sand of Alabama
     backyards playing baptizing and preaching, and doc-
     tor and jail and soldier and school and mama and
     cooking and playhouse and concert and store and
     Miss Choomby and hair and company;

128

For the cramped bewildered years we went to school to
learn to know the reasons why and the answers to and
the people who and the places where and the days
when, in memory of the bitter hours when we discovered we were black and poor and small and different
and nobody wondered and nobody understood;

For the boys and girls who grew in spite of these things to
be Man and Woman, to laugh and dance and sing and
play and drink their wine and religion and success, to
marry their playmates and bear children and then die
of consumption and anemia and lynching;

For my people thronging 47th Street in Chicago and Lenox
Avenue in New York and Rampart Street in New Orleans, lost disinherited dispossessed and HAPPY people filling the cabarets and taverns and other people's
pockets needing bread and shoes and milk and land
and money and Something—Something all our own;

For my people walking blindly, spreading joy, losing time
being lazy, sleeping when hungry, shouting when bur-
dened, drinking when hopeless, tied and shackled and
tangled among ourselves by the unseen creatures who
tower over us omnisciently and laugh;

For my people blundering and groping and floundering in
the dark of churches and schools and clubs and so-
cieties, associations and councils and committees and
conventions, distressed and disturbed and deceived
and devoured by money-hungry glory-craving leeches,
preyed on by facile force of state and fad and novelty
by false prophet and holy believer;

For my people standing staring trying to fashion a better
way from confusion from hypocrisy and misunder-
standing, trying to fashion a world that will hold all
the people all the faces all the adams and eves and
their countless generations;

Let a new earth rise. Let another world be born. Let a bloody
peace be written in the sky. Let a second generation
full of courage issue forth, let a people loving freedom
come to growth, let a beauty full of healing and a

129

strength of final clenching be the pulsing in our spirits and our blood. Let the martial songs be written, let the dirges disappear. Let a race of men now rise and take control!

Molly Means / MARGARET WALKER

Old Molly Means was a hag and a witch;
Chile of the devil, the dark, and sitch.
Her heavy hair hung thick in ropes
And her blazing eyes was black as pitch.
Imp at three and wench at 'leben
She counted her husbands to the number seben.
  O Molly, Molly, Molly Means
  There goes the ghost of Molly Means.

Some say she was born with a veil on her face
So she could look through unnatchal space
Through the future and through the past
And charm a body or an evil place
And every man could well despise
The evil look in her coal black eyes.
  Old Molly, Molly, Molly Means
  Dark is the ghost of Molly Means.

And when the tale begun to spread
Of evil and of holy dread:
Her black-hand arts and her evil powers
How she cast her spells and called the dead,
The younguns was afraid at night
And the farmers feared their crops would blight.
  Old Molly, Molly, Molly Means
  Cold is the ghost of Molly Means.

Then one dark day she put a spell
On a young gal-bride just come to dwell
In the lane just down from Molly's shack
And when her husband come riding back
His wife was barking like a dog
And on all fours like a common hog.
    O Molly, Molly, Molly Means
    Where is the ghost of Molly Means?

The neighbors come and they went away
And said she'd die before break of day
But her husband held her in his arms
And swore he'd break the wicked charms;
He'd search all up and down the land
And turn the spell on Molly's hand.
    O Molly, Molly, Molly Means
    Sharp is the ghost of Molly Means.

So he rode all day and he rode all night
And at the dawn he come in sight
Of a man who said he could move the spell
And cause the awful thing to dwell
On Molly Means, to bark and bleed
Till she died at the hands of her evil deed.
    Old Molly, Molly, Molly Means
    This is the ghost of Molly Means.

Sometimes at night through the shadowy trees
She rides along on a winter breeze.
You can hear her holler and whine and cry.
Her voice is thin and her moan is high,
And her cackling laugh or her barking cold
Bring terror to the young and old.
    O Molly, Molly, Molly Means
    Lean is the ghost of Molly Means.

October Journey / Margaret Walker

Traveller take heed for journeys undertaken in the dark of
    the year.
Go in the bright blaze of Autumn's equinox.
Carry protection against ravages of a sun-robber, a vandal,
    and a thief.
Cross no bright expanse of water in the full of the moon.
Choose no dangerous summer nights;
no heady tempting hours of spring;
October journeys are safest, brightest, and best.

I want to tell you what hills are like in October
when colors gush down mountainsides
and little streams are freighted with a caravan of leaves.
I want to tell you how they blush and turn in fiery shame and
    joy,
how their love burns with flames consuming and terrible
until we wake one morning and woods are like a smoldering
    plain—
a glowing caldron full of jewelled fire:
the emerald earth a dragon's eye
the poplars drenched with yellow light
and dogwoods blazing bloody red.

Travelling southward earth changes from gray rock to green
    velvet.
Earth changes to red clay
with green grass growing brightly
with saffron skies of evening setting dully
with muddy rivers moving sluggishly.

In the early spring when the peach tree blooms
wearing a veil like a lavender haze
and the pear and plum in their bridal hair
gently snow their petals on earth's grassy bosom below
then the soughing breeze is soothing

and the world seems bathed in tenderness,
but in October
blossoms have long since fallen.
A few red apples hang on leafless boughs;
wind whips bushes briskly.
And where a blue stream sings cautiously
a barren land feeds hungrily.

An evil moon bleeds drops of death.
The earth burns brown.
Grass shrivels and dries to a yellowish mass.
Earth wears a dun-colored dress
like an old woman wooing the sun to be her lover,
be her sweetheart and her husband bound in one.
Farmers heap hay in stacks and bind corn in shocks
against the biting breath of frost.

The train wheels hum, "I am going home, I am going home,
I am moving toward the South."
Soon cypress swamps and muskrat marshes
and black fields touched with cotton will appear.
I dream again of my childhood land
of a neighbor's yard with a redbud tree
the smell of pine for turpentine
an Easter dress, a Christmas eve
and winding roads from the top of a hill.
A music sings within my flesh
I feel the pulse within my throat
my heart fills up with hungry fear
while hills and flatlands stark and staring
before my dark eyes sad and haunting
appear and disappear.

Then when I touch this land again
the promise of a sun-lit hour dies.
The greenness of an apple seems
to dry and rot before my eyes.
The sullen winter rains
are tears of grief I cannot shed.

The windless days are static lives.
The clock runs down
timeless and still.
The days and nights turn hours to years
and water in a gutter marks the circle of another world
hating, resentful, and afraid
stagnant, and green, and full of slimy things.

The Fishes and the Poet's Hands / FRANK YERBY

I

They say that when they burned young Shelley's corpse
(For he was drowned, you know, and washed ashore
With hands and face quite gone—the fishes had,
It seems, but small respect for Genius which
Came clothed in common flesh) the noise his brains
Made as they boiled and seethed within his skull
Could well be heard five yards away. At least
No one can hear *mine* as they boil; but then
He could not *feel* his burn; and so I think
He had the best of it at that. Don't you?

II

Now all the hungry broken men stand here
Beside my bed like ghosts and cry: "Why don't
You shout our wrongs aloud? Why are you not
Our voice, our sword? For you are of our blood;
You've seen us beaten, lynched, degraded, starved;
Men must be taught that other men are not
Mere pawns in some gigantic game in which
The winner takes the gold, the land, the work,

The breath, the heart, and soul of him who loses!"
I watch them standing there until my brain
Begins to burn within my head again—
(As Shelley's burned—poor, young dead Shelley whom
The fishes ate) then I get up and write
A very pretty sonnet, nicely rhymed
About my latest love affair, how sad
I am because some dear has thrown me for
A total loss. (But Shelley had me there.
All his affairs turned out quite well indeed;
Harriet in the river drowned for love
Of him; and Mary leaving Godwin's house
To follow where he led—quite well—indeed!)

III

You see, this is ironical and light
Because I am so sick, so hurt inside;
I'm tired of pretty rhyming words when all
The land where I was born is soaked in tears
And blood, and black and utter hopelessness.
Now I would make a new, strong, bitter song,
And hurl it in the teeth of those I hate—
I would stand tall and proud against their blows,
Knowing I could not win, I would go down
Grandly as an oak goes down, and leave
An echo of the crash, at least, behind.
(So Shelley lived—and so at last, he died.
The fishes ate his glorious hands; and all
That mighty bulk of brain boiled when they burned him!)

Weltschmerz / FRANK YERBY

For they who fashion songs must live too close to pain,
Acquaint themselves too well with grief and tears:
Must make the slow, deep, throbbing pulse of years
And their own heartbeats one; watch the slow train
Of passing autumns paint their scarlet stain
Upon the hills, and learn that beauty sears.
The whole world's woe and heartbreak must be theirs,
And theirs each vision smashed, each new dream slain.

But sing again, oh you who have the heart,
Sweet songs as fragile as a passing breath,
Although your broken heartstrings make your lyre,
And each pure strain must rend the soul apart;
For it was ever thus: to sing is death;
And in your spirit flames your body's pyre.

Wisdom / FRANK YERBY

I have known nights rain-washed and crystal-clear
And heavy with the mellow, mingled scent
Of honeysuckle, rose, and pine, while near
The shadowed ghosts of trees the new moon bent,
And touched your eyes with silvered ecstasy.

Then I believed in Magic, Youth, and Spring,
Then parting was synonymous with Death;
And every note I heard the night birds sing
Caused fitful haltings in my labored breath.

How strange that now I look into new eyes
In utter calm, yet with a deeper awe,
And know so well that when the old love dies
A new is born, as Spring from Winter's thaw
Arises in new light and loveliness.

And yet it is not quite the same to know
How transient grief, how fleeting, pain;
What prosaic love to stand and watch you go,
And, in a month, to be at peace again!

You Are a Part of Me / FRANK YERBY

You are a part of me. I do not know
By what slow chemistry you first became
A vital fiber of my being. Go
Beyond the rim of time or space, the same
Inflections of your voice will sing their way
Into the depths of my mind still. Your hair
Will gleam as bright, the artless play
Of word and glance, gesture and the fair
Young fingers waving, have too deeply etched
The pattern of your soul on mine. Forget
Me quickly as a laughing picture sketched
On water, I shall never know regret
Knowing no magic ever can set free
That part of you that is a part of me.

Calm After Storm / FRANK YERBY

Deep in my soul there roared the crashing thunder,
And unseen rain slashed furrows in my face;
The lightning's flame with tendrils fine as lace,
Etched intricate designs, too keen for wonder
Upon my dull-eyed soul. And that rich plunder
Of stolen joys, snatched in the little space,
Between the dawn and dark, had caught the pace,
This rip-tide of the heart, and was drawn under.

But this slow calm, this torpid lack of caring,
Creeping along, a drugged dream of content,
Kills no less surely than the storm's duress;
Better the winds, like thin whip-lashes sparing
No proud young heart until their force is spent,
Than this vague peace, akin to nothingness.

A Moment Please / SAMUEL ALLEN

When I gaze at the sun
    I walked to the subway booth
    for change for a dime.
and know that this great earth
    Two adolescent girls stood there
    alive with eagerness to know
is but a fragment from it thrown
    all in their new found world
    there was for them to know
in heat and flame a billion years ago,
    they looked at me and brightly asked
    "Are you Arabian?"

that then this world was lifeless
    I smiled and cautiously
    —for one grows cautious—
    shook my head.
as, a billion hence,
    "Egyptian?"
it shall again be,
    Again I smiled and shook my head
    and walked away.
what moment is it that I am betrayed,
    I've gone but seven paces now
oppressed, cast down,
    and from behind comes swift the sneer
or warm with love or triumph?
    "Or Nigger?"

    A moment, please
What is it that to fury I am roused?
    for still it takes a moment
What meaning for me
    and now
in this homeless clan
    I'll turn
the dupe of space
    and smile
the toy of time?
    and nod my head.

To ~~Satch~~ / Samuel Allen

Snatch

> Sometimes I feel like I will never stop
> Just go forever
> Till one fine morning
> I'll reach up and grab me a handful of stars
> And swing out my long lean leg
> And whip three hot strikes burning down the heavens
> And look over at God and say
> How about that!

Here and Now / Catherine Cater

> If here and now be but a timely span
> Between today's unhappiness, tomorrow's
> Joys, what if today's abundant sorrows
> Never end, tomorrow never comes, what then?
>
> If youth, impatient of the disrespect
> Accorded it, yearns to be old,
> Age chafes beneath the manifold
> Losses of its prime and mourns neglect;
>
> So let it be for here and now, my dear,
> Not for the when of an eternity;
> No gazer in the crystal ball can see
> The future as we see the now and here.

Flags / GWENDOLYN BROOKS

Still, it is dear defiance now to carry
Fair flags of you above my indignation,
Top, with a pretty glory and a merry
Softness, the scattered pound of my cold passion.
I pull you down my foxhole. Do you mind?
You burn in bits of saucy color then.
I let you flutter out against the pained
Volleys. Against my power crumpled and wan.
You, and the yellow pert exuberance
Of dandelion days, unmocking sun;
The blowing of clear wind in your gay hair;
Love changeful in you (like a music, or
Like a sweet mournfulness, or like a dance,
Or like the tender struggle of a fan).

The Old-Marrieds / GWENDOLYN BROOKS

But in the crowding darkness not a word did they say.
Though the pretty-coated birds had piped so lightly all the
        day.
And he had seen the lovers in the little side streets.
And she had heard the morning stories clogged with sweets.
It was quite a time for loving. It was midnight. It was May.
But in the crowding darkness not a word did they say.

Piano After War / GWENDOLYN BROOKS

On a snug evening I shall watch her fingers,
Cleverly ringed, declining to clever pink,
Beg glory from the willing keys. Old hungers
Will break their coffins, rise to eat and thank.
And music, warily, like the golden rose
That sometimes after sunset warms the west,
Will warm that room, persuasively suffuse
That room and me, rejuvenate a past.
But suddenly, across my climbing fever
Of proud delight—a multiplying cry.
A cry of bitter dead men who will never
Attend a gentle maker of musical joy.
Then my thawed eye will go again to ice.
And stone will shove the softness from my face.

The Chicago *Defender* Sends a Man to Little Rock, Fall, 1957 / GWENDOLYN BROOKS

In Little Rock the people bear
Babes, and comb and part their hair
And watch the want ads, put repair
To roof and latch. While wheat toast burns
A woman waters multiferns.

Time upholds or overturns
The many, tight, and small concerns.

In Little Rock the people sing
Sunday hymns like anything,
Through Sunday pomp and polishing.

And after testament and tunes,
Some soften Sunday afternoons
With lemon tea and Lorna Doones.

I forecast
And I believe
Come Christmas Little Rock will cleave
To Christmas tree and trifle, weave,
From laugh and tinsel, texture fast.

In Little Rock is baseball; Barcarolle.
That hotness in July . . . the uniformed figures raw and
      implacable
And not intellectual,
Batting the hotness or clawing the suffering dust.
The Open Air Concert, on the special twilight green . . .
When Beethoven is brutal or whispers to ladylike air.
Blanket-sitters are solemn, as Johann troubles to lean
To tell them what to mean . . .
There is love, too, in Little Rock. Soft women softly
Opening themselves in kindness,
Or, pitying one's blindness,
Awaiting one's pleasure
In Azure
Glory with anguished rose at the root . . .
To wash away old semidiscomfitures.
They reteach purple and unsullen blue.
The wispy soils go. And uncertain
Half-havings have they clarified to sures.

In Little Rock they know
Not answering the telephone is a way of rejecting life,
That it is our business to be bothered, is our business
To cherish bores or boredom, be polite
To lies and love and many-faceted fuzziness.

I scratch my head, massage the hate-I-had.
I blink across my prim and pencilled pad.
The saga I was sent for is not down.
Because there is a puzzle in this town.

The biggest News I do not dare
Telegraph to the Editor's chair:
"They are like people everywhere."
The angry Editor would reply
In hundred harryings of Why.

And true, they are hurling spittle, rock,
Garbage and fruit in Little Rock.
And I saw coiling storm a-writhe
On bright madonnas. And a scythe
Of men harassing brownish girls.
(The bows and barrettes in the curls
And braids declined away from joy.)

I saw a bleeding brownish boy . . .
The lariat lynch-wish I deplored.
The loveliest lynchee was our Lord.

The African Affair / BRUCE McM. WRIGHT

Black is what the prisons are,
The stagnant vortex of the hours
Swept into totality,
Creeping in the perjured heart,
Bitter in the vulgar rhyme,
Bitter on the walls;

Black is where the devils dance
With time within
The creviced wall. Time pirouettes
A crippled orbit in a trance,
And crawls below, beneath the flesh
Where darkness flows;

Black is where the deserts burn,
The Niger and Sasandra flow,
From where the Middle Passage went
Within the Continent of Night
From Cameroons to Carisbrooke
And places conscience cannot go;

Black is where thatched temples burn
Incense to carved ebon-wood;
Where traders shaped my father's pain,
His person and his place,
Among dead statues in a frieze,
In the spectrum of his race.

Sonnet / Alfred A. Duckett

Where are we to go when this is done?
Will we slip into old, accustomed ways,
finding remembered notches, one by one?
Thrashing a hapless way through quickening haze?

Who is to know us when the end has come?
Old friends and families, but could we be
strange to the sight and stricken dumb
at visions of some pulsing memory?

Who will love us for what we used to be
who now are what we are, bitter or cold?
Who is to nurse us with swift subtlety
back to the warm and feeling human fold?

Where are we to go when this is through?
We are the war-born. What are we to do?

Sunset Horn / MYRON O'HIGGINS

*Enduring peace is the only monument civilization can raise
to the millions who have perished in its cause.*

I

Block the cannon; let no trumpets sound!
Our power is manifest in other glory;
Our flesh in this contested slope of ground.

In thin silences we lie, pale strangers to the corn-gold
> morning,
Repeating what the fathers told . . . the promised legacy
> of tall sons:
The hushed sibilants of peace; and the far tomorrow on the
> hills.

O we went quickly or a little longer
And for a space saw caste and categories, creeds and race
Evaporate into the flue of common circumstance.
We sought transcendent meaning for our struggle,
And in that rocking hour, each minute, each narrow second
Fell upon us like a rain of knives.
We grappled here an instant, then singly, or in twos or tens,
> or by bewildered hundreds,
Were pulverized . . . Reduced . . . Wiped out—
Made uniform and equal!
> And let us tell you this·
Death is indiscriminate . . . and easier . . . than sorrow,
> fear, or fallen pride.
There is no road back. We rest in ultimates;
In calmness come abrupt by bomb, or bullet, or abbreviated
> dream;
With conflicts spent.
This stark convergent truth continues,
Linking us through slim unseen dimensions—we to you, we
> to you . . .

While you cry Victory! or Surrender!
Turn these figures in the head,
Clean impersonal round numbers,
Ordered inventory of the dead.

Regard these slender nines and ones;
These trailing threes and fives; these fours and sevens, bent
    and angular;
Delicately drawn, divided into ranks by commas,
Staggered down the page in regimented squads and columns:
These are our mute effigies, trim and shining,
Passing in review . . .
                O Drummer, obediently we come,
Down through the assassin's street,
The company of death in splendid array! . . .

But leave us to the terrible fields.
Yours is the pomp of brasses, the counterfeit peace, the
    dynasty of lies . . .
We are but dabs of flesh blown to the cliffs,
Or ragged stumps of legs that moved too slowly toward the
    brush.
And our song: we joined no swelling harmony of voices.
Those final incoherent sounds we made;
Those startled oaths that bubbled through the blood bogged
    in our throats;
That last falsetto cry of terror;
Were a jagged threnody, swallowed whole and drowned in
    cacophonic floods.
This was our sunset horn . . .

Let these be added with the spoils for quick division!
Set these down in sharp italics on the page
For scholars' documents!

Raise no vain monuments; bury us down!
Our power is manifest in other glory;

Our flesh in this contested slope of ground.
There is no more but these, a legacy, a grim prediction . . .
Let the scent and sounds of death go limp
And flounder in the valleys and the streets.
And for those crafty ones—those who speak our names in
    brief professional remembrance
To garner votes and profits, or practice quick extortion—
Let other music find their ears.
And give them for a souvenir this clown's disguise
Of swastikas and Roman standards, of scythes and suns and
    dollar signs . . .
One day the rest of you will know the meaning of annihilation.
And the hills will rock with voltage;
And the forests burn like a flaming broom;
And the stars explode and drop like cinders on the land.
And these steel cities where no love is—
You shall see them fall and vanish in a thunder of erupting
    suns!

O you shall know; and in that day, traveler, O in that day
When the tongues confound, and breath is total in the horn,
Your Judas eyes, seeking truth at last, will search for us
And borrow ransom from this bowel of violence!

And on This Shore / M. CARL HOLMAN

Alarm and time clock still intrude too early,
Sun on the lawns at morning is the same,
Across the cups we yawn at private murders,
Accustomed causes leave us gay or glum.

(I feel the streaming wind in my eyes,
the highway swimming under the floor,
music flung comically over the hills,

Remember your profile, your pilot's body at ease,
the absolute absence of boredom, the absence of fear)

The swingshift workers are snoring at noon,
The army wife's offspring dumb in his crib,
The private, patron of blackmarket still,
Sleeps long past reveille stark on his slab.

(The chimes were musing far beyond soft hills,
I brushed an ant from your arm,
The leaves lifted, shifted like breathing to pour
Light on your lids, seemed then no end of time)

The streets rewind to spools of home,
Dials usher in the bland newscaster,
From the mailbox's narrow room
Lunges the cobra of disaster.

(Kissed and were happy at the door,
showered, pretending this would last,
Stones down dead wells, the calendar
counts summers that are lost, are lost)

II

Is it yourself he loves
Or the way you arranged your hair?
The book which taught you to listen while he talked?
The cute dance steps and that night on the Navy pier?
Did he see yours or another's face when he waked?
On what does this shadow feed
And shall it not fade?

Is it yourself she loves
Or the easy-come money you breezily spend?
The 4-F, convertible, "A" coupons, dark market Scotch?
Would she stick if she found she could interest your friend:
When the man on her dresser returns will you prove his
       match?
On what does this shadow feed
And shall it not fade?

Is it yourself they love
Or the victories panted with vibrant voice?
(Mellow for brave boys sleeping their last long sleep)
Will sponsor and fan abide when bulletins burst in your face,
Raw stumps and barricade explode through the map?
On what does this shadow feed,
And shall it not fade?

Is it yourself they love,
You brief-cased and lens-familiar,
Invoking spring from the smoke of our heaviest winter?
Their mouths adore—but fangs may lurk for anger;
Watching night wither do you not sometimes wonder
On what does this shadow feed
And shall it not fade?

Letter Across Doubt and Distance / M. CARL HOLMAN

I dreamed all my fortitude screamed
And fled down the strict corridor,
Entered in greedy and unashamed
At the seductive door;
Or your eyes winked from the tabloid,
Your silence raised a wraith
Which lured me nearer that void
Where fact prepares its ambuscade for faith.

Carved keen in the spring-green bark
Your long absence does not congeal,
No cement sutures the cruel crack
Where the hot sap weeps still
And will furrow and blister this sand
Though vanes claim weather is north

Until your gifted hand
Heals the shocked tissues and late buds flame forth:

O girl waking now where the swirl
Of gulls scatters across white hulls
And the wind hurtling the marshy field
Spurs the green bay into hills,
All my pain falls at your power,
Slacks and comes softly to rest.
Calmed, as that gray church tower
Checks the wild pigeons taking them to breast.

Notes for a Movie Script / M. Carl Holman

Fade in the sound of summer music,
Picture a hand plunging through her hair,
Next his socked feet and her scuffed dance slippers
Close, as they kiss on the rug-stripped stair.

Catch now the taxi from the station,
Capture her shoulders' sudden sag;
Switch to him silent in the barracks
While the room roars at the corporal's gag.

Let the drums dwindle in the distance,
Pile the green sea above the land;
While she prepares a single breakfast,
Reading the V mail in her hand.

Ride a cold moonbeam to the pillbox,
Sidle the camera to his feet
Sprawled just outside in the gummy grasses,
Swollen like nightmare and not neat.

151

Now doorbell nudges the lazy morning:
She stills the sweeper for a while,
Twitches her dress, swings the screendoor open,
Cut—with no music—on her smile.

Song / M. CARL HOLMAN

Dressed up in my melancholy
With no place to go,
Sick as sin of inwardness
And sick of being so

I walked out on the avenue,
Eager to give my hand
To any with the health to heal
Or heart to understand.

I had not walked a city block
And met with more than ten
Before I read the testament
Stark behind each grin:

Beneath the hatbrims haunting me,
More faithful than a mirror,
The figuration of my grief,
The image of my error.

Christmas Lullaby for a New-Born Child / Yvonne Gregory

"Where did I come from, Mother, and why?"
"You slipped from the hand of Morn.
A child's clear eyes have wondered why
Since the very first child was born."

"What shall I do here, Mother, and when?"
"You'll dream in a waking sleep,
Then sow your dreams in the minds of men
Till the time shall come to reap."

"What do men long for, Mother, and why?"
"They long for a star's bright rays,
And when they have glimpsed a tiny light
They follow with songs of praise."

"Where does that star shine, Mother, and when?"
"It glows in the hearts of a few.
So close your eyes, while I pray, dear child,
That the star may shine in you."

Far From Africa: Four Poems / Margaret Danner

"are you beautiful still?"

1. GARNISHING THE AVIARY

Our moulting days are in their twilight stage.
These lengthy dreaded suns of draggling plumes.
These days of moods that swiftly alternate between

The former preen (ludicrous now) and a downcast rage
Or crestfallen lag, are fading out. The initial bloom;
Exotic, dazzling in its indigo, tangerine

Splendor; this rare, conflicting coat had to be shed.
Our drooping feathers turn all shades. We spew
This unamicable aviary, gag upon the worm, and fling

Our loosening quills. We make a riotous spread
Upon the dust and mire that beds us. We do not shoo
So quickly; but the shades of the pinfeathers resulting

From this chaotic push, though still exotic,
Blend in more easily with those on the wings
Of the birds surrounding them; garnishing
The aviary, burnishing this zoo.

2. DANCE OF THE ABAKWETA

Imagine what Mrs. Haessler would say
If she could see the Watusi youth dance
Their well-versed initiation. At first glance
As they bend to an invisible barre
You would know that she had designed their costumes.

For though they were made of pale beige bamboo straw
Their lines were the classic tutu. Nothing varied.
Each was cut short at the thigh and carried
High to a degree of right angles. Nor was there a flaw
In their leotards. Made of leopard skin or the hide

Of a goat, or the Gauguin-colored Okapi's striped coat
They were cut in her reverenced "tradition."
She would have approved their costumes and positions.
And since neither Iceland nor Africa is too remote
For her vision she would have wanted to form

A "traditional" ballet. Swan Lake, Scheherazade or
(After seeing their incredible leaps)
Les Orientales. Imagine the exotic sweep
Of such a ballet, and from the way the music pours

Over these dancers (this tinkling of bells, talking
Of drums, and twanging of tan, sandalwood harps)
From this incomparable music, Mrs. Haessler of Vassar can
Glimpse strains of Tchaikovsky, Chopin
To accompany her undeviatingly sharp
"Traditional" ballet. I am certain that if she could
Tutor these potential protégés, as
Quick as Aladdin rubbing his lamp, she would.

3. THE VISIT OF THE PROFESSOR OF AESTHETICS

To see you standing in the sagging bookstore door
So filled me with chagrin that suddenly you seemed as
Pink and white to me as a newborn, hairless mouse. For

I had hoped to delight you at home. Be a furl
Of faint perfume and Vienna's cordlike lace.
To shine my piano till a shimmer of mother-of-pearl

Embraced it. To pleasantly surprise you with the grace
That transcends my imitation and much worn
"Louis XV" couch. To display my Cathedrals and ballets.

To plunge you into Africa through my nude
Zulu Prince, my carvings from Benin, forlorn
Treasures garnered by much sacrifice of food.

I had hoped to delight you, for more
Rare than the seven-year bloom of my
Chinese spiderweb fern is a mind like yours

That concedes my fetish for this substance
Of your trade. And I had planned to prove
Your views of me correct at even every chance

Encounter. But you surprised me. And the store which
Had shown promise until you came, arose
Like a child gone wild when company comes or a witch

At Hallowe'en. The floor, just swept and mopped,
Was persuaded by the northlight to deny it.
The muddy rag floor rugs hunched and flopped

Away from the tears in the linoleum that I wanted
Them to hide. The drapes that I had pleated
In clear orchid and peach feverishly flaunted

Their greasiest folds like a banner.
The books who had been my friends, retreated—
Became as shy as the proverbial poet in manner

And hid their better selves. All glow had been deleted
By the dirt. And I felt that you whose god is grace
Could find no semblance of it here. And unaware

That you were scrubbing, you scrubbed your hands.
Wrung and scrubbed your long white fingers. Scrubbed
Them as you smiled and I lowered my eyes from despair.

4. ETTA MOTEN'S ATTIC

(Filled with mementos of African journeys)

It was as if Gauguin
had upset a huge paint pot
of his incomparable tangerine,

splashing wherever my startled eyes ran
here and there, and at my very hand on
masques and paintings and carvings not seen

here before, spilling straight as a stripe
spun geometrically in a Nbeble rug
flung over an ebony chair,

or dripping round as a band on a type
of bun the Watusi warriors
make of their pompadoured hair,

splashing high as a sunbird or fly moving
over a frieze of mahogany trees,
or splotching out from low underneath as a root,

shimmering bright as a ladybug grooving
a green bed of moss, sparkling as a beetle,
a bee, shockingly dotting the snoot

of an ape or the nape of its neck or as clue
to its navel, stamping a Zulu's
intriguing masque, tipping

the lips of a chief of Ashantis who
was carved to his stool so he'd sit
there forever and never fear a slipping

of rule or command, dyeing the skirt
(all askew) that wouldn't stay put on the
Pygmy in spite of his real leather belt,

quickening and charming till we felt the bloom
of veldt and jungle flow through the room.

The Slave and the Iron Lace / MARGARET DANNER

The craving of Samuel Rouse for clearance to create
was surely as hot as the iron that buffeted him. His passion
for freedom so strong that it molded the smouldering
        fashions
he laced, for how else could a slave plot
or counterplot such incomparable shapes,

form or reform, for house after house
the intricate Chatilion Patio pattern, the delicate
Rose and Lyre, the Debutante Settee
the complex but famous Grape; frame the classic vein
in an iron bench?

How could he turn an iron Venetian urn, wind the Grape
        Vine chain
the trunk of a pine with a Round-the-Tree-settee,
mold a Floating Flower tray, a French chair, create all this
in such exquisite fairyland taste, that he'd be freed
and his skill would still resound a hundred years after?

And I wonder if I, with this thick asbestos glove of an
attitude, could lace, forge, and bend this ton of lead-chained
      spleen

surrounding me?
Could I manifest and sustain it into a new free-form screen
of, not necessarily love, but (at the very least,
for all concerned) grace.

A Private Letter to Brazil / G. C. ODEN

The map shows me where it is you are. I
am here, where the words NEW YORK run an inch
out to sea, ending where GULF STREAM flows by.

The coastline bristles with place names. The pinch
in printing space has launched them offshore
with the fishbone's fine-tooth spread, to clinch

their urban identity. Much more
noticeable it is in the chain
of hopscotching islands that, loosely, moors

your continent to mine. (Already plain
is its eastward drift, and who could say
what would become of it left free!) Again,

the needle-pine alignment round S/A,
while where it is you are (or often go),
RIO, spills its subtle phonic bouquet

farthest seawards of all. Out there I know
the sounding is some deep 2000 feet,
and the nationalized current tours so

pregnant with resacas. In their flux meets
all the subtlety of God's great nature
and man's terse grief. See, Hero, at your feet

is not that slight tossing dead Leander?

The Carousel / G. C. ODEN

*"I turned from side to side, from image to image to put you
down."*—Louise Bogan

An empty carousel in a deserted park
rides me round and round,
forth and back,
from end to beginning,
like the tail that drives the dog.

I cannot see:
sight focusses shadow where once
pleased scenery,
and in this whirl of space
only the indefinite is constant.

This is the way of grief:
spinning in the rhythm of memories
that will not let you up
or down,
but keeps you grinding through
a granite air. rock

". . . As When Emotion Too Far Exceeds its Cause" —Elizabeth Bishop / G. C. ODEN

You probably could put their names to them.
The birds, I mean.
Though I have often watched their rushing
about the upper air
(deliberate as subway riders
who are not anywhere near
so orderly),
I have never stopped to inquire the name
of that one or another.
Still, I did take time
to observe them in their dips and circles
and jet-propelled ascendancies.

It's all in the wings I am told.
That could be said of angels.
I grant it may be true;
undoubtedly is,
since my informants know more
than I. But,
still, I wonder,
and harbor fear that we all are wrong
to think that birds do fly.
What if, one day, upon the ground with us
we found them;
their wings unable to lift them
anywhere except into a deeper stratum
of despair.
Would it all be a matter of wings?
Does flight depend upon such feathered things?

Or is it air? I do not trust the stuff.
Seeing the birds beating about in it,
I want to say, "Take care; and
don't believe in what it seems you do!"
Sometimes I stray across a small one

I should have said it to;
one who for all his modern design
to sweep and arch the atmosphere
had plummeted, instead, to earth
and worms that do not care about horizons.
If I retreat,
too shocked to cast the benediction
of a single leaf,
understand why:
I know the error in invisible support;
in love's celestial venturing
I, too, once trusted air
that plunged me down.
Yes, I!

The Map / G. C. Oden

My rug is red. My couch, whereon I deal
in dreams with truths I never live, is brown;
a shading more intense than that by my
skin declared. Richer it is, too, than of
any of the eight clear hues coloring
my wide, world map soldiering the white wall
there behind it. This map is of the world.
It says so. In type ½″ high: WORLD;
and with what I know of maps I do, in
deed, believe it—though over it, in type
now smaller by one-half, I read the word
"COSMOPOLITAN," and over that, in
type yet smaller by one-half, these gentile
modifiers "RAND McNALLY."

                                The seas
square off in blue. Or, ought the word be "sea?"
Uniformly bright, planed by a tone so
mild you might suppose the North Sea twinned the
South and that the Moskenstraumen was (for
the most part) Poe (quote) SAILING DIRECTIONS
FOR THE NORTHWEST AND NORTH COAST OF
          NORWAY
(unquote) to the contrary; seven diminishes
to one, where none arrests attention.

                                Not
so the land. Flowering forth as spring in
May will settle down to deed, it woos us
with such yellows, pinks and greens as would, I'm
sure, lure the most selective butterfly;
and each trim hue is sized the living room
of nations.

                    America (U. S.) is
daffodil; Canada carnation; while
leaflike as an elephant ear, Greenland
hangs indifferent to those arctic winds parching
the cell-like bounds of Russia (here halved and
showing both to the left and right of this
our hemisphere—indeed, as is a good
part of the orient split, some even
to doubling appearance.)

                        Europe (also)
lies fragmented; though from nature's—not the
mapmaker's—division. Ireland off-
set from England, offset from France (feigning
oasis besides the rot-brown fill to
Germany) supplies one awkward revel
of abstraction as that gross bud of Spain
(with Portugal) patterns another; not ·
to mention Italy's invasion of
the sea.

Norway, Sweden, much as giraffes
must bend, towards Denmark group in restricted
covenant; yet, though this canvas—Europe—
at its center holds, such unity rests
more upon imagination than that,
let's say, of Africa islanded in
those deeper latitudes.

There, it is the
green (again) I think. Incandescent flood
like the dead reckoning of spring; at four
points edging sea; it seems a fever of
the mind within that broad head housed (it shapes
—Africa—a head to me!) which in its
course will blaze the length of continent as
now it fires breadth.

And who will say it
won't? Not the mapmaker, surely, who must
exact truth. Not I, high hoisting same to,
state whirlwind. Will you, because you might not
particularly care to see it so?

The Rebel / MARI E. EVANS

When I
die
I'm sure
I will have a
Big Funeral . . .
Curiosity
seekers . . .
coming to see

if I
am really
Dead . . .
or just
trying to make
Trouble. . . .

When in Rome / MARI E. EVANS

Marrie dear
the box is full . . .
take
whatever you like
to eat . . .

> (an egg
> or soup
> . . . there ain't no meat.)

there's endive there
and
cottage cheese . . .

> (whew! if I had some
> black-eyed peas . . .)

there's sardines
on the shelves
and such . . .
but
don't
get my anchovies . . .

        they cost
        too much!

                (me get the
                anchovies indeed!
                what she think, she got—
                a bird to feed?)

there's plenty in there
to fill you up . . .

                (yes'm. just the
                sight's
                enough!

                Hope I lives till I get
                home
                I'm tired of eatin'
                what they eats in Rome . . .)

The Emancipation of George-Hector
(a colored turtle) / MARI E. EVANS

        George-Hector
        . . . is
        spoiled.
        formerly he stayed
        well up in his
        shell . . . but now
        he hangs arms and legs
        sprawlingly
        in a most languorous fashion . . .
        head rared back
        to

be
admired.

he didn't use to
talk . . .
but
he does now.

Raison d'Etre / OLIVER PITCHER

Over the eye behind the moon's cloud
over you whose touch to a Stradavari heart shames
the chorale of angels
over Mr. Eros who tramples the sun-roses
and sits amid willow trees
to weep
over the olive wood
over the vibrant reds, blacks, luminous golds of
decay
over the strength of silence and advantages of
unwareness
over the Rosey Eclipse
over the geyser in the toilet bowl
over the cynical comma
over the madness itself
the occupational hazard of artists
over the catcher caught in his catcher's mitt
over oil and opal, blood and bone of
the earth
over the iron touch behind pink gloves
over retired civilizations sunken below levels
shimmering in rusty lustre
over myself
I wave the flag raison d'etre

Four Questions Addressed to His Excellency, the Prime Minister / JAMES P. VAUGHN

Sir

I read of late
you have tired of roses
their habit of unfolding
a beginning middle and end

The stenographer unbuttons her blouse
spring rains
porcelain is everywhere

On a ledge
high above the stunned constituency
the cabinet sits
in cold tuxedos

Sir

Is it true
that when the idea is cut out
there is profuse bleeding
in the mind

around her gilded neck
Madame la Femme
Winds and winds
her silken drama

tassels wrestle
together
create a slight colloquial rhyme

Sir

if labor agrees
and management agrees
where does the grammarian
put the prefix

however nimble
skulduggery
the electorate stands pat
and opposition of weights
is felt

Shhh

Madeline is entering
her tomb appears surprised
sit sit

Sir

according to one historian
snow is a visual cadenza
remember

swiftly the skier passes
deeper and deeper into silence
the telephone rings
hello hello hello

the caretaker
boards the windows of the summer cottage
the lord chamberlain shivers
a moment sped by

So? / James P. Vaughn

Nothing if not utterly in death
    So let us now demur flowers
    Say you saw us in patience
    Gently remove wrath from thorn
    And nod "Morning" to moon passing

Happy if merely knowing light
I cannot grasp substances, but
If by chance, I drop my world
And hear it smash in the basin
I rejoice in the sound, if not fancy.

Let it stand at that. If with
These eyes I encourage the
Great Distances to move closer
And sit here with me in silence
Then will such bright candles as these
Be not held hostages too soon.

At War / RUSSELL ATKINS

Beyond the turning sea's far foam
a tender ephemera
of a moment's dawn in a fantastic place
sudden'd its appear
and was gone!

was gone
out, as a young man farewell'd to all
         but arms!

don't ask me more
what of it, of it why
I cannot explain it any—
no don't ask me, I insist—
some dared and
died—

Listen a moment—! Sh! Listen—!
that hurrying as of a shore of
fugitives!

Irritable Song / Russell Atkins

Says-so is in a woe of shuddered
    leaves
Foreboding huskily.
For who returns (said by its rasp)
Save leniently chanced
To the begun? There is fatal
    instance.

A low hanging of bough
Plucked my eye; automobile
Wheels, furious by,
Stuck objects upon
Of a deadly bruise
And strew the stone;

A footfall behind'll
Be the gunman's I swear.
None the worse when I
Am in the hearse.
Should I return, the house
(What less?) is gone:
Burned into none.

Or say upon return
Coronary farewell
Leaves me lie. Ugh!
Dare, sir? Be nay'd
Tomorrow, tomorrow
    in today?

It's Here In The / RUSSELL ATKINS

Here in the newspaper—the wreck of the East Bound.
A photograph bound to bring on cardiac asthenia.
There is a blur that mists the page!
On one side is a gloom of dreadful harsh.
Then breaks flash lights up sheer.
There is much huge about. I suppose then
      those no's are people
   between that suffering of—
    (what more have we? for Christ's sake, no!)
Something of a full stop of it
crash of blood and the still shock
    of stark sticks and an immense swift gloss,
And two dead no's lie aghast still.
One casts a crazed eye and the other's
Closed dull.
     the heap up twists
        such
as to harden the unhard and unhard
the hardened.

Lester Young / TED JOANS

Sometimes he was cool like an eternal
    blue flame burning in the old Kansas
    City nunnery
Sometimes he was happy 'til he'd think
    about his birth place and its blood
    stained clay hills and crow-filled trees

Most times he was blowin' on the wonderful
    tenor sax of his, preachin' in very cool
    tones, shouting only to remind you of
    a certain point in his blue messages
He was our president as well as the minister
    of soul stirring Jazz, he knew what he
    blew, and he did what a prez should do,
    wail, wail, wail. There were many of
    them to follow him and most of them were
    fair—but they never spoke so eloquently
    in so a far out funky air.
Our prez done died, he know'd this would come
    but death has only booked him, alongside
    Bird, Art Tatum, and other heavenly wailers.
Angels of Jazz—they don't die—they live
they live—in hipsters like you and I

Voice in the Crowd / Ted Joans

If you should see/a man/walking
    down a crowded street/ talking aloud/ to himself
    don't run/in the opposite direction
        but run toward him/for he is a *poet!*

        You have nothing to fear/from the poet
        but the truth

Harlem Sounds: Hallelujah Corner / WILLIAM BROWNE

Cymbals clash,
and in this scene
of annulled jazz,
gay-stepping stompers
roll in
shouting 'Hallelujah'
at a deposed 'Spirit'
until,
like a mimic-child,
it rages,
stumbles,
and lies exhausted,
strung like Jesus.

The honky-tonk
riffs,
runs,
and breaks,
are superimposed
on the sounds
of
weeping
amens.

The mandrill sounds
of tuba snorts,
coned by applauding tambourines;
laugh
at the banjo-dance
of amen-women
shouting
at the
boogie-woogie
voice
of God.

The Voyage of Jimmy Poo / James A. Emanuel

A soapship went a-rocking
Upon a bathtub sea.
The sailor crouched a-smiling
Upon a dimpled knee.

Young Neptune dashed the waters
Against enamel shore,
And kept the air a-tumbling
With bubble-clouds galore.

But soon the voyage ended.
The ship was swept away
By a hand that seemed to whisper
"There'll be no more games today."

The ship lay dry and stranded
On a shiny metal tray,
And a voice was giving orders
That a sailor must obey.

Oh captain, little captain,
Make room for just one more
The next time you go sailing
Beyond enamel shore.

The Treehouse / James A. Emanuel

To every man
His treehouse,
A green splice in the humping years,

174

Spartan with narrow cot
And prickly door.

To every man
His twilight flash
Of luminous recall

   of tiptoe years
   in leaf-stung flight;
   of days of squirm and bite
   that waved antennas through the grass;
   of nights
   when every moving thing
   was girlshaped,
   expectantly turning.

To every man
His house below
And his house above—
With perilous stairs
Between.

Get Up, Blues / JAMES A. EMANUEL

Blues
Never climb a hill
Or sit on a roof
In starlight.

Blues
Just bend low
And moan in the street
And shake a borrowed cup.

Blues
Just sit around
Sipping,
Hatching yesterdays.

Get up, Blues.
Fly.
Learn what it means
To be up high.

Four Sheets to the Wind and a One-Way Ticket to France, 1933 / CONRAD KENT RIVERS

As a Black Child I was a dreamer
I bought a red scarf and women told me how
Beautiful it looked.
Wandering through the heart of France
As France wandered through me.

In the evenings,
I would watch the funny people make love,
My youth allowed me the opportunity to hear
All those strange
Verbs conjugated in erotic affirmations,
I knew love at twelve.

When Selassie went before his peers and
Africa gained dignity
I read in two languages, not really caring
Which one belonged to me.

My mother lit a candle for King George,
My father went broke, we died.
When I felt blue, the champs understood,

And when it was crowded, the alley
Behind Harry's New York bar soothed my
Restless spirit.

I liked to watch the Bohemians gaze at the
Paintings along Gauguin's bewildered paradise.

Bracque once passed me in front of the Café Musique
I used to watch those sneaky professors examine
The populace,
American never quite fitted in, but they
Tried, so we smiled.

I guess the money was too much for my folks,
Hitler was such a prig and a scare, they caught
The last boat.
        I stayed.

Main street was never the same, I read Gide
And tried to
Translate Proust. (Now nothing is real except
French wine.)
For absurdity is reality, my loneliness unreal,

And I shall die an old Parisian, with much honor.

To Richard Wright / CONRAD KENT RIVERS

You said that your people
Never knew the full spirit of
Western Civilization.
To be born unnoticed
Is to be born black,
And left out of the grand adventure.

Miseducation, denial,
Are lost in the cruelty of oppression.
And the faint cool kiss of sensuality
Lingers on our cheeks.

The quiet terror brings on silent night.
They are driving us crazy. And our father's
Religion warps his life.

To live day by day
    Is not to live at all.

Preface to a Twenty Volume Suicide Note
LeRoi Jones
(For Kellie Jones, born 16 May 1959)

Lately, I've become accustomed to the way
The ground opens up and envelops me
Each time I go out to walk the dog.
Or the broad-edged silly music the wind
Makes when I run for a bus . . .

Things have come to that.

And now, each night I count the stars,
And each night I get the same number.
And when they will not come to be counted,
I count the holes they leave.

Nobody sings anymore.

And then last night, I tiptoed up
To my daughter's room and heard her
Talking to someone, and when I opened

The door, there was no one there . . .
Only she on her knees, peeking into

Her own clasped hands.

The Invention of Comics / LeRoi Jones

I am a soul in the world: in
the world of my soul the whirled
light from the day
the sacked land
of my father.

In the world, the sad
nature of
myself. In myself
nature is sad. Small
prints of the day. Its
small dull fires. Its
sun, like a greyness
smeared on the dark.

The day of my soul, is
the nature of that
place. It is a landscape. Seen
from the top of a hill. A
grey expanse; dull fires
throbbing on its seas.

The man's soul, the complexion
of his life. The menace
of its greyness. The
fire, throbs, the sea
moves. Birds shoot

from the dark. The edge
of the waters lit
darkly for the moon.

And the moon, from the soul. Is
the world, of the man. The man
and his sea, and its moon, and
the soft fire throbbing. Kind
death. O
my dark and sultry
love.

As a Possible Lover / LeRoi Jones

Practices
silence, the way of wind
bursting
its early lull. Cold morning
to night, we go so
slowly, without
thought
to ourselves. (Enough
to have thought
tonight, nothing
finishes it. What
you are, will have
no certainty, or
end. That you will
stay, where you are,
a human gentle wisp
of life. Ah . . .)
          practices

loneliness,
as a virtue. A single
specious need
to keep
what you have
never really
had.

The End of Man Is His Beauty / LEROI JONES

And silence
which proves but
a referent
to my disorder.
               Your world shakes

cities die
beneath your shape.
               The single shadow

at noon
like a live tree
whose leaves
are like clouds

weightless soul
at whose love faith moves
as a dark and
withered day.

They speak of singing who
have never heard song; of living
whose deaths are legends
for their kind.

A scream
gathered in wet fingers
at the top of its stalk.
—They have passed
and gone
whom you thought your lovers

In this perfect quiet, my friend,
their shapes
are not unlike
night's

Celebrated Return / CLARENCE MAJOR

1. a circus of battieships carrying heavy laughter passes beneath a bridge which may be lifted and each has been assigned a draft and thus lifted but those laughing were ficti-
   tious representatives of the human race no matter how more
   harmonious they were they had just left the land where
   dromedaries are plenty and men go in droll groups in robes
   with beards but their laughter was an excavated kind of shelter from the dubious plight of anger.

2. ashore gawky measures of folk of the nature of insubstan-
   tiality waited in dull booming upon the science of the earth
   for the circus of mirth which now pushed the waves forward
   as the battleships of embellishment encircled the geometry
   of the solid sunstruck people shouting now at last.

   Gloria in Excelsis
   Gloria in Excelsis
   Gloria in Excelsis
   > Gloria Patri
   > Gloria Patri
   > Gloria Patri

No Time for Poetry / JULIA FIELDS

Midnight is no time for
Poetry—
　　The heart is much too
calm
　　The spirit too lagging
　　and dull—
But the morning!
With the sunshine in one's eyes
and breath—
And all the pink clouds
Like chiffon in a dressing gown
And the orange-white mists
That leap and furl—

Ah, I should greet the morning
　　As though I never saw a morning before
And only heard that it
　　was this or that,
Gossip that was good either way,
There being nothing derogatory to say.

And in that strange-white mist
I'd be content to go upon the paths
with neither shoes nor hat
winding my way away from home
much like a
　　cornerless cat
Holding vibrations of laughter in my
Fur
　　That floated from who knows where
　　and goes who-less-could-care.

There are no orange-white mists
　　at midnight
　　They are a world away
　　And so
　　Midnight is not time for Poetry

The Bishop of Atlanta: Ray Charles /
HORACE JULIAN BOND

The Bishop seduces the world with his voice
Sweat strangles mute eyes
As insinuations gush out through a hydrant of sorrow
Dreams, a world never seen
Moulded on Africa's anvil, tempered down home
Documented in cries and wails
Screaming to be ignored, crooning to be heard
Throbbing from the gutter
On Saturday night
Silver offering only
The Right Reverend's back in town
Don't it make you feel all right?

Two Jazz Poems / CARL WENDELL HINES, JR.

#

yeah here am i
am standing
at the crest of a tallest
hill with a trumpet
in my hand & dark
glasses
on.
   bearded & bereted i proudly stand!
     but there are no eyes to see me.
   i send down cool sounds!
     but there are no ears to hear me.

184

my lips they quiver in aether-emptiness!
there are no hearts to love me.
surely though through night's grey fog mist
of delusion & dream
& the rivers of tears that flow
like gelatin soul-juice
some apathetic bearer of
paranoidic peyote visions (or some
other source of inspiration) shall
hear the song i play. shall
see the beard & beret. shall
become inflamed beyond all hope
with emotion's everlasting fire
& join me
in
eternal
Peace.
& but yet well
who knows?

#

there he stands. see?
like a black Ancient Mariner his
wrinkled old face so
full of the wearies of living is
turned downward with
closed eyes. his frayed-collar
faded-blue old shirt turns
dark with sweat & the old
necktie undone drops
loosely about the worn
old jacket see? just
barely holding his
sagging stomach in. yeah.
his run-down shoes have
paper in them & his
rough unshaven face shows

pain
in each wrinkle.

but there he stands. in
self-brought solitude head
still down eyes
still closed ears
perked & trained upon
the bass line for
across his chest lies an old
alto saxophone—
supported from his neck by
a wire coat hanger.

gently he lifts it now
to parted lips. see? to
tell all the world that
he is a Black Man. that
he was sent here to preach
the Black Gospel of Jazz.

now preaching it with words of
screaming notes & chords he
is no longer a man. no not even
a Black Man. but (yeah!)
a Bird!—
one that gathers his wings & flies
   high
      high
         higher
until he flies away! or
comes back to find himself
a Black Man
again.

Cocoa Morning / BOB KAUFMAN

Variations on a theme by morning,
Two lady birds move in the distance.
Gray jail looming, bathed in sunlight.
Violin tongues whispering.

Drummer, hummer, on the floor,
Dreaming of wild beats, softer still,
Yet free of violent city noise,
Please, sweet morning,
Stay here forever.

I Have Folded My Sorrows / BOB KAUFMAN

I have folded my sorrows into the mantle of summer night,
Assigning each brief storm its allotted space in time,
Quietly pursuing catastrophic histories buried in my eyes.
And yes, the world is not some unplayed Cosmic Game,
And the sun is still ninety-three million miles from me,
And in the imaginary forest, the shingled hippo becomes
        the gay unicorn.
No, my traffic is not with addled keepers of yesterday's
        disasters,
Seekers of manifest disembowelment on shafts of yesterday's
        pains.
Blues come dressed like introspective echoes of a journey.
And yes, I have searched the rooms of the moon on cold
        summer nights.
And yes, I have refought those unfinished encounters.
        Still, they remain unfinished.
And yes, I have at times wished myself something different.

The tragedies are sung nightly at the funerals of the poet;
The revisited soul is wrapped in the aura of familiarity.

African Dream / BOB KAUFMAN

In black core of night, it explodes
Silver thunder, rolling back my brain,
Bursting copper screens, memory worlds
Deep in star-fed beds of time,
Seducing my soul to diamond fires of night.
Faint outline, a ship—momentary fright
Lifted on waves of color,
Sunk in pits of light,
Drummed back through time,
Hummed back through mind,
Drumming, cracking the night.
Strange forest songs, skin sounds
Crashing through—no longer strange.
Incestuous yellow flowers tearing
Magic from the earth.
Moon-dipped rituals, led
By a scarlet god,
Caressed by ebony maidens
With daylight eyes,
Purple garments,
Noses that twitch,
Singing young girl songs
Of an ancient love
In dark, sunless places
Where memories are sealed,
Burned in eyes of tigers.

Suddenly wise, I fight the dream:
Green screams enfold my night.

Battle Report / BOB KAUFMAN

One thousand saxophones infiltrate the city,
Each with a man inside,
Hidden in ordinary cases,
Labeled FRAGILE.

A fleet of trumpets drops their hooks,
Inside at the outside.

Ten waves of trombones approach the city
Under blue cover
Of late autumn's neoclassical clouds.

Five hundred bassmen, all string feet tall,
Beating it back to the bass.

One hundred drummers, each a stick in each hand,
The delicate rumble of pianos, moving in.

The secret agent, an innocent bystander,
Drops a note in the wail box.

Five generals, gathered in the gallery,
Blowing plans.

At last, the secret code is flashed:
Now is the time, now is the time.

Attack: The sound of jazz.

The city falls.

Forget to Not / BOB KAUFMAN

Remember, poet, while gallivanting across the sky,
Skylarking, shouting, calling names . . . Walk softly.

Your footprint on rain clouds is visible to naked eyes,
Lamps barnacled to your feet refract the mirrored air.

Exotic scents of your hidden vision fly in the face of time.

Remember not to forget the dying colors of yesterday
As you inhale tomorrow's hot dream, blown from frozen lips.

Remember, you naked agent of every nothing.

Hearing James Brown at the Café des Nattes (Sidi-bou-Saïd, Tunisia) / RICHARD A. LONG

Yes, brother your word had come
                              Don't want nobody
                              Give me nuthin
Crowning this hilltop, long ago's lighthouse
                              Open up the do'
                              Git it myself
Your word comes, thanks to God and Marconi
To this eyrie where I sit
Mint tea before, serenaded by caged birds
And the undulating arias of Arabia,
Her last vestige of empire.

In waves, over the waves it comes
                              Don't want nobody
Mingling with birdsong and arabesques
                              Give me nuthin

Floating over an Andalusian mise en scène
(I remember Cordova)
                              Open up the do'
It pierces the blanched housetops, the waiting sea
                              Git it myself

You moan, Dido plunges into the flames
You groan, Hannibal embarks
You shriek, Cato's vow is fulfilled
You sigh, the sea roars beside a silent shore

Flaring into this moment
Your voice, snatched from beyond Sahara's sands
Crosses the western sea, enters familiarly
This concatenation of Africa's time
Flavoring mint, infusing birdsong, merging into the endless
vocalize.

Juan de Pareja: Painted by Velázquez

/ RICHARD A. LONG

(IN MEMORY OF ALAIN LOCKE)

Amused contempt, is it, that scintillates
        From your velvet domain
Or contempt for the bemused who throng
        The dim ascetic space?

Under the scrutiny of brown eyes and blue
        You view Rome's seven hills
Thinking, perhaps, of vacant yellow sands
        undulant, limitless.

Though chaotic and obscure the furies
        Who decree your present part,

191

Though anguished and confused the hungry eyes
  Feeding upon your flesh,
You mediate the sordid encounter,
  Osculant, putrid, rank
And regard, serene, the ceaseless discourse
  Of wisdom and folly.

If You Come Softly / AUDRE LORDE

If you come as softly
As wind within the trees
You may hear what I hear
See what sorrow sees.

If you come as lightly
As threading dew
I will take you gladly
Nor ask more of you.

You may sit beside me
Silent as a breath
Only those who stay dead
Shall remember death.

And if you come I will be silent
Nor speak harsh words to you.
I will not ask you why now.
Or how, or what you do.

We shall sit here, softly
Beneath two different years
And the rich earth between us
Shall drink our tears.

Young Negro Poet / CALVIN C. HERNTON

Young Negro poet
came from 'way down South,
Tennessee, to be exact,
    thought he had some verse,
    thought he could write,
    real well
    as a matter of fact.

Young Negro poet
came from 'way down South
up North,
New York City,
    found that he had no verse,
    couldn't write so well,
    folks back home had lied—
    what a pity, what a pity.

Young Negro poet
came from 'way down South
just to sleep on the cold ground,
Central Park,
to be exact . . .

        Wake up o jack-legged poet!
        Wake up o dark boy from 'way down South!
        Wake up out of Central Park, and walk
            through Harlem street.

        Walk down Seventh Avenue, Eighth,
        Madison, Lenox, and St. Nicholas,
        walk all around—
            it's morning in Harlem.

        Wake up jack-legged poet!
        Wake up dark boy from 'way down South!
        Wake up out of Central Park—
        wash your face in the fountain water,

take a long stretch,
light up a cigarette butt, and walk defiantly
through the streets of Harlem town.

Affirmation / HELEN ARMSTEAD JOHNSON

Barren cross-ties of penny-whistle twigs
Mating and parting as the wind
Beats the rhythm of sad songs
With black shafts once hung in gold.
Basketweave tears of ancestral black
Fall in arcs as the ruthless sun
Seeks the heart warm with traces
Which now the snow paints in crushing white.
But upward thrusts defy the requiem
And glisten in black affirmation
Of orchestrated songs to be sung tomorrow.

Philodendron / HELEN ARMSTEAD JOHNSON

I watch the calligraphy of shadows
Transform the evening wall
As the soft wind from the windows
Wafts secret patterns
To the split green leaves
Whose veins are only candle bright.

194

The ribless shapes
Join and cross,
Draining from memory
Other veinless, once green forms
That joined and crossed
Before eroding days
Etched split green patterns,
Which even now
Inform the evening wall
In candlelight.

Woman with Flower / Naomi Long Madgett

I wouldn't coax the plant if I were you.
Such watchful nurturing may do it harm.
Let the soil rest from so much digging
And wait until it's dry before you water it.
The leaf's inclined to find its own direction;
Give it a chance to seek the sunlight for itself.

Much growth is stunted by too careful prodding,
Too eager tenderness.
The things we love we have to learn to leave alone.

Good Times / LUCILLE CLIFTON

My Daddy has paid the rent
and the insurance man is gone
and the lights is back on
and my uncle Brud has hit
for one dollar straight
and they is good times
good times
good times

My Mama has made bread
and Grampaw has come
and everybody is drunk
and dancing in the kitchen
and singing in the kitchen
oh these is good times
good times
good times

oh children think about the
good times

Malcolm X—An Autobiography / LARRY NEAL

I am the Seventh Son of the Son
who was also the Seventh.
I have drunk deep of the waters of my ancestors
have travelled the soul's journey towards cosmic harmony
the Seventh Son.
Have walked slick avenues
and seen grown men, fall, to die in a blue doom

of death and ancestral agony,
have seen old men glide, shadowless, feet barely
touching the pavements.

I sprung out of the Midwestern plains
the bleak Michigan landscape, the black blues of Kansas
City, the kiss-me-nights.
out of the bleak Michigan landscape wearing the slave name—
Malcolm Little.
Saw a brief vision in Lansing, when I was seven, and in
my mother's womb heard the beast cry of death,
a landscape on which white robed figures ride, and my
Garvey father silhouetted against the night-fire, gun in hand,
form outlined against a panorama of violence.

Out of the Midwestern bleakness, I sprang, pushed eastward,
past shack on country nigger shack, across the wilderness
of North America.

I hustler. I pimp. I unfulfilled black man
bursting with destiny.
New York City Slim called me Big Red,
and there was no escape, close nights of the smell of death.
Pimp. hustler. The day fills these rooms.
I am talking about New York. Harlem.
talking about the neon madness.
talking about ghetto eyes and nights
about death protruding across the room. Small's paradise.
talking about cigarette butts, and rooms smelly with white
sex flesh, and dank sheets, and being on the run.

talking about cocaine illusions, about stealing and selling.
talking about these New York cops who smell of blood and
        money.
I am Big Red, tiger vicious, Big Red, bad nigger, will kill.

But there is rhythm here. Its own special substance:
I hear Billie sing, no good man, and dig Prez, wearing the
        Zoot

suit of life—the porkpie hat tilted at the correct angle.
through the Harlem smoke of beer and whiskey, I understand
the
mystery of the signifying monkey,
in a blue haze of inspiration, I reach to the totality of Being.
I am at the center of a swirl of events. War and death.
rhythm. hot women. I think life a commodity bargained for
across the bar in Small's.
I perceive the echoes of Bird and there is a gnawing in the
maw
of my emotions.
and then there is jail. America is the world's greatest jailer,
and we all in jails. black spirits contained like magnificent
birds of wonder. I now understand my father urged on by the
ghost of Garvey,
and see a small brown man standing in a corner. The cell.
cold.
dank. The light around him vibrates. Am I crazy? But to
under-
stand is to submit to a more perfect will, a more perfect order.
To understand is to surrender the imperfect self
for a more perfect self.

Allah formed brown man, I follow
and shake within the very depth of my most imperfect being,
and I bear witness to the Message of Allah
and I bear witness—all praise is due Allah!

But He Was Cool
or: he even stopped for green lights
DON L. LEE

super-cool
ultrablack
a tan/purple
had a beautiful shade.

he had a double-natural
that wd put the sisters to shame.
his dashikis were tailor made
& his beads were imported sea shells
    (from some blk/country i never heard of)
he was triple-hip.

his tikis were hand carved
out of ivory
& came express from the motherland.
he would greet u in swahili
& say good-by in yoruba.
wooooooooooooo-jim he bes so cool & ill tel li gent
        cool-cool is so cool he was un-cooled by
              other niggers' cool
        cool-cool ultracool was bop-cool/ice box
              cool so cool cold cool
        his wine didn't have to be cooled, him was
              air conditioned cool
        cool-cool/real cool made me cool—now
              ain't that cool
        cool-cool so cool him nick-named refrigerator.

cool-cool so cool
he didn't know,

after detroit, newark, chicago &c.,
we had to hip
        cool-cool/ super-cool/ real cool
   that

to be black
is
to be
very-hot.

Assassination / DON L. LEE

it was wild.
the
bullet hit high.
                    (the throat-neck)
& from everywhere:
        the motel, from under bushes and cars,
        from around corners and across streets,
        out of the garbage cans and from rat holes
        in the earth
they came running
with
guns
drawn
they came running
toward the King—
                    all of them
                    fast and sure—
as if
the King
was going to fire back.
they came running,
fast and sure,
in the
wrong
direction.

Education / Don L. Lee

I had a good teacher,
He taught me everything I know;
how to lie,
    cheat,
       and how to strike the softest blow.

My teacher thought himself to be wise and right
He taught me things most people consider nice;
    such as to pray,
        smile,
          and how not to fight.

My teacher taught me other things too,
Things that I will be forever looking at;
    how to berate,
       segregate,
        and how to be inferior without hate.

My teacher's wisdom forever grows,
He taught me things every child will know;
    how to steal,
       appeal,
        and accept most things against my will.

All these acts take as facts,
The mistake was made in teaching me
How not to be BLACK.

Stereo / Don L. Lee

I can clear a beach or swimming pool without
    touching water.
I can make a lunch counter become deserted
    in less than an hour.
I can make property value drop by being seen
    in a realtor's tower.
I ALONE can make the word of God have little
    or no meaning to many
    in Sunday morning's prayer hour.
I have Power.
BLACK POWER.

My Poem / Nikki Giovanni

i am 25 years old
black female poet
wrote a poem asking
nigger can you kill
if they kill me
it won't stop
the revolution

i have been robbed
it looked like they knew
that i was to be hit
they took my tv
my two rings
my piece of african print
and my two guns

if they take my life
it won't stop
the revolution

my phone is tapped
my mail is opened
they've caused me to turn
on all my old friends
and all my new lovers
if i hate all black
people
and all negroes
it won't stop
the revolution

i'm afraid to tell
my roommate where i'm going
and scared to tell
people if i'm coming
if i sit here
for the rest
of my life
it won't stop
the revolution

                    if i never write
                    another poem
                    or short story
                    if i flunk out
                    of grad school
                    if my car is reclaimed
                    and my record player
                    won't play
                    and if i never see
                    a peaceful day
                    or do a meaningful
                    black thing
                    it won't stop
                    the revolution

the revolution
is in the streets
and if i stay on
the 5th floor
it will go on

Nikki-Rosa / NIKKI GIOVANNI

childhood remembrances are always a drag
if you're Black
you always remember things like living in Woodlawn
with no inside toilet
and if you become famous or something
they never talk about how happy you were to have your
      mother
all to yourself and
how good the water felt when you got your bath from one of
      those
big tubs that folk in Chicago barbecue in
and somehow when you talk about home
it never gets across how much you
understood their feelings
as the whole family attended meetings about Hollydale
and even though you remember
your biographers never understand
your father's pain as he sells his stock
and another dream goes
and though you're poor it isn't poverty that
concerns you
and though they fought a lot
it isn't your father's drinking that makes any difference
but only that everybody is together and you

and your sister have happy birthdays and very good
      christmases
and I really hope no white person ever has cause to write
      about me
because they never understand Black love is Black wealth and
      they'll
probably talk about my hard childhood and never understand
      that
all the while I was quite happy

Knoxville, Tennessee / NIKKI GIOVANNI

I always like summer
best
you can eat fresh corn
from daddy's garden
and okra
and greens
and cabbage
and lots of
barbecue
and buttermilk
and homemade ice-cream
at the church picnic
and listen to
gospel music
outside
at the church
homecoming
and go to the mountains with
your grandmother
and go barefooted

and be warm
all the time
not only when you go to bed
and sleep

The Funeral of Martin Luther King, Jr.
NIKKI GIOVANNI

His headstone said
FREE AT LAST, FREE AT LAST
But death is a slave's freedom
We seek the freedom of free men
And the construction of a world
Where Martin Luther King could have lived and
    preached non-violence

Kidnap Poem / NIKKI GIOVANNI

ever been kidnapped
by a poet
if i were a poet
i'd kidnap you
put you in my phrases and meter
you to jones beach
or maybe coney island
or maybe just to my house

lyric you in lilacs
dash you in the rain
blend into the beach
to complement my sea
play the lyre for you
ode you with my love song
anything to win you
wrap you in the red Black green
show you off to mama
yeah if i were a poet i'd kid
nap you

A Robin's Poem / NIKKI GIOVANNI

if you plant grain
you get fields of flour
if you plant seeds
you get grass
or babies
i planted once
and a robin red breast flew
in my window
but a tom cat wouldn't let it
stay

No Smiles / FRANK LAMONT PHILLIPS

We are with one another
sometimes
and there are no smiles
no easy togetherness
only one and one
against the grain
we speak
sometimes and
nothing
is said
but where we are
apart
there is longing
and pain
like arguments within
ourselves
that will not end

Genealogy / FRANK LAMONT PHILLIPS

The magnolia trees
that blossom in summer sun
on summer days
in the south
have my mother's name
written
on each leaf
where her hands
touched saplings that tore

my back
long ago in summer heat
after day
when mama bent
over cotton plant
and sang
in fields where her
mama had worked
before she was born
and had sung
songs too
full of grief for tears

Maryuma / FRANK LAMONT PHILLIPS

at seventeen your
thoughts were younger
than your face
and your smile
mirrored in dishwater
was mississippi pleasant
you had large eyes
and larger hopes of marrying
somebody rich
or famous or something
you settled for a little house
so close to the tracks
that the sound of a train shook
some of everything
you settled for a boy
with eyes larger than
your own

you settled for dishwater
just as deep
as that you knew
at home

And She Was Bad / Marvin Wyche, Jr.

she slid past
so fly & outtasight
that whistles
didn't phase her
her strut putting   roosters
to shame
had a keyhole figure
that would open any door
had knobs
that would turn any head
she was   bad   jack
awww she was fly

she had the brown   est of eyes
matching a smooth ebony complexion
glimpsed now and then
through tons of cream-style
makeup
her dress was mini's mammy
revealed   beaucoup booty
and her stockings changed colors
every five miles.
she was decorated in
silver-dipped jew els
imported from
                    jap—an

her fingernails
were miniature
rainbows
man she was up on   all
the latest fashions
cause she was bad
yeah she was fly

her afro wig
was shaped
to bring out its fullll
        naturalness???
her lips were painted by
max factor   himself

myself
scoped her   and said:

        hey sister
        like whuss your name?

and she looked around
to see if my   SISTER

was as bad
as she was

We Rainclouds / Marvin Wyche, Jr.

        black people, we rainclouds

        closer to the sun and full of life.
        soaking up the knowledge of the earth
                                        and

storing it within ourselves

                             moving on
to spread truth throughout the world

we black clouds.
loved and feared.
ready to explode and give new life
to a dying planet

beautiful dark clouds
casting shadows of blackness
shadows of dignity
shadows of

                          love

giving of ourselves to promote life

                                while

realizing our ability to destroy

rainclouds
           we are
nature
nature
nature

natural!!!
black people, we rainclouds

closer to the sun and full of life

Leslie / Marvin Wyche, Jr.

that same look.
eyes wide in puzzlement
confusion.

you wonder why
i act the way
i do
and i wonder
why
you think i'm acting

Five Sense / MARVIN WYCHE, JR.

morning.
and she awoke to
see
the same sameness:
      basement bedroom
      dusty mirror
      scattered cosmetics

      half empty double bed

she awoke   to
smell
the plastic flowers
on the dresser
(a gift of an ancient anniversary)
and her memories
became
tears   defiantly tracing
her
swelling
brown
cheeks

213

she awoke
to   hear
herself cussing
cussing
a nickel hearted absence
sour/sweet thought
that
nickel hearted
absence
she awoke
to   taste
the bitter loneliness
of life
without her man

morning.
and she awoke
to   feel

forgotten

BIOGRAPHICAL NOTES

SAMUEL ALLEN (1917–   ) was one of James Weldon Johnson's students of creative writing at Fisk University. He also attended Harvard Law School and has studied at the Sorbonne in Paris, where Richard Wright discovered his poetry and had it published in *Présence Africaine*. A collection of his poems, *Elfenbein Zänne* (*Ivory Tusks*), signed Paul Vesey, was brought out in 1956 by Wolfgang Rothe Verlag in Heidelberg. Allen has been connected with the Legal Department of the United States Information Agency and has taught at Tuskegee Institute in Alabama and Wesleyan University in Connecticut. At present, he is a professor in the Afro-American Studies Program at Boston University and has recently compiled an anthology of African poetry. His other publications include *Poems* and *Voice Not Our Own*.

RUSSELL ATKINS (1926–   ) has had poems in avant-garde journals since the forties. He still lives in Cleveland, Ohio, the city where he was born and educated, and he presently edits *Free Lance*.

GWENDOLYN B. BENNETT, born in Giddings, Texas, attended elementary school in Washington, D.C., before moving on to Girls' High School in Brooklyn, New York, where she was graduated in 1921. Subsequently, she studied at Columbia University and at Brooklyn's Pratt Institute. An early interest in the fine arts also led to study at the Académie Julian and the École de Panthéon in Paris.

HORACE JULIAN BOND (1940–   ), lives in Atlanta, Georgia, as did his late father, Dr. Horace Mann Bond. He took an active part in the student movement that was responsible for sit-ins and other attacks on segregation in his home city, which casts a sidelight on his often-quoted couplet:

> Look at that gal shake that thing—
> We can't all be Martin Luther King.

Since that campaign, he has won a seat in the Georgia Legislature, had it denied him, had the denial overruled; and has had his name placed in nomination for Vice-President of the United States, even though he was too young to qualify. His most recent book was *A Time to Speak, A Time to Act,* published by Simon and Schuster in 1972.

ARNA BONTEMPS (1902–73) was editor of *Golden Slippers,* an anthology of Negro poetry for young people, and co-editor with Langston Hughes of *The Poetry of the Negro: 1746–1949.* His own poetry appeared in magazines between 1924 and 1931. His most recent books of prose include *The Harlem Renaissance Remembered* (1972), *Young Booker*

(1972), and *The Old South: "A Summer Tragedy" and Other Stories of the Thirties* (1973). He also wrote a number of books for children and was librarian at Fisk University for many years.

WILLIAM STANLEY BRAITHWAITE (1878–1962) was born in Boston, of West Indian parents. His career as a poet began in 1904 with the publication of *Lyrics of Life and Love*. A second volume, *The House of Falling Leaves*, followed two years later. In 1946, his *Selected Poems* appeared. Between 1913 and 1929 Braithwaite edited an annual *Anthology of Magazine Verse* and presented the work of American poets such as Edgar Lee Masters, Vachel Lindsay, and Carl Sandburg before they were widely recognized. He also edited other general anthologies and served on the editorial staff of the *Boston Transcript*.

GWENDOLYN BROOKS (1917–), awarded the Pulitzer Prize for poetry in 1949 after the publication of *Annie Allen*, has since written fiction as well as verse for children and more poetry. Her first collection, *A Street in Bronzeville*, was published in 1945; *The Bean Eaters* in 1961. She read her poems for the National Poetry Festival at the Library of Congress in 1962. She won the Friends Literary Award for Poetry in 1964 and in 1970 taught poetry at Northeastern Illinois State College; Columbia College, Chicago; and Elmhurst College, Elmhurst, Illinois. She is the Poet Laureate of Illinois, succeeding Carl Sandburg. Her most recent works include *Jump Bad: A New Chicago Anthology* and *The World of Gwendolyn Brooks*, both published in 1971.

JONATHAN BROOKS (1904–45) and his widowed mother worked a share-croppers' farm in Mississippi until he was fourteen, when he began the uphill struggle for an education. When he died in 1945, he was working in the post office at Corinth. *The Resurrection and Other Poems*, his only book, was published posthumously.

STERLING A. BROWN (1901–) has had a distinguished career as a member of the faculty of Howard University. Educated in the schools of Washington, D.C., and at Williams College and Harvard University, he taught at Fisk University and Lincoln University in Missouri before beginning the long association with Howard which led to his selection in 1961 to write a history of that university. His published books include *Southern Road*, 1932, a volume of poetry; *The Negro in American Fiction*, 1938; and *Negro Poetry and Drama*, 1938. He served as senior editor of *Negro Caravan*, first published in 1941 and revised in 1969.

WILLIAM BROWNE was born in New York, where he now lives. A student of clinical psychology, he has traveled widely, worked at many jobs, and occasionally published poems in the *Pittsburgh Courier*.

CATHERINE CATER (1917–), daughter of a college dean, holds academic degrees from Talladega College in Alabama and the University of Michigan. She has been a librarian and a professor of English.

MARCUS B. CHRISTIAN (1900–), a self-educated printer-poet and Louisiana history buff, wrote for the Negro History Unit of the Federal Writers' Project in New Orleans. His poems and articles have appeared in anthologies and periodicals, and a book, *High Ground,* was printed on his own press in New Orleans in 1958, commemorating the U.S. Supreme Court's decision of May 17, 1954. His latest book is *Negro Ironworkers of Louisiana,* published in 1972.

LUCILLE CLIFTON (1936–   ) was born in Depew, New York, and attended Howard University in Washington, D.C., and Fredonia State Teachers College. She is married and the mother of six children. Her collection of poems, *Good Times* (1969), includes some poems previously published in *The Massachusetts Review.* She has also written *Some of the Days of Everett Anderson* (1970), *Good News About the Earth* (1972), and *Everett Anderson's Christmas Coming* (1972).

LESLIE M. COLLINS (1914–   ), born in Alexandria, Louisiana, was educated by the Sisters of St. James before he attended Straight College and Dillard University in New Orleans. He holds advanced degrees from Fisk and Western Reserve universities and taught for eight years before joining the English faculty at Fisk in 1945.

COUNTEE CULLEN's (1903–46) literary talents developed in the parsonage of a large church in Harlem. Reared by foster parents, he won poetry prizes as well as scholastic honors at Dewitt Clinton High School and at New York University. Before graduating in 1925, he had already had poems published in leading magazines and his first book, *Color,* had appeared. A graduate degree from Harvard followed. Then in 1927 two more collections of poetry were published, *Copper Sun* and *The Ballad of the Brown Girl. The Black Christ* (1929) was written in France on a Guggenheim Fellowship. His other books include *One Way to Heaven* (1932), a novel; *The Medea and Other Poems* (1935); *The Lost Zoo* (1940); *My Nine Lives and How I Lost Them* (1942); and *On These I Stand,* which appeared posthumously in 1947. Cullen edited *Caroling Dusk* (1927), an anthology of American Negro poetry, and collaborated with Arna Bontemps in the dramatization of *St. Louis Woman,* from Bontemps's novel, *God Sends Sunday* (1931).

WARING CUNEY (1906–   ) attended schools and conservatories in Washington, D.C., his birthplace, and Pennsylvania, Boston, and Rome. While he was still a student at Lincoln University, his "No Images" won a national poetry contest. It was widely reprinted in 1926 and has often been anthologized, as have some of his later poems. Several of his poems of protest, sung by Josh White, have been recorded and issued as an album under the title *Southern Exposure.*

MARGARET DANNER (1915–   ), who now lives and works in Detroit, was born in Pryorsburg, Kentucky, but has spent the greater part of her life in Chicago, where she was at one time associated with *Poetry: The Magazine of Verse.* A selection of her poems appearing in that magazine prompted the John Hay Whitney Opportunity Fellowships Committee to offer her a trip to Africa. In 1962 the literary group with which she is associated in Detroit was featured in a special issue of the *Bulletin of Negro History.* She is interested in French and African art, and published a collection of verse in 1968 entitled *Iron Lace.* In that same year she

217

received an award from Poets in Concert, and in 1970 she was poet-in-residence at Virginia Union University in Richmond.

FRANK MARSHALL DAVIS (1905–   ) left a career in journalism, mainly with the Associated Negro Press, for the tropical attractions of Hawaii, where he now lives with his growing family. Three volumes of his free verse (Chicago style) have been published: *Black Man's Verse* (1935), *I Am the American Negro* (1937), and *47th Street* (1948).

CLARISSA SCOTT DELANY (1901–27), beautiful and talented, was a magazine cover girl the year she graduated from Wellesley. She was a teacher in Dunbar High School in Washington, D.C., when she married Hubert Delany in 1926.

OWEN DODSON (1914–   ), head of the Department of Drama at Howard University in Washington, D.C., has been involved with poetry and poetic drama since his own school days. A graduate of Bates College and Yale University, he had two of his plays, *Divine Comedy* and *Garden of Time*, produced at Yale while he was working toward his Fine Arts degree. Others have since been presented on other campuses, and in 1946 a collection of his poems, *Powerful Long Ladder*, was published. In 1967 he received a Doctor of Letters from Bates, and during the spring of 1969 he was poet-in-residence at the University of Arizona. Broadside published his *Confession Stone* in 1970.

ALFRED A. DUCKETT (1918–   ) is a public-relations man in New York and has had broad experience in journalism, with the *Amsterdam News, New York Age,* and *Pittsburgh Courier.* His early poems occasionally reappear in anthologies, and he is the author of *Changing of the Guard: The New Black Breed of Black Politicians,* published by Coward in 1972.

PAUL LAURENCE DUNBAR (1872–1906) was discovered operating an elevator in Dayton, Ohio, in 1893. One might almost say a new era began that year for the American Negro in literary expression. His *Oak and Ivy,* privately printed in 1893, attracted little attention, and his *Majors and Minors* (1895) made a similarly small impression, but together they paved the way for *Lyrics of a Lowly Life* (1896). This book won for the poet a national reputation and enabled him to pursue a literary career for the rest of his life. A Negro poet had not won recognition in the United States in the century and a quarter since the family of John Wheatly of Boston emancipated their slave girl, Phillis, in recognition of her *Poems on Various Subjects, Religious and Moral* (1773). Dunbar's life was short, as was Phillis's: both suffered from tuberculosis. In spite of illness, Dunbar wrote prose as well as poetry in the decade following *Lyrics,* and his *Complete Poems* (1913) has retained a warm appeal for many readers.

JAMES A. EMANUEL's (1921–   ) doctoral dissertation at Columbia University in 1962 was concerned with the short stories of Langston Hughes. Emanuel's poems have appeared in *Phylon* and other magazines and newspapers. He lives with his young family in Westchester County, New York, and teaches at the City College of the City University of New York.

218

His most recent works include *Dark Symphony: Negro Literature in America* (1968), *Treehouse and Other Poems* (1968), and *Panther Man* (1970).

MARI E. EVANS, born and raised in Toledo, Ohio, now lives in Indianapolis, Indiana, where she has worked as a civil-service employee. She was a John Hay Whitney Fellow in 1965–66. Her poetry has appeared extensively in textbooks and anthologies. Producer/director of a weekly half-hour television series, she has also been writer-in-residence and instructor in Black Literature at Indiana University and Purdue University. In 1970 she published *I Am a Black Woman.*

JULIA FIELDS (1938–   ) returned to her native Alabama to teach high school in the steel city of Bessemer after she graduated from Knoxville College in Tennessee. But her first summer vacation after her return was spent in a very different setting—the Bread Loaf Writers' Conference in New England. She published a collection, *Poems,* in 1968, and her work has also appeared in *Massachusetts Review, Riverside Poetry* II, *Beyond the Blues, New Negro Poets,* and *Negro Digest.*

NIKKI GIOVANNI (1943–   ) was born in Knoxville, Tennessee, and educated at Fisk University in Nashville. She has been associated with Rutgers University, has contributed poems to various black publications, has read poems on educational television and published several collections of poetry, including *Black Judgement* (1968). She is also the author of *Gemini* (1972), a volume of prose.

YVONNE GREGORY (1919–   ) frequently contributed poems to the *Fisk Herald* when she was an undergraduate. Since then, her occasional appearances in magazines have all been in prose.

ANGELINA W. GRIMKE (1880–1958) spent the last years of her life in quiet retirement in New York City, but before that she had been for many years a teacher of English in the Washington, D.C., high schools. Her three-act play, *Rachel,* was published in 1921.

ROBERT HAYDEN (1913–   ), born in Detroit, attended Wayne State University and the University of Michigan, where for two years he held a teaching assistantship. In 1938 and again in 1942, he received Avery Hopwood awards for poetry at Michigan; and in 1940 a collection of his poems, *Heartshape in the Dust,* was published in Detroit. In 1946 he joined the faculty of Fisk University, where his teaching was occasionally interrupted by fellowships for creative writing. His poems have appeared in *Poetry, Atlantic Monthly,* and other periodicals and anthologies. A brochure, *The Lion and the Archer* (1948), presented a group of his poems with some of Myron O'Higgins's. *A Ballad of Remembrance* (1962) was published in London and won first prize at the First World Festival of Negro Arts, held in 1965 in Dakar, Senegal. In the United States, he has published *Selected Poems* (1966), *Kaleidoscope* (1967), and *Words in the Mourning Time* (1970). He was visiting professor of English at the University of Michigan in 1968, and at the University of Louisville, Kentucky, in 1969.

DONALD JEFFREY HAYES (1904–   ) has long been interested in music as well as poetry, but beyond high school his education has been gained through private study. He has worked for many years as a counselor with the New Jersey State Employment Service in Atlantic City, where he lives. His poems have appeared in *Harper's Bazaar, Good Housekeeping,* and *This Week,* and some have been set to music.

CALVIN C. HERNTON (1932–   ) is a native of Chattanooga, Tennessee. He studied sociology at Talladega College in Alabama (B.A., 1954) and at Fisk University (M.A., 1965). He has taught at other, previously all-black colleges in the South and has been employed by the New York Welfare Department. His poems were first published in the journal *Phylon* (1954), but he has been writing since his early teens. His prose writings include *Sex and Racism in America* (1965). A book of his poetry appeared in a limited edition in 1964 under the title of *The Coming of Chonos to the House of Nightsong: An Epical Narrative of the South.* Hernton is now teaching in the department of Afro-American Studies at Oberlin College in Ohio.

CARL WENDELL HINES, JR. (1940–   ), had his own jazz combo and played for dances as a student at Tennessee Agricultural and Industrial University, where Wilma Rudolph, Ralph Boston, and other Olympic athletes have studied. Not until he graduated in 1962, however, was his real secret revealed: he had been writing some of the most authentic jazz poetry of this period. He is a native of Wilson, North Carolina, and went to A. & I. to study engineering but switched to science education. He has never studied music formally.

M. CARL HOLMAN (1919–   ) has been president of the National Urban Coalition in Washington, D.C., since 1968. A native of Minter City, Mississippi, Holman spent his youth in St. Louis. He holds academic degrees from Lincoln University in Missouri, the University of Chicago, and Yale University. While at Chicago, he won a Fiske Poetry Prize and was granted a Rosenwald Fellowship for advanced study in creative writing. Since 1949, Holman has taught at Clark College in Atlanta, Atlanta University, and Hampton Institute in Virginia. From 1960 to 1963 he was editor of the *Atlanta Inquirer.* Before joining the Coalition he was a member of the U.S. Commission on Civil Rights.

FRANK HORNE (1899–   ) is a New Yorker. The background of his widely reprinted poem "To James" would seem to be his own experience on the track team of the College of the City of New York. His subsequent career has included graduate and professional studies at the Northern Illinois College of Ophthalmology, Columbia University, and the University of Southern California. As a Doctor of Optometry, he practiced in Chicago and New York. A period of college teaching followed before he began the long and distinguished service in government which earned him prestige as a leading authority on housing. He has contributed to *Opportunity, The Crisis,* and *Carolina* magazines.

LANGSTON HUGHES (1902–67) wrote poetry, plays, and short stories, as well as the *Langston Hughes Reader* and *I Wonder As I Wander: An*

Autobiographical Journey. He began writing poetry as a student at Central High in Cleveland, Ohio, and even before he graduated from Lincoln University in Pennsylvania, he was supporting himself by writing. His public readings of his poetry, which began after the publication of *The Weary Blues,* his first book, in 1926, were always warmly received. Langston Hughes also wrote novels, newspaper columns, books for children, song lyrics, and even works of historical interest, including the story of the NAACP. In fact, books and doctoral dissertations are already being written about him. He held Guggenheim and Rosenwald Fellowships and an American Academy of Arts and Letters grant. The Free Academy of Arts in Hamburg honored him in 1964, and Emperor Haile Selassie of Ethiopia decorated him in 1966. Two of the last books published before his death are *Simple's Uncle Sam* (1965) and *The Sweet Flypaper of Life* (1967).

TED JOANS (1928–   ) was born Theodore Jones on a riverboat at Cairo, Illinois, on July 4, just after the annual street parade ended. Twelve years later to the hour, he recalls, his riverboat-entertainer father put a trumpet in his hands and put him off the boat at Memphis. A wanderer thereafter, Ted somehow managed to stay put long enough to get a degree from Indiana University. In 1951, he says, he "joined the Bohemia of Greenwich Village, U.S.A." His painting and his poetry have been exhibited and published, often in connection with the Beat Generation. His most recent works are *Black Pow-Wow* (1969) and *Afrodisia: New Poems by Ted Joans* (1971).

FENTON JOHNSON (1886–1958) was once a dapper fellow who drove his own electric automobile around Chicago at the end of the first decade of this century. Since he was an only child in a family of some means, he was able to pursue his interest in the arts. One of these was writing and producing plays at the old Pekin Theatre on South State Street. Another was editing and publishing little magazines. More enduring than either of these, however, was his love for poetry. His first collection, *A Little Dreaming,* came out in 1914. *Visions of the Dusk* and other volumes strongly influenced by Paul Laurence Dunbar followed in the next few years. By the twenties, times had changed for the Johnsons, and young Fenton succumbed to a more rugged influence, which showed in his later verse, including the posthumously published *42 WPA Poems.*

GEORGIA DOUGLAS JOHNSON (1886–1966) was born in Atlanta, Georgia. She studied music at Oberlin Conservatory in Ohio but soon gave up her early ambition to become a composer. She had been working as a school teacher when her husband was appointed Recorder of Deeds under President William Howard Taft and they moved to Washington, D.C. Later she was employed in government agencies, but writing became her principal occupation. Published collections of her lyrics include *The Heart of a Woman* (1918), *Bronze* (1922), *An Autumn Love Cycle* (1928), and *Share My World* (1962).

HELEN ARMSTEAD JOHNSON (1920–   ) is a professor of English at York College of the City University of New York. She holds a Ph.D. degree and is a specialist in black-theater history, as indicated by her article

"Black Theater: 1960 and After" in *The Afro-American Reference Book* (1973). She is a Fellow of the School of Letters at Indiana University, and she has received other scholarly recognition as well.

HELENE JOHNSON, born in Boston, was the youngest of the young poets and writers who brought about the Negro renaissance, as it was called in Harlem in the twenties. She contributed to *Opportunity: A Journal of Negro Life, Vanity Fair,* and other magazines.

JAMES WELDON JOHNSON (1871–1938) created "small literary works, unpretentious but remarkably durable, in a variety of forms." His autobiography, *Along This Way* (1933), however, is a large and enlightening work. He often observed that the years of his life seemed to move in cycles of seven, and these included periods of high-school teaching and administration, diplomatic service as a U.S. Consul in Latin America, an exciting seven years as a lyricist on Broadway, a notable span as Executive Secretary of the National Association for the Advancement of Colored People, and a final phase as professor of Creative Literature at Fisk University. But poetry was the thread that pulled all of them together. Johnson was born in Jacksonville, Florida. His books of poetry include *Fifty Years and Other Poems* (1917), *God's Trombones* (1927), and *St. Peter Relates an Incident* (1930).

LEROI JONES (Imamu Baraka) (1934–) has appeared in a number of publications, including *Yugen,* his own avant-garde magazine. His first collection was a paperback called *Preface to a Twenty Volume Suicide Note* (1961); his second was *The Dead Lecturer* (1963). Among other recognitions of promise, he received a John Hay Whitney Opportunity Fellowship for creative writing. He also received a Guggenheim Fellowship in 1964–65, and his plays and productions have won several awards, including an Obie for *Dutchman* in 1964 and an International Art Festival Prize at Dakar, Senegal, in 1966. His publications include *Home* (1966), *Black Music and Tales* (1967), *Raise Race Rays Raze* (1972), and *African Congress: A Documentary of the First Modern Pan-African Congress* (1972). He has taught at the New School for Social Research and at Columbia University, and he founded the Black Arts Repertory Theatre School in Harlem and the Spirit House Movers and Players in Newark.

BOB KAUFMAN (1925–) was published in *Broadsides* by City Lights in San Francisco as early as 1959 and 1960. The first collection of his poems was *Golden Sardine* (1967), published by the same company. In 1965, his poetry of the past ten years and some of his prose were collected in *Solitudes Crowded with Loneliness,* a New Directions Paperback. Kaufman himself, a member of the San Francisco group of poets who made the "renaissance of the 1950s" in that city, appears to have dropped out of sight just as his poetry has begun to win a wider audience. In France he has been called the "Black American Rimbaud," and his reputation is even greater in Europe than in the United States.

DON L. LEE (1942–) was born in Little Rock, Arkansas, but was reared and educated in Chicago. His *Think Black* (1967) was a sensation

222

of the "new Black consciousness" and it was followed by quick reprints and revisions as well as other collections of poetry: *Black Pride* (1968), *Don't Cry, Scream* (1969), and *We Walk the Way of the New World* (1970). Lee has been a writer-in-residence at Cornell University and a teacher at several other universities and colleges, especially in the Chicago area. As editor of Third World Press, he puts out a bibliographical magazine, *Black Books Bulletin*, and publishes broadsides and books. He also edited, with James A. Emanuel, *Dynamite Voices: Black Poets of the 1960's* (1971).

RICHARD A. LONG had been known for his scholarship and his standing in the academic community long before his poetry appeared. His impressive two-volume collection, *Afro-American Writing*, edited in collaboration with Eugenia W. Collier, became available from New York University Press in 1972. A collection of his poems is pending. He is associated with Atlanta University and has been a lecturer at Harvard and elsewhere.

AUDRE LORDE (1934–   ) is a New Yorker born and bred, as rural folks might say. She has taught at the City Colleges of New York and served as poet-in-residence at Tougaloo College in Mississippi under a National Endowment for the Arts grant. Her first collection of poems is *The First Cities* (1968). A second volume, *Cables to Rage* (1970), was published in London.

CLAUDE McKAY (1891–1948) was first published in his native Jamaica, British West Indies. In his early twenties, however, he came to the United States to study agriculture at Tuskegee Institute in Alabama and then at Kansas State University. After two years, he moved to New York City, where he was drawn into the literary life. He went to Europe for the first time in 1919, spent a year in London and published there a slight volume of poems, called *Spring in New Hampshire* (1920). Back in the United States again, he became associate editor of the *Liberator* under Max Eastman. *Harlem Shadows* (1922) was his next collection of poems. For the rest of his life McKay published only prose, but off and on he wrote poetry, and some of his later pieces are included in the posthumously published *Selected Poems* (1953).

BRUCE McM. WRIGHT (1918–   ) graduated from Lincoln University in Pennsylvania in 1942 and then served in the First Infantry Division in Europe during World War II, where he was wounded twice and received several decorations. He was trained for the law at Fordham University and Yale University Law School; at Yale he was quondam Chief Justice of the Yale Law School Moot Court of Appeals. Since 1970, he has been a judge in the Criminal Court of the City of New York. While he was still in the army, McM. Wright's poems, *From the Proud Tower* (1944), were published in Wales. Since then, his poetry has been featured in French, Swedish, Slavic, as well as English anthologies, and President Leopold Sedar Senghor of Senegal plans to have McM. Wright's *Collected Poems* published in a bilingual edition in Dakar.

NAOMI LONG MADGETT (1923–   ) was born in Norfolk, Virginia, but grew up in East Orange, New Jersey, and St. Louis, Missouri. Since 1956

223

she has lived in Detroit, where she was a high-school teacher for thirteen years. In 1965 she was the first recipient of the Mott Fellowship in English at Oakland University. Thereafter she taught at Eastern Michigan University in Ypsilanti, where she is Professor of English. She is the author of four volumes of poetry, among them *Star by Star* (Harlo Press, 1965, rev. 1970) and *Pink Ladies in the Afternoon* (Lotus Press, 1972). Her poems have appeared in more than fifty anthologies and a number of journals in this country and abroad, and her papers are being collected in the Special Collections of the Fisk University Library. She is a graduate of Virginia State College and Wayne State University.

CLARENCE MAJOR (1936–   ) was born in Atlanta, Georgia, but grew up and attended school in Chicago. His poems have been published in *Black Orpheus* and other small magazines, for which he has also written about painting. Occasionally he contributes short stories. He now lives and teaches creative writing in New York City. Author of the novel *The All-Night Visitors*, he has also published several collections of poems, such as *Swallow the Lake* (1970) and *Symptoms and Madness* (1971) and has appeared in many anthologies, including *Black Voices* (New American Library), *In the Time of Revolution* (Random House), *The Writing on the Wall* (Doubleday), and *Where Is Vietnam* (Doubleday). He served two terms as writer-in-residence at the Pennsylvania Advancement School.

PAULI MURRAY (1910–   ) has written a family history, *Proud Shoes,* published in 1956. Like Samuel Allen and Bruce McM. Wright, she is an occasional poet and a practicing lawyer. Born in Baltimore, Maryland, Miss Murray began her education in North Carolina and continued it in New York and California, among other places. Her poetry has appeared in *Common Ground, South Today,* and *Saturday Review of Literature.* Her most recent collection is *Dark Testament and Other Poems* (1970).

LARRY NEAL (1937–   ) was born in Atlanta, Georgia, and reared in Philadelphia. He has a degree from Lincoln University in Pennsylvania and was a graduate student at the University of Pennsylvania. He has served on the staff of magazines such as *Liberator* and *The Cricket* and contributed to *Journal of Black Poetry*. He edited *Black Fire* (1968) with LeRoi Jones.

EFFIE LEE NEWSOME (1885–   ) has lived most of her life in Wilberforce, Ohio. Her book *Gladiola Garden* (1940), a collection of poems for children, is mainly concerned with nature.

GLORIA C. ODEN (1923–   ) was a member of the staff of *The Urbanite: Images of the American Negro. The Naked Frame: A Love Poem and Sonnets* (1952), won for her a John Hay Whitney Opportunity Fellowship for creative writing. Her college was Howard University in Washington, D.C. She is teaching in the English Department of the University of Maryland in Baltimore.

MYRON O'HIGGINS (1918–   ), born in Chicago, belongs to the tribe of wandering poets. At Howard University in Washington, D.C., he came under the influence and guidance of Sterling A. Brown, but his writing earned him Lucy Moten and Julius Rosenwald Fellowships, the army took him abroad, and so his travels began. His poems have been published in magazines and anthologies and in *The Lion and the Archer* (1948), which he and Robert Hayden put out privately in a limited edition.

FRANK LAMONT PHILLIPS (1953–   ) was born in Elroy, Arizona. He is at present an undergraduate at Fisk University. He submitted poetry to contests while in high school and was awarded honorable mention in the *Scholastic Magazine* contest and a merit award in the *Atlantic Monthly* Creative Writing Contest for 1971. He came to Fisk as a freshman and was married soon after. He works in the Nashville Public Library system while continuing his college studies.

OLIVER PITCHER (1923–   ) is a playwright, poet, director, and teacher. Born in Massachusetts and educated at Bard College, the Dramatic Workshop of the New School, and the American Negro Theater, he has had works published both here and abroad. Recently, his play *The One* was presented by The Negro Ensemble Company in New York and was published in *Black Drama Anthology*. Two other plays, *Shampoo* and *Crap Game*, are scheduled for off-Broadway production. A booklet of poems, *Dust of Silence*, was published in 1958. Mr. Pitcher has taught black theater at Vassar College and at present is poet-in-residence at Atlanta University Center, where he teaches poetry and creative writing. He also teaches at Emory University.

DUDLEY RANDALL (1914–   ) is the poet-founder of Broadside Press in Detroit, Michigan. A former librarian and teacher, he revived the old custom of printing single poems on broadsides at a few cents each. The success of this avocation led to expansion of the operation. In 1966 he visited Paris, Prague, and the Soviet Union, with a delegation of black artists. That same year, he received the Wayne State University Tomkins Award for Poetry. Since 1969, he has been poet-in-residence at the University of Detroit. His latest works include *Love You*, second edition, and *More to Remember*, both published in 1971, and *Black Poetry: A Supplement to Anthologies Which Exclude Black Poets*.

CONRAD KENT RIVERS (1933–68) was born in Atlantic City, New Jersey. His poems have been published in the *Antioch* and *Kenyon Reviews*, and a booklet of his poems appeared in 1959 under the title *Perchance to Dream, Othello*. *These Black Bodies and This Sunburnt Face* was published in Cleveland in 1962. Breman brought out his fourth volume of poetry, entitled *The Still Voice of Harlem*, and in 1971 Broadside published his *Wright Poems-Essay by Ronald Fair*.

ANNE SPENCER (1882–   ) has lived for most of her life in Lynchburg, Virginia, where she was for years the librarian of the Dunbar High School. Tending her garden has been a long-time interest. In 1970, the Friendship Press published her *African Panorama*.

MELVIN B. TOLSON (1898–1966) was an English teacher at Wiley College in Marshall, Texas, and at Langston University in Oklahoma after he graduated from Lincoln University in Pennsylvania and Columbia University in New York. He was a debating coach, worked with drama clubs, and gave many public readings of his poetry. His "Dark Symphony" appeared in *The Atlantic Monthly* after winning a poetry prize in Chicago and was included in his book *Rendezvous with America* (1944). His *Libretto for the Republic of Liberia* was published in 1953 with an introduction by Allen Tate. His *Harlem Gallery* (1965) was introduced by Karl Shapiro.

JEAN TOOMER's (1893–1967) poems, sketches, short stories, and plays of Negro life appeared in the early twenties. They received praise from Sherwood Anderson, Hart Crane, Gorham Munson, John McClure, and many others, and his book *Cane*, in which they were collected in 1923, was introduced enthusiastically by Waldo Frank. About ten years later, Toomer "disappeared," so far as most of his former literary associates were concerned. Recently his papers, his correspondence, his unpublished manuscripts, the record of his exile, if that is the word, have been found. In any case, Toomer was born in Washington, D.C., the grandson of P. B. S. Pinchback, the Negro who served for a short time as acting governor of Louisiana and was then elected to the United States Senate but denied his seat.

JAMES VAUGHN (1929–   ) was born and educated in Xenia, Ohio. After serving in the army, he earned two degrees at Ohio State University and was for a time an English teacher at Southern University in Louisiana and at West Virginia State College. From 1966 to 1970 he taught at the University of Riyadh, Saudi Arabia, and since the fall of 1971 he has taught at the Herbert H. Lehman College of the City University of New York.

MARGARET WALKER (1915–   ) wrote a collection of poems which was accepted by the State University of Iowa in place of the usual Master of Arts dissertation, and she was awarded the degree in 1940. She has since been a teacher of English at Jackson College, Jackson, Mississippi; Livingston College, Salisbury, North Carolina; and West Virginia State College. She was born in Birmingham, Alabama, the daughter of a minister, and has herself reared a large family. Her first novel, *Jubilee* (1966), was awarded a Houghton Mifflin Literary Prize and became a ringing success in a paperback edition. She holds a Ph.D. from the University of Iowa. Her work has been included in *Black Voices* (1968), and her recent collections are entitled *For My People* (1968) and *Prophets for a New Day* (1970).

CHARLES ENOCH WHEELER (1909–   ) was born in Augusta, Georgia, but later attended school in New York.

RICHARD WRIGHT's (1908–60) autobiography, *Black Boy*, was a sensational Book-of-the-Month selection in 1945. Five years earlier, his hardfisted novel, *Native Son*, had a similar impact. Since his death in 1960, the meteoric career of this Mississippi-born writer has frequently been recalled, and some previously unpublished poetry has come to light. After the struggles detailed in the autobiography, Wright lived and wrote in

226

New York for a while, traveled extensively, but spent most of his later years with his family in Paris.

MARVIN WYCHE, JR. (1951–   ), described himself at one time as "a twenty-one-year-old blood from Englewood, New Jersey." He went on to say: "As a first-year poet, I've attempted to reproduce personal experience in hopes of reaching as large a section of black and oppressed people as those experiences will allow. As a second-year poet, I will do the same." He attracted attention as a college junior by winning a national poetry contest sponsored by the United Negro College Fund in association with *Reader's Digest* (1972).

FRANK YERBY (1916–   ) is noted for his brightly colored historical romances, but his writing career began with poetry and short stories in the *Fisk Herald* when he was a student, about the time of Samuel Allen, Yvonne Gregory, and their group. The true Yerby fan, of which there are many indeed, should be able to relate the poetry to the prose without difficulty. Among his latest books are *Judas, My Brother* (1968), *Speak Now* (1969), *Dahomean* (1971), *Vixens* (1972), *The Girl from Storyville* (1972), *Flood Tide* (1972), and *Golden Hawk* (1972). Yerby was born in Augusta, Georgia, but in recent years he has made his home in Spain.

INDEX OF TITLES